A SHOT WORTH TAKING

A BAD KARMA SPECIAL OPS NOVEL

TRACY BRODY

This novel is entirely a work of fiction. The incidents portrayed in it are the work of the author's imagination. Any resemblance to actual persons, living or dead, events or localities is entirely coincidental, unless you're my friend as I do occasionally, with their permission, name a character after friends as a thank you for their support. So be nice to this author and you can show up in a book.

A Shot Worth Taking

Copyright © 2020 by Tracy Brody Books 2020

ISBN: 978-1-952187-05-6

First Edition

Also available as an ebook

ISBN: 978-1-952187-04-9

❁ Created with Vellum

To my awesome and supportive husband and family.

To our military members and their families. Thank you for all you sacrifice.

To all the aspiring writers with a dream of sharing their love of story telling.

PRAISE FOR TRACY BRODY

"The Bad Karma series just gets better and better. Do yourself a favor and start reading. You won't be able to put them down." ~ Liliana Hart, New York Times Bestselling Author.

"What do you get when you have a kickass female Black Hawk pilot, a sexy Bad Karma Special Ops elite soldier, and a deadly cartel out for revenge? You get toe curling romance, heart-stopping suspense, and a daring rescue that will keep you reading late into the night. Deadly Aim is a book you won't be able to put down." ~ Sandra Owens, author of the bestselling K2 Team and Aces & Eights series.

"You're going to love this Army Special Ops team and Tracy Brody's authentic stories." ~ Angi Morgan, USA Today and Publisher's Weekly Bestseller.

"Seat of the pants action with true military insight!" (Deadly Aim) ~ Robin Perini, Publisher's Weekly Bestseller.

GET THIS PREQUEL FOR FREE!

Dear Reader,

Thank you for choosing this book to read! I love the heroes of the Bad Karma Special Ops team, and I hope fall in love with them, too.

I've written a short story detailing the joint operation where Tony Vincenti first meets FBI Agent Angela Hoffman. This story is FREE, but available EXCLUSIVELY as a thank you to my newsletter subscribers.

You may want to read this story before you begin A SHOT WORTH TAKING. To get your link for the free download to UNDERCOVER ANGEL, subscribe to my newsletter at this link or via https://www.tracybrody.com/newsletter-signup.

ONE

KANDAHAR, Afghanistan

"PORTER, I'm talking to my mom. Can you keep your shorts on a second?" Tony turned his chair and laptop, so the bunks became the background on his Skype session.

Too late. Mom got an eyeful, based on her wide eyes. By now, he was oblivious to the overexposure of his teammates' junk, but was it too much to ask for ten minutes of privacy a week? The fun factor of "camping out" with eight of his closest friends only lasted the first month or two, max, of a deployment. Five and a half months into sharing a space barely larger than his folks' living room tested the most patient of souls at times—like right now.

His noise-canceling headphones kept him from making out any response to his request. Probably for the best, because if Dominguez made another wisecrack about Tony's weekly call to his family, today's call could turn into a lecture about his use of profanity.

"Sorry, mom. What were you saying about Mrs. Pesci?"

"That she ran into Carla last week at the market."

Lord, not again. "She's married and has kids, and I'm—"

"But she wasn't wearing her wedding ring. You should get in touch with her."

He worked not to go cross-eyed. Weren't seven grandkids enough, at least for now? "I can handle my own love life. Thanks."

"Really?"

Ouch. Now would be a good time for the shitty internet connection to go out.

It didn't.

He swallowed and shifted on the hard chair trying to avoid his mom's convicting stare. Even traveling a few thousand miles through his screen, it didn't lose any impact.

Okay, he didn't have anyone special in his life. Hadn't in, oh, say a decade, but what he and Carla shared years ago had as much chance of being resurrected as the two US troops and nearly a dozen locals killed by a suicide bomber last week.

None.

He never told his mother—or anyone—the whole story, and he wasn't going to now. Carla still lived in Amherst. No pointing in trashing her good-girl reputation.

Porter motioned to him while pulling on the uniform pants he'd shed a minute ago. Something was up based on the spate of activity in the room.

Tony lowered the headphones to his neck as Chief Lundgren closed in.

"Eyes on LaRuh. We're rolling." Lundgren lifted his M-4 from the hook on the wall.

Eyes on! Seriously? Tony's heart pounded against his ribs like the thud of mortar fire. His body went on autopilot. The laptop rocked on his lap as he began to rise, then sat again. He yanked the headset back on.

"You love kids," his mom continued without missing a beat. "You're both still—"

"Mom, I gotta go."

"You said you weren't going out until tonight. Anthony Salvatore Vincenti, are you trying to get out of this conversation? Because I know how—"

"The team's going out on patrol. I'll talk—"

"What for? Is something wrong?" Her pitch rose, and her face scrunched in worry.

"It's a routine patrol." He stared right at the computer screen and lied to his mother.

His mother's eyebrows arched, the left higher than the right in the manner she'd perfected raising four kids.

He didn't flinch or let his gaze deviate from the screen.

She made the sign of the cross, then leaned closer to the screen. "I'm headed to the market. I'll stop by St. Benedict's to light a candle and say a prayer for you."

Busted. He never could fool his mother's bullshit detector.

"Thanks." He and his team could use the extra prayers, even to patron saints, about this mission. *Father, forgive me for lying to my mom.* "Give my love to Pop and the family. I'll talk to you next week and see you soon."

That made her smile, and the wrinkles on her forehead disappeared. "Be safe. Email me later, so I know you're okay."

"We'll be fine. I gotta go."

"Routine patrol, huh?" Lincoln Porter grinned at him and pulled on his Kevlar vest.

Tony shook his head. Not exactly routine. If they nabbed Samir al-Shehri, aka LaRuh, the guru of recruiting suicide bombers, it would be like getting extra cheese and double meat on a deep-dish pizza. However, there were a lot of things family was better off not knowing.

"How good's the intel on this?" he asked Lundgren.

"A local told a patrol team from the 173rd he saw al-Shehri going into a home this morning. At least that's what they got out of the translation. I wouldn't bet a month's pay on it."

Tony wouldn't, either. They were oh for three when it came to translators they shared with another unit.

The first translator had been good. Good enough to get shot in a drive-by assassination. The second stopped showing up, likely after he was threatened by insurgents. The third "translator" fired off one shot, hitting Rozanski in the vest, before the team took him down.

Lundgren spoke Pashto better than their translators spoke English, and Tony couldn't think of anyone he trusted more. Well, he could think of one linguist who would have their backs, but he doubted Angel Gilbert—the alias he'd known FBI Special Agent Angela Hoffman by—knew Pashto. Besides, her being here could be a major distraction to the guys on the team, and him most of all.

Time to gear up, load up on ammo, and pray this intel proved reliable and didn't send them into an ambush. Then it'd be time for the strike team to live up to their name and deliver bad karma to deserving jihadists.

TONY HELD the door handle as the caravan of Humvees bumped down a pothole-rutted street. Outside the vehicle, a sandstorm raged. It sounded like rain as it beat against the metal and glass, only instead of water, the wipers swept aside the grains. An eerie red glow reflected off the blowing sand and distorted the already shitty visibility.

They braked to a quick stop before the concrete wall of the house. They'd been down this street on routine patrols a handful of times. This evening was different.

A thousand mini shocks of electricity danced on the surface of his body and his pulse rate jumped as if someone floored his heart's gas pedal when he and the team poured out of the vehicles onto the narrow street.

The sand infiltrated his uniform's neck and sleeves. With his gloved hand, he pulled the *shemagh* scarf higher to cover his nose. He never thought a sandstorm would be good for something. But the storm kept the locals hunkered down inside their mud-walled homes. Still, he scanned what he could see of the residential street. Only flat rooftops peaked over the high walls that protected the homes.

Tony didn't let the deserted streets lull him into an over-confident state. Not here. Not *ever* in Afghanistan. Just because he didn't see anyone didn't mean an enemy sniper wasn't there watching. Waiting.

The team fell into place behind the eight-foot-high wall near the locked metal gate. Porter shifted his M4 Carbine rifle to his back. Tony and Lundgren clasped their hands to each other's forearms. Porter placed one foot on their arms, and they boosted him up. He peered over the top before swinging his legs over the ledge. Within seconds, he gave the all clear.

They boosted Juan Dominguez next. He kept an eye out while Porter dropped to the ground on the inside. Metal grated metal when Porter unlocked the gate for the team to enter.

Time to start this party. Two of the team guarded the entrance while another pair took Dita, the team's working dog, and headed toward the back courtyard.

Tony sprinted to the side of the target residence with Porter, Lundgren, and Dominguez. They edged their way to the main door.

The walls decreased the amount of blowing sand to improve visibility by a few feet, yet dust rolled in waves along the base of the house. It drummed against the surrounding walls, masking most of the noise they made.

The mud house had a metal door. Solid metal, not a sheet of corrugated or scrap metal. Hardly standard Afghan construction. Major red flag. The fight-or-flight instinct hit and pumped adrenaline through his veins. No brainer. Fight. He'd do his part to stop one more zealot from persuading kids to strap on bombs. Who the hell decided being a martyr got you a shitload of virgins in heaven? *Gimme a freakin' break. Sounds more like hell.* He'd take a woman with experience any day.

Lundgren tried the doorknob. No-go. He nodded to Porter, who opened his ordnance pack.

Porter looped detonation cord and taped it to the wall near the door. For the tighter quarters, Tony pulled his Kimber .45 from the holster on his protective vest. After Porter inserted a blasting cap into the C4, the team stepped clear of the blast zone.

Tony turned his face away. The vibration rocked his body though the earpieces of his communication headset muffled the explosive *crack* when the charge detonated. A poof of smoke mixed with the sand in the air. They ducked through the opening into the house, weapons raised.

He tugged the scarf below his chin and pulled his dusty goggles from his face. Sand rained down. He licked the rough grains from his chapped lips.

The pungent aromas of fresh herbs hung heavy in the air.

Dinnertime. Somebody's home.

Lundgren and Dominguez veered to the right. Tony followed his nose, and Porter trailed him through the doorway to their left. A few steps in, a shadow appeared on the floor of the narrow hallway.

His gaze shot to the dark-gray fabric that billowed into the hall, and his weapon tracked with his eyes. A figure covered in a *burqa* emerged. Definitely not al-Shehri, but Tony's heart rate yo-yoed when the woman squawked and stopped dead. He held his index finger to his lips and aimed his weapon away from her chest.

She hobbled a step toward them on a crutch carved from a branch. Her gravelly voice fussed at them in rapid Pashto. He couldn't make out all of what she said, but the tone and gnarled finger she waved clearly conveyed her message: *Get the hell out of my home!*

He advanced, trying to force the old woman back into the kitchen. Except she refused to budge.

"Move," he growled through clenched teeth and resorted to waving his pistol to direct her. She rattled off a fresh litany of complaints, something about American troops and invasions. Behind him, Porter cleared his throat, probably to keep from laughing at the diminutive menace.

Damn, she reminded him of his Nonna Sofia. Stubborn cuss. Rules of engagement dictated the only way he could touch her was if she were in danger or presented a physical threat. Smacking his legs with her stick probably didn't qualify. Just as reprisal wasn't an option when Nonna's cane accompanied a swift reminder to behave like a good Catholic boy.

A noise came from the next room. Tony rushed forward. Using his body as a shield, he spun the woman and lifted her out of the potential line of fire.

Her crutch clattered to the floor. Thin arms and legs

flailed at him and Porter, who surged past them. A heel smashed him in the shin. He reared his head back to avoid the clawed hand that reached for his eyes.

"I'm not going to hurt you!" he said in Pashto. He couldn't protect her and cover Porter, but he didn't dare release her. She didn't weigh half of what he bench-pressed, but holding onto her was like trying to cuddle a feral cat. Covered head to toe in the *burqa*, she could be hiding something. Something other than the ragged fingernails that raked his cheek. He didn't need a mirror to know she drew blood.

She jabbered while Porter searched the kitchen. People in the house next door probably heard her since she was louder than the blast from the hole they blew in the wall.

He shifted her slight figure and held her to his side as he backed into the kitchen. With no viable options, other than to flex-cuff her, which he couldn't bring himself to do—yet—he dragged the kitchen's wooden worktable to the doorway and deposited her in the hallway. He wedged the table in the doorframe hoping that would keep her out while he joined the hunt.

Heat radiated from the brick oven to his right. Loaves of bread sat on the rough-hewn shelf along the wall. Four loaves. The hairs on the edge of his scalp bristled. Porter made eye contact, then nodded to the floor-length, crimson curtains that separated the kitchen from another room, likely the communal dining room.

Porter pointed, then held up one finger.

Please, let it be al-Shehri. Tony would take him dead or alive. Preferably alive to see what information they could garner from him, but …

He indicated for Porter to go low.

Behind him, the woman yammered away. Her pitch rose,

making it more difficult to decipher her words. As Porter whipped back the curtain, Tony translated her last phrase.

Don't lay a hand on her.

Her?

Oh, shit!

Too late, he realized he was wrong.

His world shifted to slow motion, and he shoved Porter aside as steaming meat and vegetables flew at them. Hot droplets of broth splattered his face. Food bounced off his body to the wooden floor, some landing on his boots.

"Whoa. Whoa. Wh-oa!" he warned a petite figure clad in a blue *burqa.* The barely teenage girl clutched the pot with its remaining contents, ready to launch a second round. He shifted from firing stance and raised both hands in a surrender gesture. He searched for the right words in Pashto. "You should save what's left of your dinner."

In the back corner of the room, a young boy crouched. His patterned *taqiyah* cap slipped to the side of his head as the child pointed at Tony. His other hand covered his mouth while he laughed.

Tony chuckled along. "I look funny, huh?" He waved a hand at the bits of herbs and vegetables that clung to his uniform.

The boy laughed harder when Tony plucked dark green leaves and onion strips from his arm. When the girl lowered the pot from the side-armed pitching position, Tony snatched it from her hands. Defenseless, she fled around the low dining table to the corner where she huddled beside the boy.

The room had two small windows high on the wall. Wooden flaps covered the openings, but sand blew in through the cracks. There wasn't another entrance to the room. It made as good a place as any to corral the house's occupants while his team cleared home in their search for al-Shehri.

"Watch them while I get the old lady," he ordered Porter.

His mouth watered like Pavlov's dog as he set the pot down beside the brick oven. The food smelled better than anything the cook at their forward-operating base had served in the past five months, but he resisted taking a bite since most of the family's dinner was on the floor. Besides, he'd bet money the old woman watched his every move. Probably gave him the evil eye from behind the veil, too.

She switched her grip to the doorframe when Tony grabbed the edge of the table and pulled it back into the room. He jerked his head to the woman. When she didn't move, he edged around her and retrieved the fallen crutch from the floor. Her age-spotted hand snatched it away. She tucked the rag-wrapped end under her arm and limped toward the eating area without any prodding.

"Did he touch you?" The woman's voice crackled with angst.

"Yes," the girl replied. A single, soft-spoken word in Pashto. And a flat-out lie.

"Wait a damn min—"

Whack!

The top of the crutch made direct contact with his nose. He felt the all-too-familiar pain.

"Fu—" Tony choked back the string of expletives about to pour out of his mouth. White spots of light obscured his vision. Bent over, one hand braced above his knee, he rode out the wave of nausea. He opened his mouth to breathe as blood dripped onto the floor.

Porter grabbed the crutch from the woman before she could strike again.

"Don't do it," he ordered before Porter could snap the crutch in half. "But keep it out of her reach!"

She wanted to protect the young girl's virtue, but he

didn't deserve a broken nose. There were plenty of other things he *might* deserve a beating for, but he hadn't laid a finger on the girl. *Damn.* A low growl rumbled in his throat.

Porter placed the crutch on top of the brick oven, then dug in a side pocket of his pants.

Tony took the offered sterile gauze pads. He rolled one up and stuffed it in his nostril to staunch the blood dripping down his face. Over the communications headset, Lundgren requested status updates.

"We've got three non-hostiles contained at our position," Porter stated.

Non-hostiles, my ass. Tony glared at the old woman while he gingerly touched his nose to determine the damage before it swelled more. He felt the bump from the first break in a high school football game. The second break came from a hand-to-hand combat exercise after he made it through Selection and into Special Forces. Those were both stories he could live down; they even enhanced his image. But conked in the face by a gimpy old lady? Hell, this was beyond embarrassing.

Minutes later, more of the Bad Karma team crowded into the kitchen.

"What the hell happened to you?" Dominguez was the first to take in the bloody scratches, protruding gauze, and damp patches on Tony's uniform.

Chief Lundgren's eyebrows rose at his appearance, too.

"Don't ask." Tony prayed Porter would keep his mouth shut. His teammates flanked a man in a flowing white *perahan tunban* over black pants. His hands were flex-cuffed behind his back. It made the throbbing pain worthwhile— until the prisoner faced him. The universe sucked his flash of enthusiasm into a black hole.

"No sign of al-Shehri, and he's not talking." Lundgren

shifted his gaze back to their prisoner. A muscle in Lundgren's cheek twitched. "Got a teen in the back bedroom. He's not talking, either—because he's in no condition to. Chemical burns on his arms, chest, and face. Wounds are infected. Dad here was praying for him, but he won't let us take the boy to the base for treatment. Grant's cleaning and dressing the burns, but ..." The grim set of Lundgren's mouth and shake of his head conveyed paragraphs of information, ending ominously.

Silence settled around them. Tony cast a glance at the shrouded woman, her arms wrapped around the children. He wanted al-Shehri. He wanted people like this family to not live in fear of al-Qaeda *or* American troops. He wanted to go home without losing more buddies in gunfights or to freakin' IEDs or mortar attacks.

Tony dug in his pants pocket and pulled out a pack of candy. He caught Lundgren's eye and jerked his head to the kid. "Let me have the picture." The idea tumbled out. "Translate for me?"

Lundgren handed over the picture of al-Shehri. "You're going to have to get your nose fixed this time."

Tony gave a resigned nod. He signaled for Dominguez to keep the prisoner out of sight before he approached the trio in the dining room. He motioned to the boy, but the old woman held him to her side. Tony pulled off his gloves to unwrap the candy, then popped a purple disk into his mouth. The boy slipped from the woman's grasp and darted to him, smiling expectantly. Tony handed the rest of the candy to the bright-eyed boy, who turned and spoke to the females, then flashed a gap-toothed grin at the men.

Lundgren snickered. "He told his grandmother not to be scared of you. That you're funny." His gaze roved over Tony's disheveled appearance in concurrence.

While tall, dark, toned, and dangerous drew women to him for one reason, kids saw right through him. They knew they had no reason to be afraid. He was Uncle Tony.

He squatted, getting on the kid's level. The boy opened his hand, offering to share the candy. Tony took a piece. The time seemed right, so he showed the picture of al-Shehri to the boy.

The kid's eyes doubled in size. The hand shoveling more candy into his mouth froze.

"He was here?" Lundgren asked in Pashto.

The boy's head bobbed in slow motion.

"He's gone now?"

This time the boy nodded more vigorously, and his features relaxed.

"When did he leave?" Lundgren probed over the chatter of the grandmother. One of his signature stares intimidated her to go silent.

"This morning," the boy answered.

Crap! Anticipation waned, and energy drained from Tony's body.

"Is he coming back?" Lundgren remained calm.

Tony's stomach muscles tightened the same way his fingers gripped his weapon in a gunfight. His trigger finger flexed and released.

This time, the boy only shrugged.

So far, Tony followed the conversation with ease—right to another dead end. Even Lundgren's shoulders sagged. So damn close. What next? What were they missing?

"How did he get out of the house?" Tony asked in Pashto.

An ornery grin tugged at the boy's lips. He pointed to the dining table.

Okay, my Pashto needs work. "Ask him how al-Shehri got out of the house," he asked Lundgren.

"You did."

Their gazes locked. Both men turned their attention to where the boy had pointed. The low dining table sat atop a deep red rug woven with an intricate pattern.

Tony stood. He ushered the boy to the edge of the room with the women, then handed him another packet of candy. The older woman was strangely quiet now, her head down while she held the girl close.

Together, the men turned the table on its side, setting it against the wall. They peeled the rug back to reveal a hole dug in the center of the room. Lundgren aimed his flashlight into the blackness and let out a whistle. It wasn't just a rat hole. It led to a tunnel.

"Bring in Dita," Lundgren said into his communications mic.

The prior adrenaline rush fizzled as every brain cell told Tony that al-Shehri had again slipped through their fingers like the fog and was gone. Long gone.

TWO

FBI SPECIAL AGENT Angela Hoffman scanned the people waiting for the next train while she walked to the middle of the subway platform. Several faces were familiar. Most she dismissed after assessing their threat level. Two bearded men with long, curled sidelocks and black Hasidic hats and coats were not a threat. Neither was the musician playing a Jimmy Buffet song.

Wish I was wasting away in Margaritaville. As Sabine, she wouldn't appreciate his music though, so instead of dropping a dollar in his open case, she continued past.

A young man in jeans and navy-blue polo with black hair and a Middle Eastern complexion stood about fifteen feet away. She'd seen him before. Today, he had a backpack slung over one shoulder and a section of folded newspaper in his right hand. His gaze flicked over her before he turned away.

This guy wasn't included in the pictures the Bureau had of Hakim's known associates. She'd spotted one of Hakim's flunkies on the train the day after "meeting" him at the gallery. She'd give up coffee for a month if the guy she spotted outside the mosque two days after their *accidental* encounter wasn't there on Hakim's orders. Was this one the Bureau missed? A recent recruit? Or a regular joe taking the New York subway?

Hakim's men weren't half bad at tailing her, but with her background, she had an edge at picking them out without acknowledging their interest in her.

She raised the coffee cup to her lips and snuck another peek in his direction. Though hating to waste perfectly good caffeine, she downed another gulp, then walked to the trash can and dropped the cup in.

Polo Guy shifted his weight and avoided eye contact. From her position, she could make out the Arabic script of a headline. Probably *Al Madar* but hard to tell which news-paper it was from this distance. If he were running surveillance on her, she'd make it easy for him.

A couple hurried past, a crying child on the young woman's hip. The stroller the mother dragged behind her bumped, and a stuffed pink bunny bounced out and landed on the platform.

Angela scooped up the toy. "Excuse me. Excuse me, miss," she called. "Is this your bunny?"

The woman glanced back, then slowed. The child reached for the toy and cradled the animal to her body, rubbing her teary face against the plush fur.

"Thank you," the young woman replied with a strong Slavic accent.

The glare the woman's partner unleashed at the sound of the approaching train made her hurry to keep up. Angela recognized several not so nice words in Russian as the man berated the young woman for landing them on the wrong platform. Probably tourists. Navigating the New York City subway system wasn't the easiest feat for a newbie. Throw in a crying child and an oppressive mate, and sympathy made Angela itch to tell the man to lighten up. However, Sabine wouldn't confront a man and insinuate herself into a domestic situation, and Angela couldn't blow her cover when she had a potential tail within earshot. *Sorry.*

Warm, stale air rushed past, and the subway train screeched to a stop. People pushed forward to board. Deliberately, she headed to a separate car than the young family and ignored the man who may or may not be one of Hakim's contacts. For all appearances, she was Sabine Deschamps on her way to work at LeBlanc Fine Arts Gallery. She needed to sell that lie for at least one more day.

Angela claimed a seat in the back corner beside an Asian woman who didn't look up from her e-reader. The car jolted forward, then built speed as it barreled through the tunnel.

At the other end of the car, Polo Guy sat with his back to her, though that didn't negate the possibility he was following her. With the majority of passengers already fixated on their phones, she pulled out her doggedly vibrating phone to check her text messages.

Three messages in ten minutes? *Crap.* It had to be important for the Bureau to send repeated coded messages. A shoe sale at Bloomies wasn't *that* urgent.

She studied the people around her before she tapped the link that would take her to the supposed sale page. Better to check it now in case they needed her to come into the office before she went to her current "job."

Please don't let anything have gone wrong. Not now. She entered her information in the customer login and password fields.

Seconds later, she read the plain text on the secure website for the FBI.

She read it again.

Her lungs forgot how to draw in oxygen. Her heart missed a beat. Then another. It didn't have to do with her case. Or did it?

Samir al-Shehri.

The name made her shiver despite the late-June heat. Her nervous system forced her lungs to work. In Afghanistan years ago, she'd witnessed the results of al-Shehri's anti-American agenda. While al-Shehri's travels throughout the Middle East to recruit impressionable dupes for his cause alarmed her when she was there, his coming to North America made her body go cold.

The alert said he'd taken a flight into Toronto. Only Canada wouldn't be his target. And if al-Shehri needed money to fund some cause, then Anmar Hakim would be the man to see.

It'd taken two months for her to get close to Hakim. Tonight, it was supposed to come together. Could she get evidence against more than Hakim? If she found something to connect the men … But what if Hakim canceled their plans? Lost in thought, she nearly missed her stop in Soho.

She got off, but Polo Guy stayed on the train.

TONY AMBLED across the pavement toward the Special Ops command post on their secure part of Fort Bragg. The temperature threatened to break ninety today. It'd still be training as usual. Could be worse. He could still be in Kandahar. The temps were pushing ninety there when they left almost three months ago.

Inside the unit's conference room, several members of his team sat at the tables.

"Was that a personal record for ya, Vincenti?" Juan Dominguez smirked. "What, like three minutes before some hot chick made her move on ya?"

Talk about business as usual. Tony ground his teeth together rather than let Dominguez bait him. He took a seat in the back of the room with Mack Hanlon and AJ Rozanski.

Dominguez swiveled around. "Told you the new GQ look worked for you. Even if you still aren't as pretty as Grant."

"Don't drag me into this. I didn't even go to Jumpy's last night," Devin Grant said.

"Where were you?" Tony attempted to shift the focus off his sex life.

"I had class."

"Class?" Dominguez targeted Grant. "What are you taking now?"

"Finance 354."

"Finance? Why you taking some lame class like that? Are there any hot chicks in it?" Dominguez was like a dog chasing a squirrel.

"Two or three, I guess." Grant rolled his eyes and shook his head.

"Just saying … So, Vincenti, the brunette. Was she the love of your life? You two didn't stay for a second drink. And, man, that woman was smokin' hot. All long legs and—"

"Shut up, Dominguez. Why all the interest in my love life? You jealous?" No, she wasn't the love of his life. Just one more woman convinced that hooking up with a Special Ops guy would be the most satisfying and memorable time in the sack ever. He didn't disappoint.

The disappointment came later. With the realization that if they were more interested in great sex than a relationship, he couldn't trust they would stay faithful. To do his job, he couldn't worry about what was happening on the home front while he was deployed.

Dominguez snorted. "Yeah, I like your pretty new look. But don't ask, don't tell."

"Shut up, Dominguez!" A chorus of voices drowned him out.

Rozanski sent a pen sailing. It hit Dominguez in the shoulder; he laughed it off.

The door opened, and Colonel Mahinis walked in ahead of Chief Ray Lundgren, who carried a tablet. The room went silent. Tony's mission radar lit up.

Within minutes, the colonel confirmed his suspicions. Every hair on Tony's body rose to attention as he stared at the surveillance photos of Samir al-Shehri on the wall screen. He'd shaved his traditional beard and wore Western-style clothing. It altered his appearance enough that, using a forged passport, he'd slipped through Canadian customs. How many hours had passed before a match triggered the potential terrorist alert?

The colonel tapped on the tablet, and the board switched to a photo of al-Shehri getting into a cab. "This is the last photo—or sighting—Homeland Security has of him. They're expanding the search, but not a single hit yet."

Of course not. It was like fog. You could see it in the distance but seemed to dissipate when you got close.

Beside Tony, Rozanski swore under his breath.

If only we'd nailed al-Shehri's sorry ass in Kandahar.

Dita hadn't found anyone hiding in the tunnel. Or the bunker under the house. They found explosive components, four AK-47s, and five crates of ammunition, but they hadn't found any intelligence data. There hadn't been any more sightings of al-Shehri in Kandahar or anywhere else—until now. *Damn.* Obviously, it didn't take as much to get past customs and airport security as it should.

Tony ran his index finger down his nose. The bruises and swelling were gone, and five weeks post-surgery, his face appeared normal—to most people.

He hadn't gotten used to his perfectly straight nose. The colonel was right. It did make sense that while fixing his nose —so he could breathe again—for the surgeon to make some minor changes. A few tweaks to modify his profile enough to fool facial recognition programs. Hopefully, he could get back into Egypt and Morocco now. Oh, and Libya. Though the intel-guys should run a test to make sure it worked before he tried to slip back into Libya. With Special Ops, he never knew where he might end up. His team only worked on US soil in unique circumstances—and their experience and knowledge of al-Shehri could sure as hell be useful now.

"We're operating under the assumption that al-Shehri has, or will, cross into the States. He'll likely skip the border checks by taking a boat across Lake Ontario to Rochester, or Lake Erie near Buffalo."

Shit. The colonel's statement jabbed Tony like a sucker punch in the stomach.

He couldn't risk breaking operational security to tell his family or old friends now might be a good time to take a vacation to Kansas or Montana. *Dammit.* He pushed those thoughts away to focus on the colonel's briefing.

That worked for like thirty seconds.

No point in attacking a low-value target like Buffalo, unless al-Shehri had a grudge against the Bills—not a likely scenario even after another dismal season. New York City or D.C. would have a higher impact.

They had no clue what al-Shehri's plans were, but Tony knew he sure as hell hadn't come to see Niagara Falls.

DESPITE THOUGHTS of Samir al-Shehri running through her head more often than political ads aired in an election year, Angela managed to concentrate on the tasks required of her at the gallery. Skipping lunch since she hardly had an appetite— a rarity for her—she wrapped up early. She tapped on Nathan LeBlanc's office door. When he glanced up from the over- sized computer screen displaying several metal sculptures, she stepped in.

"I sent an invoice and money transfer instructions to the buyer in Hamburg. I also left a voice mail for the gallery in Cannes, with their shipment update and customs claim number." She spoke each word clearly, in the manner associ- ated with someone communicating in a second language.

"You're amazing. I don't know what I did without you."

She flashed a modest smile. "You managed quite well. However, I am more accurate than online translations sites. You're the art expert."

Nathan's inability to communicate with the surge of inter- ested foreign buyers—some real, some fictitious—made it ridiculously easy for her to get a job at the gallery with her fluency in several European languages. The part-time job provided the perfect cover and inroads for her current assignment.

She enjoyed this side "job" more than she'd anticipated and admired Nathan's eye for art. She wouldn't mind his help picking out a painting for her apartment back in D.C. after this assignment wrapped. Soon. If tonight went as planned, she wouldn't return to this up-and-coming gallery. She could wrap things up in a few days, be out of New York, and back to her friends and pragmatic life in D.C. doing her regular job.

"Unless there's anything else you need, I'll be leaving for the day."

Nathan pursed his lips. "That's all for now. Have a nice evening, Sabine."

"Adieu," she added in Sabine's refined French accent. Yes, hopefully, tonight will be the end of playing the submissive-Sabine persona. Time to get back to her home turf.

ANGELA TOOK a seat at the rear of the subway car, then observed the occupants in the same discreet manner as always. While she didn't recognize any faces around her, that didn't mean anything. At this point, she couldn't afford to slip out of character. Her covert experience kept her alive, despite the half-million-dollar bounty the Vazquez family had on her life—or more accurately, her death—and had gotten her up close and semi-personal with Anmar Hakim after the Bureau's other failed attempts. Diligence. She should have made that her middle name. Too late now, and she hoped she wouldn't have to change her name again.

The energy that thrummed through her body kept her alert.

By the time she transferred lines and took the short walk to her cramped one-bedroom apartment, her expectations for tonight had climbed to a nine. With al-Shehri possibly crashing the party, she refrained from getting overconfident.

In her mailbox, she found the package she'd expected from the Bureau. After working together in Afghanistan, Jarrod should trust her to get the job done *her* way. She climbed the stairs carrying the nauseous sensation that came from wanting a do-over in life. Only you don't get do-overs once you pass adolescence. What you got were you-know-better-than-to-repeat-that-shit life experiences.

Inside her apartment, she opened the envelope and inspected the pair of large silver earrings. A "stone" was inset in the pattern. They were well-crafted with a wire the same deep brown as her hair. No valid excuse to refuse to wear them came to mind—other than if Hakim discovered the wire, he wouldn't hesitate to turn her over to the people he employed. While Hakim himself didn't pose a threat, some of his associates wouldn't mind dealing with a spy. She shoved the thought aside.

As crucial as this op was to Jarrod—*how the hell had he risen to supervisory special agent already?*—she had to believe he had good reason other than micro-managing to make her wear a two–way wire. It's not like she was averse to risk. However, there were two kinds of self-preservation: preservation of your life and preservation of your moral integrity. Both mattered to her, while Jarrod proved he only cared about the first. And his *own* preservation over anyone else's.

After changing into a high-neck dress, she pulled the sleeves down to cover her wrists. With almost every inch of her skin covered, it left everything to a man's imagination. She clasped a silver chain around her neck. The oblong pendant hung above the curve of her breasts. She'd chosen the necklace to draw Hakim's gaze and make him use his imagination about what lay beneath the forest-green fabric.

She sent a text before inserting the first ornate earring into her right lobe. Double-checking the other earring, she used her clear-glossed fingernail to nudge on the tiny power switch, then fastened the post and wrapped the wire behind her ear, inserting the listening piece.

"You there, Cal?" She arranged her hair to cover the thin filament wire. "Talk to me."

"You want me to tell you that your eyes are more beautiful than a goat's to get you in the mood for tonight's date?" The familiar voice of FBI Special Agent Michael Weiss, instead of Cal, came through her earpiece seconds later.

"No." She bit her tongue to keep from pointing out how offensive that comment came across. *Be a team player. Be a team player.* Working undercover required the same disciplines, whether it was for the Bureau or the Agency. You didn't take the trash talk seriously, especially when she needed to trust these guys to have her back. Trusting others, however, wasn't her strongest attribute. It worked out about half the time. Jarrod Carswell happened to be in the half that did not work. "Where's Calomiris?"

"He's talking to Carswell. Audio is great."

Since joining the Bureau, the assignments where she'd stepped out of her linguist role to go undercover had all worked out. She needed to bank on continuing that track record. Crashing a few embassy parties were minor, and the agents in charge had given her latitude to do things her way. Jarrod knew her history, her track record. That's why his micromanagement grated her nerves.

"I'm ready." If she'd known she'd be working with Jarrod when the New York office asked for her help on this case, would she have passed? Maybe. It was her own fault. Her ego kept her from asking questions when the Bureau needed her unique skills. It seemed easy enough. Cozy up to Hakim to get solid evidence of his involvement financing terrorist activities. It wasn't that different from getting the inside track on a drug or arms dealer's operation. You just needed the right connection.

Finding the right connection to get close to Hakim definitely provided a challenge. But she'd done it. Because everyone had a soft spot or weakness—even if they didn't know it. The key was finding it, then exploiting it. Jarrod had taught her that lesson—by finding her soft spot.

She rearranged her hair to better camouflage the wire. Her smile looked forced. Her history with Jarrod could be to blame for making her skittish—like the way a normal person reacted after hearing an unidentified noise in the middle of the night.

Be prepared for anything, but don't obsess on what could go wrong. She and the team of FBI agents could do this. Her past and upbringing were why the Bureau first pulled her from linguistics to infiltrate the bad-ass Coyotes biker gang. When that assignment turned up leads on stolen military weapons, she requested back up rather than try to handle it on her own—not that she'd expected the Bureau to send in an Army Special Ops team.

She'd accepted their help, and those guys quickly earned her loyalty, in large part because they'd listened to her input and trusted her skills, even without knowing her background with the Agency. "Jake," with his chiseled biceps and delicious sense of humor, had watched over her back then. No point in going there, though. That fantasy ended when that mystery man disappeared back into his Special Ops world.

She stood straighter, tilting up her chin and staring at her reflection, then slid a silver bracelet over her wrist. Until this morning, she wanted to gather enough evidence to put Hakim behind bars, so she could get out of New York City and back home. But Hakim could lead them to Samir al-Shehri, and bringing him in would be a nice little "up yours" to Al-Qaeda and the Agency. There was so much riding on tonight. On her abilities.

No pressure.

THREE

THE HOSTESS LED ANGELA, trailed by Hakim, through the dimly lit restaurant. Hakim hadn't canceled dinner, and on the cab ride to the restaurant, he acted normal—for him. Cal and Weiss were in place, and everything was going according to plan.

Square tables for four filled the center of the room, with round tables for larger parties nestled in specially designed alcoves. Along the perimeter, narrow rectangular tables backed up to a booth seat. Her eyes moved left to right, perusing the diners' faces. A man with short, Nordic-blond hair seated at a table in the back dragged a memory into the light of day. A large floral arrangement blocked her from getting a better view.

The hostess led Hakim to a booth. Not her first choice, but it allowed her a prime view of the dining room, so she slid in. Taking the menu from the hostess gave her a chance to check out the blond man's profile. Thank goodness Hakim didn't see her do a double take when she noticed the blond's dining companion.

Her heart raced, and it took a concentrated effort to

control her breathing. While Hakim studied his menu, she cut her eyes to the table at the back of the restaurant again.

It wasn't her imagination. The six-and-a-half-foot blond was memorable enough, but it was "Jake" she recognized most after two years. Tonight, his black hair was short and styled. Clean-shaven and in a navy suit and yellow tie, he bore little resemblance to his Harley-riding, ex-con character, Jake, from their Texas assignment. But she recognized the deep-brown eyes. The way he sat. The intense way he stared at Hakim. Based on the pair's scrutiny, they knew exactly who Hakim was.

When Jake's gaze shifted to her, she squelched her instinct to wink. Instead, she lifted her eyebrows enough to convey she recognized him. His eyes widened, and he broke into a smile that made her stomach flip. He spoke to his team leader. She made out his mouth forming the name Hakim before he turned his face enough that she couldn't read his lips.

She shifted her attention away, to Hakim, then to her menu. *Get a grip.* One look at Jake had her forgetting her mission and her heart doing a sensual dance, sending blood and energy south.

What were they doing here? The Bureau wouldn't call them in for backup without alerting her. Operating on different mission plans could get tricky. And messy. *Great.* Okay. She could make this work—if she could get a minute alone with one of them. Preferably, Jake. And she knew exactly how to communicate that to him.

After giving Hakim another minute to read over the menu, Angela asked, "Any recommendations?"

Hakim, a self-proclaimed foodie, began his usual line-item analysis of the menu. He paused when the waiter arrived and listened to the specials. That gave her the opportunity to flash a *T* in sign language to Jake under the edge of the table. Jake caught the movement. She repeated it, then flashed the number seven. A peek toward him garnered his nod of acknowledgment.

"Would you care for a drink or an appetizer?" The waiter's gaze brushed over her to land on Hakim.

"I would like a cup of hot tea. And …" He hesitated long enough to give her the opening she needed.

"Would you care to share the seafood plate?" She gave a shy, hopeful smile.

Hakim's mouth tightened, clueing her in it wasn't his first choice, but it made her plan plausible. "That will be fine," he said to the waiter.

"I'll put that order in while you look over the menu."

Though it didn't take long to pick what she wanted, she stared intently at the menu—not at Jake—and ran through scenarios to get to her outcome. Her prior apprehension faded simply by having Jake and his boss in the room. By the time the waiter came to take their order, she'd come up with her tentative game plan. A direction the Bureau might not love, but it was her ass on the line.

Jake disappeared down the hall to the restrooms. Time to make this work.

"Excuse me. I'm going to slip to the ladies' room before the appetizer comes."

Hakim stood while she rose. She needed to break him of those gentlemanly habits for tonight to come to fruition, though she'd brought insurance.

"We've got company." She kept the movement of her lips to a minimum and spoke softly as she passed the tables of diners.

"Al-Shehri?" The excitement in Special Agent Calomiris' voice shrilled in her ear.

"No. JSOC."

"What the …? This can't be happening," Special Agent Weiss grumbled.

"We cannot let some military Special Ops group pick up Hakim now," Cal stated the obvious.

"I'm on it. Give me a minute to deal with them." She turned the corner, and Jake stepped inside the restaurant's unisex, handicapped bathroom. Perfect. She caught the door before it closed and slipped inside, locking it behind her.

"You clean up nice." She looked him over and got another jolt of arousal.

"Thanks. You, too. Almost didn't recognize you." Jake's eyes drifted downward, though the conservative dress didn't invite the same heated perusal her more revealing biker attire had.

"I noticed you seemed more interested in my date."

"We hoped Hakim might be meeting someone else."

"Al-Shehri? Sorry to disappoint you."

"No offense to you."

"None taken." She understood a shot at al-Shehri trumped everything—even any naughty fantasies about Jake. "Looks like we're after the same men. Our bosses should talk more. Could have saved you a trip."

"You have intel connecting them?"

"Not yet."

Jake's mouth shifted, and he studied her with a hopeful expression.

"Since we're all here and want to keep the same individuals from inflicting terror around the planet, we could work together," she said.

"Wait! What are you doing?" Weiss roared in her ear.

She winced and turned her head.

Jake chuckled and stepped closer. "Your team protesting that idea?"

"How could you tell?"

He touched her cheek near the earring and probably saw the wire.

She turned her face toward his hand, prolonging his touch for another precious second. "You know how it goes."

While their higher-ups preached interagency cooperation, experience demonstrated that talk and reality were two different things. Egos and jurisdictional conflicts led to posturing and power plays that didn't always make for the best working relationships.

She'd been surprised when the Bureau tasked a military team to join her investigation in Texas and more surprised when Jake and his team hadn't been the take-control alpha males she'd feared.

"How long have you been working Hakim?" He kept his tone businesslike.

"Me? Two months. The Bureau, a lot longer."

"What's your plan?"

"Hoping to get lucky. Have him invite me back to his place so I can copy his hard-drive and gather intel."

A muscle in Jake's jaw twitched.

While not exactly in the scope of job duties of a linguist, he didn't know her complete work history, and now wasn't the time nor the place to explain. "Hopefully, we'll find something to tie them together or, better yet, lead to al-Shehri. Unless Hakim gets picked up now. Then that's shot to hell." She touched her earpiece to clue him in and continued. "We on the same page here?"

He smiled, and his head bobbed, catching her drift. Smart man.

"That's more solid than anything we've got. Best to let your plan play out," he said for her fellow agents to hear.

"Good. Have your boss talk to Special Agent in Charge Grochowski if you guys want in. We've got a mobile surveillance team in the flooring truck a block down. Maybe you can join forces. Special Agent Weiss likes an audience." She ignored Weiss's continued protest. "I better get back before Hakim gets antsy."

"We'll get it worked out."

"Then, I'll probably be seeing you." That idea shouldn't give her as much of a thrill as catching al-Shehri. Shouldn't.

Jake did a quick check of the hallway before he ducked out and left her alone.

She inhaled and took a second to close her eyes. Her hands trembled a bit as she freshened up her neutral-beige lipstick. Hours ago, Jake invaded her thoughts, and now he appeared like she'd rubbed a genie's lamp. He certainly stood a chance to make it into the top three on her wish list. Maybe even number two, if they could catch al-Shehri.

Finding out Jake's real name would be nice, too. Working clandestinely, it was better not to know things that could break cover. When his Spec Ops team joined her mission working the Coyote motorcycle gang, she stayed in character and didn't ask questions that could get her or someone on her team killed.

When that mission wrapped, she had only a few, too brief, minutes with him before his team loaded up the recovered weapons. He'd given her one final sexy smile before he disappeared back into his Black Ops world. Tonight, he wore a wedding ring, which meant he probably went home to his wife, two rambunctious sons, brown-eyed, pig-tailed daughter, and dog—she pictured a Labrador Retriever.

Damn. She'd tried not to think about that before, though it

explained why he hadn't taken advantage of them sharing a room at the Deluxe Stay Motel back in Texas. Not knowing his relationship status, she'd kept things professional other than a little flirtation—which had been necessary for their cover.

Not that she hadn't indulged in a few explicit fantasies starring Jake. That needed to be in the past. It wasn't right to lust over a married man. Fantasies could be so much easier than real life.

No time for fantasies or distractions tonight. She pushed Jake into a locked compartment of her brain to refocus. Right now, she was Sabine, and Sabine Deschamps did not know Jake, and he was not her type. Damn. She disliked being Sabine more by the minute.

Back at the table, she avoided looking in Jake's direction. No more signals under the table. Nothing to make Hakim suspicious. When the waiter brought their food, she handed him her appetizer plate and seized the opportunity to slip the libido enhancer into Hakim's tea.

While they dined, she kept things low-key. The conversation centered on France and their shared passion for art. She prayed the Cialis would kick up his primal urges. "The next artist Nathan plans to showcase is not my style. He's talented with clean lines and interesting uses of color, but his work is too modern and interpretive for my taste. You robbed me of my favorite piece. I'm glad you're happy with the painting, but I miss the chance to admire it." She stuck out her bottom lip, playing her role of the demure widow to the hilt.

"It looks magnificent with the adjustable lighting I had installed. Would you care to see it in its new location?"

While Angela refrained from jumping at *his* suggestion, her pulse got a powerful jumpstart, and her toes curled inside the conservative black pumps. "I—I would like that." She met his eyes before looking down at her hand and toyed with her fork. *Score!*

She didn't follow the movement when she glimpsed Jake and his boss pass on their way out of the restaurant. Emptiness settled in her chest while she listened to Hakim, and she repressed a shudder when he trailed two fingers down her forearm to her hand. His touch left her feeling tainted—like a sacrificial lamb for "the greater good." She returned his gentle squeeze, letting her hand remain in his—distancing herself from Angela. She had to be Sabine. To protect herself, she had to keep up the façade.

FOUR

OUTSIDE THE RESTAURANT, Tony split from Lundgren and walked down the block. The drizzle of rain barely registered. Why was Angela working undercover again? That question rattled around in his brain while he'd watched her and Hakim interact over dinner. Each bashful look and shy smile, each touch the two exchanged, made him want to hurt someone—and his stomach still threatened to expel his dinner all over the sidewalk.

The two minutes he spent with her inside the bathroom brought back a flood of memories—of how it felt to have her riding behind him on the Harley, her arms wrapped around his torso; of his dread and her calm demeanor when the Coyote's ringleader held a gun to her head; of her trust in his team's ability to shoot the bastard dead.

Afterward, he'd proposed Angela switch from linguistics to a field position. *Leave my safe cubicle to have a gun held to my head? No thanks,* she'd replied, then given him one of her trademark winks and somewhat-suggestive smiles. Yet here she was, undercover again, this time on one of the highest priorities on Homeland Security's watch list. Not exactly on par with translating documents in the confines of a cubicle in the Washington, D.C. office.

He hadn't seen her since he, Mack, and Dominguez roared away on the FBI's confiscated Harleys—but he'd thought of her. Even dreamed of her on more than one occasion. When he'd been in D.C. a year ago, he wanted to call her up to see if they could get together. Of course, there wasn't an Angela Hoffman listed in the phone directory. Something, mostly the probability she was married, made him cop-out rather than call the FBI office to track her down. But now, here she was, and watching her cozy up to a known money-mover for terrorists was not his idea of fun.

He turned the corner and picked out the rectangular work truck with the name of a flooring company on the side. It was a good setup for the FBI to listen in, especially being a block away and out of sight. It wouldn't stick out to most people, except the truck was still there at nine thirty at night.

He scanned the street before he slipped between a parked car and the rear of the truck, then rapped on the door. Silence. He ticked off the seconds in his head. "I can pound on the door, but that might draw unwanted attention," he said, loud enough that the agents inside should hear. "I'm not going away." He detected the muffled sound of conversation before the back door cracked open.

"What can I do you for?" asked a guy with a heavy Brooklyn accent who wore a T-shirt with a logo matching the one on the side of the truck.

Nice touch. "I want to see if you do Brazilian hardwoods." Tony yanked open the door and climbed into the truck, forcing the agent to back out of the way.

"What the …?" the agent blustered.

Tony pulled the door shut behind him. "Sergeant First

Class Anthony Vincenti. Army Special Operations. Which one of you is in charge?"

The older agent, seated in front of the bank of listening equipment and computer monitors, rolled his shoulders back and looked Tony up and down. "I am. But we have this covered. Besides, there's not really room for one more in here."

You gotta be shitting me. Tony's jaw clenched to keep from saying it aloud. Despite the smell of pastrami and stale coffee, it was luxurious compared to some of his past assignments.

"Look, we're on the same team here. You guys can take all the credit for bagging Hakim and al-Shehri. No one wants them to pull off something *we* could have prevented but didn't because of politicking. You going to play nice, or do I go over your heads to Grochowski, who cleared it?"

There were only two chairs in the vehicle. Though tempted to pull a power play and slip into the vacant one, it was more important he get their buy-in, so he perched on the corner of the counter holding the equipment. And waited. The two FBI agents exchanged a look. He took the slight tilt of the senior agent's head as a sign of consent. Good enough.

Tony loosened his tie and shrugged out of his jacket. "Got another set of headphones?" Apparently, the agents weren't going to offer anything up freely.

The senior special agent jerked his head to the younger agent, who took his time retrieving a set of earbuds from a cabinet built into the truck.

Angela's sultry voice purred in his ears, speaking fluent French.

"Jackpot. Hakim offered to take her home to show her the painting and, no doubt, his private collection," the agent with the heavy New York accent announced.

Tony snuffed out the impulse to wipe the smirk off the agent's face. Must be Weiss, the guy she mentioned in the bathroom.

"So, how did Special Agent Hoffman ID you?" the senior special agent asked.

"We worked together a while back," Tony answered in French to see the dumbfounded look on Weiss's face at the realization he understood what Hakim and Angela were saying—mostly. Man, she sounded like a native speaking at such a rapid clip.

"What did you guys need our help with?" Weiss wore a patronizing smile.

"Special Agent in Charge Minton from the Dallas office called *us* in to assist their investigation locating weapons, including stolen shoulder-launched multipurpose assault weapons." He wasn't sure if it was the part about the missiles or that the FBI approached Spec Ops for help, but it was enough to shut Weiss up.

Though Angela knew her fellow agents were listening in, Tony still felt like a voyeur as he continued to monitor the conversation in the restaurant. When Hakim told the server to keep the change, the senior special agent took off his headset. "Let's move out." He slid back a partition to maneuver into the driver's seat.

Tony took the vacated seat. Weiss didn't speak to him while the truck snaked through the ever-present New York City traffic. Angela's chitchat with Hakim didn't seem pertinent, but he concentrated on the nuances of their voices, in hopes he'd pick up something useful.

Hakim used a respectful tone with their cab driver, who spoke with a heavy Middle Eastern accent, but his reply to the night doorman at his building sounded condescending, and though it was only two words, he swore Hakim's clipped greeting to the concierge bore an air of smugness. He filed away that information.

After circling a city block, Special Agent "Cal" Calomiris —he finally asked Weiss for his name—parked the truck. Tony stood and relinquished his chair when Cal slid the divider back and squeezed through to rejoin them in the rear of the truck. Before sitting, Cal produced a collapsible stool from the equipment closet and handed it to him.

Figures. He took the chair, ticked neither agent had the courtesy to offer it up earlier when he balanced on the counter by half a butt cheek. He bit his tongue and accepted it as a peace offering.

The amount of static from Angela's audio increased. Calomiris pressed his middle finger against the earpiece, then pulled off the headset.

"She's in!" Weiss pulled off his headset, too. "Jackpot! Finally! Anmar Hakim, we are gonna nail your ass."

Panic poured into Tony's chest like quick-set concrete. "What's up with the signal?"

"Hakim installed a top-of-the-line security system. The vibration scrambler renders transmitters useless as tin cans on a string," Calomiris said.

Should have known that. Only he didn't have the inside info the agents did. "Guess he doesn't use a landline, either."

"No. He's paranoid when it comes to security."

Tony wanted to be a fly on the wall, or better yet, a spider in a web waiting to catch his prey. "Couldn't slip the concierge or super enough to get in and disable it?"

"Why didn't we think of that? Oh, wait! We did," Weiss said.

"System uses a keypad and palm scanner. No one gets in without Hakim," Calomiris said. "Tried to use our guys to deliver and hang the painting he bought from the gallery

Hoffman's working at, but no go. Hired his own crew to mount it and do the lighting work. Not worth tipping our hand to try and get in another way."

"In case you thought you'd rappel down the building and cut a hole in the window to plant a bug or do some peeping GI Joe surveillance," Weiss added.

"I could if you need me to." Tony ran through the possibilities of inserting himself through a window, wall, the ceiling, or even the floor. "What's the plan once she's in?"

"Well, she didn't give us all the juicy details, but once Hakim's asleep"—Weiss paused, letting that register, before he continued—"she's supposed to disable the scrambler, copy his hard drive, clone his cell's SIM card, and bug the apartment."

Tony knew all agents had field training, but they were expecting a helluva lot from a linguist. There was some piece of the puzzle he didn't have. "Looked like she slipped something into his coffee cup at dinner." He and Lundgren had watched her closely, but neither was positive—she was that good.

"She did requisition Cialis. You know, talk of the Louvre and art only go so far toward him wanting to take her home to unveil her masterpiece."

The desire to forcibly shut Weiss up tripled. The need to remain professional and not blow this strained cooperation trumped Tony's personal agenda—barely. He'd hoped she roofied the asshole, not helped him get it up.

The idea of Angela having no way to communicate left him unsettled to his core. The idea of hearing everything going on inside appealed even less now, though. Bile burned all the way up to his throat. How far would she go? "Is she married?" The question slipped out.

Weiss shrugged. "Don't think so."

"She have a boyfriend or fiancé?" he asked, more because of his own curiosity.

"Other than Hakim?"

He refused to answer Weiss. Angela was smart. Creative. And in a very precarious position. If anyone knew firsthand how a mission could put an operative in a compromising situation, he did. He didn't want her sleeping with a skeevy terrorist, but it was a better alternative than her being dead. While they waited, he prayed that her plan, whatever it entailed, worked.

"CAN YOU STOP THAT?" Calomiris stared at Tony's fingers tapping on the countertop.

"Sorry." He stilled his hand. In the thirty-seven minutes since they'd lost Angela's audio feed, he'd endured Weiss's litany of questions, until the two found something to bond over—the lousy performance of the Buffalo Bills the past few seasons. But that only distracted him to an extent. He'd chewed the inside of his cheek raw. What the hell was going on in there, and how long would this take? He blew out a breath, which drew another pained look from Calomiris. This could take hours, and he'd better find a way to chill before Calomiris kicked him out or killed him.

Both men jolted when the cell phone lying on the counter vibrated. A smile broke across Calomiris' stressed face when he saw the display.

"Talk to me. Great."

"Put it on speaker." Weiss nearly tipped off the stool as he leaned closer to hear.

Tony's muscles relaxed when Calomiris punched the speaker button.

"Systems are linked now," an unfamiliar voice broadcast, likely an FBI computer tech. "I'll run the list of possible passwords based on your data before it begins the full decryption—"

"Shit! Gotta go!" Angela's words rushed out before the call disconnected.

In the truck, silence loomed.

FIVE

THE CONTENTS of Tony's stomach churned. *Damn.* This was worse than the waiting earlier. He'd abandoned the back of the truck to sit in the driver's seat, where he could watch the building's windows for a flash of gunfire. Nothing—thankfully. And, so far, no sirens from a neighbor's call to report a woman screaming or—

Stop letting your imagination go worst case!

She was probably being cautious. It's not like she'd said, "Help. He's going to kill me."

Hakim was a businessman. He laundered and moved money. Probably didn't own a gun. However, Tony could envision the guy with a deadly looking ceremonial dagger.

He shook his head to dispel those visions. Somehow, he couldn't shake this deep-seated compulsion to protect Angela. Maybe because, as a linguist, she wasn't trained to handle someone like Hakim. Though it could be that he was already thinking ahead to when this mission ended—when things didn't have to be all business.

The phone finally rang. Tony whirled.

"Everything okay? You had us worried." Calomiris asked.

Weiss motioned, and Calomiris put the phone on speaker.

"Sorry," she spoke softly. "Hakim was throwing up again. I didn't want him to find me with his phone, hacking his computer. Get anything yet, Singh?"

Throwing up? Her apparent ingenuity let Tony breathe easier.

"Hoffman, it scares me how deep you are in Hakim's head. Hit his password in under two minutes. Who's Fatima?" Singh, the tech, asked.

"A cousin, but I think there's more to it. Might want to see what info you can dig up on her."

"We'll do it." Calomiris scribbled on a notepad.

"We're set for you to plug in the drive. It might take a while depending on how much is on there," Singh instructed.

"His hard drive is near capacity, plus he has two backup drives. Okay, I'm going to make the adjustments to the security system, now. Ready, Weiss?"

"Always."

Weiss brought up the security system's schematics on the monitor. Tony reclaimed his stool and observed.

"I'm there," she said.

Weiss talked Angela through rewiring the system to disable the scrambler without tripping a warning. The guy knew his stuff, so Tony kept his mouth shut to not step on any toes.

"All right. Let me mute the phone and see what you can hear."

Though there was white-noise interference, they could decipher her words.

"Not perfect, but we can use it," Calomiris said.

"Okay." Angela switched back to the phone. "Let me— wait. Shit! We've got another problem. Hakim's got an RF detector. And it's not the cheap off-the-internet kind. Oh, yeah," she said after a pause, "he uses this, he finds the surveillance bug, and it'll point right to me."

Calomiris growled. "Skip the bugs. We have too much invested. Switch out the SIM card on the phone. We'll set up parabolic mics across the street if needed. You going to be able to get the files out tonight?"

"There're too many files to upload or email from here. Hakim set the security system. Unless he tries to shoo me out later, I'm here for the night."

"We'll be here all night, too, then," Calomiris said.

"Have fun," Weiss added.

"At least I get to sleep horizontal."

"Rub it in." Weiss griped and reached for the coffee thermos.

Tony glanced at his watch. It was going to be a long night. While, thank God, he wouldn't spend it listening to Angela having sex with Hakim, she wasn't out of the woods, or that locked-down condo, yet.

SIX

ANGELA HEARD Hakim move about in the bedroom, then brush his teeth. She'd pay a hundred dollars for a toothbrush and minty toothpaste right now. Instead, she laid still on the couch.

In her purse two feet away, she had the information the Bureau worked over a year to get. She'd also snuck in his bedroom and replaced the SIM card in his phone. She was close now. So close. It made her mouth water and her pulse race. She needed to keep up the pretense for a few more minutes.

I'm Sabine. Sabine. She forced her breaths into a deep, steady rhythm. Her heart slowed its frantic pace. Sabine had foul-smelling breath from throwing up, too.

Innocent Sabine had no reason to be afraid of Anmar Hakim. If she'd gone to bed with him, and he woke to find her with his phone or computer, *that* would have been a death sentence.

Angela resisted the urge to open her eyes before his hand touched her shoulder, gently rousing her.

"Sabine." His voice was raw, hoarse.

She grumbled and stretched, then blinked several times before she struggled to sit up. "How are you feeling?" She rubbed her stomach for emphasis, then laid her hand on his arm, careful to downplay the fact she heard him puking his guts out last night.

"Horrible."

"I'm sorry. Not a pleasant end to an otherwise wonderful evening. I just had to order the seafood plate for us."

"You think it was bad shrimp?"

"What else could it have been?" She massaged her brow and looked toward the window. "What time is it?"

"Around seven."

She groaned. "Thank you for letting me pass out on your sofa. The thought of trying to make it home in a cab was … well, more humiliating than …" She dropped her gaze to the floor. Her breaths came easier now.

"Yes, I—I understand."

She slipped her feet into her pumps, stood, and swayed a bit. "Would you call down for a cab? I should get home."

Everything in the apartment was in its original place. Another minute and she'd be out of here. This critical phase of mission complete!

The adrenaline rush of living on the edge, when discovery of her deceptions could lead to mortal jeopardy, was one incredible aphrodisiac. Not that she would benefit from it. And Hakim sure as hell wouldn't, either.

The doorman had a cab waiting when she exited the building. The flash of headlights from the white truck parked half a block away confirmed Cal or Weiss saw her. She couldn't risk going straight to the FBI offices in Federal Plaza, so she kept up the French accent and gave the cabbie her home address, then settled back against the worn vinyl seat.

Outside, the tall buildings blocked most of her view of the sky, the sun nowhere in sight. She'd enjoyed the bit of the city's culture she'd managed to partake in.

When she'd walked the city streets or ridden the subway, she'd heard dozens of languages spoken every day. It'd given her a chance to brush up on her skills. But there were too many people here. Too many unfamiliar faces that kept her constantly alert in an exhausting way.

Reggae music played on the radio, and she fantasized about relaxing on a sunny beach, listening to waves break against the shore instead of the current honking of cars.

The cab pulled to the curb in front of the six-story building where the Bureau had set up the tiny apartment for her as Sabine. Her bosses may be desperate to get the files on the zip drive in her possession, but they were going to have to wait a few minutes longer.

Upstairs, she shoved a change of clothes in her gym bag and brushed her teeth. She tuned out the coffeemaker's siren song calling to her—no time to wait for it to brew. Almost feeling like a civilized human again, she switched out her pumps for walking shoes. She retrieved the lockbox in her closet and removed her FBI credentials and tucked the zip drive in the holder.

Please, let this have solid information. It only took one thread to unravel a money-laundering syndicate. One email or file could tie Hakim to al-Shehri. She hurried back down the two flights of steps and was back on the street in under five minutes.

She scanned the street on her way to pick up the number four subway line, checked out the other riders, and the people she passed during her walk to Federal Plaza. She was too close to blow her cover by getting tailed now. As much as she wanted to go the additional block and get some good coffee, she figured there'd be a ten-minute wait. Duty won out, and she turned down Duane Street. A cup of crappy coffee would suffice until she could slip out after she turned the files over.

As she passed through building security, reality reached a climax. The information she held could lead to major breakthroughs and help locate terrorist cells. Today might turn out to be a great day. A twelve on a scale of one to ten kind of day.

She approached the elevator humming "God Bless America." Two men in expensive suits and power ties, both toting thick leather satchels, shot her amused looks as they waited. She finished the line, then switched to sing in her head.

"Don't stop on my account. I like a patriotic woman," said the shorter one. The elevator doors opened, and he motioned her in with a gracious wave of the hand that held a coffee cup emitting a delicious aroma.

She pushed the button for the FBI's counter-terrorism offices.

"Twelve, please." He checked her out head to toe. "Not in uniform today?"

"Uni—" Oh, the stereotypical dark suit. "Cocktail Wednesday," she quipped.

He gave a pleasant laugh. "What time do they start serving? If I'm done with my cases, I'll come join you for a drink."

"Not until after five. Silly rules and regs." The guy wasn't bad looking—for a lawyer. She preferred less hair gel. And muscular arms. She'd always had a thing for great arms—like Jake's.

Last night, she'd laid on Hakim's couch and pictured Jake's arms and his eyes. His smile. His firm abs.

She'd drifted off to sleep indulging in fantasies she couldn't resist after seeing him again. A sexy aura of danger emanated from the man, but there was more. Something she'd glimpsed when they worked together nearly two years ago. He definitely put this attorney in the "average" category by comparison.

"Maybe I'll see you." The lawyer stepped out of the elevator behind his colleague, leaving her alone for the remainder of the ride.

"Special Agent Hoffman." Angela flashed her credentials to the young receptionist.

"Grochowski's been asking for you. Wanted you in his office an hour ago," the woman said.

Do not pass Go. Do not collect much-needed coffee first. At least she'd taken the time to brush the fuzz off her teeth.

The special agent in charge was already on his feet and rounded his desk to meet her.

"Calomiris tell you we couldn't plant the bugs?" she asked.

"He left me a message. You still made my day. Actually, my year." Grochowski took the zip drive from her and led her out of his office and down the hall.

"Get on this. Top priority." He handed the drive to the technical analyst who lit up like a kid getting candy on Halloween, then turned to Angela. "You want to transfer here, I've got a spot for you."

"You have more terrorists for me to date? Wow. That's an offer I can refuse."

"Can't blame me for trying," Grochowski pressed as they left the tech. "I'll have my assistant find you office space downstairs."

"While she does that and we're waiting for him to access and download the files, I'm going to change."

Angela headed to the locker room, ready to dispense of

her Sabine persona now that she was in the office for the first time in nearly two months.

She longed for a scalding shower to wash away the dirty taint clinging to her but settled for rinsing her face. If the computer files uncovered any terrorist cells or gave them information that led to Hakim's arrest, it was worth every bit of the distasteful sucking up she'd done. If it led to al-Shehri, that'd be better than hitting the lottery.

"She's in here," Weiss called out. He made his way across the locker room while she buttoned the fresh, crisp white shirt.

"Oops. Sorry."

She recognized the rich baritone voice immediately and glanced over her shoulder. That Jake caught her getting dressed, brought to mind some of the more intimate moments forced on them at the Deluxe Stay Motel.

Jake set the tray with two large coffees and a bakery bag down on the bench, then took a seat as she folded the dress. She swore she saw a flash of heat in his dark eyes. There had been that touch of her cheek last night, too, which she'd attributed to him checking for the wire. Okay, married but male.

"*You* were in the truck with those two?" She jerked her head toward Weiss as Cal entered the locker room.

"I volunteered."

"But all night?"

Jake shrugged. "So, Hakim got food poisoning?"

"He thinks so, thanks to a little tetrahydrozoline in his nightly tea."

"You dosed him with eye drops?" He laughed, smiling at her with an incredulous expression.

"They're good for more than getting the red out." She gave him a lecherous smile as he handed her a coffee. She inhaled the tantalizing scent, then took a sip and luxuriated in the smooth taste of the vanilla latte. "Mmmm ... heaven."

Undercover work meant having to remember cover identities: names, accents, associates, backgrounds, and more, but Jake remembered her favorite coffee. He sure wasn't making it easy to keep her thoughts semi-pure. When he opened the bag, she salivated for more than him.

"Blueberry muffin or sausage, egg, and cheese croissant?"

Her lust for this man jumped yet another notch. She looked from one to the other, debating.

He gave another sexy, throaty chuckle, then cut the croissant in half. "I thought you might be hungry. You didn't dose yourself, did you?"

"No. Fanciest dinner I've had in probably three years, and I had to stick my finger down my throat to make sure I didn't get kicked out."

"Better plan than the alternative Weiss thought you'd employ."

"That doesn't surprise me." She shook her head and accepted half of the sandwich. "Thanks. I'm glad *someone* is a gentleman *and* thoughtful enough to bring me coffee and something to eat," she jabbed at her fellow agents.

"Hey. I would have gotten you coffee, but I had to circle the block in the truck. No place to park," Cal said in his own defense.

She took a bite while Jake cut the muffin in half. *Is this what falling in love feels like?* Because these small gestures made her want to kiss him. She was probably being overdramatic after years of providing for herself with no one watching her back. But, still, it was beyond nice.

Another gulp of coffee gave her time to regain her composure.

"Yeah, we woulda, but the Boy Scout had it covered." Weiss' tone held a hint of mockery.

"It's Tony. Vincenti. And I'm not a Boy Scout!" He rolled his eyes.

Tony Vincenti. Finally. She'd figured he was of Italian heritage. Joey, Frank, Vinnie were all names she'd run through, but Tony fit him better. Knowing his real name would surely play into any future fantasies.

Damn. Somebody was a lucky woman. She needed to get control of herself. She polished off the remainder of her croissant and closed her locker.

Angela studied him as he ate and watched her with an adorable grin. Something was different—other than his haircut and clothes. *His nose.* Before, it had a bump on the bridge and hooked a bit to the left. His jaw appeared broader, too, though it could look different without the sexy scruff he had in Texas. Remembering how soft it had been against her cheek inspired an urge to stroke his face. Another impulse to resist.

He handed her half of the blueberry muffin, then took a bite of his. Leaning in, he spoke in a low tone. "When this is over, maybe we can go out to dinner. Make up for you losing yours last night."

A date? Was he serious? Or … "You, uh, don't have family to get home to—back at your *secret* base?"

"Special Ops Command at Bragg isn't exactly a secret. Wait—family? The ring?" Understanding registered across his features. He held up his left hand and pulled off the gold band. "A prop for last night. I promise. Did you think—when we were in Texas …?"

A flush shot her body temperature up a few degrees. How did this man read her like a giant billboard? "I didn't see why not. I mean, you behaved like a gentleman—or a married man."

"No. Not married." He shook his head. "Or in a relationship. I was being professional, and you, uh,"—he glanced over at Cal and Weiss to make sure they weren't listening —"didn't offer any overt invitations. I kinda thought *you* were married or involved with someone. Too bad we didn't talk about that." His smile broadened, and his eyebrows hitched up.

"We didn't exactly have that opportunity." Not with the surveillance camera planted in her room. While they'd put on quite a show pretending to be lovers in public, she'd focused on the assignment. Resisted the temptation.

Her past, the choices she'd made, and the contract on her life meant serious relationships were not an option. Probably never would be. But she could see having a little fun. "You're planning to stay in the city for a while?"

"With the right incentive." Again, one side of his mouth turned up in that appealing, make-her-stomach-flutter manner. "The colonel's been on me to use some of my accrued vacation time. I was thinking about heading upstate to see family for a couple of days. First, we could get tickets for a show. Have a nice dinner. See some sights." His gaze held hers.

She wanted to say yes—*if* he was being honest with her about not being married. She'd been burned before. Could she trust him?

Hell, she could find out. After all, she was with the FBI.

SEVEN

SEEING Angela had been an invigorating turnaround to Tony's morning after a long night in the van. He'd love a twenty-minute power nap, but the rest of the Bad Karma team had arrived, and they'd all been relegated to a windowless FBI conference room. At least the Bureau higher-ups hadn't told the team, *'Thanks, but we don't need your help'*—yet. It would suck if they got sent home before he could honor his promise to take Angela out. Their exchange in the locker room gave him a double incentive to tackle the stacks of paper covering the table, hoping to find anything useful in locating al-Shehri or convicting Hakim.

"What," a booming voice interrupted their work, "there aren't enough assholes running around in Afghanistan to keep you guys busy? Now you gotta come to the big city and play here, too?" Jarrod Carswell, former Bad Karma team leader, stood in the doorway, grinning at the men.

"Look at you, Captain." Lundgren rose to his feet.

"Not Captain anymore. *Supervisory* Special Agent Carswell now." Carswell threw back his shoulders and puffed out his chest, posing in his dark-gray suit and yellow tie.

"What are you doing here? Last I heard you were working for that private contractor, Dileas." Lundgren shook Carswell's hand.

"Yeah, well, that gig ended. Joined the Bureau four years ago. Here I am, running my first show when Grochowski calls last night, saying Hoffman requested to bring in outsiders. I said, 'Hell no.' We're this close." Carswell held his thumb and index finger an inch apart. "Then Grochowski says some Spec Ops team is about to pick up Hakim, and we've got to play ball. When he mentioned Colonel Mahinis, I figured it could be like old times. Didn't know I was saying yes to my Bad Karma team. Might not have said yes if I'd known I was bringing you yahoos in."

"Bullshit!" Mack Hanlon protested with a broad grin.

"Hanlon, Vincenti, you still dishing out bad karma?"

"Every chance we get," Tony said. He and Carswell only served on the team together for a year, but they'd been knee-deep in serious shit on more than one occasion.

Lundgren introduced Carswell to the newer members of the team.

"How're Cheyenne and the kids? Glad to have you home for a change?" Mack asked.

"Hardly," Carswell grunted. "She'd be happier if I were overseas and bringing in the triple-digit paycheck. Flipside is I get to see the boys more."

It sounded like married life wasn't paradise for Carswell on this second go-round. Still, Tony wanted more than the string of short-term, shallow relationships that only satisfied his physical needs.

It was his own fault. Picking up women in bars—or being picked up as was the case over half the time—was not the ideal way to meet women who were interested in what he could offer beyond the bedroom.

A familiar longing sucker-punched him in the chest when Mack showed Carswell pictures of his daughters and new wife, Kristie. Finding a woman who understood and supported guys in their line of work was rare. Most bailed when reality didn't live up to their romanticized versions. Too many, like Mack's first wife, couldn't handle the danger. Then there were those, like Carla Ciancio, who couldn't be trusted to stay faithful during a deployment.

Angela hadn't been fazed by his dangerous career when they were undercover together—though they'd both been playing roles. They were together for a purpose, not because they wanted to get to know each other. But maybe things could be different now.

"What happened with the security job?" Mack's question pinged Tony's brain.

He hadn't seen Carswell—who'd come up with the name for Bravo Company—since he left the Army for the big bucks that private security companies paid to lure operators away from Special Forces.

"Things were going pretty well. We were working with the CIA in Afghanistan when they nabbed one of al-Shehri's couriers. Best lead in years, only he wouldn't give up anything. So, the Agency tasked us to bring in the courier's daughter as motivation to talk. I mentioned the assignment to one of the CIA agents. She went ballistic—I didn't think they'd be keeping secrets from one of their own, you know—and she went off on her boss. Wanted to question the courier and try to get intel without involving the kid. The Agency sent us out anyway, then I took the heat when their agent got her panties in a wad and quit, and I got blackballed over a little pillow talk."

"You two were, uh …" Tony interrupted.

"Hey, you're not married when you're overseas." Carswell raised a closed hand for a fist bump.

Tony wasn't a prude. Far from it. But marriage was a commitment. A covenant. Some tenets of the Catholic faith were still engrained in him. He left Carswell hanging.

"Anyway, bitch of it all," Carswell continued, "is the whole thing was a setup. Guy didn't have a kid. We drove into an ambush. Lost one guy and two of us were airlifted out and sent stateside. After I rehabbed, I joined the Bureau. Spent a year in Cincinnati before being promoted and landing here."

Typical Carswell. Like a cat, he always seemed to land on his feet. He could walk through a pile of shit, and it wouldn't stick to him. Something about the guy drew others to him, but Carswell liked living on the edge. Too close to the edge for Tony's comfort. If he had to pick who to follow into battle, he'd pick Lundgren's level-headed leadership style and the way he looked out for the guys on the team above himself any day.

"I've got to get to a meeting. Told my staff to take care of you. Let them know if you need anything." Carswell gave a two-finger salute, then strode out the door.

THE BRUNETTE JUNIOR agent eyed the men. "Can I get you gentlemen more coffee?"

"The other gal just brought us some, but thanks." Lundgren rubbed the bridge of his nose.

Juan Dominguez groaned when she set down another armful of documents on the conference table. "What are we? Grunt labor?"

"To stay involved, we agreed to help with whatever they needed," Lundgren reminded the group after she left.

Devin Grant flagged a page and set it aside. He reached for another document, jostling Tony in the process.

"How do you do that, man?" Mack flipped his hand at the pile Grant had already gone through, outpacing the rest of the team.

"Speed-reading. You look for the keywords." Grant's head moved left to right as he turned pages at a dizzying rate.

"We can't all be geniuses. And the more he reads means less for us," Dominguez said.

"It'd help us all if you didn't whistle while you read, Dominguez." Porter fixed him with a pointed stare.

Tony shook his head. Eight action-oriented Alpha males crammed in a conference room reading over the files from Hakim's computer was hardly an ideal situation. It'd only been four hours since they started, but the constant interruptions and movements distracted him. Plus his thoughts kept wandering down the hall.

He rose and made a show of stretching. "Be back in a few." Someone snickered, and he overheard Dominguez whisper Angela's name the second he turned out of the doorway.

After making a pit stop in the restroom, he ambled further down the hall and paused in the doorway of the small office where Angela sat engrossed in a document. She glanced up from the printout in her hand and gave him one of those demure smiles that sent electricity coursing through him.

"Come on in. How's it going down there?"

He rolled his eyes and chuckled. "I give it another half an hour max before someone goes looking for rope to string up Dominguez or rappel down the side of the building to escape."

"Too much testosterone in the room?" she asked with a laugh.

"Not our typical workday. Close quarters and way too sedentary. People keep coming in every five minutes with more coffee or files that are all crap. Haven't found anything useful."

"They're probably giving you guys the low-priority documents. Tech said there are *thousands* of saved files. Mostly inane stuff probably loaded to make it harder to find what we're looking for. And you'll likely keep getting offers of coffee—and more—based on the inquisition I've gotten from half the female staff already. You guys are way more interesting than agents investigating white-collar crimes. Becca, the brunette junior agent, is on the rebound, and she's drooling over the redhead from the Texas op."

"That's Mack. He just got remarried. She won't get anywhere with him or the chief. Now, the rest of the team, that's another story. And you might want to warn them about Dominguez, who you knew as Carlito."

"Really?"

"Trust me," he warned, envisioning Dominguez disappearing into a supply closet with one of the junior agents. His gaze settled on the script of the top document on her desk. "Arabic? But you were speaking French with Hakim ... Because you didn't want him to know you can read or speak it." *Duh!* He realized it after the words were out.

She winked at him. "He's quite enamored with all things French. We used that angle to get him interested."

"Speaking of languages, what are you doing out in the field again?" The Bureau putting a linguist undercover on something this big didn't add up. Every time he tried to deduce their reasons, it interfered with his concentration.

"They had someone else working Hakim, but she wasn't getting anywhere. Either not his type or he was suspicious."

"And the Bureau didn't have anyone else?"

"Weiss speaks French and Arabic, but he wouldn't shave his legs and put on a dress. I was bored." Her head and shoulders did a little dance.

Tony grimaced at the image of Weiss in a dress trying to entice the devout terrorist. Angela's being bored didn't explain it, and the curiosity that pricked his mind wouldn't let him drop it. "They don't typically send linguists into the field. Texas, I could understand because of your relation to Brock, but this is different. You are good—as if you were trained for undercover work ..."

All traces of her smile disappeared. "Close the door."

The command got his attention. Her giving him orders was also kind of a turn-on, which sent blood pouring into his groin again. He closed the door, then sat in the chair opposite her desk.

"Before this, I worked in a different capacity—for *another* government agency."

Agency? "*The* Agency?" He held his breath.

She nodded.

"Wow. The CIA." If she'd been an operative for the CIA, it explained why the Bureau would utilize her and her adeptness for undercover work. He and the team had never worked with a spook like her before.

"One of my professors at Northeastern thought I had skills they could use and arranged an interview. I was headed to law school on scholarship, so I passed on their offer."

"What changed your mind?"

"9/11." Angela broke eye contact and took a deep breath in the silence that followed. "My fiancé was on American's Flight 11."

A sickening feeling rolled through Tony's core. "The first plane to hit the World Trade Center."

"Yeah. He'd come east for a friend's wedding and stayed to spend some time with me. I drove him to the airport for his flight before my classes. When I first heard a plane hit one of the towers, I envisioned a tourist prop plane. When I went to the student union, it was on every television. One look and I knew it was something big. I watched the second tower come down. I didn't know then … Dammit." She swiped away a tear with her fingertips, leaving a wet streak across her cheek. "Anyway, a week later, I contacted the CIA. A week after that, I withdrew from law school to start training at The Farm."

Sympathy swelled. So many lives damaged by 9/11. His cousin's husband was a firefighter who died when the first tower collapsed. Everyone back home in Amherst knew someone who died that day. It obviously changed the trajectory of Angela's life. That she'd decided to go after the sons of bitches responsible was appealing, too—not that he'd tell her that, especially now. Better to keep on track.

"So, how'd you end up working as a linguist for the Bureau?" Based on his experience, the two groups didn't exactly mesh, and the Agency would've given her a better opportunity to get payback against Al-Qaeda for 9/11.

"We may be at war, but there are certain lines that shouldn't be crossed—especially when it comes to innocent civilians and children. It makes us no better than the terrorists we're after. I couldn't condone some of the methods they used. So, I resigned. The FBI was a good fit for my linguistic skills."

"And yet you still venture into the field." Compared to being a CIA operative, he could understand how confining and boring—and safe—her job could be. "Arabic, French,

Spanish. How many languages do you speak?" He switched the topic to a less dark subject.

"Fluently? Seven. My Pashto is passable. I'm proficient in sign language, and I'm learning Mandarin. Based on my forays into Chinatown, though, my Chinese pretty much sucks."

"Still"—a gruff laugh escaped him—"that's impressive."

"I also have a list of keywords and phrases memorized in another seventeen." She gave a subtle shrug, but the corners of her mouth curved up for a moment.

Holy shit. His fluency in Italian, Spanish, and French, and limited ability to communicate in Pashto and Korean sounded average now. He shook his head. "Were you a child prodigy?"

"No, the environment I grew up in. My mom was Louisiana Cajun, and I was born near New Orleans, so I grew up speaking English and French. My dad is an engineer in the oil industry. We went where the work was. We lived in Venezuela, Brazil, and the United Arab Emirates before I was twelve. I came back to the States with my mom for a while. Later, I lived with my dad in Germany, until my stepmother decided a foreign-exchange program in France seemed like 'an excellent educational opportunity.' So, *voilà*. Here I am."

"I can't imagine living in that many places." His parents lived in the same house where he'd grown up. He'd gone to school with all the same kids from kindergarten to graduation. Until he'd left for basic training, he'd never been out of the Northeast, though he'd been to Canada a few times to see Niagara Falls and hockey games.

"I lived in some interesting places. There were some benefits to always being the new kid. Drawbacks, too."

Based on the way she averted her gaze, he'd picked another touchy subject. *Great.*

She closed her eyes and exhaled audibly. "After a while,

my mother didn't like the moves. The money was great, but even that couldn't keep her in the Middle East. She left my dad and brought me back to the States with a roughneck she hooked up with. That didn't last, and she went from one bad relationship and crappy job to another until she ended up with Ronnie. Stepdad of the year." Disdain accompanied the shaking of her head.

"Brock's dad?" He knew about her stepbrother from their prior mission with the Coyotes gang; however, her reaction whenever he came up roused his curiosity on the degree of their relationship. The tug in his gut made him push. "You and Brock were close?"

She sighed again. "I wouldn't say we were close. I mean, we lived under the same roof, but I was rarely there. I tried to avoid *home* as much as possible."

Tony waited, allowing her to drop it or change the subject. To keep her secrets. Why should she trust him enough to open up? He was just some guy she worked with for a few days. A virtual stranger. Someone she'd have dinner with, and based on the earlier looks and innuendo, she'd have sex with. Hot, up-against-a-wall-then-in-the-bedroom-and-later-in-the-shower sex. Unless he blew it. Which he was on the cusp of doing. Typically, he didn't dig into a woman's past. Angela, however, wasn't the typical woman.

"Home wasn't a safe place." She talked without looking at him—her voice flat and her face devoid of emotion. "People coming and going. Drugs. Sex. Guns. I stayed at school or the library. People knew my family. I was guilty by association."

She met his eyes finally, seeming on the brink of a major disclosure. He should interrupt. Avoid the responsibility of shared secrets.

What kind of flawed individual got a hard-on going head-to-head with an enemy, but broke out in a cold sweat at the mere notion of revealing past hurts? God, no wonder he sucked at relationships for anything beyond casual sex. She probably thought he shook his head in response to her tale of woe instead of self-deprecation.

"One night, a biker came looking for a fix. Ronnie and my mother were out somewhere—who knows where. The guy didn't believe I didn't know where their stash was, so he decided to get his high another way. My screams woke up Brock. He pulled the guy off me. The fight didn't last long, but the biker spent a few days in the hospital after surgery to sew him back together.

"That served as a wake-up call to my mother. She'd always relied on someone else to provide for her needs, only she wasn't the twenty-year-old beauty anymore. She was doing the best she could, but when she saw what it was doing to me, she sent me to live with my dad in Germany. I wouldn't have gone if I'd known they'd charge Brock. He was defending himself. Trying to protect me." She paused, her mouth pinched with emotional pain. "But he had a record, so they sentenced him to prison. When I came back for college, I found out he'd gotten out and was riding with the Coyotes."

"It's not your fault." Tony read it on her face, in her tone: the guilt, the blame.

"If I'd been here, I could have testified."

"You were what? Seventeen or eighteen?"

"Sixteen."

His hand balled into a fist, and he swallowed the lump of rage cutting off his air supply. Sixteen. And she still blamed herself for how much of it? That had to fuck up her ability to trust people. With her background and no close family, no wonder it made her a perfect candidate for the CIA.

"It wasn't fair. Brock deserved better."

Tony didn't know the "right" thing to say. If her hands were closer, he could have reached out to her, but he doubted she would appreciate him coming around the desk to give her a sympathetic hug.

Instead, silence settled like a cold, wet blanket.

"They ever find out who killed him?"

"No one was ever charged. Not sure anyone cared enough to work that hard."

He was saved from not knowing what to say again by a knock on the door. The brunette agent cracked the door and peeked in.

"Singh found more documents the program couldn't translate and asked me to bring them to you." She eased into the room and handed a few pages across the desk.

Angela's eyes narrowed, and her mouth pursed as she scanned the top printout. "Thanks. Oh, and Becca, the redhead in the conference room is newly married. He's off-limits."

The young woman's eyes went wide, and her body stiffened. Tony witnessed the quick jerk of her head in his direction.

"And, uh—he is, too." Angela pointed her pen at him. She smiled but kept her gaze fixed on the junior agent.

"I'll, um, make sure that's, uh, understood." Becca backed into the doorframe, then fumbled for the doorknob.

Tony raised a hand to his mouth to cover his amusement.

Angela shifted her gaze to him and leaned back in her chair. "She was talking about you, too. I figured I'd be more productive if she wasn't flirting with you."

He mentally pumped his fist. Dinner was still on—and the after-activities that would require his mother to light a candle on his behalf. If his mom could read his mind right now, she'd scurry down to St. Benedict's and light a candle for every dollar she had in her purse.

Did Angela have a clue what a turn-on her smile was?

"I guess I better let you get back to work," he said before he forgot why he was here and indulged his graphic imagination.

"You get any sleep last night?"

"A little. We traded off."

"Well, if you need a power nap, come on back. It's not the Ritz," she motioned to the two office chairs across from her desk, "but it's quiet."

"I won't distract you?" he asked, unable to keep from teasing her.

"It'd be a welcome distraction."

Great. He was definitely walking back in the conference room with a full-on boner.

EIGHT

"I THINK SOMETHING'S GOING ON." Tony used his chopsticks to pick another piece of chicken out of the box. He craned his neck to see out the doorway into the area filled with cubicles.

"Why? 'Cause the gals haven't checked back to see if we need drink refills in the past twenty minutes?" Mack smirked.

"What's up with that anyway?" Dominguez's eyes drilled Tony.

He ignored Dominguez. "There's movement and raised voices."

"And we didn't get invited to the party?" Lundgren's eyebrows rose in contemplation. "Go." He gave the nod.

Tony grabbed his cup to provide a pretense while he attempted to gather intel. Angela came down the hallway. An agent he hadn't met was on her heels.

"There's no point in waiting for Wetzel when these guys can probably tell us what the hell it is." She made straight for Tony. "You guys are familiar with a variety of explosive devices, right?"

Whoa! "Yeah. We all are. What do you need?" The intense look on her face and her question shattered the lethargy that plagued him after hours of reading bogus documents.

"I need you to see if you can make heads or tails of these. It's out of my area of expertise." She relinquished the papers despite the grumbled protests of the other agent.

Tony gave the sheets a cursory glance. He pivoted and ushered her to the conference room. "Take a look." He turned the papers over to Lundgren.

The chief studied them for a moment. "Make room," he requested.

The team scrambled to clear the stacks of papers and takeout containers strewn over the large table's glossy wood surface. Tony picked up the box of sesame chicken while Lundgren spread out the hand-drawn sketches. Grant and Porter crowded in to get a better look.

"You got my sesame chicken?" Angela frowned.

"Yours? They just brought us …" Guilt, and her adorable pout, won out. He held out the container. "Sorry. I didn't know."

"I got some lo mein. I wanted sesame chicken, though." She gave him a coy smile and used his chopsticks to help herself to the chicken and broccoli.

He'd give this woman anything she asked for. Watching the food disappear into her mouth made the blood rush to his groin again. Man, he couldn't wait until this mission wrapped up.

"Those two know what they're doing?" She leaned closer while Porter and Grant shuffled papers around.

Her shoulder brushed against his bicep, giving him a fraction of the body contact he yearned for. It took Herculean control not to slip his free hand to her hip to keep her close. He settled for eye contact. "Porter likes to blow things up, and Grant's our resident genius." He pointed out his teammates while he talked. "If it's any type of explosive device, they'll know. What made you suspect it could be a bomb?"

"I translated the word 'detonator.' That kinda raised a red flag."

The sketches didn't resemble any bomb he'd seen. Detonator, however, was pretty damned specific.

"He really a genius or you picking on him?" She studied Grant's profile.

"Depends. You like the genius type?"

She gave a low, lusty chuckle. "They aren't usually the best conversationalists. Course, he might not steal my sesame chicken." Her voice dropped lower, adding to the seductive lilt.

"I said I was sorry. Guess I'll have to buy you Chinese another night."

"Sounds good to me." She dug out another piece of chicken, then returned the chopsticks to the box.

"What are you lookin' at, Dominguez?" Great. Dominguez grinned in that annoying way that told Tony he'd be grilled later.

"I'll leave those sketches to see what you guys can make of them." She gave him a subtle wink when she passed him on her way out.

"Excuse me. Ma'am?" Grant stopped her. He dug out his notepad from the pile of papers they'd shoved aside and tore off the top sheet. He rounded the table and gave her the sheet. "Can you ask your techs to eliminate all saved files with these sentences? I found them randomly inserted into documents. And this list on the right, I think they're words inserted because they would set off the alarms and whistles. I thought the request might be better received coming from you."

Tony's jaw muscles tightened when Grant flashed Angela his all-American, boy-next-door pearly whites, but Tony nodded to reassure her there must be a solid reason to his teammate's analysis.

"O-kay," she drawled. "I'll ask."

———

"I FOUND SOME MORE ..." Angela stopped a step inside the conference room. She stared at the image projected onto the cream-colored wall. It resembled a drawing made by a spirograph. "What is that?" she asked the team of men.

"We're still working on it. Things aren't lining up right," the man with the shaved head and goatee who Tony had identified as Linc Porter answered. His tilde-shaped eyebrows gave the sexy operator an aura of perpetual concentration as he adjusted one of the transparencies in the stack layered on the overhead projector.

"Here are the sketches with everything translated. We found a few more sketches, and this. I don't know if it's related or not, but these symbols here"—she pointed —"there's one on each of the sketches."

"Ah-ha! I knew it. Thank you! And this"—the genius, Grant, took the sheet she'd pointed to and gripped it in both hands like it was the Holy Grail—"has to be the key." He snatched up the entire stack of transparencies and shuffled through them. He conferred with Porter, and they turned the slides at different angles. "I need transparencies of these new ones."

"I'll go ask Becca to make them. Give 'em over." Dominguez acted downright gleeful at the excuse to escape the room and seek out the flirty junior agent.

"He's easy to make happy, huh?" she said to Tony, who had already made his way to her side. He stood close enough that she could feel the heat radiating from his muscled body.

She forced her attention back to the image. "So, it's like a puzzle?"

"And it's driving Grant nuts that he can't figure it out."

"I have more good news. He was right about the dummy phrases. Singh did as he asked, and it eliminated all but like seventy-three files. They're printing those off now, and we'll get you copies."

"We've spun our wheels reading all this crap for nothing?" Mack tossed several pages on top of a pile to his side.

"I wouldn't say for nothing. What he discovered helped a lot. There are encrypted files they're trying to crack, and Singh said they'll run an algorithm on those secret code words."

"'Secret code words'? You sound like such a spy." Tony chuckled.

She shot him a mock scowl. He laughed harder, and his fingers touched her low back. His touch didn't last long enough. Her eyes locked and held on his. What was it about this man that could make her melt with a look, or a touch, and bare her soul? While she hadn't run a background check to verify his marital status because of everything else going on, she'd flirted and conveyed her interest. Now, if she found out he'd lied and had a wife or fiancée, she might have to kill him.

Since he didn't know her entire past, he didn't have the good sense to run. And telling him would be presumptuous. Besides, he wasn't looking for anything serious. Just fun and sex. Then he'd be gone. She could live with that—couldn't she?

Of course.

She had to.

Her mouth turned up in a smile that didn't sync with the empty ache inside her. She needed to get out of this room.

Now. Before her thoughts went down that dusty road to nowhere.

"Good luck with the puzzle, guys. If I find anything else, I'll be back."

"See ya." Tony discreetly touched her arm.

"Thanks." Grant took the briefest moment to glance up before resuming his frenetic manipulations of the transparencies.

She hurried back to the safety of her temporary office and sank into her chair. When she finished this assignment, she'd be like the ghost she'd been as an operative working for the CIA. She'd disappear and leave behind no trace of being there. Only a memory in the minds of those she had contact with. No one would miss her.

They might miss her work. That's what she excelled at. It was where she could make a difference—protect the innocent. After one more heavy breath and glance around the sterile office, she went back to doing what she did best.

NINE

"GROCHOWSKI NEEDS everyone in the main conference room. Now." Weiss interrupted Angela's reading.

"They find something?" She stared at his mischievous grin for a moment before it hit her. He'd spoken in Arabic, and she'd responded in kind. Shouldn't surprise her after reading documents in Arabic for the past few hours.

Weiss laughed and switched to English. "Singh broke the encrypted files, and your fan club found something that has Grochowski in there—and Hollis."

Hollis? She sprang to her feet. The director of local Homeland Security and the special agent in charge of the FBI's New York office didn't call joint conferences every day. More like every half-decade. Her mind raced over the implications. She hurried down the hallway after Weiss and crowded into the conference room.

"Here you go, ma'am." Tony's teammate Kyle Liu, who hadn't previously spoken two words, got to his feet and motioned for her to take his seat.

After the past two hours at her desk, she preferred to

stand—right beside Tony Vincenti. The chair afforded her a prime spot to observe his profile, though.

The navy tie Grochowski wore with his charcoal-gray suit complemented Hollis in her navy suit and butter-yellow blouse. Both wore matching grim expressions.

"Hakim's banking records show three high-six-figure money transfers out in the past four months," Grochowski started once everyone settled in. "The money hit an account in the Caymans. Singh is working on where it went after that."

That garnered Angela's full and undivided attention. She'd bet the worst was yet to come.

"We have an idea what it might be for. Chief Warrant Lundgren."

Lundgren shifted his impressive frame, sweeping an arm toward the fair-haired genius. "Staff Sergeant Grant will brief you on his findings. In civilian speak," he added in a low tone.

Grant turned on the power to the projector. Two separate images appeared on the whiteboard. His gaze swept over her as he began speaking. "Thanks to Special Agent Hoffman"—*Great.* She really didn't want to take credit for this find—"we found this series of sketches that were individual files. When compiled correctly, they're schematics for building a shockwave-type bomb. But our major concern is that this second diagram indicates plans to incorporate radioactive material—creating a dirty bomb."

Several gasps reverberated throughout the room. The contents of Angela's stomach bubbled like lava before an eruption.

"They'd need radioactive material to make that happen. So far, we haven't had any viable threats." Calomiris downgraded the threat.

"True. But it doesn't have to be weapons-grade," Grant continued. "It could be radioactive material used for research or medical purposes. There are thousands of orphan sources. Stolen materials and high-security risk elements that disappeared after the collapse of the Soviet Union. This bomb wouldn't have the destructive capability of a nuclear weapon, but depending on where it's detonated, it could kill thousands. Sicken hundreds of thousands. And apart from the human cost, it would create mass hysteria and cost billions in cleanup."

Weiss whistled through his teeth. One of the male agents in the back of the room muttered an expletive.

Grochowski exhaled a lament. "We don't know for certain that it's gone beyond getting the design for the bomb. However, the amount of money that Hakim's moved makes us think they could have acquired the materials. And, if so, we have no idea of their target—or when."

"Special Agent Hoffman?" Homeland Security Director Hollis scanned the females in the room and settled on her before she nodded in acknowledgment. "Does the name Ahmad Bin Faud ring any bells? Someone Hakim might have mentioned doing business with?"

Angela couldn't suppress the rueful laugh. "No. Hakim *never* discussed business associates. Paranoid is his MO. He doesn't even mention where he eats a meal. Makes it hard to carry on a conversation."

"We found a receipt for an airline ticket booked under that name in his emails. We don't have a record of anyone entering the States under that name. We're checking visas and passports issued abroad," Director Hollis explained.

"Where was the ticket to?" she asked, trying to follow the evidence trail.

"LaGuardia to Paris. Two days from now and returning in three weeks."

"Leaving—for France? I think we may have a problem." Angela swallowed the lump in her throat only to have it crash in her chest.

"Why?" Director Hollis asked.

All eyes were on Angela. What if she were wrong?

"I think the name is an alias." She struggled to get the words out. Her tongue seemed too large for her mouth. "He wouldn't—I—I can't see him having that on his computer for someone else. It doesn't make sense."

"Singh also found porn on his computer." Grochowski didn't even crack a smile at the implication. "That doesn't fit what we know of him, either."

"Porn?" Her brain threatened to explode. He was right. That didn't fit Hakim's profile. She'd heard reports that one of the 9/11 hijackers called for a hooker the night before their attack, and another watched pay-per-view porn in his hotel room. Those terrorists were radical extremists, too.

"It was just one downloaded video. We can check his surfing history, though," the tech, Singh, said.

"I …" She hesitated and ran a hand through her hair. "I think he's skipping the country. Going to France fits. It's the one thing he *does* talk about. And how he loved it there. Says 'America is a den of iniquity.'"

"Hakim's not perfect, either. He planned to do the deed with Sabine. You guys aren't married," Weiss rationalized.

She wanted to strangle Weiss. His implication made heat rise to her face.

"Hoped to." Tony's hard tone challenged anyone to make another insinuation.

She couldn't meet his eyes. She'd done it before—slept with a man she'd rather have killed. But she'd done what she had to do to get the job done and stay alive. And she would have slept with Hakim if she had no other choice.

"We need you all looking for any mention of dates, locations. Anything that could be related. Anything out of the ordinary," Grochowski instructed.

"Our last option is to detain him at the airport to make sure he doesn't flee the country," Hollis said. "That would tip our hand, though."

The room remained silent as people filed out to go back to work. Detaining Hakim wouldn't stop anything already in the works. The airline ticket told her Hakim didn't want to be in the proximity of a dirty bomb, but would he talk to save himself? When the alternative meant spending the rest of his life in prison, no. Not without some form of torture—the line she'd swore she wouldn't cross. Making him puke his guts out was nothing compared to things she'd seen in the past. But with so many lives at risk, would she sacrifice her moral high ground? Even suggest a specific form of torture?

THIS MORNING'S meeting had derailed Angela's train of thought. With so much on the line, it had taken her twice as long to translate the documents. And nothing had stood out. Maybe Weiss would see something she missed.

As she approached his office, it was the moans of pleasure that stopped her more than the five people sandwiched inside.

"We've got a potential dirty bomb threat, and you guys are watching porn? Unbelievable!" She shook her head at the men—and Becca—all facing Weiss's computer, that now issued a woman's accented voice.

"Relax. It's not even good porn." Weiss grinned at her.

"We're following Grochowski's orders. Seeing if there's anything in the video that would explain your boyfriend's interest in it."

"It could be because the woman looks and sounds like she's from a Middle Eastern country. And he's right, it's not good porn." Dominguez didn't show the least trace of being embarrassed, unlike Liu, who had the good graces to tear his gaze from the screen. "Look. Seriously," Dominguez continued when Angela crossed her arms and held her ground. "The woman looks like she's drugged out."

"Probably some amateur who answered a casting call," Weiss explained. "They're desperate for money and their big break to stardom, so they believe the guy who tells them they only have to let someone touch them a little. Producer gives them something to help them relax. Next thing they remember is waking up and being given a couple of hundred bucks for a few hours of work. I worked human-trafficking cases here. Same ploy. I'm not totally devoid of scruples," he admonished. "And get this. The name of the film is *Den of Iniquity*. See? Valid research." He turned the screen to show her.

"See what you can find on the *stars* of the film," she suggested. "That *may* be helpful."

She disregarded the scantily clad body of the woman on the screen and studied her face. A pang of compassion rippled through her. And the tiniest bit of relief that Tony wasn't in here watching the video. "I didn't find any clues in these. Take a second look. Anything else you need me to take a look at? Besides the video." She handed Weiss the documents.

"Naw, I'm good. But this really is work." He couldn't quite keep a straight face.

She understood the need to take a break from reading and translating Hakim's documents. Her own eyes stopped focusing half an hour ago. She needed to get caffeine and clear her head. Okay, and a glimpse of Tony would help her get a second wind.

In the break room, she slipped a dollar into the vending machine for a Butterfinger. *Oh, seriously.* She cursed the anonymous dolt who left enough for two swallows in the coffee pot. She poured it into a foam cup, dug out a new packet, then filled the machine with water. *See, it's not that hard people.*

While she waited for fresh brew, she twirled the cup in her hands. There might be coffee in the carafe in the conference room, though those guys were mainlining it. It gave her an excuse to go in, get her little bonus thrill.

Her pulse quickened as she made her way down the hall. *Breathe normally. You're just getting coffee.*

She breezed into the conference room, then fought to keep from pouting that Tony wasn't there. "How's it coming?" Trying for nonchalant, she reached for the nearest carafe and filled her cup.

"Nothing new since this morning's bombshell." Mack winced at his own choice of words. "Tony ducked out a few minutes ago," he added.

"Just needed a refill." She waved the coffee cup. "Back to my cell." So much for playing it low-key.

Halfway back to her office, the top of Tony's head appeared over the partitions on the central office floor. He rounded the corner and broke into a smile when he spotted her.

"Need a pick-me-up?" His head bobbed toward the coffee and candy bar.

"Yeah." Oh, she needed a pick-me-up—one besides a sugar buzz. "Sometimes, a change of scenery helps me see things in a new light."

"I know what you mean. Thought seeing you would get my blood flowing again."

Oh, my. "Well, I was kinda hoping to—"

"Hey, Vincenti." Jarrod's voice cut off her words. "Oh, hi, Ang." He paused, his eyes shifting from Tony back to her. His lips twisted in a half smile.

Crap. Jarrod discovering her interest in Tony was the last thing she needed. "I've got more documents to translate. Catch you later." That thrill was short lived.

TEN

"You okay?"

Tony's question forced Angela's eyes open to find him standing in her office doorway—as though she'd mentally summoned him after Jarrod waylaid him a few minutes ago. "Yeah. Just doing mission prep."

"Really? Because it looked like you might be praying."

Her chin jutted up. "Maybe prayer *is* a part of my planning." He had no clue what worked for her or had kept her alive while working undercover to bring down people who had no compunction against killing anyone who got in their way.

He stepped into the room and closed the door behind him. "Good." He came around the desk, leaned over, and pressed a gentle kiss to the top of her head, surprising the hell out of her.

It wasn't a romantic kiss. Certainly not the steamy, passionate, melt-your-insides, start-peeling-off-the-clothes kiss she'd imagined all day. This kiss ignited a different heat deep inside that radiated all the way to her toes and fingertips.

He lingered over her, his fingers touching her, for a few glorious seconds.

"Thanks."

He mumbled a contented noise, then eased away and sat on the corner of her desk. "I saw the big kahuna was in here. What's up?"

"Grochowski wanted to discuss options to get back into Hakim's apartment to plant a bug in case I don't hear from him. If you consider the morning after is awkward enough when you do get what you want, imagine the morning after when you spent time in adjacent bathrooms puking. I don't expect him to call for a do-over, especially if he's getting ready to leave the country." She met his eyes, which were locked on her.

"True," he agreed.

"Maybe I'll get lucky and not need to go. Your genius find anything on a date or location? Because I sure haven't."

The pile of papers on her desk mocked her, and her stomach muscles clenched in a painful knot. There had to be a clue somewhere, but with each passing hour, she grew more convinced Hakim didn't have any information saved about a possible attack. He'd probably learned better from other plots being uncovered on confiscated computers.

"Nothing solid." Tony looked discouraged, too.

"How do you guys do it?"

"Do what?"

"Deal with knowing this kind of shit is out there. I mean, I've dealt with drug and arms dealers, but this … It's not about money. I lived in the Middle East for years and never had anyone come right out and want to kill me. The Muslims I knew were warm, loving people. I know there are extremists —but I don't get why some radical psychos want to go on a jihad to kill thousands of people. It's … warped. Wanting to kill innocent people. For what? Attention? Because they live their lives differently than you?" She rubbed her temple, but it didn't relieve the throb.

"You gotta realize that it's not up to *you* to save the world. It's bigger than you. You do what you can. And you have made a difference. We've got time. Don't go getting all doom and gloom on me. We have a date when this is over." He winked.

"You come in to give me a pep talk?" She managed a smile. His presence, his reassurances, was what she needed. He made it easier to draw a breath, despite the rapid heartbeat his nearness inspired.

"Actually, to get a smile and take you up on your offer of a place to crash for a power nap. I'm fading, and my patience is shot. Dominguez is trying to trace the girls in the porn flick, so you can imagine …"

"I don't think I want to. Help yourself. I'll try not to sing or hum."

"Trust me, it'd be better than what I've been listening to." He turned the chairs on the other side of the desk to face each other. Settling in, he slid low enough to rest his head on the top of the chair and propped his legs on the other.

"You can slip off your shoes if you want."

"My feet might stink." His bashful look endeared him all the more.

"Go ahead," she chuckled. "If they do, I'll tell you."

"Please do." He leaned forward enough to untie the laces and slip off the dress shoes. "Ah, that feels good." He wriggled his toes and feet.

"I know." She spun her chair and raised a leg to reveal her bare foot. He scanned her unpainted toenails—yet another concession to playing Sabine—up her leg, and met her eyes, raising his eyebrows. Her muscles constricted in arousal.

It'd been less than twenty-four hours since she spotted him in Pera's, and now she knew his real name and had a date planned with him. They just had to find out if there was a bomb planted somewhere and make sure it didn't go off first. That little detail kept her busy rather than admire him while he slept for the next twenty-three minutes.

Reading Hakim's emails proved to be an exercise in futility. No dates. No places. And, certainly, no outright exposition on where he or his group might target. He was cautious, but there had to be something. Some clue she'd missed. But what? She rolled her neck, then shook her arms to get her blood moving. Might as well indulge in a small reward. She turned her attention to the man asleep just feet away.

This morning, Tony shed his suit jacket. Sometime before lunch, he'd ditched the tie. The rolled-up sleeves of the white button-down highlighted the tan on his face and sculpted forearms. Stubble on the verge of being scruff shadowed his face. Even in the relaxed state of sleep, his arms and chest filled out the dress shirt.

She wanted to see his eyes, though. Eyes that could be as cold and dark as a starless night, or bright, intense, and downright mesmerizing.

Tony's head bobbed, then jerked up. His lids opened widely as if on command. Startled, she jolted.

"Nice nap?" She hoped he wasn't aware she'd been staring.

He stretched—the simple act playing into her fantasies.

"Yeah. That's what I needed. Thanks."

"I think the idea of an afternoon siesta is way underappreciated in this country."

"You didn't stare at me the whole time, did you?" He bestowed her with a rakish smile.

She cleared her throat, sure her face turned a healthy flush. "Not the whole time," she admitted.

"Good. I didn't want to be a major distraction, but you might hurt my feelings if you ignored me like you did last night." He put his shoes back on.

"Trust me, I would rather have you as my dining partner. But until we get this case wrapped up …"

"Case first, *and* we can't be seen together. Too risky. I know." His head rocked back and forth, and the left side of his mouth skewed up in a grimace.

He understood. It reminded her she couldn't invite him home tonight, even if it would help her sleep. Instead, she envisioned hours of staring at the ceiling, trying to think like Anmar Hakim. Crawling into Hakim's head was about as distasteful as the idea of crawling into his bed. She needed something positive to offset the dark places her mind would be going.

Tony rose. She got to her feet, too, and skirted the desk before he moved to the door.

She blocked his exit. He watched her with an intense gaze. His head tilted lower, inviting her.

She slid her hand to the firm muscles of his bicep. Her other hand went to the side of his head. She lifted her face and kissed him.

It only took a second for his hands to grip her hips, to pull her body closer, and give her the contact she craved. His tongue skimmed her lips, encouraging them to part, which they did willingly. He smelled and tasted like spearmint, fresh and cool. Better yet, he felt like heaven.

She backed off, already at risk of getting swept away. It had been months since she'd been with a man. The holding hands and clumsy kisses with Hakim had hardly been intoxicating like this.

Tony's thumbs rubbed over her hips, not releasing his hold on her.

"Those times I kissed you when we were in Texas, I enjoyed it, but it was for show. This"—she smiled at him —"was because I *wanted* to."

"Me, too," was all he said, his voice husky, aroused.

He kissed her again. She bet he thought along the same lines—*the door's closed, so go for it.* As enticed as she was, she figured it would only be minutes before Weiss, Grochowski, a junior agent, or one of Tony's team came knocking and would know exactly what was going on.

Self-denial was not one of her stronger virtues—more like a learned, life-sustaining trait. With an anguished murmur, she ended the kiss. His warm fingers caressed her jawline; his thumb stroked her cheek. She turned her head and kissed his thumb, then stared into his smoldering eyes.

Seconds ticked by. His expression changed, softened. He blew out a breath with a soft *whew.* A subdued smile tugged up the corners of his mouth.

"Guess I better get back to work before rumors start flying. But I'll see you."

She edged aside to allow him access to the door. "We've got to find something."

"If it's there, we'll find it."

She noticed he didn't make empty promises.

ELEVEN

"STILL NO WORD FROM HAKIM?" Special Agent in Charge Grochowski leaned on the doorframe to Angela's office. Lines etched his haggard face. The threat of a dirty bomb meant no one had left at five o'clock. The buzz of activity had slowed though once the sun had set and the support staff trickled out.

"No," she drawled and shook her head. "Anything on the bomb?"

"Zero. Maybe that's good news. We've been through the main files. Now we're going through the ones that look to be clutter. Intelligence is monitoring all the audio chatter. I think we need to call it a night in case Hakim has someone watching your place. I know," he interrupted when she started to protest, "but it's possible. I want to nail this bastard. Can't risk making him suspicious. At this point, I'm praying to Saint Jude, Saint Michael, and Saint Thomas More that finding nothing means no imminent threat. If Bin Faud is Hakim, maybe he's making a pilgrimage to see the Eiffel Tower."

She wished she believed his assessment, except impending doom weighted her limbs. She began to regret her decision to douse Hakim with the eye drops. If she had slept with him, he'd be more inclined to call or let her in the door if she just showed up at his apartment. Only she hadn't known what they'd find in his file might require more interaction with him. What if her decision cost innocent people their lives? Would she be able to live with that?

She remembered Tony's remark that it wasn't all up to her. Still, she might be the only one in a position to get the information they needed. "What about al-Shehri? Anything on him?"

"He must be holed up someplace. We've alerted border entry points and agencies throughout the state. So far, no hits from them or from facial recognition. He may not be a part of this, though the timing seems coincidental."

Besides al-Shehri's recent work in Afghanistan, his history included time in terrorist training camps and suspected ties to the group that bombed the hotel in the Philippines. She wanted al-Shehri even more than Hakim.

"If it weren't for the information on the bomb, our sole focus would be on him. Pack it up. I want everyone in at eight, and we'll do a briefing to evaluate at eleven." Grochowski walked toward Weiss and Cal's offices.

Angela gathered the pages stacked haphazardly on her desk. She locked them up. Taking them home would be a security risk and probably keep her up all night, which wouldn't help. She'd translated them and then read over the content again without finding anything useful. Maybe tomorrow, with fresh eyes, she'd find something. She could hope.

She picked up her bag in the locker room before heading to the elevators. A chorus of voices carried to her. She scanned the group consisting of Becca, Jarrod, and the suit-clad operators. Catching sight of Tony again set off a flutter in her stomach.

"You guys get kicked out, too?" She incorporated everyone in her field of vision.

Mack talked on his cell a few steps away from the group as Grant carried on an animated conversation with Singh, the technical analyst, in front of the elevator doors.

"Just for the night," Porter said.

When the elevator doors slid open, she heard someone—it had to be Tony—clear his throat. Subtle, but she got the message and hung back, waiting while the others crowded into the elevator.

"We can squeeze you guys in." Grant took a half step backward, only to jostle forward.

"They can take the next one." Lundgren issued it like an order, though a grin played across his face. "Mack?"

Mack held up a finger only to have the elevator doors close, leaving him behind, too.

She caught the glower Tony shot at the closed doors, then at Mack, who continued his conversation.

"Best laid plans," Tony muttered and punched the down button before turning his sexy smile on her.

Oh, the fantasies he inspired. In an elevator, no less. It was probably a good thing Mack was there to chaperone them.

"And they're sure?" The stupefied grin on Mack's face couldn't get any bigger. "You did? Oh, babe, this is great."

The elevator finally arrived.

She and Tony stepped in, and for a second, it looked like they'd get a solo trip after all.

"Hang on a sec," Mack called to them. "I'm sorry I

couldn't be there, but we'll celebrate when I get back. Okay? Gotta run."

He joined them, lost in his own world as he pulled up something on his phone.

Tony peered over at Mack, his face scrunched. "What is up with you, dude?"

Mack glanced up. "Sorry," he said. "You, uh, remember me saying Kristie hadn't been feeling well. She finally went to the doctor today, and they sent her to a specialist."

"But she's okay?" Tony asked with authentic concern.

Angela had no doubts about what was coming out of Mack's mouth next.

"Better than okay. She's pregnant!" He turned his phone to show them a fuzzy black-and-white ultrasound image.

"That's awesome, man. Another girl!"

"Most likely." Mack grinned at the screen.

"For all his shortcomings, he does produce great kids. Show her a picture of the girls. You know you want to," Tony teased.

"This is Amber." Mack pulled up a picture of a blonde teenager. "And this is Darcy."

"Isn't she the cutest thing?" Tony said. "She's got this adorable giggle, and, man, all she has to do is bat those lashes and give a pout, and you'll do whatever she wants."

Angela had to agree about the impish grin and deep dimples of the young girl with red curls. She peeked up and saw Tony looking at the picture on Mack's phone. What she read on his face, in his eyes, was the missing piece of Tony Vincenti.

When he told her he wasn't married, she attributed his bachelorhood to him making the same conscious decision that marriage and a family weren't compatible with their chosen careers. She'd been wrong. His answer wasn't a "hell no!"

denial. He wanted the same things she used to dream of having.

The picture on Mack's phone became blurrier as her past taunted her. Being an au pair for the Vasquez boys started out as her favorite undercover role. It had given her a glimpse of non-dysfunctional family life, despite their mother's ties to her brother, Tito's, cocaine empire. Elena's boys weren't her children, but Angela had come to love them, nonetheless.

The irony that their father put a contract on her life still speared her soul. She'd been so close to getting Elena and the kids out of the house before the Agency's raid. If Tito hadn't brought his teenage daughter, Abi-Maria, with him, they would have been at the park, and Elena and Abi-Maria would be alive. Everything would be different. She might be able to show off pictures of her own family one day. But having a contract on her life extended to that dream family. It nailed the door shut and locked out that possibility.

"She's not gonna be my baby anymore." Mack swiped the screen to stare at the ultrasound picture again.

In the minute it took the elevator to descend twenty-two floors, her daydreams of an occasional weekend rendezvous with Tony plummeted to the basement of the Not-Likely-to-Happen Hotel. He wanted the honeymoon suite and all that went with it. She only needed a comfortable room as her safe place to crash until she had to move on. Their futures were booked at different resorts.

MACK'S good news countered the shit piling up all day and reinforced why they did what was needed to protect the people they loved. Still, a twinge of jealousy jabbed at Tony.

He wanted a woman he loved to come home to. Kids. The

whole close-knit, loud, Italian family like he'd grown up in. Like he always thought he'd have by now.

Did Angela want that, too? What thoughts went through her mind when she'd looked up at him then diverted her gaze? May be something to explore after they wrapped up this mission and could do dinner and —more.

He tabled those thoughts as the elevator doors slid open. They joined the group in the lobby, where they were now talking with Carswell.

"We're going to have drinks at the bar across the street from our hotel. You want to join us, Angel-a?" Dominguez belatedly added the last syllable.

"I wish. I could use a drink right now. But I have to get back to 'Sabine's apartment.'"

"Sorry. Maybe next time." Dominguez turned his attention back to Becca.

"Somebody should probably tag along with Agent Hoffman to make sure no one is watching her place." Tony looked to the chief.

"Not a bad idea after last night and what we learned," Carswell agreed.

"If Hakim does have someone watching, Vincenti and I might be recognized from the restaurant." Lundgren shot down Tony's plans.

"I'll take point," Mack offered.

Lundgren eyed Dominguez, who avoided his gaze like the plague. "Liu. Check in with me later."

Liu nodded and drifted to the side with Mack as Angela gave them directions to the City Hall subway station and the route she'd take.

"You coming, Vincenti?" Carswell asked as the remaining group headed in the opposite direction.

Apparently, Carswell wanted to relive his team days rather than go home to his family.

"Yeah." Lundgren made the best pick. Liu would blend and fade into the background and not draw notice from any of Hakim's men nosing around Angela's. Since Plan A tanked, Tony could use a beer or two before turning in for the night.

Once the group made it to the bar, the agents and his team crowded around an available table. Tony had spent enough time on his butt today, so he joined Carswell at the bar and signaled to the bartender.

"I hear you guys worked with Hoffman before, and that's how you recognized her last night."

"Actually, she recognized us first." Tony didn't give him details of their prior mission.

"She is good at what she does," Carswell admitted. "But we have serious business at hand. I know she's easy on the eyes, and in the sack, I'm telling you, she's got no inhibitions. But now—"

"Wait. You and Angela?"

Carswell's wicked grin made Tony's skin crawl. "Like I said, overseas, there's no rules. But watch your back, 'cuz it may not be worth it. Besides, your priority is finding if there's a bomb out there." He took a sip of his drink, while his eyes bored into Tony's in warning.

Carswell joined the others at the table, but Tony stayed at the bar drinking his beer and mulling over what Carswell had said.

Angela fooled around with a married man? That didn't add up to how things went when they'd worked together in Texas. Or this morning, when she probed to find out if he was married after he asked her to dinner.

Maybe Jarrod was bullshitting him. Maybe he thought telling him this would steer Tony away so he wouldn't distract Angela at a critical time. If it were true, though, would it change his feelings? With Tony's history, he couldn't judge her for her past.

He downed the rest of his beer and paid the bartender. Time to catch up on sleep and try to get the image of Angela with his former teammate out of his head.

TWELVE

THE GROWL of Angela's stomach echoed in Cal's office.

He grinned at her. "Need to run down to the café?"

"Maybe." She needed food and a decent cup of coffee. Her stomach rejected the idea of food at five in the morning when she'd given up the notion of going back to sleep. After two cups of rotgut office coffee, lethargy still muddied her brain after a restless night.

Another glimpse of Tony Vincenti would get her energized again. His team had come in around seven, but she hadn't gotten two seconds alone with him. She could take five minutes to grab the cup of yogurt she'd brought, and while she was on their floor, poke her head in the conference room.

"I got the information you asked me to look into." Singh stepped into Cal's office before she got to her feet. He handed a thin file to Angela. "Fatima bin Muhammad is a second cousin to Hakim."

She opened the file to the top page. "Pretty girl. Are you sure she's the right one? She's really young." She studied what she could see of the girl's face, her forehead and hair covered by the traditional hijab, then handed the picture to Cal.

"She was only fourteen in that picture. It's from her original passport. Her family fled Saudi Arabia and settled in Saint-Etienne, France," Singh continued.

France. "Was Hakim already there?" she asked.

"Yes, he moved there right after the first Gulf War."

That made sense, along with bringing his family to France.

"There's not much information on her or her family before she went missing."

That got her attention. "Missing?"

"A week before the family planned to return to Saudi Arabia. Records the French authorities sent us said the family indicated the trip back home was for Fatima to marry a Sheik. I checked. The guy was sixty-two then. My guess is she got cold feet because when police investigated, they found she had bought an airline ticket—with cash—to JFK."

"Gee, doesn't sound like a love match," she said.

"You don't think? The guy was probably rich and had a harem. It could be worse," Cal cracked.

She tsked at Cal's rejoinder. "Did you check to see when Hakim came to the States?" She tried to put the pieces together.

"I figured you would ask that." With a smug smile, Singh pointed to the file. "He came to New York a couple weeks later."

"Where is Fatima now?"

"That's a good question. She came in on a student visa but never enrolled. No tax records. No death records under her name that match her age. No record of her leaving the country. Nothing."

"So, she's a dead end." *Crap.* Another lead that went nowhere.

"Looks that way." Singh shrugged.

"Maybe she got a taste of freedom in France. Decided she didn't want to be the wife of a guy two or three times her age. She comes up with a plan to get out of the marriage. Either Hakim wants to help or thinks she wants to be with him, so he funds her escape," she speculated.

"Only she gets to the States with some money and runs to avoid ending up as Hakim's child bride instead." Cal picked up the thread. "He gets here. Fatima isn't waiting with open arms. He thinks someone hurt the woman he loves, so he blames evil Americans?"

"Either way, it could add to the litany of reasons he doesn't like Americans, Jews, Christians, women who look men right in the eye, and women who carry little dogs around in their purses." She reflected on comments Hakim made during their time together.

"I'm with him on the dog-in-the-purse thing," Singh agreed. "Let me know if you need anything else."

Singh took off. Angela scanned the copy of the French police report. Even with nothing substantial to base it on, her sense that the girl was a part of this somehow made her nerves tingle. Was she part of the "business" that had kept Hakim in the States this long?

Her cell phone rang. Only there was an unknown number on the screen. Could it be Hakim? She held up a finger to Cal for quiet.

"Hello," she answered with Sabine's soft voice and accent.

"Hoffman?" Grochowski barked.

"Yes, sir."

"I need you in my office. Now."

"Be right there." He disconnected before she got the words out. "Grochowski needs me," she relayed.

"He say what for?" Cal leaned forward as she got to her feet.

"No." But her spidey-sense tingled as she hustled down the hall. In her years as an operative, it rarely failed her.

"Go on in," the receptionist outside Grochowski's office said.

Inside, the special agent in charge had loosened his tie, and his mouth was set in a grim line. "There was a call made to Hakim's cell phone a few minutes ago. I need you to ID his voice and translate." He motioned her to the chairs across from his desk and pushed a legal pad and pen toward her, then tapped on his keyboard.

The first voice she heard she didn't recognize. "That's Hakim," she identified the second. A third voice joined in. Educated, but submissive. This unknown sounded younger than both Hakim and the first unsub.

She didn't make notes as she listened, trying to keep up with the cryptic conversation between the three men. Her stomach tightened when the youngest-sounding mentioned "the item"—the bomb?—was nearly complete. Her eyes closed when he mentioned the final materials being delivered.

The conversation didn't last long, but she had to fight nausea roiling in her gut. "They never used names or used the word bomb," she filled in Grochowski, "but the last man to speak was suggesting the tenth for a delivery date to tie in with a reminder celebration on the eleventh. Hakim was insistent that he's funding this adventure and wants to stick to the fourth of July date."

Grochowski grumbled, and his scowl deepened.

"It gets worse."

"How?"

"The second unsub assured the other that the 9/11 cele-bration would be on time."

"Two? Son of a bitch," he muttered. "Did they mention any names or places?"

"Not that I picked up. I need to listen to it again." Once the initial shock passed, she might pick up something she missed.

"I want you to translate *every* word they said. I'll get Weiss up here for secondary verification.

ANGELA FIDGETED IN THE CHAIR, looking to Weiss while Grochowski and Jarrod compared the two transcripts of the conversation. Voiceprint identification confirmed one of the unsubs was Samir al-Shehri. Going from planting roadside IEDs and training suicide bombers to building a dirty bomb was a big leap, but his involvement confirmed this threat's credibility.

The idea of them planning a second attack changed the game, too. They weren't going for coordinated attacks like 9/11 from the sound of it. There would be enough time for people to calm down and lower their defenses after the first attack. With the heads up, they had time to stop both attacks —if they could determine the target locations.

She'd painstakingly translated every word and listened for clues. There were none.

Voices outside the office pulled her from replaying the conversation over in her head. Grochowski pushed to his feet as William Harkins, the Assistant Director of the Bureau's D.C. office, was escorted in, along with her friend, Special Agent in Charge Kathryn Barnsley.

Angela rose to greet them. "What are you …?"

"I called the D.C. office after you translated." Grochowski spoke over her. "Felt they should be involved, because if they follow the pattern of 9/11, D.C. is the most likely target."

"Could be the initial target since the D.C. attacks weren't nearly as catastrophic as planned," Harkins agreed. "If they take out a significant portion of the country's leaders and create mass panic on our Independence Day, it'd be a huge win for them."

Security in D.C. was always tight, but they could use the Potomac River to transport a bomb. Avoid cameras and authorities. It could be anywhere around D.C.—Capitol Hill, Georgetown, Arlington.

As much as Angela hated the idea of another attack on New York, especially because Stephan died here, D.C. was her home. Where her friends lived. She'd do whatever it took to prevent an attack there.

"We flew up as soon as we heard," Kathryn said. "Outstanding work. Not that I'm surprised."

"It was a team effort," Angela said.

Jarrod got to his feet to join the senior agents. "We've got a lot of people working on this. It's top priority."

"We couldn't have done it without her," Grochowski jumped in to praise her. "I'll call Director Hollis. We need to strategize."

TONY SHIFTED HIS WEIGHT. He locked his jaw to keep from griping. The briefing should have started ten minutes ago. Instead, everyone stood around—or sat on their asses—waiting. His team had joined the FBI agents in the larger conference room. Well, most of the agents. Grochowski, Carswell, the technical analyst, and Angela were all MIA. The churning in his gut grew each minute that ticked by. Why weren't they here?

He'd seen Angela earlier—the highlight of his morning—so he knew she was here. Somewhere.

Dominguez sat at the table between two of the youngest FBI agents, carrying on a conversation laced with touches that made Tony wonder what happened after he left the bar last night. Once he'd sprawled out in the hotel bed, lack of sleep took its toll, even pushing Carswell's comments out of his head.

The tension in the room ramped up the instant a group led by Grochowski filed in. In addition to Angela, Weiss, Director Hollis, Carswell, the tech guy, were a man and woman, both in navy suits. All of them together, a picture of total seriousness.

Angela met his eyes for a mere second before diverting them without a trace of her usual flirty smile. Mack motioned to her, offering her his seat. She gave a quick shake of her head and held her position near the head of the table.

Grochowski introduced the director of the Bureau's D.C. office and the female special agent in charge, piquing Tony's curiosity on why they were here.

"Thanks to Agent Hoffman cloning Hakim's SIM card, we intercepted a call this morning. *The* call," Grochowski stated. "Singh."

The tech typed on his laptop, then nodded.

"Voiceprint identification confirms the first voice is Samir al-Shehri. The second voice you'll hear is Anmar Hakim. Confirmed by Special Agent Hoffman."

Yes! Murmurs rippled through the room at tying the two together.

Based on the way Angela's cheek muscle twitched and

her visible swallow, Tony bet he wasn't going to like the conversation they were about to hear.

"We're running the third voice against known voice clips. It was a three-way call al-Shehri originated from a pre-paid cell," Singh continued. "They're speaking Arabic. Subtitles are on the screen."

Tony read the words but concentrated on the voices. July 11. Shit, Dad's birthday.

Chill, Vincenti. We're going to stop this.

Hakim spoke next, demanding July fourth. The eleventh would give them an extra week to find it. Now they were talking days.

The unidentified man asking for more time gave Tony some hope that the bomb builder would fuck up the assembly in his rush to complete it. Of course, if he screwed up, there would still be a nuclear incident. Deaths, sickness, panic. That wasn't happening on his watch.

Wait. What? Were they referring to a second bomb?

Somebody let out a low whistle. A few people swore, and everyone glanced around the room at the other faces, looking for a ray of hope—and not finding it.

Tony's hands balled into tight fists under his crossed arms. Safer than punching a hole in the wall. Two bombs. Two targets. That explained the presence from the D.C. office.

Another reminder of 9/11. He tried to quiet the voice in his head that was screaming profanities unsuitable to say aloud.

Grochowski gave everyone an opportunity for the initial shock to pass and their brains to process the details of the call. "We were only able to track the call as far as a cell tower in East Brunswick, Jersey."

"What about locating the nuclear materials?" one of the agents asked.

"We have a credible threat, so we'll try. But first, we have to pinpoint the target city, or cities, and call in NEST teams to blanket those areas," Homeland Security Director Hollis explained. "It sounds like they're not planning simultaneous attacks; however, we can't rule that out based on the available information. At this point, we assume they are targeting something in the New York vicinity, especially with Hakim planning to leave here."

"There's a Yankees game on the fourth that could be a prime target," Jarrod said. "Over 50,000 capacity in the stadium, and with it being a holiday and followed by fire-works, it's a sellout. You've got a lot of people in close prox-imity. There are also home games in Boston, Philly, and D.C."

"Hakim has never mentioned baseball," Angela said.

Jarrod's jaw clenched, and he cut his gaze her way as she continued to speak.

"Other than soccer, he's never mentioned sports. Some-thing tells me this is personal. That he's not picking a random target even for maximum impact."

"We cannot afford another 9/11." Grochowski punctuated each word. "The Bureau got a black eye for not following up on leads then. Unlike 9/11, there's been no chatter or leaks on a pending attack or targets. They've kept this close to the vest. We're going to monitor local mosques Hakim has attended for any change in attendance levels and run down *any* potential leads. Alerts are going out to every FBI and Homeland security office and to local authorities."

"Will a terror warning be issued for New York?" Becca asked.

A palpable silence settled over the room with all eyes on Grochowski and Hollis.

"Not without a solid lead. It was a joint decision from Washington," Hollis answered. "It would create mass panic. We can't evacuate every major city. We don't have much time, so we need to work the contacts we have."

Being part of the team getting the job done, Tony was used to carrying the weight on his shoulders. Fixated on Angela, the weight settled into his chest instead. The "contact" they planned to work was her.

THIRTEEN

"WOW. YOU, UH, LOOK LIKE A TOURIST." Angela did little to suppress a smirk. "You've got mustard on your shirt."

Tony stepped into her office and pulled off the Yankees baseball cap, then frowned and rubbed at the mustard on the new Yankees T-shirt. Bummer that mustard stains didn't always come out; the Yankees were his team. Not that he followed baseball like he did football. "Would you believe me if I said it was intentional? Part of my cover?"

She just cocked her head at him.

Oh, well. "Yankees won four to two. Barely saw any of the game, though. NEST guys didn't pick up any readings in the blocks around the stadium, but there are plenty of places nearby to stash the kind of bomb we're looking at."

"Did Weiss fill you in?"

"Cal did." And Tony didn't like it, but he also didn't have a say. "Grochowski agreed to let our team help provide surveillance and backup. We're rolling back in now." Most of the Bad Karma team spoke at least limited Arabic, Pashto, or Dari, so they'd split up and gone on reconnaissance after this morning's meeting. They dressed like tourists on the off chance they'd overhear something. A remote, pick-the-right-planet-in-the-vast-cosmos chance. One that hadn't panned out yet.

He'd heard that Nuclear Emergency Support Team, or NEST, sent over a hundred of their people hoping to pick up any radioactive material with their equipment. Maybe they'd have better luck. While he'd scouted around Yankee Stadium, Angela had changed clothes, too. He hoped she had a weapon concealed under the conservative black dress she wore in hopes of meeting with Hakim.

"You get any lunch?" he asked.

"I wasn't hungry."

Stress strained her features and robbed her of her usual confident aura. He took hold of her hand. It was icy in his.

"Come here." He pulled her up to cradle her against his chest.

"What if this is my chance, and I don't find anything? What if something like 9/11 happens?" Her voice was a desperate whisper.

After losing her fiancé, he didn't doubt it would devastate her if they missed stopping another major attack. "Don't give up. You're not trying to get out of dinner, are you?"

She chuckled. "No. Though worrying about stopping a bombing is kind of a mood killer."

"Really? 'Cause I've heard that when people are looking at a potentially life-ending situation, they tend to have sex. A one-last-chance thing. I'm just saying …"

She put a sliver of space between them, taking in his facial expression. "I think that's when you think you're *going* to die."

"Oh."

"Nice try, though."

It might be worth it. He shrugged, and she gave him the

first smile he'd seen from her since this morning. "Look, the chance that they have enough radioactive material to make a dirty bomb is slim to none." It's what he'd told himself all afternoon.

"I pray you're right." She rested her head against his shoulder again.

There hadn't been a credible dirty bomb threat in the States to date. They'd track down this bomb, and it'd just be a bomb, probably not well constructed—not on the scale of the Oklahoma City bombing or the first World Trade Center. They'd laugh over drinks about being so worried. Put it out of their minds. They'd undress each other. And after one long night of mind-blowing sex, they'd joke about sending Hakim a thank-you note for bringing them together again. Yeah. That all sounded great.

He gave her a squeeze to reassure her. "We'll be right outside the building. If you need anything, just whistle."

"I can't whistle," she said with a trace of despondency in her voice.

"Everybody can whistle. You know. Put your lips together and blow." He hadn't meant it literally. She had to know the movie. Right?

"I can't whistle." She pulled away and blew a weak *fwoo* sound through her front teeth.

"Okay, then." He laughed. "If you need me, um ... I don't know ... say orange or purple. Some art thing."

"Something artsy? I'll bring up Picasso if I need help."

"Picasso? I don't get his stuff."

"Not my style, either. I prefer to look at something and can tell what it is. Okay. Picasso. And if I hit pay dirt, I'll bring up architecture."

"Use your many charms to get in and plant that bug. Then get the hell out. Remember, it's not up to you to do this on your own. Be careful, because if Hakim's invested beyond financially, he could be dangerous."

"I'm used to dangerous," she reminded him, though her smile hinted she didn't mind the warning. "I don't scare easily."

She pinched the front of his T-shirt below his navel and gave it a tug, sending his libido into overdrive again. She had that sultry, expectant look in her eyes.

He wrapped an arm around her waist. His right hand cupped her neck, and his thumb stroked her smooth cheek.

She responded willingly when he lowered his face and claimed her mouth. Desire and need drove him. He pulled her body closer and let her feel exactly the effect she had on him.

Her lips parted, and their tongues met. He tasted cinnamon. She pressed her hips against his aroused body, nearly sending his impulse control out of the galaxy. A passionate half-murmur, half-moan escaped. Before he reached to close the door and start on fantasy number one of three hundred and twelve, she pulled back, panting. She bit on her lower lip.

Damn. Wrong place. Bad time.

Her head tilted back. She took a deep, controlling breath. "I need to get in the Sabine mindset. That's hard enough with you in the room, much less kissing me senseless."

Okay, maybe it was the wrong time, but the way she expressed it gave him a buzz better than alcohol or the rush of freefalling from 15,000 feet. He swallowed. "Sorry. Didn't mean to mess up your mission planning."

"Don't apologize. Give me a rain check for later." She winked. "And thanks for the injection of optimism. I needed that."

"Anytime. Glad to help."

She shooed him out, but he couldn't resist. He leaned

over and kissed her again. A gentle kiss with the promise of "I'll see you later."

He hadn't been able to get her out of his mind since they recovered the missiles in Texas. This time, he was making sure they got a chance to explore this attraction for long-term possibilities. Despite what Jarrod implied about them sleeping together, he wanted to believe Angela was the faithful type.

FOURTEEN

"YOU CAN KEEP THE CHANGE." Angela handed a twenty over to the cabbie, her stomach tighter than a new pair of shoes. That nervousness kept her in character while she exited the cab in front of Hakim's building. She walked the few steps to the entrance, conscious of nearly a dozen pairs of eyes and ears tuned in to her every word and move.

The doorman on duty was the same as the night she'd come with Hakim. His wide-eyed expression meant he recognized her. The left corner of his mouth rose, though he didn't say more than, "Good evening, ma'am."

The concierge set down the sports page of the New York Times. He made eye contact with the doorman before he stood. "What can I do for you?"

"I need to see Anmar Hakim." She laid it on thick with the accent, her gaze fixed on the desktop.

"Is he expecting you? I don't have you on the list."

She doubted Anmar had ever put any woman on the list. "No, he is not. But I need to see him." She raised her eyes to his, hoping her face flushed.

"I'll have to call up." The concierge gave her a once-over while he punched numbers on the phone. "Your name?"

"Sabine Deschamps." She fidgeted while the concierge spoke with Hakim. He handed her the phone rather than allow her to proceed.

"Hello. I'm sorry to show up unexpectedly, but I need to see you." She spoke softly in French and turned away from the concierge's curious stare.

"Speak up. I can't make out what you're saying." Hakim sounded more confused than irritated.

"I'm sorry. I was trying to keep this between us. I, um, left something the other night—"

"You can come up. Put the concierge back on."

Score!

"He asked to speak with you again." She handed back the phone, working hard to suppress a triumphant smile. Moments later, she was ushered to the elevator.

The elevator made its slow ascent to the ninth floor. She breathed easier. Hakim would let her in, but the tricky part remained.

"Okay, guys. Halfway there." *Sabine. Sabine*, she chanted. She shook her arms and rolled her neck against the rising wave of adrenaline that always accompanied an undercover assignment. Then she closed her eyes and exhaled slow and long. Sabine Deschamps rapped twice on the solid wood door and startled when it opened immediately.

Hakim motioned her in, peering out into the deserted hallway before he closed the door and locked it. "This is unexpected. What brought you here?" He scrutinized her, keeping a bit of distance between them.

"I realized my silver bracelet is missing. I must have left it here when … well, the other night. My grandparents gave it to me. I'd hate to lose it."

"Are you sure you had it on?"

"Yes, I only wear it for special occasions. I hope I didn't lose it somewhere else." She frowned and rubbed her fingers over her wrist. "Though I admit I wanted an excuse to see you."

His eyebrows quirked up, and a flash of heat flared in his eyes. "You did?" He stepped closer and reached a hand to her face. His fingertips touched the earring dangling from her left ear.

Her stomach lurched, and her heart skipped a beat. His thumb stroked her cheek, and angling his head, he slipped his other hand to her waist. *Great! Now he's going to get it up. Dammit. If I have to do him with Tony and the whole damn team listening, I swear I'll kill Hakim afterward. Slowly and painfully.* Time to redirect.

"The other night didn't, uh ... Well, I ... I hope you're feeling better." She broke eye contact and glanced around the room. "Do you mind if we look for my bracelet? It has sentimental value." Biting the inside of her lip, she braved meeting his eyes again.

He huffed and dropped his hand from her face. When she stepped around him, she snuck a peek at his crotch. Oh, yeah, something was definitely up with him tonight. "If you can check around the couch, I'll look in the bathroom."

While he was lifting sofa cushions, she headed down the hallway to the bathroom. She placed a bug over the doorframe to his office before flipping on the light in the half bath. Then she moved the hand towel and kicked the trashcan aside enough for Hakim to notice.

Returning from the bathroom, she spied a cardboard box on the floor in front of the bookcases lining the back wall. It appeared half-packed. A prickling that started in her core raced upward, then down her arms and legs. She needed to keep him distracted—preferably with their clothes on—to plant the second bug and see what was in the box. "It's not in the bathroom. Any luck?"

"I didn't find anything. Are you sure you wore it the other night?"

"Yes. But if I lost it in the cab or restaurant … I guess it's gone." She pouted and edged a step closer to the box. "Look, I've never done this before"—she gave him a shy smile and shifted her weight from one foot to the other, then back—"but there are free concerts in the park next week. I hoped you'd like to go. With me."

"I can't," he answered without the slightest hesitation.

"Oh." She waited, hoping he'd provide a reason or excuse. Which he didn't. "Was I too forward in asking?" She wandered the length of the couch, stopping near the box, and kept her gaze on him.

"I'll be out of town."

A chill invaded her body. "And when will you be back?" This could back up her theory that the ticket was for him.

He frowned, and his eyes narrowed. "I'm not sure."

"Is this a business trip or …?" She pressed her luck.

"You're asking a lot of questions."

"Forgive me. But you don't share much. I want to get to know you better." With her eyes downcast, she studied the contents of the box. She could only make out two framed pictures, but not who they were of or what was below them. "What's this? Are you—packing?" She took the last step to reach the box.

"I'm putting some things in storage." He waved his hand, though his tone had a panicked edge. It made her more determined to see what the box contained.

She picked up the top picture and the one below and resorted to flattery. "You look so handsome." In the picture with Hakim were a young woman and another young man. The woman had the same mole beside her right eye as the woman in the video on Hakim's computer.

Jackpot!

"Is this the bridge in St. Etienne? I love the architecture there. And the young woman is beautiful. Who is she?" She turned the frame toward him. She'd bet her life savings that it was the mysterious Fatima.

Hakim's face contorted. "Put it back."

"This trip isn't to see another woman, is it?" She angled her head, taking the jealous-woman route.

"No," Hakim snorted. "She … she's dead—to me."

"I'm sorry. Were you close?"

Hakim's speed surprised her. He grabbed hold of the picture. It wasn't the only thing he wrenched from her hand. The dime-sized disk concealed between her middle and ring fingers flew out and skittered across the floor.

FIFTEEN

TONY STRUGGLED to translate the rapid French, but he had no trouble deciphering the word "architecture." Angela had picked up on something, not that he had any idea what based on their conversation.

The change of tone in Hakim's voice tempered Tony's excitement, and he shifted back from the edge of his seat in the surveillance van. He'd missed the last exchange and didn't like the Weiss way shook his head.

"What?" he mouthed to the agent.

Weiss, his face scrunched in concentration, ignored him.

Tony closed his eyes and listened, trying to catch up and picture what was happening. Man, he wished they had eyes on the inside. But putting a camera on her would have been too risky. He couldn't figure out why she'd talk about the hanger for the picture frame until she compared Hakim's face to a Picasso.

Picasso!

Oh, shit! Something had happened. He bolted toward the van's back door.

"Where are—" Weiss reached out, trying to stop him.

"She's in trouble. Bravo team, move in!" he yelled into his commlink.

"How do you—"

"Because she said Picasso," he answered before Weiss finished.

He burst out of the back of the van to see Grant and Porter converging on the building from their posts. None of his Bad Karma team questioned his cryptic request.

"Hold your positions!" Cal ordered his agents. Fortunately, he didn't try to stop Tony's team.

Tony dodged traffic to cross the street. A cabbie slammed on his brakes and laid on the horn as he vaulted across the front of his yellow cab to avoid becoming a hood ornament. Only he couldn't evade the cab in the other lane, and it clipped his leg. He spun but managed to remain upright.

Pain shot from his thigh to his toes and back up to his hip. Each step sent crushing pain through his leg. His gait uneven, he plowed forward.

Cal's loud string of profanities clued Tony into his presence, only feet behind him. Lundgren appeared, weaving through the pedestrian traffic.

The doorman took a defensive stance at the sight of the charging men.

"FBI! Stand down!" Cal yelled, hopefully to the doorman because Tony wasn't slowing down. He trusted Angela wouldn't give the panic word unless it was serious.

Porter and Grant pushed past the doorman into the breezeway, where the beefy concierge was on his feet, maneuvering to intercept them. Tony cringed when he saw the Taser in the concierge's hand—in firing position. The wired electrodes shot out and connected with Porter's torso. His body went stiff, and he cried out from the electricity surging through him. His knees buckled, and he collapsed to the tile floor.

"FBI!" Cal shouted again, holding up his badge to the concierge.

Grant dropped to his knees to check on Porter.

"Shit! How the hell was I to know you guys are Feds?" The concierge knelt next to Grant.

"He's good. Go!" Grant hollered to them.

"Elevator." Cal jabbed the button.

Tony hesitated. Normally, he could sprint the nine floors, no problem, but his leg hurt like hell, and the numbers above the door showed the elevator descending past the third floor.

"We'll take the stairs." Lundgren disappeared through the metal door to the stairwell, with Grant on his heels.

The elevator doors slid open. A silver-haired woman holding a small dog frowned at them blocking her exit.

Cal flashed his badge. "Official business, ma'am."

She didn't move fast enough. Tony gripped her above both elbows to lift her out of the way. The little mongrel yipped ferociously, his bark shriller than the woman's surprised outburst. He set her on her feet outside the doors. She stopped blustering when they drew their handguns before the doors shut.

"Sitrep, Weiss!"

Tony silently thanked God for Cal asking what they'd missed in the commotion.

"Something is up. I think he found the bug. She's trying to talk her way out of it, but—hang on …"

Could this elevator move any slower? Tony gritted his teeth, tracking the slow ascent. He listened to what Angela was saying, but the poor reception inside the car made the foreign words almost impossible to make out.

"How'd you know?" Cal turned his head to him.

"We talked about it before. A code word." God, he'd only been joking with her. A hundred-pound weight settled in his chest. His hand gripped the butt of his Kimber tighter. He rocked on the balls of his feet, willing the car to rise faster. His thigh had started to swell and tighten.

"We need Hakim alive." Cal's voice was even, authoritative.

Tony swore, unable to meet Cal's eyes. He tried to swallow, only his mouth was as dry as the Iraqi desert.

Seventh floor. Eighth.

He might not be able to make out the French dialog, but the sound of flesh striking flesh was clear. His blood boiled. If it would speed things up, he would pry the doors apart. Instead, he was trapped in this cage. A deep growl emitted from his throat.

"All FBI personnel maintain watch for al-Shehri!" Cal said, only the words were punctuated by the sharp crack of small-arms fire.

Tony squeezed through the opening doors and dashed to the right. He had to believe she got to her weapon and defended herself. If Hakim was dead, he didn't have a problem with that. Angela might have the information they needed based on what she hinted to him earlier.

Two shots destroyed the lock. Despite the pain in his leg, he shouldered his body into the door, which swung open into the spacious marble foyer of Hakim's apartment. He held his breath, listening, desperate to hear Angela call out that all was clear.

What he heard instead was Hakim cursing in Arabic. Tony's heart froze in his chest and blood roared in his ears. He motioned for Cal to cover the near side of the foyer.

During the split-second dash to the far side of the foyer, he caught a glimpse of Hakim—arm raised; gun pointed. Tony tried to channel his rage, maintain his professional bearing. It wasn't working.

"FBI! You've got nowhere to go, Hakim. Give it up," Cal called out.

A shot hit the foyer wall in response to Cal's attempt to defuse the situation.

Ray Lundgren peered around the corner, his eyes narrow and hard.

Tony motioned for Lundgren and Grant to enter. *Where the hell was Angela?* Her silence amplified the *thwump-thwump* of his heart. Unable to take it anymore, he gave Lundgren a signal to go high and one to Grant to go low. He started to count down.

"Alive," Cal huffed.

Fine, but I can make it painful. He visualized a shot to the groin. Three … two …

Another shot rang out, followed by a *wummph* sound of a large object—or body—hitting the floor.

A cautious peek around the corner showed Hakim crumpled on the floor. Thank God.

"Angela!"

"Here." A weak, pained cry answered him. Tony kept his weapon trained on Hakim's unmoving body—eyes open but unseeing. Blood pooled under his head. His mouth was set in a twisted grin. A gun lay on the floor near his body.

Conservative heels and delicate ankles rested on the plush Persian carpet. Tony spun and dropped to where Angela slumped against the sofa, her face contorted in pain.

"Call for a bus!" he yelled as he took in the wet stain of blood near her left shoulder.

Lundgren edged past him and moved to check Hakim's body.

"Weiss already has one on the way," Cal answered.

Tony gently examined her wound. "You'll be all right," he assured her.

"That's not … the one … worried … about." Her words came in ragged gasps, and her gaze dropped from his eyes. Her hand pressed against her side, and dark blood seeped between her fingers.

Shit. This was bad. Panic stole his breath, and his heart pounded. *No, don't lose it, Vincenti!* He eased her to a prone position and pressed his hand to her side to staunch the flow of blood.

"I know … where … target is." Her body shook with the effort to speak.

"Hakim's dead. Save your strength. Tell the medics to hurry," he cried, afraid she might go into shock.

She gripped his arm with a blood-soaked hand. "Plan's … set. Gotta stop it. Girl in … movie is … Fatima." Pained whimpers punctuated her words. "Target's L.A. or Holly … wood. Check studio … filmed … *Den of Iniquity*." She grimaced, struggling for breath. "Promise … you'll stop 'em."

She was losing so much blood. Her face was ashen, and her lips were turning blue. He pressed harder on her side, even though it would hurt. His emotional pain mirrored her physical pain.

Don't let this happen, Lord. Please. His eyes misted over, and his nostrils flared and tingled from the burn. "We'll stop it. I promise. I owe you a dinner." His voice cracked. *Where the hell were the medics?*

She choked on a pained sob, tears escaped and ran into her hair at her temple. "I really … wanted … that …" Her voice faded, her eyes closed, and her grasp on his arm relaxed until her hand slipped limply to the floor.

"Angela. Angela! Stay with me."

Her eyes fluttered halfway open, then closed again.

SIXTEEN

TONY STOOD out of the way to allow the medics to work, but close enough to watch the slight rise of Angela's chest with each strained breath. The men worked quickly to control the bleeding and set up an IV. Their serious tones and expressions only added to his nausea.

He turned away from the sight, his gaze landing on Hakim's body. His fingers itched to empty his entire magazine into him. Only the bastard put a bullet through his own brain and wouldn't feel a thing. Life was not fair.

His heart sank further when the medics transferred Angela to the gurney, leaving a pool of blood on the carpet. He trailed them out of the apartment. Dried blood covered his hands. It coated the underside of his short nails.

"We've lost her pulse. She's crashing!" the bald medic exclaimed, watching the portable monitor at the foot of the gurney.

"Charge the paddles," his partner ordered, already pushing the gurney into the elevator Rozanski held.

The medic ripped open the defibrillator pads. The doors slid closed in Tony's face. His arms hung slack. All energy drained from his body. The world spun around him. He closed his eyes and fought to suck in a breath.

"You okay, man?" Rozanski interrupted his silent plea for God to intervene, not that he deserved for God to answer his prayers.

He wanted to vomit. His knees threatened to buckle under him. He needed to sit down. Or punch someone. Or a wall. Maybe that would expel this helpless anger. Unable to answer his friend, he shook off Rozanski, who went back into the apartment, leaving him alone.

The strength of his emotions surprised him. He and Angela had never been on an actual date, nor had sex, yet he was more comfortable around her than any woman he'd spent time with in over a decade. She understood him. Trusted him. And he'd let her down in the worst possible way.

The anguish of losing her before having a chance to see where it could go bore down on him. It blackened his perspective on life and killed the hope that had started to take hold. His head dropped; his foot tapped on the marble floor. He wanted payback.

Revenge.

But Hakim was already dead. The only thing he could do was fulfill his promise to stop whatever the hell Hakim had set in motion.

What had she said?

He concentrated. Angela's last words replayed through his mind. Energy charged up and spread, replacing the numbness. She'd figured it out and had given him the key they needed.

He limped back in, ignoring the corpse and the stain of Angela's blood, to interrupt Carswell's conference with Lundgren and Calomiris.

"How is she?" Lundgren asked.

Cal leaned closer.

We've lost her pulse. She's crashing! Tony swallowed the wave of torment. "It looked bad." All that dark blood meant the bullet must have hit an organ.

"Shit." Lundgren shook his head.

"I wanted to believe otherwise, but …" Cal exhaled. "And we still don't know—"

"Actually …" That word was enough to make Cal shut up and Carswell to snap to attention. "She got a lead on a possible target."

Cal's jaw dropped. "How? Spill it!"

"I don't know how. She said architecture—"

"Another code word?"

"Yeah. But she"—Tony pointed to the spot where Angela had lain, bleeding, desperate to tell him what she'd risked her life for—"she said the woman in the porn movie was Fatima. The cousin? Something made her think the place they filmed the movie is the target. In California. Not here."

Carswell wasted no time getting on his cell phone. "Sir, we have a lead on the target. Hoffman thinks." He paused. "She thought Hakim might be planning to bomb the studio where the porn film we found on his computer was made. Have Singh review the conversation and see what he can make out to back that up." Carswell stepped away while he wrapped up the call.

Carswell rejoined them a minute later, his phone still in his hand. "We need to do damage control and set back up to have a shot at al-Shehri. If he gets word, he'll slip away for sure." He scanned from the body on the floor to the destroyed door, his face grim. "I'm going down to talk to the doorman and concierge. I'll get you updates on what Singh learns about the film-studio lead. What are you thinking?"

"That my team needs to head to California," Lundgren answered without hesitation.

Tony nodded in response. With all the commotion on the street, the ambulance, curious bystanders, al-Shehri wouldn't show here. The Bureau could handle things on this end. No time to grieve or mourn. They had terrorists to stop and a bomb to find.

He'd promised.

IT'D ONLY TAKEN a few hours for the Bad Karma team to evacuate their hotel and get to the airport where the NEST team had loaded their equipment on their transport plane. A somber mood had permeated the combined group ever since they'd listened to the recorded conversation between Angela and Hakim shortly after takeoff. While nothing Hakim said identified the target, Tony's gut instinct told him to trust Angela. She'd put her life on the line to get it. It had to mean something.

"Listen up." Lundgren garnered the attention of the Bad Karma team. "The Bureau's got an address for the studio. It's north of L.A. in the San Fernando Valley. Grochowski has alerted the Los Angeles FBI office and local NEST team that we'll be working with them."

A quick examination of Hakim's living room had turned up the picture that Angela referred to, backing up her theory. Hopefully, the Bureau would scrounge up information on the "actress" in the movie to lead to a break.

"Coordinates are being sent now. We'll need an analysis of the surrounding area," Lundgren continued. "The studio is the last chance for stopping the bomb. We need to find it before they put it in place."

"If it were me assembling a bomb according to the specs we found, I wouldn't do it someplace where I'd have to mess with stairs. It's too volatile. Rule out apartments. Too many people around in crowded buildings that might ask questions," the SEAL leading the NEST team speculated.

"Rule out any middle-class or above, predominantly white neighborhoods. Our guys would stick out there, raise suspicions," Porter added.

"They might not be smart enough to think that through," Dominguez said.

Grant leaned back, crossing his arms over his chest. "No. The unidentified guy on the three-way call with al-Shehri and Hakim was educated. You could tell by his word choice. Probably got a degree in this country. I wouldn't write him off as some backwoods, downtrodden recruit. He's probably thought this through to cover his ass."

"Agreed," Porter continued. "Ideally, I'd set up shop in a rental house near a nuclear power plant to mask any radiation. Maybe a big hospital. I'd want to be within twenty miles of the target. Pick a poorer neighborhood with a diverse mix. Mostly Latino and African American to blend better. Probably work in the garage."

"It's a hell of a lot of territory to cover. We're gonna need to narrow that down." Lundgren focused on the NEST team leader.

"I'll make the call. Our aircraft will start a grid search. See if we pick up any readings."

"Since this could turn into an urban assault mission, Colonel Mahinis is sending out Alpha team as backup. They'll bring out the gear we need. Until we get more to work on, I suggest you grab what sleep you can. Could be a busy few days." Lundgren stepped to loom over Tony. "You need to let Grant take a look at your leg."

"It's just sore."

"I didn't make you go get checked out in New York 'cuz I knew you'd want to be here. So, drop your pants, Vincenti." No trace of his dry humor was present.

"First time he's heard that from a guy," Dominguez cracked.

"At least without punching him," Rozanski said through laughter, the tension in the plane easing a little.

Tony ground his teeth together. Lundgren didn't back away. Even though the NEST guys were also doing little to hide their amusement, Tony stood and unfastened his pants. He couldn't go with the paramedics working on Angela and he'd promised her he'd stop this attack, so there was no way he'd sit on the sidelines during this mission.

He grimaced when Grant probed his bruised and swollen thigh with his fingertips. His body jerked when Grant felt further up his leg. "You go any higher, and I will kill you."

"This is no picnic for me, either." Grant continued his physical exam. "It's definitely bruised, but since you can walk, doesn't seem to be torn ligaments. I'll wrap it and give you something for the swelling and pain."

"Fine. Hurry up."

"Don't get your briefs in a bunch." Grant couldn't maintain a straight face as he moved to get his medical kit.

Dominguez stared at Tony from across the aisle. "I'm sorry about Angela, man."

Tony gave an abrupt nod, not in the mood to get into a discussion about his relationship with her. Or, more accurately, the lost possibilities. He'd rather sit half-naked the rest of the flight. Grant ambled back and handed him two tablets.

"I'm capable of doing that myself." He took the elastic bandage from Grant.

"Whatever. Just doing my job."

If he'd been in the battlefield or seriously hurt, he would have accepted the help. Confined in this plane with no place to escape, he needed something to do.

Only it didn't take his mind off Angela. He couldn't banish the memory of her warm, sticky blood on her hands. On his hands. The rug. The smell of singed flesh still filled his nostrils. At Hakim's, he'd washed his hands three times, but now he picked at the blood caked under his cuticles. A dark cloud engulfed him, forming an invisible barrier to keep everyone at a distance.

The fact that Lundgren hadn't given any info on her condition after talking with the Bureau didn't bode well. He needed to know. One way or the other.

Mack Hanlon had been outside the building when the medics brought Angela out. His eyes were closed, but Tony reached over and tapped his arm anyway. Mack's eyes flew open. He stared at Tony—waiting.

"When they came out—what'd you see?"

Mack's Adam's apple bobbed, and he swallowed visibly. "I was watching the street for al-Shehri. I ... I didn't see much."

"What. Did. You. See?" Tony asked through clenched teeth.

Mack hesitated again. "One of the paramedics was bagging her, and they had the portable defibrillator on the gurney. That means she was still alive," he said, but couldn't maintain eye contact.

SEVENTEEN

"YO-HO! THE A-TEAM IS HERE!"

Tony recognized Alpha Team leader, Dale Simpson's jovial greeting when he entered their temporary command post in the FBI's Los Angeles field office. While the Bravo team deconstructed cubicle partitions and moved empty desks around to set up the past few hours, they'd given Tony space. No more.

He sucked in a deep breath before he checked his phone for the umpteenth time—in case he'd missed a callback from the voice mail he'd left Carswell.

"Better than the Cavalry. You candy-asses want to give us a hand with this shit? Half of it's your gear since you did a piss-poor job of packing." Jeremy Milledge took the first good-natured jab to start the ribbing between the teams.

"Can't help it if the brass tasks *us* first for the big missions one after the other and uses you guys as backup." Mack punched Milledge in the arm on his way past.

"Your wife can call me for backup anytime she needs to." Laughing, Milledge threw up his hands.

The men guffawed, and Mack pointed his thumb and forefinger at Milledge, then pulled an imaginary trigger.

"Speaking of lovers, we brought your boyfriend, Grant," Leon Hightower's voice sang out.

"Boyfriend? What the—Dita!" The Belgian Malinois nearly knocked Grant over.

The team's working dog slobbered all over Grant's face. It almost made Tony smile. Almost.

Porter issued a sharp whistle. Dita ditched Grant for Porter, who ruffled the dog's fur and made baby-talk noises. The dog made his rounds, getting affectionate pats from the rest of the Bad Karma team.

Dita padded over to where Tony sat on a rolling chair. The dog nuzzled his arm, but he wasn't in the mood to play. Only Dita didn't go away. Instead, he laid his face on Tony's leg, staring up with big, sad eyes, whining as if sympathizing with him. Man's best friend.

He scratched Dita between the ears and ran his hand through the thick, silky fur on the dog's neck, drawing comfort from the contact before he roused himself to his feet to help unload their equipment.

When he hauled in a crate of weapons and ammunition a minute later, Tony sensed a change in the room. Several pairs of eyes fixated on him.

Great. Someone, probably Dominguez, had filled in Alpha team on what happened in New York. About Angela. Despite the silent camaraderie, his *relationship* with Angela didn't compare to the loss all these men had experienced: friends, teammates, marriages.

He kept moving to avoid conversation. Each hour that passed without word on Angela pushed him closer to the edge. He needed information so he could concentrate on the mission. They had their hands full in New York trying to track down al-Shehri, but couldn't Carswell spare two fucking minutes to call him? Unable to take it any longer, Tony slipped outside and called the New York FBI office again.

"Supervisory Special Agent Carswell isn't in the office," the operator said.

Though he hadn't expected him to be in, Tony debated whether to leave another message. "Can I talk to Special Agent Calomiris or leave him a voice mail?" With Jarrod and Angela's past, he might have better luck with Cal.

Halfway through the message for Calomiris, the back door opened, and Dita bounded out, followed by Hightower and Grant. Tony inserted a finger in his ear to block out the distraction of the men's voices while they tossed a tennis ball for the dog to retrieve.

He ended the call but stayed put with his back against the warm, rough wall, watching the sunlight fade. Time to go to work.

God, Angela had to be right about the studio. If not, they were beyond screwed. And so were the people in the proximity of the bomb—wherever the hell it was.

———————

TONY HELD his phone to his ear and drummed his fingers on the desktop beside his empty second cup of morning coffee.

"Hoffman? She is not a patient here," the hospital receptionist said.

Sequestered in a quiet office away from the two teams, Tony drew a line through yet another hospital name on the list. Over one hundred and eighty freakin' hospitals and medical facilities in New York City. He'd already called the ones closest to Hakim's apartment. Now he ran through the bigger hospitals—ones that had trauma centers.

This could take all day, and he didn't have that kind of time—or fortitude. With each "I'm sorry. We don't have a patient by that name" response he got, his hopes took another hit. He should call the New York FBI office again. Someone there had to know something. Beat making a hundred more calls.

Ten minutes later, he wanted to punch through a wall. The FBI receptionist didn't give him any information on Angela, transferring him to another voice mail every time he got routed back to her. He tried Carswell, Weiss, then Calomiris. Who next? Special Agent in Charge Grochowski? That junior agent, Becca-somebody?

Why was no one at the FBI talking? He could think of one reason. One he didn't want to accept. Rather than continue this merry-go-round, he hung up.

He pinched the bridge of his nose, which did nothing to relieve the dull throb in his skull. He needed to catch a few hours of sleep while the team had downtime. Be ready to go when they got information or activity.

Last night, the NEST guys flew a drone over the area around the building that housed the studio. They hadn't picked up any radiation readings—not that he'd expected it to be that easy.

The teams had spent hours in the gloom of night scouting the surrounding area and looking at places they might find a bomb. Any busted locks or things out of the ordinary. They'd strategically placed surveillance cameras in the block around the studio to monitor activity around the building and the more likely spots they'd place the bomb—in case they didn't find it beforehand.

What if the target wasn't the studio itself? They were

checking on who owned the porn-film company and any prior locations used. Also, the male lead in the video. It's not like Los Angeles was a small area to cover. The drone picking up a radiation reading was about their only shot.

They were down to two days now—and everyone was aware of that.

This morning, they'd used incoming intel to eliminate possible areas targeted by NEST reports.

"Hey, Vincenti. Lundgren needs everyone for a sitrep." Rozanski roused him from across the desk.

Tony picked up his phone and checked for messages as he got to his feet.

Rozanski stared at the printed list of hospitals. "You find out anything yet?"

"No."

"You're calling hospitals?"

He nodded. "The FBI can't be bothered to return my calls."

"Have you, uh, called the morgues? 'Cuz I can do it for you if you want."

He'd been putting that off. Paralysis gripped him. "We'll see."

The two joined the group of men gathered around the conference table, some already chowing down on deli sandwiches. Tony perched on the edge of his seat, ready for action while Rozanski grabbed an unclaimed sandwich.

"Listen up," Lundgren commanded everyone. "We've got a potential location. NEST aerial surveillance picked up higher levels of radiation a couple blocks from Northridge Hospital. They've gotten as low as they can with the Van Nuys airport nearby. Alpha team, I want you to do a drive-by and see if we'll need to do some street recon."

About fucking time. The weight on Tony's chest lightened by a brick or two.

———————

TONY SCOWLED when Alpha team's Jeremy Milledge tried to turn Hightower's black ball cap backward. "No! And give him the belt to hold his damn pants up."

"Thank you." Hightower smacked Milledge's arm away.

"Come on. Let him bring out his inner gangsta," Milledge persisted.

"I grew up in rural Georgia. I'm not some gangster." Hightower flipped off Milledge.

Tony grabbed the belt. He wanted to kick Milledge's ass for antagonizing them. Or maybe he wanted to because he wanted to go undercover and case the neighborhood, not set Hightower up to do it.

He chalked up Lundgren's insistence on using Hightower since he was Dita's regular handler—and not because Tony was too personally involved. "Trust me." He clipped the leash onto Dita. "We want him to fit in the neighborhood, not have people watching him or calling the police on him."

Milledge gave a resigned sigh under Hightower's I-told-you-so-asshole look.

After they dropped Hightower and Dita off two blocks from the suspects' house, Tony and Lundgren waited in the van in a convenience store parking lot. The cell rang a few minutes later.

"Closing in on the house. I am seeing evidence of families in the vicinity. Minivan. Toys in the yards. Backyard playset. Whoa, Dita's picking up on something," Hightower added a minute later. "Bingo. Come on, boy. Come on."

"Families. Great." Lundgren huffed. "Okay. I'm calling in

the NEST team. See what else you can gather about the area without raising suspicions."

Tony grimaced. Innocent Americans were not acceptable collateral damage. If—*if*—they got confirmation from the nuclear experts that this could be the location tangos were assembling a bomb, the teams would require a lot of planning for a tactical strike. Planning time they didn't have.

EIGHTEEN

"WE KNOW WHERE THE BOMB IS." Twenty-three pairs of eyes fixed on Chief Lundgren when he paused.

Did they ever. The radiation readings picked up by the NEST team's equipment left no doubt. Tony shifted his weight to his good leg.

"In a residential neighborhood," the SEAL leading the NEST team cut off Chief Lundgren in front of the teams gathered to formulate their attack plan.

Silence settled, amplifying the tension that filled the room.

"While we have reason to believe the intended target is the film studio," Lundgren continued, wearing a forced patient expression, "there's no solid evidence on that. We run the risk of losing them if—"

"That's remote with a drone tracking them," the SEAL interrupted again.

Lundgren's jaw clenched. "Remote. Not impossible. Buildings. Parking decks. The target could be someplace with higher population density, too. And ready to be activated then. If—*when*—we recover the bomb, anyone at the house goes down for it. If we take them down at an alternate site, we might not be able to link the subjects to the bomb. They could land back on the street."

This time, no one on the NEST team protested the idea of taking out the terrorist cell at their safe house.

Tony crossed his arms over his chest. It wasn't gonna be a safe house anymore. Not with the Bad Karma team in proximity. Though they were only doing surveillance tonight to plan the joint takedown with the Bureau tomorrow night, the team geared up like this was the real thing. He might not be a Boy Scout, but he sure as hell adhered to the "Be Prepared" motto.

While putting fresh batteries in his night-vision goggles, his phone vibrated in his pocket. He dropped the goggles to grab his phone. The text message was from the 212-area code. New York City. His arm froze mid-movement. He swallowed, then stepped away from the tables serving as the staging area and clicked to open the message.

Medics revived Hoffman. Crashed again during surgery.
No alshehri. Sucks. Find the fucking bomb.

Crashed again.
Reading the text that had to be a response from the voicemail he'd left Jarrod, Tony's throat swelled shut.
Sucks.
That was an understatement.
He stared at the generic art hanging on the office wall until it went blurry. He'd wanted answers, only he hadn't expected knowing she hadn't made it to hit him like a runaway truck—one barreling down the side of a mountain.
His lungs worked to draw in several deep, even breaths.
He'd seen all that blood. The pallor of her face.

He wanted to think he'd have been able to tell, though. That he'd feel the loss of their connection. It wasn't until now that the earth moved underneath his feet. And it wasn't a California earthquake throwing him off balance.

Around him, the drone of voices and movements continued as if the world hadn't changed. His friends prepped to make sure it didn't change for the residents of Van Nuys and San Fernando. Life wasn't fair, but these men were determined to keep the playing field level. He couldn't stop, either. He picked up the empty magazine for his baby Glock and numbly loaded it.

"We've got a problem," Rozanski said.

The quiet suddenly blanketing the room captured Tony's attention more than the words.

Lundgren stalked over to Rozanski. The two stared at the live feed from the camera the NEST team had planted two doors down from the suspected target house.

"What the hell …?" Lundgren groused.

"A pre-fourth of July party?" Rozanski guessed.

"In the fricking front yard? Shit." Lundgren's mouth pursed.

"Can we not get a single break?" Tony muttered to Mack.

"If it's a block party, that could work for us," Simpson, the perpetually upbeat Alpha Team Leader, said.

We could only be so lucky.

"All right. I want every piece of information you can get on the occupants of the party house. Names. Ages. Jobs. Relatives. Anything you can dig up. Then get names of whoever's living down the street. Let me know if any neighbors are set up to be in on the 'block party.'" Lundgren's voice dripped with skepticism. "Either way, we're going to use this, and somebody is crashing their party. Porter, we'll need to devise some distractions."

NINETEEN

Two hours later, Tony strode past the cars lining the street. All the other vehicles would make the surveillance team less conspicuous.

There looked like thirty people mingling in the front yard now. He walked straight into the center of the revelry.

"Can I help you?" a dark-haired guy with a buzz cut and medium-brown skin asked Tony.

Crap. That didn't take long. Here goes nothing. "Where should I put the beer?" He raised the two cases he toted.

"Uh, who are you?"

"Tony. Mandy invited me," he mumbled in hopes that, with all the noise, the guy heard a name that clicked with some invited guest. Mandy, Sandy, Brandy, or even Amanda.

The guy's head jerked back. His mouth opened, and his gaze dropped, then drifted from Tony's thighs back to his eyes, telling him that Dominguez's research on the homeowner's friends and coworkers scored a hit on the name that he'd suggested. "Really?"

"Yeah. We're meeting here. Guess I'm early. Don't want the beer to get warm."

"Um, in the tub over there."

"I don't know anyone else here. You mind introducing me?" He started unloading the first case.

"Uh, I'm Albert." Either the need to be a gracious host, curiosity, or the two cases of beer trumped his reservations. Based on the way Albert gave Tony another dubious once-over, he must not be Mandy's usual type, or the chick was majorly unattractive.

With the path paved, he mingled for the next half hour. More guests joined the party. Mostly Caucasian and Asian, and they appeared a bit younger than him, but not enough to account for the way a number of them studied him—blatantly. The men were more decked out than the women, but Tony's jeans and T-shirt blended in for the occasion. He took the initiative to strike up conversations rather than wait to be approached.

The guests he'd talked to weren't from the neighborhood, so he hadn't dug up nothing useful so far. He sipped a beer but kept his mouth shut with the group bitching about politics. Trying to remain inconspicuous, he went and dropped the now lukewarm beer in the trashcan. Scouting the crowd for new faces, he grabbed a fresh, cold beer.

He turned around and came face-to-face with the man he'd seen talking to Albert. His hair shone from the hair gel or spray that held it in place and the collar on his light-blue polo shirt turned up. Tony took a step back, but cologne filled his nostrils enough to taint his sip of beer.

"We haven't met. I'm Jody." Tony's new friend—*Jody?*—checked him out in nearly the same way Albert had earlier. "You can do better than Randall. *Randy.*" He gave a dismissive chortle.

Hehkkh. Tony choked on the beer. It suddenly made sense. The homeowners were Albert and Jody—as in two guys. That confirmed the skewed number of what appeared to be same-sex couples. "Um, who's Randall?"

He'd told Albert he was a friend of Mandy's because Dominguez said Jody worked with enough nurses with similar-sounding names that he could bluff. But now he had to decide which route to take.

Shit. He'd bet twenty bucks that Dominguez and Porter had scrounged up a picture of *Jody*—his hospital ID badge picture or headshots from his portfolio—and knew what Tony was walking into. It would have been nice to get a heads-up with so much on the line.

"Albert said you're a friend of his."

"Not Randy. Mandy. She works with the people having the party." Tony played dumb. "She's running late. I thought she'd be here by now."

"I don't work with anyone named Mandy."

"Amanda. Mandy for short?"

Jody shook his head, and his eyes narrowed. The way his lips shifted to the side and up sent stabbing pinpricks up Tony's arms.

Busted. If he went with Plan B, he could still salvage this or get decent intel. *What is Plan B?*

"Shit. I left the address at home. I remembered the street name, and when I saw the party, I just thought this had to be it." He shook his head and gave a self-deprecating laugh.

Jody didn't look convinced.

"God, Mandy is gonna be pissed thinking I blew her off. And the beer I bought for that party is already half gone. Shit, this is embarrassing." He stared at the tub of beer like he might reclaim what remained of his contribution. "She said it was a get-together at her friend's. I think it was Tina or Trina. Hell, I don't remember. You know someone on the street it might be?"

"Afraid not. So, you're not Randall's *friend*?" Jody's head and shoulders did a seductive little dance.

"Uh, no." Tony scanned the houses on the street, keeping up the pretense, but with this one spiraling down, he'd better take a more direct approach to gathering intel. "Guess you'd know if it was one of your neighbors. You know the people in the third house down?"

"Three down? That's Becky and Judy. They're older than your mother and not the party-throwing type, but they're sweet and lived here for a long time. They may know who you're looking for."

Hmm, they might be worth talking to since they've had a front-row seat to the comings and goings of the suspects.

"What about the tan house over there?" He pointed to the target house.

"I don't think so. A couple of Middle Eastern-looking guys moved in there. Not very sociable."

"Maybe they're terrorists," Tony said, adding a snort. Reality made the laugh ring hollow, even to him.

Jody's eyes widened momentarily. He leaned closer and kept his voice low. "Well, last week, some kids kicked a soccer ball into the bushes by the front of that house. When they went to get it, one of the guys came out yelling for them to stay out of their yard. I mean, it was over the top. I said the same thing—about them being terrorists—but Albert said they're students and probably sick of always getting profiled and mistreated. We can relate. I guess he's right. I have seen them going out with backpacks." He cast another wary glance at the house.

Backpacks? Warning bells clanged in Tony's head. What if instead of building one major dirty bomb, they were split-ting nuclear material into a couple of smaller devices? He tried to swallow the lump lodged in his throat. It didn't budge.

Finally, he was getting some usable intel. The key now meant not blowing it by being overly inquisitive or needy. "I should text Mandy and get to the right party."

Jody shrugged as if agreeing.

Time to cast his net if he had any chance of a worthwhile haul before he moved off. He took a long pull of beer. "Does anyone around here have a dog? 'Cuz I was in this movie where—"

"Wait. You're an actor?"

Suddenly he had Jody's total attention. "Yeah, I act." *I'm doing it right now.*

"Anything I would have seen?"

"Maybe. Mostly bit parts with a few lines. I've done some work internationally. South America. Europe." *The Middle East. Africa.* Keep it simple like Mrs. Boone taught for improvisation. As appalled as he'd been to have Coach stick him in drama for an easy *A*, that class saved his butt more than any other class he'd taken. "I've got a good shot at a recurring role on this paranormal show."

"Which one? I auditioned last week for a part as a zombie." Jody's eyes shone, and he invaded Tony's personal space.

Despite them not clarifying that Jody was a guy, Tony was going to owe Grant a cold one for digging up his profile. "I can't say until it's a done deal." He lowered his face. "But there are bloodsuckers in it." Close enough. "Anyway, in this movie I was in, the terrorist had a bomb in his backpack, but this Doberman smelled the explosive stuff and chased him down."

"I think I saw that! What character did you play?"

"I was an FBI agent." He said the first thing that popped in his head. A chill coursed through him at the reminder of Angela. *I should have said a soldier.* No matter. Jody apparently bought the overused plotline. "Anyway, I was thinking if you had any vicious dogs on the street, you could have them follow those guys and see what happens. Be kinda cool if it was like in the movie."

"Not cool if you live here." Jody chewed on his lower lip.

"True," he agreed.

"The sisters have two dogs. But the only danger from their yappy little fluffball would be to your ears. And Logan, their Lab, would retrieve their backpack and return it for a pat on the head."

"No other attack dogs you can use? Guess you're out of luck."

"There are lots of dogs on the street. Mostly inside ones, though."

That was good to know. The breeds that scared most people didn't bother Tony as much as noisy little dogs, which posed more of a threat to a covert mission. He finished the text message to "Mandy" and hit send.

His phone vibrated a minute later. The message acknowledged his warning about the presence of dogs and asked if the party might break up soon.

Not likely, he replied. He shouldn't have brought so much beer.

Stay as long as you can fly under radar, read Lundgren's response.

"Did she give you the right address, or is she pissed?" Jody asked.

"I'm off the hook. A coworker didn't show, so now she's pulling a double shift. She feels bad for ditching out, and I didn't have to fess up." He tossed the beer bottle into the nearby can. "Guess I'll head out."

"No need to rush off. Have another beer."

Bingo. An official invite to the party.

For the next half hour, Tony did his best to bluff about his "acting career." He diverted attention by asking Jody questions about his roles as an extra, and they'd attracted a small group at the edge of the yard by the time he picked out Dita leading Hightower down the road. From the opposite end of the street, Porter meandered their way.

Tony positioned himself to face the target house when the white van turned the corner and cruised down the street.

When the firecrackers started going off, Dita began barking. Tony refrained from turning toward the source of the noise with the other partiers.

Before the van reached the suspects' house, it slowed to a crawl. It didn't stop, but three shadowed figures darted from the side door and crossed the sidewalk. The first figure, which had to be Rozanski, took hold of a low limb on the tree in the neighbor's front yard and vanished into the foliage. The other two disappeared around the side of the adjacent house. Mack stared straight ahead as he drove the van past the party.

The fireworks, followed by Porter and Hightower's shouting and Dita running free, held the attention of everyone in Tony's field of vision. All clear.

"Police."

Police? Tony's head whipped left. Albert was on his phone, watching the escalating conflict between Hightower and Porter. Shit! Tony snatched the phone out of Albert's hand.

"Excuse me. What do you think you're doing?" Albert blustered.

"9-1-1. Where is your emergency?" the operator asked. Tony's mind whirled, and his blood pressure shot up a thousand points.

He stepped back out of Albert's reach, using his height and bulk to keep control of the phone. Time to bank on his acting skills. "Sorry. It's okay now. My, uh, sister's ex showed up and wouldn't leave. Now that I called 9-1-1, he's getting in his car. Sorry for the false alarm." He disconnected before the operator could respond.

The police were the last thing the team needed. *Hi, officer. I can explain being up a tree staking out this house. Fan-fuck-ing-tastic.* They could blow this op because Hightower and Porter oversold it.

"What makes you think you—"

"If the police show up," he cut Albert off, "they may start issuing bullshit citations about open containers on public property." He nodded toward the group standing on the sidewalk.

"Well, if those gangbangers get in a shootout—"

Gangbangers? He tried not to smirk. "If they're gang-bangers, do you want them or their friends coming back for retaliation because you called the cops on them?"

"I didn't think about that." Albert backed down with a sigh and nervously glanced toward the street.

Hightower whistled; Dita heeled, then dashed to his handler.

Tony held Albert's phone out to him. "Looks like one's leaving, and the other is trying to get his dog. If they start back up, then call the cops."

Albert pocketed the phone. Disaster averted. Now they could get down to the business of gathering intel before they kicked in the door tomorrow night.

TWENTY

"Well, hello. I'm Randall." The short, balding newcomer sidled between Tony and Jody.

Damn, if Tony checked out a woman the way Randall sized him up, he'd deserve to be slapped.

"Albert said you were looking for me." Finally, Randall looked him in the face.

"There was a little mix-up. I said Mandy; he heard Randy."

"Well, that's disappointing." Randall pouted, his gaze fixed again on Tony's chest. "Yet, you're still here."

"We got talking about acting gigs." Oh, and I'm staking out some terrorist sons of bitches so my team can stop an attack and send their asses to prison for life—as their best-case scenario. A better scenario than Angela got.

"I thought maybe you were doing research in case you got called for a role playing a gay character," Jody teased.

"What? You could tell right away I was straight?" Tony hoped his smile took the edge off his sarcasm, not entirely sure he bought into the gaydar concept. "Was it the shoes? Or am I stereotyping or being politically incorrect?"

Fortunately, both men laughed with him. It was the first time he'd laughed in days.

Randall stuck around, making it harder for Tony to mine any more information about the neighbors from Jody. Hopefully, his team had knowledge of how many subjects occupied the house since this fact-finding mission had run dry. Time to head out and see where else he could be useful.

Tony wished Jody luck with his next audition and headed to his vehicle. He pulled up short when he spotted the team's white van coming back down the street. Watching it approach, he froze. He whipped out his cell phone. No, he hadn't missed a text or call. When the van neared, he'd see if Mack gave him any signal.

It clicked that the white van was a different make than the team's van. Tony made out a young male driver with a dark complexion and hair. Another man slouched in the passenger seat. A buzzing sensation filled Tony's head when the brakes lights flashed, and it pulled into the driveway of the target house.

His heart thumped a steady cadence, even as he reasoned they wouldn't need a van for backpack bombs. It could be their everyday vehicle. Or were they prepping for tomorrow? Shit. Shit. Shit!

Two men emerged from the house, and the driver and passenger got out of the van. The four stood in a tight group and alternated looks toward the party. Better than spotting Rozanski in the tree.

Tony needed to be in the loop. Now.

He navigated past the guests into the house and found the bathroom. Inside, he removed the earpiece from his pocket and inserted it. Silence. If this damn thing doesn't work— then he heard it. A slight rustling and faint male voices—not his team's—speaking what sounded like Arabic. Possibly another Middle Eastern dialect.

"Sounds like they're bitching about the party," Lundgren interpreted. "Trying to decide what to do."

"How many—" Tony broke off. No comms link meant he couldn't talk to the team. This sucked. The rest of the team had thermal-imaging goggles to see how many subjects and were clued in on their activities while he was flying blind. He sent a text to Lundgren to tell him he was listening in and asked for the 411.

"Vincenti's live," Lundgren informed the team. "We've got eyes on six counting the two who just arrived. One pair is getting up from their beauty rest."

Tony liked those odds.

"Garage door is going up," Rozanski relayed.

"Vincenti, see if your friends have seen that van before."

Great. Not the plan of action he wanted. Hopefully, the partiers wouldn't notice the earpiece. At least his jeans concealed the ankle holster holding his baby Glock.

"They're turning the van around and backing it in," Dominguez said.

Tony exited the house to rejoin the party. He grabbed a water bottle from the tub and stood where he had a clear view of the house. The van's headlights were off now, but the red glow of the brake lights reflected off the garage walls as it angled in. It maneuvered several times before the man in the driveway waved his arms, signaling the driver, who got out.

"These idiots can't open the van's back doors because then they don't have room to close the garage door."

Tony could barely make out Rozanski's whispered update.

"Can you see anything of interest inside?" Lundgren asked.

A chorus of "negative" responses shot down Tony's hopes of solid photographic evidence to guarantee a search warrant.

"I thought you'd left." Jody popped up at his side, dogged by Randall.

"Decided I'd better lay off the beer and wait a while before heading out. Figured you wouldn't mind if I hung out longer."

"No problem, especially if you'll put in a word for me with your agent."

He nodded. If everything went as planned, they'd take down the tangos in the gloom of night tomorrow and be gone before the neighbors woke to see the house cordoned off with crime-scene tape. No future acting gigs with Jody. *Sorry, dude.* "Your neighbors have that van long? 'Cuz they sure can't seem to park it."

Jody turned to look. "I don't recall seeing it before, but who knows." He shrugged. "There've been several cars and trucks over there since they moved in last month."

"Looks like the subjects are carrying something heavy through the house," Rozanski said.

Tony scrutinized the thick blanket of leaves hiding his teammate from sight as Jody spoke to Randall.

"Anyone able to get a look into the garage?" Again, Lundgren's question brought a round of negative responses. "Everyone hold your position. They could be loading up in preparation for tomorrow."

"I'm sorry. What?" Tony had missed whatever Randall said.

"Randall's ranting about how Hollywood keeps ruining classics with second-rate remakes. We don't listen to him anymore, either."

This time, Tony half listened to the conversation, though his focus kept shifting to the house less than a hundred yards away and the possibility it contained a weapon of mass destruction. He could be vaporized in a matter of minutes.

Every muscle fired warning shots through his body when Rozanski reported someone getting behind the wheel again. The van pulled forward in the drive, then backed straight into the garage. Seconds later, the garage door closed. Both Jody and Randall turned to stare at Tony when he audibly exhaled the breath he'd been holding.

Maybe Lundgren was right. But why leave the bomb in the van tonight? He managed to ditch Randall and mill around where he didn't have to participate in a conversation. Hearing surveillance updates about the men assembled in the kitchen of the target house gave him hope they'd all sit down for a terrorist-style family dinner.

"Two subjects entered the garage." Dominguez's voice had that singsong quality Tony associated with a mission about to go down.

Dammit. Tonight was supposed to only be surveillance. What if the bad guys had other plans? Thank God, the team members were armed and prepared for this contingency.

He hesitated. Did he have time to sprint to the car for more firepower? The garage door going up answered that question.

"Go! Go! Go!" Lundgren called out before the van cleared the garage.

Tony freed his Glock from under his pant leg in one fluid motion. A nearby woman saw the gun and screamed, then jumped out of his way. Across the street, the dark forms of his teammates materialized from their concealed positions, rapidly converging on the van and house.

The driver hit the brakes. From more than one direction, voices yelled to stop and exit the vehicle.

Tony cringed when the van surged forward, tires squealing. Bodies jumped out of the way. Rage fueled him as he skirted the guests and rushed toward the street.

Albert stood wide-eyed, his mouth gaping.

"Take cover! Get in the house!" Tony slowed long enough to shove a few guests in the direction of the small brick home in hopes it would offer protection.

"Tires! Tires! Tires!" voices yelled.

The first gunshots rang out. The van veered off the driveway onto the front lawn.

Following their hasty plan for this possibility, Tony focused on stopping the van. He had ten rounds. Each shot counted.

He fired at the front driver's side tire as the van navigated down the driveway next door.

Though confident he hit the tire, the van kept coming— for him, or to inflict carnage among those at the party. He raised his arm, taking the shot he didn't want to, praying it didn't set off the very thing they wanted to avoid.

The windshield shattered. The driver's head jerked back against the headrest, then slumped over the steering wheel. The passenger lunged for the wheel, but the van slowed and crashed into one of the parked cars lining the road.

No explosion.

Tony didn't have time to catch his breath before the occupant in the passenger seat ducked behind the dash, then slammed open the door to squeeze out the wedge of space. The staccato cadence from the automatic gunfire confirmed the passenger was well armed. Tony crouched low, using the front of the van as cover when a few poorly aimed shots came his way.

Heat radiated from the van's engine, reminding him he lacked a bulletproof vest. But he couldn't play it safe with his team taking fire and all the civilians in the danger zone. "I'm sorry, Mom," he muttered and duckwalked to the back of the van.

The target beat him there, yanking open the doors. The metal door shielded most of his body, but Tony fired at the terrorist's exposed calf.

The man wailed and crumpled to the pavement. He still managed to fire at Rozanski and Porter, who returned fire as they advanced. The terrorist's body jerked, and he cried out in anguish. His weapon clattered to the ground, and Tony kicked it away.

"I got him." Porter dropped to a knee next to the man.

Rozanski closed the distance, dragging his left leg.

"Checking the driver." Tony kept one eye on the house. It only took seconds to confirm his head shot proved fatal. He secured a .9mm Beretta from the driver and scoured the van's cab for other weapons.

The gunfire died out, and silence reigned. The remainder of the team reported they'd secured the house.

"We're clear. Rozanski needs a bus," Porter said.

Tony stood over the passenger, who lay on his back a few feet away from the vehicle. Blood soaked a large portion of his plaid shirt and one leg of his khakis. His strained breathing made it clear they weren't getting him before a jury. It also reminded Tony of Angela's struggle for life and sent a chill through his sweaty body.

Porter motioned to Tony to change places, then climbed into the back of the van. He circled the crate, not touching it. "Size matches the specs on the computer."

"How bad is it?" Tony asked Rozanski.

Rozanski winced. "I'll live—provided that bomb doesn't go off. It in there?"

Tony stared at the crate. "Looks that way." *What if ...? No. No point in going there now.* "Here come the NEST guys." He cut away the fabric of Rozanski's pants. "It's just a graze." A deep graze bleeding badly, though. He dug a dressing out of Rozanski's medic pack and wrapped his buddy's leg.

Porter stepped out of the van, allowing the NEST agents access to the suspected bomb.

"Low-grade radiation reading," one said after they conferred. "Appears the crash didn't compromise the integrity."

Tony knew that comment was directed at him. He'd gone with his instinct. It'd worked out. So far.

Porter laid the top of the wooden crate against the side of the van, then was handed another piece of the crate.

"There's a timer. And it's counting down," one of the NEST guys announced.

Tony locked eyes with Porter. Neither breathed.

"How long?" Porter asked.

The NEST pair climbed out, lingering near the wounded subject. "It's set for—" The SEAL member's mouth pursed as he examined his watch. He tsked. "Nine eleven p.m. on the Fourth of July."

The significance wasn't lost on the gathered men.

"We've got all the time in the world and the bomb's specs." The SEAL's confidence let Tony breathe.

Angela had been right. They found the bomb. The experts could defuse it.

Dominguez ambled out of the house and over to help Porter place the driver into a body bag. "He say anything?" Dominguez nodded toward the passenger.

"No dying confession. Just an 'up yours' in Arabic." Porter laid an empty body bag on the pavement beside the passenger. "Any survivors inside?"

"One. Think he's the scientist. Claims he doesn't speak

English. Chief is trying to ID him now," Dominguez answered.

"What else did you find?" Tony asked.

"Airline tickets for tomorrow. Bags of bundled cash. Guess they finally wised up and decided being suicide bombers wouldn't be so great if their virgins-in-paradise were virgins for a reason. As in, they aren't young or hot."

A gruff chuckle escaped as Tony envisioned strict Catholic nuns as the *reward* for killing infidels.

The scream of sirens grew louder, then flashing lights appeared. Two police units turned onto the street. Based on their speed, or lack of, Lundgren or the FBI had updated dispatch on the situation to prevent them from becoming targets themselves. The team produced IDs when the cops emerged with weapons drawn.

TWENTY-ONE

THE ARRIVAL of the local FBI agents squared things away with the police. The ambulance was cleared to leave with Rozanski, and Alpha team was allowed in to help establish a perimeter.

Lundgren hauled the handcuffed surviving target across the lawn to the van. "Meet Fariq Shah. He graduated from the University of New Mexico two years ago."

Lundgren's ominous tone gave Tony goosebumps. *I don't speak English, my ass.* He sized him up.

"He's got a graduate degree in nuclear engineering. How 'bout that?"

The man shrunk into himself, unable to vanish from the angry stares fixed on him.

"I want a lawyer." His accent was pretty understandable for someone who didn't speak English. He also sounded like the unidentified voice on the call with Hakim and al-Shehri.

"No problem. Once that bomb is disabled—or detonated —we'll get on that."

Under Lundgren's saccharine smile, Shah shook, and his glance darted to the back of the van.

"The police have the perimeter established and the area cordoned. Time to take a look." The NEST explosive ordnance disposal (EOD) expert set his tools on the floor of the van. "Ideally, with this much time, we'd move it to a remote location. However, with three flats and its current parking spot, this van's not going anywhere right now."

Tony looked him in the eye. Refusing to squirm, he owned up to his actions. He'd take any heat that came from it later. Right now, he wanted these guys to do their job and disarm the damn thing.

"No bomb suit? He's got brass kahunas," Dominguez stated.

Tony rolled his eyes. "It's nuclear. Suit won't protect him." Or us.

"We should step back."

"Better be one helluva step." Tony held his ground, putting his trust in these guys. After a closer examination, they'd determine whether it could be moved or if they needed to evacuate the surrounding area—creating mass panic—to disarm it here.

The EOD tech snapped pictures. He handed his partner the camera, then proceeded to open the timer casing. "We'll double-check before we make a—Oh, fuck!" His hands jerked back. He lost his balance and landed on his ass.

"What is it?" The tech's partner moved closer.

"The timer reset."

The tech's partner blocked the view inside, but his urgent tone had the same effect as touching a live wire.

"We have twenty-two minutes."

They'd gone from nearly two days to twenty-two fucking minutes to defuse the bomb? Just like that? Tony thought these guys knew what the hell they were doing. It wasn't supposed to go down like this.

Okay. Calm down. Not their fault. Twenty-two minutes. Could they clear the area in that time? The street, maybe …

Lundgren forced the prisoner's face into the back of the van.

"You added a tripwire on the timer. You do anything else different than the specs?"

Shah shook his head.

Tony looked to see if the guy pissed himself. Wouldn't be the first time that happened when Lundgren was incensed.

Lundgren's head swiveled from the van to take in the neighboring houses—some brave, or curious, residents started to emerge. "Alpha team, get as many people to evacuate as you can. Don't use the word nuclear." He dropped his voice. "Tell them not to pack. To leave now!" He checked his watch. "Mack, back our van up to the house. Bravo team, grab every bit of potential evidence. Bodies, too. I want everything and you loaded up and out of here in nine minutes. No exceptions. Go."

The team raced to secure anything in the house that might lead to additional terror cells, plots, another bomb, or something that would point them to al-Shehri. In under seven minutes, other than furniture, most everything the occupants possessed—electronics, notebooks, mail, flash drives, backpacks, books, even toiletries—had been shoved into trash cans, laundry baskets, random boxes, or wrapped in blankets and stowed in the van.

Tony helped Mack grab the ends of the last body bag. They loaded it on top of the other bodies and slammed the doors shut with a minute to spare.

Tension hung in the stagnant air around the group while the EOD techs compared the printed specs with the actual device in the back of the van.

"Load up!" Lundgren commanded the men.

"After you, Chief." Tony planted himself at Lundgren's side.

Lundgren cocked his head at the challenge. "I have—"

"You have a wife and kid," Tony talked over him.

"We don't have time for this. Mack! You're driving this out. I want the rest of you in our vehicles and—"

"While you decide, I'm going to work because we have nine minutes and seven seconds left. Six. Five. Four," the EOD tech said.

"I get the picture. Just get started," Lundgren snapped. He fixed his hypnotic do-as-I-say stare on Tony. "You need to go."

"I need to stay."

"It won't bring her back."

"I—" He couldn't finish. The emotions hit him, nearly dropping him to his knees. Angela risked her life to stop this bomb. He couldn't drive away. He planted his feet and crossed his arms over his chest. They'd have to manhandle him into a vehicle. Good luck with that.

Lundgren growled. He gave a resigned jerk of his head to the team, already loaded in their vehicles. Tires squealed and left rubber on the road peeling out to deliver everything to the FBI.

"You know this is insubordination." Lundgren didn't look at him.

"Can you hold off on the court-martial until they defuse it?"

"I guess so." Lundgren turned to Shah and got so far in his face that the man nearly collapsed backward. "What do you know about a second bomb?"

"Nothing."

"Somehow, I don't believe you." Lundgren's voice cooled the sultry night air.

In the moonlight, the guy's face lightened a few shades. Hell, Lundgren's tone gave Tony chills, too.

"I was to complete this. That was all."

"Where is al-Shehri?" Lundgren's tone turned lethal.

Fear shone in Shah's eyes. He shook his head with his jaw clenched. Tony wasn't sure if he feared Lundgren, the bomb, or al-Shehri more. All equally lethal, which could explain Shah refusing to say anything as Lundgren and a SEAL flanked him, neither speaking another word aloud while the minutes ticked by.

A running litany of confession for his sins ran through Tony's mind. Fortunately, he could go straight to the source rather than try to find a priest to confess to. It gave him more time.

"Which wire do I cut?" the EOD asked the prisoner.

"The blue." It took a second for Shah to reply. His gaze flickered up before dropping to the pavement, then his eyes closed. His arms twitched.

Tony closed his eyes, too. *And forgive me for not—*

"Done." The EOD tech eased out of the van. Sweat dripped off his face.

"But, I … I …" the prisoner stuttered.

"I didn't expect you to tell me the truth." He flashed a cocky smile from Shah to the SEAL holding onto him.

Tony concurred. Eternity in an American jail or complete the jihad? Shah had no motivation to help them out.

He breathed easier than he had in days as the EOD tech swaggered away. Lundgren grinned, though Tony didn't feel the same sense of satisfaction.

Thanks, Ang. It didn't feel like a win even though they'd saved countless lives tonight because of her sacrifice.

TWENTY-TWO

THE TEAM'S flight touched down at Simmons Army Airfield at Fort Bragg mid-afternoon. Despite getting a couple hours of sleep on the plane, Tony still felt bone-weary. He was emotionally spent. Once they stopped the bomb, he thought it would stamp out most of the anger—only an emptiness persisted.

Colonel Mahinis waited for the team off the tarmac. While the men unloaded their bags and gear, Lundgren strode over to talk to the colonel. The team converged minutes later.

"Well done, men. Though I'd appreciate you not cutting it so close next time." A smile broke out over the colonel's usually serious face.

"I'd prefer not having a 'next time' on something like this," Mack chimed in. He scanned the airfield, probably hoping to see his wife, Kristie.

Tony's heartbeat echoed in the cavity in his chest. It'd sure as hell be nice to have someone to come home to after a mission like this.

"I hear you. Let's debrief after you stow your gear so you can enjoy your day off tomorrow." The battle-hardened veteran gave a nod of dismissal. "Vincenti." The colonel stopped his departure.

"Sir?"

"I got a call from Special Agent Calomiris in the New York field office. He asked if I'd pass details about Special Agent Hoffman on to you." The colonel extended a folded sheet of paper.

Tony stared at the paper. His blood froze in his veins, and his limbs became blocks of ice. His windpipe constricted to the point that he couldn't speak. He wanted to take her flowers, not send them to her funeral. Who would be there to mourn her? In slow motion, he reached for the paper.

"If you want to take a couple of days, I checked, you've got two months of leave accrued."

He nodded numbly. "Yes, sir. When is the service?"

"'Service?' That's the hospital information." The colonel pointed to the paper, his brow creased in confusion.

"Hospital? But Jarrod said she …" His hands shook as he unfolded, then read the words on the paper. Disbelieving laughter erupted. "Thank you, God."

"Must have been bad. Calomiris said she wasn't conscious yet. Anyway, take all the time you need, and give her my thanks. The rest of the team can handle the debrief. Dismissed."

Tony clutched the piece of paper like it was a winning Powerball ticket—or a gift from God. He wanted to be on the next plane to New York City. After all the stress the past few days, he could probably fly there on his own.

CRUISING off the elevator at New York Presbyterian Hospital, Tony only slowed enough to look at the directional plaque on the wall for the ICU desk.

"Can I help you?" A blonde nurse in pink scrubs glanced up from an iPad screen when he leaned over the counter.

"I'm … I'm looking for Angela Hoffman."

"Hoffman. We don't have any patients by that name in this unit," the nurse said.

"Can you see if she was transferred?" He fought the panic that raced through him. He'd left post to go home, book a flight, shower, and pack, then he raced like a madman to the Raleigh airport, making it through security and to the gate minutes before they closed the door. It hadn't occurred to him to call the hospital—hadn't thought it necessary.

They moved her to another room because they'd upgraded her condition. That's it. He refused to let the grim reaper's shadow overtake the euphoria of learning Angela survived.

"We haven't had anyone in critical care by that name. Maybe she was in a different unit." She tapped on the keyboard. "No, I don't see—"

"Are you sure? She was shot twice. In the shoulder and the abdomen." He motioned, rattling off details. His voice grew louder, his words more urgent. The nurse's head whipped from side to side, her eyes wide, heightening his sense of alarm.

A woman wearing a white lab coat over her scrubs, her raven hair in a low bun, hurried over. "Sir, you need to calm down."

Calm down? He hadn't gotten started yet.

"Come with me," the doctor instructed in an authoritative tone. Her direct stare said more than her words, compelling him to comply. She led him a few steps away. "Who told you this person was here?" *Dr. Sarah Saba* was stitched on her jacket.

"Um, Special Agent Calomiris. He's with the—"

"Yes. I know," she interrupted. With a quick nod of her head, she walked away from the desk; he followed.

Dr. Saba pushed open the door to Room 4585 without knocking. His heart skipped a beat. The surge of relief from his core to his limbs left him dizzy. He moved past the doctor to the side of the bed, where he reached out to stroke Angela's cheek with the back of his fingers. She didn't stir.

"Special Agent in Charge Barnsley requested that we list her under an alias for her protection—and not advertise that she's with the FBI. We have her listed as Elizabeth Sutcliff. So, you might not want to go around shouting her real name."

"Sorry. I didn't know." That made sense with al-Shehri still out there and his money-launderer dead. "How ... how is she?"

The doctor cocked her head. "Stable now. She went down twice. Fortunately, she had the best medic in the city respond. Course, I might be biased."

He picked up on her pride. "Husband or boyfriend?"

"My brother. And she had a kick-ass trauma surgeon ..."

"You?"

"If I say so myself." Her chin jutted up.

"Thanks." He gave her an appreciative nod. Emotion made his throat tight.

Her gaze dropped to his left hand. "Are you family?"

"Uh, not exactly. The only family she has is her dad. I think he lives in Germany." Had the Bureau let him know? Would he come? The idea of having no one else here for her hit him hard.

Dr. Saba hesitated, studying him before she spoke. "She lost a lot of blood, and I removed nearly a third of the right lobe of her liver to stop the bleeding. However, she can function without it, and the liver can regenerate. She's going to need time to recuperate, but she should make a full recovery. We've been keeping her heavily sedated to control the pain while she's healing."

He squeezed Angela's limp hand.

I'll be here for you. You aren't alone.

TWENTY-THREE

PAIN RADIATED through Angela's body. Apparently, she was not in heaven. It was so dark she couldn't see anything, but she could hear. Background noise. A rhythmic beeping of machinery. The smooth, sexy voice of Jake pierced through the fog enshrouding her brain. *No, not Jake. Tony—Tony Vincenti—mmm ...* Though some woman was talking. The damn woman drowned out his voice.

"Come on. Open your eyes, Elizabeth. You can do it."

Angela willed her eyes to open to see who the woman was talking to, but her world stayed dark.

Maybe she was in purgatory. She couldn't see Tony, couldn't make out what he was saying. What if they were both here and never able to be together? Never touch or kiss. *That* would be her definition of hell. She wanted to revert to the floating sensation, the one without the physical pain. But what if Tony were here? Was he dead, too?

"The bomb?" she forced the words out. At least she thought she did.

Again, the woman spoke, then Tony's voice. He sounded

far away, and she couldn't understand what he said before she slipped back into the soothing weightlessness.

———————————

WHEN ANGELA MOVED, Tony's head jerked up. He leaned forward to caress her hand. "Come on, Ang. Time to wake up."

Her eyelids fluttered open, then closed, and she murmured something.

His name.

It sent a bolt of electricity through him. "Yeah. I'm here."

This time her eyes opened and her head turned toward him. As she focused on his face, a dreamy smile altered her features. Then her eyes shot wide open and scanned the room. "The bomb?"

Unlike earlier in the day, this time when Angela asked, she had the clarity of mind to be sure the room was clear first. A good sign, though he'd covered when she asked the nurse on the last shift before drifting back into unconsciousness. "We found it in time. Everything's good."

She sank into the pillow behind her, still fighting the lull of drug-induced sleep. "Where?"

"You were right. We found one at their safe house outside Van Nuys. Near the studio. We couldn't have done it without you." He didn't tell her that he thought she'd given her life for that information or how freaking close they'd been. "Al-Shehri? Please tell me you got him."

"No. Nothing." The man was like a magician's assistant—disappearing into thin air.

"Dammit."

He gave her a moment to deal with the frustration.

"What day is it?"

"The fourth. They kept you sedated for a few days."

The fingers on her left hand moved as if counting. Her mouth tightened, and he guessed she realized al-Shehri could be anywhere by now.

"Why are you here? Was Grochowski afraid I'd talk while drugged up or …?"

"No. I, uh …" *Great.* What should he tell her? He couldn't man up and go for soul-baring honesty. Not yet. "We have a date. Remember?"

"Yeah, but …" She attempted a smile. "How long have you been here?"

"I got in yesterday afternoon."

"I'm afraid it's going to be a while before I'm up for—a date." Her fingers tickled his palm.

Oh, man. Even lying in a bed, pale and so weak she couldn't hold her head up, her subtle innuendo gave him a hard-on. "I can wait. I'm a patient man. Get some sleep," he suggested.

"I think I've slept enough," she mumbled.

"You need to heal. I'm not going anywhere." He brushed her hair back from her face and lightly kissed her forehead.

———

Jeez. Didn't the nurse just leave? Tony squinted against the light that streamed into the room. The door closed quickly this time. He bit his tongue. He shouldn't harass the nurses checking on Angela to manage her pain. Only the person who moved into the room this time was male and wore a ball cap.

Tony dug his elbow into the corner of the recliner and pushed himself upright. The figure jerked back, then froze.

"Vincenti? What the hell are you doing here?" Jarrod

Carswell kept his voice low and stepped further into the room.

"Better question is, what are *you* doing here? What the hell time is it?" It had to be well after midnight. Tony stroked a hand over his jaw rather than go for Carswell's throat after the text message that misled him to think Angela died.

"Wanted to check on her. Been a crazy few days."

Carswell took another step toward the bed.

Tony's nerves jangled. He repressed the urge to take hold of Angela's hand. Instead, he rose and joined Jarrod at her bedside. "Anything on al-Shehri?"

"Nothing. Guy's a damn ghost. He's gotta be pissed, but if he's planning another attack, he could still be in the States. We have an alert out at all major transportation centers here and Canada. Nice work locating the bomb by the way," Carswell added.

"Couldn't have done it without her." He glanced down at Angela, oblivious to the conscious world. The remnant of rage over her being put in such a dangerous position had waned. Though it was in line with Jarrod's typical MO to send her back in, he hadn't been the one who'd asked. From what Tony knew about Angela's psyche, she would have volunteered to go, regardless. It drew him to her—even if it scared him, too.

"True. She's headstrong but good. Especially with using her assets to get what she wants from a guy."

A grumble elicited from Tony's throat at Carswell's statement.

"Grochowski said it's a miracle she pulled through. That they kept her in an induced coma, and there could be permanent impairment—if she woke up. Buzz at the office is she's out of the coma." In the dim light, Carswell's gaze fixed on Angela.

"She's more alert each time she wakes up. Doc said brain function looked normal. She made sense talking." Especially the last time when she'd been awake long enough to eat something. He never thought watching her eat a few cups of Jell-O in a hospital bed would be foreplay, but when she offered him a taste, he nearly went in search of a cold shower. Or a hot shower with—

"Like I said, she's headstrong enough to survive this." Carswell's hard-edged tone and statement interrupted Tony's trip down fantasy lane. "Hey, you need a ride to your hotel?"

"Naw. I'm staying here."

"For how long?"

"Don't know. Couple of days."

"If you need a place to stay, we can get you a reasonable rate through the Bureau."

"I've slept in way worse places than this."

"You can say that again." Carswell hesitated, focused on Angela. "Guess I'll try to come by when she might be awake."

"I can give her any message. Save you the trouble of another trip down." Angela needed rest, not stress from dealing with Jarrod.

"No message. She may not want to hear from me right now anyway."

Or ever.

Maybe Carswell had the decency to feel bad for treating Angela like shit now that she nearly died. Maybe he had lingering feelings and wanted to check on her himself. Maybe it was his own jealousy that Carswell had a past with Angela, but his interest kept Tony's nerves on edge when Jarrod ducked out of the room after one last glance at her still form.

TWENTY-FOUR

ANGELA GRIMACED as the doctor secured a fresh dressing after examining her abdominal incision. It was going to leave a nasty scar. Tony winked when she met his gaze, reducing her self-consciousness from the wound's appearance. Maybe when it healed, she'd finally get the dragonfly tattoo she wanted and position it to camouflage the scar.

"When can I get out of here?" she asked.

Dr. Saba shook her head. "You're doing well—all things considered. I'd say two more days."

"I was hoping tomorrow," Angela persisted.

"You getting tired of our hospitality and fine cuisine?" The doctor looked to the Chinese-takeout containers and pizza box leaning against the trashcan.

"I can sleep better at home. Your nurses keep coming in to check *him* out." She nodded to Tony, who turned up his hands helplessly.

Dr. Saba laughed. "I overheard something about a shower and a scar on his arm, and there's been speculation behind how he got it."

Tony gave a sheepish grin and tugged down the left

sleeve of his T-shirt to conceal the bullet wound on his bicep that hadn't been there when he and Angela worked together in Texas. "Can't say. It's classified."

"That's only going to increase the frenzy of inquiring minds," the doctor said with an eye roll.

The man wasn't shy about his toned body, but he appeared to blush at the stir he'd caused since he emerged from Angela's hospital bathroom in only a towel after taking a run yesterday. Not that the physical therapist minded based on the way she'd checked him out.

He'd grabbed his clothes and dressed in the bathroom, depriving Angela of a peek as well. That Tony hadn't reacted to the therapist's obvious interest elicited a needy hunger in Angela. A hunger that could lead to starvation if she weren't careful.

"So, Doc, any chance …?" she pressed.

"You're recovering nicely—but—I don't want you over-doing it. Do you have someone who'll help you for at least a week or two?" Doctor Saba asked.

"I've got home health care lined up in D.C." Angela didn't waver under the doctor's dubious scrutiny.

"I'm taking her back there, and I'll stay to make sure she doesn't try to say she doesn't need them."

He hadn't mentioned that, but one glance told Angela he was serious, not just covering for her. Part of her melted at the idea of time together. Another part wanted to protest the idea of him sacrificing more of his leave time sitting at her bedside.

Other than a daily run, trips to get food, and going to her apartment here to pack up her clothes, Tony had been at her side every minute the past few days. She felt terrible that he missed his dad's birthday celebration. He hadn't told her about it in advance because going to Buffalo meant an overnight trip. This wasn't how she'd envisioned spending time with him.

"We'll see tomorrow. No promises. Especially with you planning to travel," Dr. Saba said.

Close enough. If Tony was going to be with her, she was making flight reservations and heading home tomorrow whether the doctor officially released her or not. The Bureau said she could stay at the apartment here, but she wanted to get home. Snuggled up to Tony in her bed in D.C. would aid her recovery more than anything the hospital offered.

TWENTY-FIVE

"TAKE YOUR TIME." Tony paused on the step next to Angela.

With her left arm in the sling, she couldn't hold the handrail, so she rested more of her weight on his supportive arm. She acquiesced to using a wheelchair at the airports because of the size and crowds, but in a minute, she'd be home and could collapse in her queen-size bed with her dignity intact. That propelled her upward to the landing of her condo.

Tony waited while she unlocked the deadbolt. Inside, sunlight streamed in to flood the living area. Through the window, she glimpsed the leaves of the maple tree dancing in the breeze. She turned to the security-system panel and punched in her code. Tony edged past her.

"Wait!" Adrenaline surged through her body. "Don't move!"

Tony turned back toward her. "What?"

She couldn't breathe as she stared at the keypad display. "Someone's been in here."

"Are you sure?"

"Yes."

"Maybe the Bureau sent someone to stock the fridge."

"They still think I'm being discharged tomorrow. They wouldn't have the code, either."

"A break-in?"

Nothing she saw in her condo appeared out of place. Her finger left a trail through the layer of dust that coated the glass-top entry table. She couldn't bend to the floor in her physical state, so she dragged the tip of her shoe across the smooth, hardwood surface.

As still as a marble statue, Tony watched her every move.

She stepped back, angling her head. No dust to show the path her foot had traced. An icy chill gripped her. "No. Someone disarmed it." Someone who didn't want her to know they'd been there. And not just 'someone.' An average intruder wouldn't have the skills to bypass her top-of-the-line system.

"We're outta here." Tony's voice dropped to an ominous level. He lifted her up and out and pulled the door closed. He wrapped an arm around her waist, and with their suitcases banging the wall, dragged them both with his one free hand.

"There another exit out of the building?"

"Behind the stairs. Out into the alley. I have a key."

It was one of the reasons she'd bought the condo. Being on the second story added a layer of security over being on street level, yet she could go out a window if needed without breaking a bone. The private entrance to the upper-level residential units also had a secondary exit that led into the alley behind the boutique and coffee shop occupying the first floor of the building. She'd hoped she'd never need to utilize any of the alternate routes.

"No security camera?" He maneuvered them around the bottom banister.

"No."

He let go of her to unlock the back door, then peered down the alley. "Cab?"

God, she loved the way he thought the same way she did and didn't act like she'd lost her mind. "Go left."

They went down the alley to the street, not stopping until they were another block away. Scanning the traffic, he let out a shrill whistle, then waved.

A light-blue cab cut over and stopped at the curb. The cabbie popped the trunk, then got out.

Tony gave her a hand inside while the driver stowed their luggage in the trunk.

"Where to?" the driver asked once he got in.

Tony looked behind them, then down the street. "Reagan National."

"Don't you think we should go to my office?" She could practically hear the wheels turning in his head, but he didn't answer. "It might not be anything."

Tony studied her. "If that were true, you wouldn't have reacted like that."

So much for her false bravado. The cabbie was on the phone, speaking in what sounded like Romanian. "Was there news coverage when I was shot? My name or picture?"

"No. And trust me, I looked."

"Then I don't see how Hakim's people or al-Shehri could have found out who I was, much less where I live."

There were other possibilities. She'd been damn good at her job. There were others that if they knew who she was— where she was … It's why she remained vigilant—even four years after leaving the Agency—and would be for the rest of her life.

Her body sagged against the seatback. Had her past caught up with her? She'd made plans for that contingency. But with barely the stamina to make it up a flight of stairs …

No. She wasn't going anywhere.

At least not yet.

TWENTY-SIX

TONY TOOK in the pallor of Angela's skin. Damn, he should have insisted she stay in the hospital another day.

Am I overreacting? Or did her near-death experience have him in overprotective mode?

Spending the past few days together, he'd gotten to know her on a deeper level. Growing up abroad made her unfamiliar with the iconic television shows of their youth. She preferred reading over television. He gathered it was her mother using her looks to get what she wanted in life that skewed Angela in the opposite direction—using her brains and work ethic to take care of herself.

And while he'd picked up on how independent she was when working together in Texas, he witnessed how hard it was for her to rely on others for help, even in the hospital after nearly dying.

He'd gained her trust based on the bits and pieces she'd told him about her family. He couldn't let her down now.

He rubbed his temple. *Think. Think. Think!*

Screw it. He needed time and information. It was better to overreact than not do enough.

He had a plan roughed out by the time the taxi took the exit for the airport. "You have something you can, uh, camouflage with after you're inside?"

"Yes," she said after a few seconds, not questioning him.

"Can you make it down to arrivals on your own?"

She nodded with her gaze fixed on his face.

"Have him circle once after you drop me off on the lower level. I'll text you when I'm coming around. You got me?"

Her head bobbed in the same near-silent communication they'd established in Texas. It'd worked then. Been on the verge of eerie how easily they read each other. It felt right in a comforting way.

THE TENSION in Tony's muscles stepped down from DEFCON 2 when he saw the text back from Angela. He pulled the car to the curb where she'd instructed—even though he didn't see her. Not that he expected to spot her immediately.

Opening the trunk, he felt the electric charge she created before he saw her. She moved slowly, bent over like an old woman. A dark scarf covered her hair like a hijab. He took her suitcase, then moved swiftly to help her slide into the passenger seat.

After he closed his door, Angela handed him a cold bottle of water. A pained wince escaped when she shifted in her seat.

"Time for more pain meds."

"Half an hour ago," she admitted, pulling the orange prescription bottle from her purse. "Wanted to wait until we were back together, though."

"Sorry. The first agency didn't have any cars with it being

the holiday." He hadn't cared if he'd pissed off the tourists waiting when he skipped the line at the next agency to inquire if they had available cars. That saved him time since the summer holiday tourist travel tapped out that place, too. He'd finally gotten a car before resorting to hotwiring one. "Did you call your office to let them know what you found?"

"Not yet. It sounded like you had a plan, and I didn't want to get ahead of you."

"Thanks." He hadn't been able to tell her the details in front of the cabbie, yet she'd shown him the amount of respect due a general by waiting instead of moving forward with her own plan. It reaffirmed their connection went beyond their similar training and work experience. "Is there someone high up you trust—implicitly?"

"With my life? Special Agent in Charge Barnsley."

"She was in NY, right? Call her. The fewer people who know, the better right now." The car in front of them pulled away, but he waited while she dialed.

"Kathryn, it's Angela."

She greeted the agent by her first name. That meant she'd called either her personal number or direct line rather than go through a receptionist. Good girl.

"They let me leave this morning. However, we have a —situation."

Ahead of them, he watched an airport police officer signal a stopped vehicle to move along.

"When I disarmed my alarm system, the code showed whoever reactivated it last was not me. I'm sure," she continued after a brief silence. "There were other signs. The floor had been swept. Can you *quietly* send a security team over to check it out?"

Tony nodded his support and pulled the car away from the curb before the cop got to them.

"Thanks. It may be nothing—but tell them to be careful."

Once past the cop, he pulled back over to keep their position fixed at the airport for the duration of the call—in case anyone tried tracking it.

Angela sighed. "You're right. We can't rule out that possibility."

Possibility of what? He didn't interrupt her to ask.

"Yeah, I'm someplace safe." She met his eyes.

She hadn't asked where he was taking her, showing Tony she trusted him. Now, saying she was safe—because she was with him—did something to his insides.

Once Angela disconnected, he edged the car into the slow-moving airport traffic to the exit.

"She have any thoughts on if this is connected to Hakim's death?"

"Too soon to tell. Thing is, I, uh, made a few enemies while I was with the Agency. One put a price on my head."

"You're serious?" One glance confirmed she was. "Who?"

"One of my early assignments was to get close enough to track Tito Vasquez."

"As in *cartel leader* Tito Vasquez?" He clenched his jaw, thinking how the Agency sent her in after one of the biggest names in the gun and drug trade.

"Yeah."

"I've heard stories. No one could get close to him." He stopped at the crosswalk for people dragging suitcases to the terminal. "How?"

"I got hired as a nanny for a friend of his sister, Elena, who offered me more money to work for her."

"Smart."

"Elena's husband, Jorge, ran the semi-legit import and export part of the family business. It took a while, but the plan was to nab Tito when he came to their estate in Venezuela. Only Tito brought his daughter. Then Elena decided to stay home with the kids."

"It got ugly?"

"Turned into a huge firefight. Two of our guys were shot by Tito's bodyguards. Those guards were killed. So was Elena. And Tito's daughter, Abi-Maria."

Tony knew from experience you could never anticipate all contingencies. "It's not your fault."

"Tell that to Jorge. He figured out I leaked the information about Tito, and they offered a sizable bounty. For me dead—or alive."

Alive so they could torture the hell out of her. They wouldn't care that she's a woman.

"Only the contract is for Raquel Decaino from Venezuela. The threat was credible enough that the Agency pulled me from South America to work in the Middle East after that. It's been over seven years, though. The timing that they would find me now—when I haven't been in D.C. in months? No. It's too remote."

She downplayed the threat. Her modus operandi.

Even though it was a long time ago, cartels had long memories, and vengeance was their brand. But she had a point, and she didn't need more stress right now.

"You're right. Let's wait and see what the Bureau's team turns up. Maybe they'll figure out the glitch with your alarm. But you're going to be stuck with me for a while longer."

"I can live with that." She winked.

He wanted both to be true—that the Bureau would find no threats, and he and Angela would have time to give this thing between them a shot. Still, his training refused to let him stand down until they had facts.

TWENTY-SEVEN

TONY's gentle tap on her leg woke Angela. It took a second for her eyes to focus on him punching the button on a ticket machine in a parking deck. She returned her seat to the upright position and shook out the headscarf she'd used as a pillow from the time they'd hit the interstate. Tony hadn't said where he planned to take her—and she hadn't asked.

He'd gotten them something to eat shortly after leaving the airport. By the time he picked up I-95 South and passed Quantico, she deduced he was headed to North Carolina. To his home.

Being with him, letting him take the lead, let her relax, breathe easier, and she'd fallen asleep. There wasn't any place, or with anyone, she felt safer.

According to the dashboard clock, she'd been asleep for over three hours—thanks to his making sure she took the full dose of pain meds.

The roar of a plane's engines penetrated the car as they circled up in the garage. He stopped on the fourth level, got out, and came around to open her door. The taillights of a black SUV flashed when he unlocked the car with the key fob.

"I'll go turn the rental back in. You okay?" He took her arm when she struggled to get out of the car.

"Yeah. I need to move a bit." Despite his mission, she needed the contact she'd longed for the past few days. Instead of moving toward his vehicle, she stepped closer to him.

As if reading her mind, his arm wrapped around her. He held her as close as the sling supporting her left arm allowed, and her head rested against his chest. She listened to his heart beat in a soothing, steady rhythm. A car drove past, but it wasn't enough to make her leave the comfort of his arms.

His right hand rose to cradle the back of her head. He lowered his face until his mouth met hers. When another car cruised past, he ended the kiss, but the look in his eyes promised more to come.

It had only taken Tony Vincenti a few days to work his way past her protective bubble. Sneaky bastard. Healing her heart and making it ache at the same time.

Waiting inside Tony's car while he turned in the rental, she inhaled his masculine scent that prevailed despite the pine air freshener dangling from the rearview mirror. The interior was clean. No empty cups, cans, or trash. It didn't surprise her, but if Tony liked his life neat and orderly, that didn't mesh with her past. With her life.

She checked her phone. No message from Kathryn yet. What if they found nothing? Anyone could turn on the alarm system with the push of the "Away" button. But she was the only one with the code to trigger the "All Clear" rather than "System Off."

If the power had been out long enough to drain the backup batteries, would it have erased the extra measures she had in place? Every cell in her body jangled with the certainty that someone had *disarmed* her security system. If not for that, she wouldn't have noticed the buildup of dust present on the side table but not on the floor. The perpetrator had been clever enough to cover their tracks.

Her mind jumped to the timing of someone possibly finding her now.

Would Hakim's men want revenge? With al-Shehri's resources, could he have figured out her identity that fast?

Her mind whirled with worst-case scenarios. It'd been years since Tito Vasquez offered the generous bounty for her head. Though there hadn't been any credible threats, she'd changed her real name after leaving the CIA. Names and faces from past cases paraded through her mind. She hadn't exactly been in the business of making friends. Powerful enemies, though …

One of Hakim's men or al-Shehri might want payback for his death and the failed bombing attempt. If they stayed at her place, Tony would have insisted on assessing the situation—only there were dozens of ways someone could get payback, depending on what they wanted. If they wanted her dead, a trigger wired to the gas stove could do it. Or carbon-monoxide poisoning. A syringe to inject cyanide or another poison through the cork into a bottle of wine. Acid placed in a showerhead to disfigure her and prolong the agony.

A dull throb built in the base of her skull. Physical exhaustion mixed with the painkiller hangover didn't make for the clearest thinking.

She was going to make herself crazy. Better to wait and see what the search turned up.

She needed a diversion. Tony had to have a handgun in his vehicle. She pulled the handle on the glove compartment. Not there. Where? Under his seat? She couldn't check, so she opened the center console instead. The breath mint she helped herself to was the same spearmint flavor she'd tasted when they'd kissed.

Satisfaction rippled when she found the small ridge for a door to a hidden compartment. She slid it open, and her fingers touched the cold steel of what felt like a .9mm and spare ammunition magazines. Bingo. She closed the compartment and console. Knowing it was there was enough.

She hit the unlock switch when Tony reached the driver's door. After he slid in, she handed him the keys. His gaze lingered on her before he started the car.

"We've got another hour. Do you need to make a restroom or food stop?" He backed out of the parking space.

"I'm good."

"Hope you're okay with going to my place …"

If only he could read my mind. "Yeah. I trust you."

He turned to see her face. She couldn't decipher his expression, and he didn't say anything, but he swallowed and turned back to navigate the parking deck.

"What?" Tony asked when he caught her staring.

"Admiring your new profile."

His eyes rolled up, and color tinged his neck. "My nose got broken again a few months ago. Had to get it fixed this time. My colonel suggested changing things up a bit. You know, in case I have to go back to one of the countries that might not be willing to let me through customs."

"Gotcha. How'd it get broken?" Her imagination got the better of her.

He grimaced before he described his encounter with the Afghan family and the old woman who broke his nose with her crutch. Despite his apparent embarrassment, he laughed at himself, making her laugh along with him.

"It wouldn't have been so bad if we'd caught al-Shehri then."

"Wait, it was al-Shehri you were after? I thought you said a different name."

"Yeah. Sorry. LaRuh is the Pashto word for fog—the nickname we gave al-Shehri."

"The Fog. It fits. And you were that close?" She groaned. If they'd caught him, that might have stopped these bomb threats.

"Missed him by hours at the most."

That connection explained his team being sent to New York and their need to end al-Shehri's reign of terror, too.

"When you were working with the CIA, did you, uh, was he one of your targets?"

"He was a target of *every* operative."

"Carswell mentioned they came close to nabbing al-Shehri when he was working for that private contractor firm, Dileas Security, over in Afghanistan." He looked at her out of the corner of his eye.

"Yes, we worked with the team from Dileas, including Jarrod, when they caught one of al-Shehri's suspected couriers. The courier wouldn't talk, so they told him they'd bring in his daughter and rape her if he didn't help them get al-Shehri."

"Jarrod and the contractors planned that?" Tony's mouth hung open, and his knuckles whitened gripping the steering wheel.

"Sorry to say, it was my higher-ups at the Agency. They kept me out of the loop. I thought they were just threatening it. But then I found out they tasked Dileas to kidnap the girl. That was the mission I quit over. Told the Agency I was done and left their camp."

"Did Jarrod request you assist the New York office because of your past work together?"

"Hardly. Our association didn't end on good terms since

he was the one who told me the plans, and I don't think Jarrod had disclosed the full mission details to his boss, either."

"Before that, you were on good terms, though?"

Was Tony digging for info? She wouldn't put it past Jarrod to somehow out their history. She didn't want to admit it or risk hurting Tony, but it was better if he heard it from her than Jarrod's potentially lurid version.

"There's something you should know." God, she hated that phrase. It was always the precursor to something people *didn't* want to know.

"Okay," Tony said but wouldn't make eye contact.

"When we were in Afghanistan, Jarrod and I … slept together a few times."

Tony finally looked at her and gave her a nod, wearing a grim smile. "I appreciate you telling me. Carswell did insinuate there was something between you, but I was hoping it was his typical BS and didn't want to believe him."

"If it makes you feel any better, I wish it weren't true. It wasn't love. It was two people in high-stress situations needing release, you know? It's also something I truly regret."

"He can be charming when he wants to be. Sorry I made you bring it up."

"It's better we got it out in the open, and now we can bury it in the past."

"Sounds good. Let's do a rewind. What were we talking about before?" He reached over and squeezed her hand. His subtle smile gave her hope that he wouldn't hold that lapse in judgment against her.

"Let's see. Oh, yeah, your nose. Did your team give you a little flack over the woman breaking it?"

"Little? Ha. That's an understatement. Mostly Dominguez. And my family."

She could see him relaxing after dropping their conversation about Jarrod. Maybe Tony wouldn't view her differently after knowing she'd been intimate with his former teammate. "How did you explain the nose job to your family?"

"Told them it was classified. My mom knew that was BS, but she dropped it."

"I'm guessing the cops interrogated you?"

"Yes, but I sure as hell was not telling my dad or brother that I got whacked in the face by an old woman with a cane."

"Why'd you join the Army instead of going to the police academy?"

"Growing up, I wanted to be a cop like my dad more than anything. Only I wasn't very athletic. One of those chubby kids who got picked last for teams in gym."

"Really?"

"When I said I was going to become a policeman, I got jokes about cops and donuts."

"Ouch," she said in sympathy.

"When I was sixteen, I grew a few inches. I was what my mom called a late bloomer. I made the football team as an offensive lineman. I started working out—a lot. I grew a few more inches, and the jokes quit. But in the wake of 9/11, as a New Yorker, I was still pissed. I wanted Bin Laden. That wasn't gonna happen as a cop here. So, I enlisted. Figured I'd get good training and experience for later. Get to go to Afghanistan."

"'Get to go?' You wanted to get Bin Laden?"

"Of course. What did I know?" He shrugged. "After the SEALs got him, I set my sights on Special Forces. I already had my Ranger tab and made it through the Q Course to be a Green Beret. By then, I didn't want to go back and be a beat cop in my dad and brother's shadow. I'm my own man. Not that chubby kid anymore."

"Definitely not." The words slipped out, but the grin he gave her was worth it. "Delta Force. Best of the best."

"A lot of what I do is hard. You probably know that. More often than not, I have to embrace the suck. But I make a difference. I didn't get Bin Laden, but the Bad Karma team likes dishing out justice to evildoers. We can get al-Shehri. We'll make you an unofficial member."

"It would be an honor." Tony Vincenti was the type of man she could happily spend her life with. He would think he could protect her. It was too damn bad she couldn't give him what he wanted.

In the hospital, she'd listened to his voice change as he talked to his family when he called during the party for his dad's birthday. It was another confirmation of what she'd picked up on when his teammate showed them pictures of his girls.

Tony didn't know all her history. With her dysfunctional upbringing and lack of maternal examples, it would be better to be alone than screw up the lives of kids. While she'd developed genuine feelings for the Vasquez boys as their nanny, she'd been playing a role. They had a mother. Elena wouldn't have won any mother-of-the-year awards, but she didn't treat the boys as if they were a burden the way Angela's mother had made her feel.

She steered the conversation to his family and soon pictured his parent's home filled with his brother, Frank, and sisters Marie and Caterina, and their spouses and kids. His mother would have a table full of food. It'd be loud and chaotic and exactly where Tony wanted to be.

Minutes after leaving the highway, he pushed a button on his rearview mirror, and the garage door to a modest one-story brick home went up. He parked next to a black Harley-Davidson motorcycle. A heavy punching bag hung from the ceiling behind the bike, and racks mounted on the walls held yard tools.

He came around the back of the vehicle. Before she could swing her legs out, he had a hand under her arm to help her.

Stepping into his home sent an unexpected tingle through her limbs, and erratic energy zipped through her.

"Time for more meds." Tony set her purse on the small kitchen table.

"They make me sleepy," she complained.

"You need a nap before dinner anyway." He filled a glass with water, keeping an eye on her to be sure she followed orders. "This way."

He guided her through the house. In the family room, an end table sat between the oversized black leather couch and chair facing a large screen TV. The early evening sun filtered through the white wooden blinds. The walls were a light gray. They passed a framed print on the wall of camouflaged figures freefalling, still above the clouds, the setting sun in the background. The picture was very badass and very Tony.

The master bedroom had a large dresser and a king-size bed. Telling, though there were no signs of a woman having lived here. Tony pulled back the covers on the bed.

"Can you help me get my dress off?"

"You want something from your suitcase?"

Her usual lack of sleeping attire might not be the best choice right now. "Can I borrow one of your tees?"

He rummaged in a drawer before he moved in front of her. His gaze didn't drift down when he eased the long, loose-fitting dress up and around her injured shoulder, then off her head. He gently helped her into the V-neck shirt.

"I'll rustle up something for dinner. I don't think I have

any Jell-O." He winked, then tucked soft sheets around her instead of undressing and sliding in beside her.

She sank into the mattress with the feeling that Tony Vincenti had already come to the realization that she didn't fit with his future.

———

TONY WALKED BACK to the kitchen. He sure hadn't expected what Angela had shared today. But she trusted him. She'd even said it. And now she was here.

He opened the fridge and set about finding something to feed her.

"Ew." Something smelled rotten after his week away. Leaving the refrigerator door open, he grabbed the garbage can and tossed out the slimy, browned head of lettuce, the baggie with half a liquefied cucumber, and take-out container he didn't bother to open. As he poured the expired milk down the sink, an unfamiliar ringtone sounded behind him.

He hesitated a moment before digging into Angela's purse for her phone. Seeing Kathryn Barnsley's name on the screen, his need for an update overrode the nudge of concern about boundaries.

His greeting was met with a moment of silence.

"I'm calling for Angela Hoffman."

"She's sleeping right now, ma'am. Did the team turn up anything at her condo?"

"If you'll have her call me on my personal number when she's able—"

"What'd they find?" His mouth went dry.

"I'm not at liberty to disclose—"

"Let's cut the bureaucratic bullshit—"

"Excuse me. I don't know who the hell you are, but this is now an active FBI investigation, and I'm not—"

"I'm Sergeant First Class Anthony Salvatore Vincenti. US Army Special Forces—Operational Detachment-Delta." That would likely get her attention. "I guarantee I've got the security clearance for whatever you're about to tell me, and more importantly, Angela trusts me. That's why she's with me. I need to be in the loop. Now, if you'd rather be the one to tell her what the Bureau turned up, fine, you deliver the news. She'll tell me. But in the meantime, if there's a credible threat, and you withholding information endangers her, I'll hold you personally responsible."

"Anthony Vincenti?" Kathryn's voice was cool and calm.

Damn, had he really mouthed off in hopes of intimidating a special agent in charge with the FBI? "Yes, ma'am." He stopped short of asking if she wanted his serial number and kept his mouth shut while the puddle of sludge in his stomach spread. His gut told him whatever they found at Angela's condo went beyond someone looking for classified case information.

Typing on a keyboard was followed by the faint tapping of fingernails on a solid surface.

"All right, Sergeant Vincenti, here's the deal."

Tony sank into a kitchen chair while she began filling him in.

TWENTY-EIGHT

IT TOOK a moment for Angela to orient herself upon waking. Darkness cloaked the world past the blinds, but light peeked in from the cracked bathroom door.

The drone of a floor fan and her folded clothes on top of her suitcase were evidence Tony had come in while she slept. She eased from the bed. A delicious aroma, laced with fresh basil and oregano, made her stomach rumble. Hunger eclipsed the pain radiating from her side and the throb in her shoulder.

Tony's voice carried to her as she headed toward the kitchen; a male voice answered. Crud. Well, Tony's shirt hung to midthigh, so she didn't bother going back to put on more clothes.

"I thought you already ate," Tony's voice grumbled as she neared.

"It wasn't as good as pasta with your mom's sauce," another voice joined the mix.

In the kitchen, Tony and three of his teammates sat around the table, which had been pulled from the wall. Dominguez stood at the stove, ladling sauce over a plate of spaghetti. Goosebumps rose on her arms at the quaint, domestic scene. Genius-boy Grant cleared his throat when he spotted her. Tony swiveled in his seat. With five sets of eyes locked on her, a freezing bolt of lightning raced down her spine—and it wasn't from her lack of pants.

Tony got to his feet in a flash. "Here," he motioned for her to take his chair. "Let me get you a plate of pasta."

The men dropped whatever they were talking about before she interrupted. Devin Grant slid a basket of bread and large bowl of salad toward her. Empty plates remained in front of AJ Rozanski and Kyle Liu. Both men gave her half-hearted smiles.

"You're looking better than …"

"Than last time you saw me?" she finished when Rozanski broke off. "That's probably not saying much." She picked up a piece of crusty bread. Tony set a plate in front of her as she bit into the warm bread.

Dominguez tapped Liu on the shoulder. Liu looked up, huffed an exasperated breath, then relinquished his seat. Angela savored a bite of spaghetti while Dominguez twirled his fork, loading up a generous mouthful.

"So, the gang's all here." She eyed the men.

"I didn't want to leave you alone, so I, uh, called Grant to make a grocery run," Tony said.

"And we all wanted to see how you were doing," Grant added.

"How sweet." She didn't buy it for a second. No one spoke, and the men avoided eye contact like she was naked instead of moderately covered by Tony's shirt. "And did he tell you about D.C.?"

"Um …" Rozanski stammered.

"Would you hand me my phone? It's in my purse." She pointed behind Liu.

"Your friend at the Bureau called," Tony fessed up. "I talked to her."

The chill in her spine turned arctic. "And …?"

"Someone did break into your place."

"What'd they find?" Her appetite dissipated.

"No fingerprints or other evidence."

Dominguez forked in another mouthful while staring at his plate. Grant picked up empty dishes from the table and carried them to the sink.

"Give me my phone." Maybe they thought her injuries made her an invalid, but she wasn't putting up with this stonewalling crap.

Tony stepped between her and the counter with her purse. "They found an explosive planted in your condo."

His statement sucked the air from her lungs. The little energy she had vanished and her arms fell limply to her sides. "What kind? Where?"

Tony swallowed and noisily exhaled. "A pressure-triggered device. Mounted between your mattresses."

"Holy shit." *My bed?* Talk about personal. She forgot how to breathe. Tony rubbed her shoulder. He could have been killed. What if he'd tossed her suitcase on the bed? Or they'd lain down together?

For years she'd taken the threat seriously, yet never quite believed anything would come of it. But now …?

"Was anyone hurt?" Dread rose as she contemplated their silence.

"No. They discovered it and sent a tech team to disarm it."

That news allowed her to breathe.

"They're going to send us the report when they finish analyzing it to determine its signature," Tony continued.

"That's not necessary. The Bureau can handle it. You guys have your own work to do."

"We couldn't have found the bomb in LA without you. And I kinda take this personally, too," Tony stated in a don't-mess-with-me tone.

"We've got your back," Rozanski added.

She scanned the men's determined faces, felt them closing ranks like a wall of muscled protectors. Maybe her defenses were down because the damn tears burned, and her throat closed. After all these years on her own, maybe the time had come to depend on someone else. She reached up and squeezed Tony's hand.

"What are you guys planning?"

TWENTY-NINE

TONY WAS in the middle of his third set of pulldowns when a scream penetrated through his heavy-metal playlist.

Angela!

He let go of the bar, and the weights crashed down as he surged up and into the hall.

"It's okay." He tried to calm both his cleaning lady as she backed out of his bedroom and Angela, who stood bent over and clutching her side. "Sorry. Rosie cleans for me. Oh, shit! You're bleeding." He rushed past Rosie to Angela as she sank onto the bed.

Blood seeped through the shirt she wore. He helped her lay back on the bed.

"I'm sorry, Mr. Tony. I didn't know you were home and had a guest. I came to strip the bed. She screamed when I came in, and I …"

"We got back last night. I forgot what day it was and didn't hear you come in." He lifted the shirt to check Angela's side, then carefully pulled away the dressing's tape. Fresh blood oozed from the wound. "Can you grab my phone from my weight room?"

Rosie disappeared.

"Does it hurt?"

"Not too bad." Angela attempted a smile, but it looked more like a wince.

Rosie slipped in and handed him the phone, looking on nervously as he dialed up Doc.

"Shelly, it's Tony Vincenti. Is Doc there?" He brushed the hair from Angela's face. "Tell him I need him at my place—ASAP—and to bring his medical bag. Thanks." He laid the phone on the nightstand. "Rosie, will you go let Doc Rivers in. He lives a few doors down and will be here in a minute."

Rosie nodded and hurried off.

"What'd you do this time, Vincenti?" Doc stopped short once he glimpsed Angela lying on the bed.

"Not me." Tony took a step back. "Rosie, sorry for the scare. Since I've been gone, there's not anything for you to do. Why don't you come back in two weeks?"

"You don't need my help?" Rosie wrung her hands together.

"Thanks, but we've got it."

Doc set his bag on the edge of the bed, then pressed two fingers over Angela's wrist, checking her pulse. "What happened?" he asked after Rosie left.

"I got spooked and jumped out of bed too quickly."

Tony shook his head and rolled his eyes. "She sustained two bullet wounds a week ago. They removed part of her liver," he clarified.

Doc gently probed her side. "Looks like you ruptured some sutures." He opened his bag and dug inside. He tore open a packet, then proceeded to clean the wound. "I'm going to put in a couple of stitches, but you should see your surgeon. He can make sure there's no internal bleeding."

"Surgeon was in New York. Can you …?" Tony asked.

"New York?" Doc shot him a questioning look and opened the suture kit. "Have them send her medical records to me, so I know what I'm dealing with."

Tony gave Angela his hand to squeeze while Doc tugged the needle through her skin. "Uh, problem on the medical records …"

"You didn't—"

"No! I didn't shoot her! Jeez. We need to keep her presence here on the q.t. Transferring her records here could put her at risk."

"We could have the hospital send the records to the Bureau," Angela suggested. "They could forward them to keep it untraceable."

"Bureau? FBI?" Doc finished and snipped the thread.

"Sorry, Doc. This is Special Agent Angela Hoffman. Ang, Doc Rivers. Badass Special Forces doctor."

"And you're here because …?"

"Long story." Tony cut off further questions.

"It looks like the bleeding's stopping, but if it starts again, get to the hospital. Have them email me the files. I'll take a look and schedule a follow-up in a few days."

"Thanks, Doc," Angela said.

"Your body experienced severe trauma. While I want you up and moving, don't overdo it. You hear me, too, Vincenti?" Doc's authoritative tone scored a direct hit—on him.

"Yes, sir."

"That extends beyond working out to *other* strenuous activities."

Heat flooded up Tony's neck. God, did everyone think he was a manwhore? He chanced a glance at Angela. She didn't look leery of him, but still, Doc's insinuation hardly encouraged her to think of him as the commitment type, and she needed to trust his ability to be faithful.

TONY TWISTED the wrench to tighten the swivel connector on the new showerhead.

"What are you doing?" Angela asked, her voice throaty from sleep.

God, she looked sexy as hell in his shirt with her sleep-tousled hair. "Didn't mean to disturb your nap."

"All I've been doing since I got shot is sleep."

"Thought this would make it easier for you to take a shower." He stepped out before turning on the water to check for leaks.

"I'm able *now*—if you don't mind helping since I can't lift my arm high enough to wash my hair."

"Now?" He could understand her wanting a real shower. This morning Doc told her she could shower as long as she was stable and the water didn't hit her wounds. Still, he wavered. With her standing inches from him and a sultry smile playing on her tempting mouth, a shower wasn't going to clean up his mind.

"Please," she pleaded.

"Let me get one of the stools from the kitchen. Make it easier for you. Be right back."

Vincenti, you're supposed to show her you don't have a one-track mind. A blind man would notice his erection. Maybe if he stayed behind her … The visions conjured by his brain overrode his good intentions of installing the new hand-held sprayer.

He carried the bar stool back to the bathroom. *Focus on the task*—help her shower and wash her hair. When she recovered her strength, they could get adventurous in the shower. The kitchen. His workout room. Shit. *Good intentions, my ass.* So much for changing his thinking.

While she brushed her teeth, he positioned the stool and adjusted the spray of water. When he turned around, she'd unbuttoned the last button of his shirt she wore. She eased it and the sling off her shoulder.

He swallowed to keep from licking his lips.

"Your turn," she prodded, using her right hand to tug the creamy lace fabric of the skimpy panties down her thighs until they dropped to the floor. The bandages covering the wounds to her shoulder and side didn't detract from the perfection of her body.

He wanted to reach for her. Instead, he grabbed the bottom of his T-shirt and yanked it over his head. His gym shorts joined the pile of discarded clothes.

Her gaze fell to his boxer briefs. "I know you don't wear those in the shower."

That was the only encouragement he needed to shed them, too. It's not as if they hid his aroused state. She stared long enough to flatter him.

"How hot do you want it?" He stuck his hand into the water, immediately aware of how his comment could be construed.

"Fairly hot." Amusement played in her voice.

He lowered the temperature, then stepped inside. "That good?" he asked when she followed him and perched on the stool.

"Perfect."

Her hair shone as the water matted it against her bare flesh. He poured shampoo into his hand, then worked it into her long, thick, silky hair.

She tilted her head back. "You have no idea how good that feels."

Rather than say anything stupid, he kept his mouth shut. He took his time, the intimacy building, while he massaged her scalp, forming a rich lather. With him blocking the direct spray of water, her dark nipples puckered into peaks making his body harden with need. Fantasies played through his mind as he freed the handheld showerhead, then rinsed the suds from her hair.

She leaned back further to keep the water from running down her face.

He was damn near coming just from touching her hair and watching the water run in rivulets over her ample breasts. While he rinsed her hair, he replayed Doc's warning in his head. He'd gone months without sex during deployments.

He could do this. He could do this. He. Could. Do. This.

Only a few days seemed like an eternity right now.

He lathered up the washcloth, then soaped her back. *Give her the washcloth to do the rest.* That'd be a safer option. He moved the cloth from the left to the right side of her neck.

She reached up, her fingers meeting his. Except, instead of taking the cloth, she guided his hand over her shoulder and down. "Here," she said in a breathy whisper, leading his palm to cover her breast.

He gave up the fight and let the cloth drop. His left hand mimicked the right. Now each cupped a breast. Angela's head lolled back against his chest, and her mouth opened when his thumbs and forefingers pinched her nipples.

"Yes." She moaned in pleasure. "I like that."

He continued to fondle her—harder when she bit her lower lip, her legs pressed together. She arched her body before settling back on the stool.

She took hold of his arm and guided him around to stand in front of her. "Hand me the soap."

He complied, staring down into her eyes. She lathered her hand. Then her warm, slick fingers wrapped around him.

"Ang, I…" he started to protest, even though it felt like nirvana.

"Let me do this for you," she stated, not a hint of hesitancy in her voice.

Her hand glided up and down his shaft. And here he hadn't thought he could get any harder. He loved how she showed no fear of touching him. "Faster," he said and braced his hands on either side of the shower.

Angela increased the tempo. He didn't want this ecstasy to end, but damn, he couldn't hold back much longer. She angled her face up, her tongue reaching to flick over his nipple. He spread his legs and leaned forward until his chest was at her mouth level. Her lips closed over his nipple, sucking firmly.

"Yes." *Don't stop.*

Her teeth bit lightly into his flesh. He desperately tried to prolong the pleasure. The water washed away the soap, providing more friction as she pumped him faster and harder. Her mouth moved to his other nipple. When she squeezed the sensitive tip of his dick, he succumbed to the inevitable. His hips bucked forward, and he came in a remarkable rush of release.

When he opened his eyes, Angela wore a generous smile as she stared up at him. "Thank you," he managed.

"My pleasure."

He snorted. *Her pleasure?* Damn, he'd give her some pleasure. Once she washed up, he grabbed the handheld showerhead again and rinsed her off, careful to avoid the bandaged areas.

He turned off the water, then tugged down the towels draped over the glass. On a mission, he wrapped one towel around her. He rubbed the excess water from her hair before drying himself.

Droplets of water glistened on Angela's skin, but he pushed open the shower door and extended a hand to her once she eased off the stool. Out of the confines of the shower, he dropped his towel to the floor and tugged hers away. He scooped her into his arms and carried her the short distance to his bed.

After placing her near the middle, he let her get situated to protect her injuries. A hungry need shone in her eyes. A need he had every intention of filling—in time.

He ran a hand up her arm and over her bare shoulder to the back of her damp neck, cradling her head. His mouth met hers. He started with brief, gentle kisses, moving his body closer to hers. The intensity of the kisses increased. Their tongues stroked and danced seductively. She smelled fresh, and her skin heated as their bodies brushed against each other and limbs intertwined.

It'd only been minutes since he'd come in the shower, but already his body demanded more. Except this time, it wasn't about him or his need.

He trailed his hand from her wet hair to her breast, kneading the soft flesh and teasing the pert nipple with his fingertips. A strained murmur escaped her. He could kiss her like this for hours, but when his hand went exploring, he was welcomed with her slick warmth. Her muscles constricted around his fingers.

She whimpered in protest when his mouth left hers. For a nanosecond, Doc's voice pecked at his conscious, then Angela's hand roamed over his chest to his biceps and silenced the voice in his head. Her fingertip traced over the scar from the through-and-through bullet wound he'd gotten in Colombia last year. She'd never mentioned it, though. She understood enough not to ask.

"Let me do the work," he ordered.

"If you insist." Her dark pupils made her eyes more erotic.

He yanked down a pillow, then lifted her to position it under her hips. Placing his hands on either side of her, he hovered over her. "This okay?"

"Almost." Her hand slid to his lower back, pressing down until his hips made contact with hers.

He supported his upper body to avoid putting weight on her injuries. His mouth hungrily melded with hers again. How many times had he wondered what she tasted like? What her body would feel like if given a chance like this? Her skin was as silky smooth as he'd imagined. Her body was firm, yet supple and not bony.

There'd been times when he'd been with a woman and would close his eyes to pretend she was Angela. Now, he kept his eyes open. No more imagining.

When she turned her face to the side, it gave him more access to her neck. He pressed kisses to the spot where her pulse throbbed below her ear, enjoying her soft murmurs as he worked his way to her tender throat.

Sliding his body lower, he ran his tongue over her breast and drew her into his mouth to swirl his tongue over the peak. She arched back her shoulders, and he switched to her other breast, wanting to indulge every inch of her body.

Propped on an elbow, he played his fingers over her other nipple. Her fingernails raked lightly over his back, then up to his scalp, sending delicious shudders through his body from head to toe. She wrapped her calves around his legs so that her intimate heat pulsed with desire, further arousing him.

He went lower, trailing kisses over the unbandaged side of her stomach, then lower, nibbling at her inner thigh. He inhaled her feminine scent. Her body writhed, and her hands clenched fistfuls of the sheet, which heightened his determination to give to her the way she had unselfishly given to him.

His tongue trailed up her thigh to circle her smooth outer lips before delving inside to taste. He slid his hands under her firm, rounded ass, lifting her higher so he could go deeper. The end of his nose rubbed against her, applying pressure and increasing the urgency of her sultry moans.

"Don't stop. Don't," she panted, inspiring him to deliver an even higher "satisfaction guaranteed" level of service.

His tongue hit her sweet spot. She gasped when he teased the hardened nub. Her leg muscles went rigid. She lifted her hips higher when the first wave of orgasm gripped her—and didn't stop.

He watched the expression on her face as she continued to clench until she finally sagged back on the mattress and gave a prolonged sigh. He eased over her legs to lay by her side. The dreamy smile plastered on her face was the best gift he'd gotten in a decade.

After he kissed her temple, her eyelids fluttered open. He didn't need to be a mind reader to guess what she was thinking—not with *that* smile.

THIRTY

ANGELA STARTLED and nearly dropped the book in her hands. Her heart pumped like it had been the starting shot for a race instead of the doorbell ringing. She slid lower on the couch and craned to see who was at Tony's front door.

A hitman wouldn't likely ring the bell. Not likely, but … Tony had to have a gun, or five, in the house. Where would he keep them? She eased off the couch.

Damn, being alone this morning and this whole bomb-in-the-bed business had her imagination running rampant. First, yesterday with poor Rosie, and now while she kept out of view of the person at the door.

Halfway up the door's side window, a small face pressed against the glass. The child's body jolted when her shiny brown eyes landed on Angela staring back at her. Next to the girl, slender fingers held a cloth grocery bag. Though Angela couldn't see the woman, the sight of the two lessened her need to be armed.

She swallowed the shrinking lump of trepidation, opened the door, and recognized the pixie with waves of red hair.

"You must be Angela." The woman greeted her before

Angela could speak. "I'm Kristie Hanlon. Mack's wife. And this is Darcy." She nodded to the girl whose smile could reform the heart of a supervillain. "We heard you were here and might need some lunch and dinner."

"You didn't have to do that," Angela said, an unfamiliar tug in her stomach.

"This is what we do in the unit." Kristie didn't move forward. She stood there, holding the bag, and waited for an invitation. Darcy leaned so far forward on the balls of her feet she had to take a step to keep from falling face down. It knocked down a chunk of Angela's protective wall.

"Thanks. Come in. Please." She stepped back to let them pass. Darcy bounced in, triggering a reminder of the look on Tony's face when Mack had shown her pictures of his family when they were in the elevator.

"The chicken and rice casserole needs to go in the fridge." Kristie carried the bag toward the kitchen. "I thought it would help out with Tony going back to work. Heating instructions are on top. And I brought several options for lunch," she continued while she unloaded the bag. "There's chicken salad, Cajun pimento cheese sandwich, and a peanut butter and jelly with banana sandwich."

"And Jell-O since you were in the hospital," Darcy added.

"So many choices."

"And fruit salad and zucchini bread." Kristie spread everything on the counter, then put the casserole in the refrigerator.

Darcy eyed the food, cementing Angela's suspicions. "Would you like to stay and join me for lunch?"

"I—" Darcy started before Kristie's hand on her shoulder stopped the girl.

"We don't want to impose," Kristie said.

"There's plenty of food, and I'd enjoy the company."

And the funny thing was, she meant it. Even if they were here to check her out, not being alone—and an opportunity to gain some insight on Tony—prompted her to open up.

"We'd love to, then."

Angela found plates in the second cupboard she opened while Kristie found glasses.

"What would you like to eat?" Angela asked Darcy, though she knew the answer.

"Can I have the peanut butter, jelly, and banana? And some of your Jell-O?"

"You certainly may. I've never heard of PB and J with banana, too," Angela said.

"It's good. I like the creamy and crunchy peanut butter mixed."

"She's a little high maintenance, but she's worth it." Kristie winked at Darcy, who wore an impish grin. She unwrapped the sandwich and set it on a plate. "Which would you like?"

"Either is fine. I recall hearing you were …" she trailed off, cutting her gaze to Darcy in case they hadn't shared the news yet.

"Expecting?" Kristie finished. "Yup. The pimento cheese sounds good."

"I'm going to be a *big* sister." Darcy beamed.

"Have you felt okay?"

Kristie laughed. "You've heard of morning sickness? It's a lie. Though if women knew it could last twenty-four seven, the human race might die out." Nevertheless, joy radiated from her.

"I'm sorry." Angela joined Darcy at the table.

"It's okay. They say morning sickness is a sign of a healthy baby. There are worse things than being nauseous. I didn't think I could have kids, so ...." Kristie set the glasses on the table.

"Why's that?" Angela remembered Tony's comment that Mack recently married, making Kristie Darcy's stepmom.

"My first husband and I were never able to conceive."

"And did you have to do anything?"

"No. Well—*one* thing." Kristie grinned, and her cheeks reddened a bit. "The doctor said it probably had something to do with me and my late husband together. They never figured out what, but it's not an issue now."

The mention of Kristie's late husband dredged up her own loss and hit Angela like a physical blow. "How did he ...?" Why couldn't she say the word?

"Eric was killed in action in Iraq." Kristie's solemn tone mirrored the sadness that clouded her eyes.

Both women took bites of their sandwiches in the stagnant silence.

Kristie had called her husband by his name. Owning their past. Though it obviously still impacted her, she'd moved on.

"So, you've known Tony a while?" Angela changed the subject.

"I've known Uncle Tony a *long* time," Darcy stated with an adorable bobbing of her head.

"All your life?" Kristie laughed.

"Maybe. He babysat me before."

Tony babysitting? Angela wanted to know how that came about.

"I'm going to marry Uncle Tony because I can't marry Daddy."

"And your dad's okay with that?" Angela asked, further taken in by Darcy's sweet nature.

Darcy nodded with the charming innocence of a child.

"I don't think we quite have Mack convinced yet. Of

course, he says the girls can't date until they're twenty-seven, kiss a guy until twenty-eight, and they have to be thirty before they can get married. Right?"

"Yup." Darcy took a bite of her sandwich, clearly not fazed by the twenty-year wait.

"I haven't known Tony too long," Kristie chimed in. "Mack and I, uh, kept our relationship quiet for a while. Since I'm a warrant officer, our relationship violated certain Army fraternization rules. And I had no intention of falling for another man in Special Ops."

"I see how that turned out." They both gave a light laugh. Angela's connection to Kristie built with each revelation.

"He's pretty persistent. And irresistible. Like this one." Kristie nudged Darcy's leg with her foot, evoking a giggle. "Took me a while to get past my own stubbornness. I finally realized that I was better off living with the fear that something *could* happen to Mack than pass up a chance to be truly happy with a man I love. And I get two incredible daughters."

"Amber's at camp this week," Darcy contributed, her mouth filled with Jell-O.

"I definitely made the right decision." The glow on Kristie's face eclipsed her words.

"And the issue of rank?" Angela asked.

"Long story, involving classified details"—she cut her eyes to Darcy—"but the Army occasionally makes exceptions if you're in different chains of commands. My commanding officer put me on inactive reserve while I recovered from a broken leg and helped us around the fraternization issue. Though now that I'm pregnant, I won't be flying and may switch to the Army Reserve or the Guard permanently after I have the baby." She rested a hand on her belly. "Especially now that the girls' mom agreed to give us more time with the girls." Kristie and Darcy exchanged smiles.

They seemed close. Far closer than Angela had been with either of her stepparents. Her throat constricted, making it difficult to swallow her mouthful of chicken salad.

All she'd wanted was a normal, happy family to belong to. Had planned that with Stephan—until terrorists killed him and her dreams. It made working for the CIA an attractive outlet for her pain—not knowing that it would annihilate any possibility of the future she'd so wanted.

Darcy's crush on Tony would surely dim and be replaced with more age-appropriate ones in the future. Would Angela's own infatuation with Tony fade? Or would he pop into her thoughts for decades?

She enjoyed lunch with a family like the one she envisioned Tony having someday, but closed the door behind them a half hour later, knowing she'd have to work hard to keep from getting sucked into an alternate reality that didn't align with her life or future.

THIRTY-ONE

ANGELA REMAINED SEATED on the couch when Tony came in from his first day back to work. He stood near the doorway, smiling at her long enough for ripples of heat to race through her. The way he swaggered over, then leaned down to kiss her before saying a word ignited a few inner fireworks.

"How was your day? Good to be back at work?" She held on to her book to keep from running her hand up his muscled abdomen and chest.

"It was okay. Had a lot of intel to catch up on, so didn't manage to slip away for lunch with you like I hoped. I missed you."

This man always had the right thing to say. She could easily get used to him coming home to her.

"You hungry?" he continued. "I thought I'd grill out some burgers."

"Kristie Hanlon brought over lunch and left dinner for us."

He gave her a hand when she shifted to stand. "Nice. I didn't know she was doing that, or I woulda called to prepare you. Sorry." He led her to the kitchen.

"It's fine. Good to have some company, and I got to meet your fiancée."

"My fian—what? Oh!" He laughed. "You mean Darcy. Isn't she the cutest thing? You aren't jealous, are you?"

"Maybe a little."

"No need to be," he assured her.

Angela opened the refrigerator and reached for the casserole dish with her good arm.

"Let me get that." He eased past her. "I'll get dinner on the table, at least."

"How is it some woman hasn't snatched you up?"

His smile disappeared, and he angled away to turn on the oven.

Why the heck did she say that? She wracked her brain for something to say to get him out of the hot seat.

He met her gaze, then sighed. "I came close. I dated this girl, Carla, for two years in high school. The fall after graduation, she went to Syracuse University, and I left for boot camp at Fort Benning. We were young and naive about how hard a long-distance relationship would be."

"It's hard." She and Stephan had been making an effort, but a young guy in the military? Far from home?

"Yeah, suddenly, she's at this big university known for its party reputation. No strict parents to answer to. Meeting new people with no boyfriend to hang out with."

This was not going down the path Angela had assumed.

"In Basic Training, you can't make calls whenever you want, and you don't have much time to write. I'd told her that, but I could tell things were starting to change when I finally got to talk to her after Basic. I went straight to Advanced Individual Training, so I didn't get to go home and see her until Christmas.

"I gave her a promise ring to let her know I was all in.

That's when Catholic guilt made her confess that she'd cheated on me. Claimed because I only called once a week, she thought I didn't care anymore, and she had gotten drunk and hooked up with some guy. She said it didn't mean anything. Begged me to forgive her."

"That's hard to move past."

"Yeah. I was hurt. Pissed, too, but I loved her. I thought she was the one. We all screw up sometimes, so I agreed to give it another shot. She, uh, tried to make it up to me."

Angela could guess what he meant by that.

"She came to see me during her spring break. I came home on leave that summer and took her on a four-day Caribbean cruise. Things seemed back on track."

"Three more years is a long time. Was getting married and her going to school where you were based an option?" she asked.

"Not really. Changing schools, credits don't always transfer. Her parents wanted her to get her degree from Syracuse since they were alumni. They were afraid she might drop out and not graduate. When she went back to school that fall, she joined a sorority, and things got —weird."

"Weird how?"

"She accused me of going to bars and strip clubs to pick up girls before I deployed to Iraq. Said there was no way I could go a year without sex."

"She was projecting because of her infidelity," Angela mused.

"That's what I thought and that she'd chill when I deployed. She wouldn't have anything to worry about when I was over there. One day I see a picture of her on social media. She's at a frat party, Solo cup in her hand, hanging on some guy. My trust level was already stretched thin. All I can think is that she's cheating again, and I'm gonna have to confront her."

A sickening feeling formed as Angela listened.

"We went out on dismounted patrol that afternoon, and all of a sudden, I'm on the ground, eating dust. My ears were ringing. It took a minute to shake it off and see our medic getting a tourniquet on what's left of my buddy Mills's leg. He stepped on an IED."

She grimaced. "Did he … ?"

"He made it, but he lost both legs. If my head had been in the game, maybe I would have seen the IED, and he wouldn't have stepped on it."

Angela touched Tony's arm. "I'm sorry about your friend, but you can't blame yourself."

"I know." His voice was gruff. "But you can't help but go there. When you're in combat, you can't afford to be distracted. It's more than your own life. I called Carla the next day." He looked away.

"How'd that go?"

"She tried to tell me she'd been at the library writing a paper on Thursday night. When I mentioned the photo, she accused me of not trusting her. Goes on and on saying I hadn't forgiven her, and four years apart was too much, and we needed to take a break." His laugh rang hollow. "Like we could just pick up again after she graduated. I couldn't trust her anymore, and I ended it. Since then I've been looking for a woman I can trust and who can trust me enough to make a go of it."

"You're right. In your line of work, having a spouse you can trust to be faithful and hold down the home front is key," Angela agreed. He wasn't looking for sympathy with all he'd shared. But there was something, at least subconsciously, he wanted her to know, and it was now plain as day. He told her what he needed, but she couldn't give him the future he wanted, so she didn't say more in the uncomfortable silence that followed.

"I'm gonna go get changed. I'll come back and put the casserole in once the oven's preheated."

"Wait." He might want more, but he didn't live like a monk. She'd thought about him all afternoon. Pictured him in the kitchen, serving her a plate of pasta. Imagined the sheen of sweat on his arms and chest when she passed the exercise equipment filling the second largest bedroom. Remembered the ecstasy on his face in the shower. Longed for his touch, and the deliciousness of his mouth when she'd lain alone in his bed to nap. Finally, he'd come home and stood close enough to touch.

She understood his physical needs. *Those* she could satisfy. The oven might not be preheated yet, but it was close enough.

"Why don't you put it in now?" She set the timer, then stepped out of his way long enough for him to shut the oven door. "It says to cook for forty-five minutes."

His raised eyebrows told her he caught the invitation in her voice.

"Forty-five minutes, huh?"

At his heated smile, she invaded his space—not that he moved back an inch. She'd had it with the damn sling supporting her left arm. With her right hand, she unfastened the clasp, releasing her arm so both hands were free to touch, to urge him closer. Her fingers slid into the soft hair above his neck to pull his face down until their mouths joined in a hungry, urgent meeting.

His hips pressed against hers. She groaned with pleasure when his hand slid down to cup her bottom and position her against the hard bulge of his arousal. His tongue swirled with hers.

No doubt, this man could use his tongue to illicit pleasure wherever he used it. Her nipples tingled, longing for his attention, but her mouth refused to give up its claim on him.

Behind her, the oven beeped—fully preheated. As if that was his signal, Tony lifted her with both hands. Her legs wrapped around his hips while he held her with powerful arms. He continued to kiss her as he carried her out of the kitchen.

He placed her on the bed, taking only a second to wrestle off the boots he wore with his uniform before he joined her. His lips pressed against her neck, slowly moving higher until their mouths meshed again. Her fingers moved to his waistband, working the fabric to undo the button. He pulled back, his breathing heavy. Heat shone in his dark eyes.

"I don't want to hurt you …"

"You won't. Besides, I heard endorphins are good for healing," she assured him.

The uncertainty fled, and he stripped off his shirt before helping her out of hers, then eased her pants down her legs. His fingers trailed a tantalizing path back up her legs.

"I'll be right back." He slipped from her grasp and off the bed.

She waited impatiently while he disappeared into the bathroom. He returned and laid a strip of condoms on the nightstand, then shucked off his pants and army-brown socks. His erection strained against the black fabric of his boxer briefs, which he quickly shed.

"Let me know if anything hurts you," he demanded, not moving until she nodded. He nudged her legs apart and settled between them, supporting the weight of his upper body on a forearm. His other hand caressed her cheek with his fingers tangling into her hair. His mouth claimed hers with urgent, possessive kisses, and their tongues engaged in an erotic dance.

With his erection pressing intimately against her, she needed more. She lifted her hips, sliding against him. A half groan, half moan of pleasure rumbled in his throat. She repeated her silent plea for more.

He dragged down a pillow and placed it under her hips. She waited breathlessly while he opened, then rolled on the condom. His intense, feral gaze never left her naked body.

How many times had she fantasized about this? How many lonely nights had "Jake" popped into her head with her wishing he were in her bed? Only he wasn't Jake. He was Tony. Hot. Hard. Ready. And incredibly real.

Poised on his knees, he edged closer. Lifting her hips, he eased inside her with his tantalizing thickness. He moved slowly, gently. His features displayed his pleasure, though he held back. He increased the tempo, thrusting satisfyingly deeper. It sure as hell wasn't only his hands and tongue he'd perfected using.

He felt impossibly good as he continued to slide in, burying himself inside her. The raised angle with the added contact of his balls slamming against her ass heightened her ecstasy. Her muscles went taut, building to a too-early climax, but she couldn't help herself. Honestly, she'd always preferred a dramatic payoff over a drawn-out performance with a modest climax. Go big or go home.

She locked her legs together over his hips. It freed up one of his hands, which went right to her breast. Long, strong fingers squeezed hard enough to amplify her aroused state, but not causing pain in a way that ruined her experience.

Reading her body like an expert, he pressed deeper inside. The hand under her back pulled her toward him, holding them together as if clinging for dear life. He gave her breast one more firm squeeze, pinching her nipple between his fingers before it ran down her stomach to where their bodies joined. He slid his thumb between them, rubbing her clitoris with the perfect amount of pressure.

That did it. She had no motivation to hold back with her reward seconds away. Better to save her limited strength for the next time—because she intended to do this again. Soon.

Her calves tightened, and her toes curled when the first wave of the orgasm rushed over her. Tony's groan mingled with hers. He pulled out enough to build momentum, then drove inside her. Her muscles clenched around him, making him her captive as much as she was his.

She held her breath to extend and increase the intensity of her orgasm.

"Breathe!" he said.

She sighed and released him so he could finish them both off with a few frenzied thrusts before she felt the pulse of him coming deep inside her.

Neither spoke while they strained to draw air. Tony leaned over her, supporting his upper body with his left arm, and lowered her hips.

"That release some endorphins?" His tempting mouth turned up into a wicked grin.

"Definitely. Though there's no such thing as too many endorphins." She ran a hand up his bicep to the back of his head so she could pull him close enough to kiss. The perfect ending to a reality that topped all fantasy.

THIRTY-TWO

THE STEADY RHYTHM of Angela's breathing confirmed she'd dozed off. Tony fought the urge to close his eyes. The aroma from the casserole cooking told him it'd be ready soon, so he lay on his side, staring at Angela. Even in sleep, a contented smile played on her luscious mouth. Her long, thick lashes curled above her lightly bronzed skin, hiding her rich brown eyes. Dark hair splayed on the pillow under her.

This time, his usual sated gratification was accompanied by something different. Something that made him content and happy and complete. Yeah, this time was different. Different because—it hit him like a solid smack upside the head—he'd *made love* to Angela.

In the years since he'd ended things with Carla, he'd been with dozens of women. He didn't keep count. There'd been a few short-term relationships. Mostly, there'd been sex. It'd been about meeting physical needs.

He didn't say he'd call those women. He didn't make promises. And he didn't *make love* to them. That would involve opening up his heart. He didn't do that with a one-night stand or woman who didn't take the time to know him or make the effort to see beneath his surface. To *trust him*.

Angela trusted him.

With her in his life, he'd be fine if he never had sex with another woman—as long as he had her. Could make love to her.

Tonight, the euphoria following great sex lingered in him. Years ago, he'd stopped bringing women to his home because they often felt entitled to stay after having sex, expected things he didn't want to offer. It was easier to go to their place. To say he snored as an excuse not to stay the night. But, now, the idea of Angela not being here created a panic that prowled around in his gut.

In the past week, his feelings for her had raced from respect, with an enormous dose of physical attraction, to a protective calling. Then to an addictive need to be with her. A very good kind of addiction.

Only someone wanted her dead, and apparently had the means to make it happen. He had to find a way to stop them —permanently—from hurting her. Once he did, would she feel safe enough to leave him, though? Go back to D.C.? That idea unsettled him nearly as much as someone placing a bomb under her bed.

"YOU WANT MORE?" Tony carried his plate to the stove for a second helping of the casserole Kristie had brought.

"I am good." While her appetite had returned, she couldn't possibly finish off the generous portion he'd served her.

He seemed different. Off. Though she couldn't put her finger on how exactly. After the verbal foreplay and preludes to lovemaking, she didn't expect the actual act would change anything. Yet when he sat back down, she noted it in his eyes and the set of his mouth. Especially in the way he avoided prolonged eye contact.

And here she'd worried about him getting too attached. She usually did a better job reading people. Evidently, she had a soft spot for him.

Though it stung, she sure wasn't going to go all needy and call him out on it. With the D.C. office developing leads on who'd broken into her home, she could be back there in a matter of days. Sooner, if needed. She'd reached the point where she could take care of herself—for the most part. No need to hamper his life.

She swallowed another bite of the casserole that had become tasteless. "Kathryn said she'd have video from the street-side surveillance cameras uploaded this evening."

"You don't sound excited." He met her eyes, taking another bite of zucchini bread. One corner of his mouth rose in a playful manner, more reminiscent of the Tony of the past week.

"Like you guys enjoyed combing through Hakim's files?" she retorted. "Even with the Bureau running through the footage and isolating faces, then running comparative analysis to eliminate the regulars, there'll be thousands of possibilities from dozens of surveillance cameras over days or weeks."

"There's a chance we'll get lucky, but I think it's a one-in-a-quarter-million shot, too. Better than one in a million, but that's why the guys and I were working up another angle."

He had her full attention.

"What if we make them think it worked?" he asked.

Maybe she'd read him wrong earlier. He could be in

mission mode. "What do you mean?" She already had a good idea.

"Set off an explosion in your place—"

"Too risky. What about my neighbors? Pedestrians on the street below?" She wouldn't take the chance of injuring others.

Based on the tilt of Tony's head and his measured exhalation, he anticipated her objection.

"It'd be controlled. Rock the place and shower broken glass on the street. We'd wait until no one was in the blast zone. Just big enough to make the neighbors call nine one one. We'd get the Bureau's buy-in to pull it off. Send in a fire department crew that was in the loop. Have a coroner wheel out a body bag."

A shiver ripped through her. How close had she—they— come to that scenario playing out for real? "How do you know whoever placed the bomb will know it went off and … and that I was 'killed'?"

"Trust me. If someone is waiting to collect that chunk of change, they've planned to follow up. They'll see it on the news. Hell, they may have stuck around or set up for a local to notify them."

Not likely with a professional who'd avoid any ties. She closed her eyes to think. The chances of her recognizing a face on the video were about the same as hitting the lottery— which is why she never bought tickets.

The Bureau comparing faces to their and Interpol's database of assassins didn't yield high odds of success. They had so little evidence to work with. "How would we know who did it?"

"DEA has a line on Vasquez's accounts," he continued. "If it's them, we follow the money. See where it goes. Then we nail the son of a bitch."

"What if they require proof before a payoff?" She played devil's advocate, toying with the idea.

"We can run an obituary with a picture they'll recognize. Stage a funeral service."

"I want to be cremated."

"How 'bout we bury these assholes instead?" Tony ignored her attempt at gallows humor.

"What if it's not them, and it's tied to Hakim and al-Shehri's bombing attempt? Or ... something else? I can't show up for work the next week."

What if she had to completely cut ties to this life and everything—and everyone—in it?

Once again, the reality of her past raised its head to mock her. What option did she have?

THIRTY-THREE

"THE BUREAU WILL NEVER GO for that." Angela ignored the narrowing of Tony's eyes and stern set of his jaw. "Besides the cost—"

"We're only talking about monitoring calls for a day or two …" Tony looked to his teammates, all crowded into his family room, for backup.

"There's the matter of people's privacy," she continued, determined to follow the spirit, if not the A-to-Z letter of the law, no matter how much it frustrated him.

"We're only interested in calls related to the bomb going off, not every drug deal or—"

"They'll shoot it down," she cut him off. "It's better not to bring it up. You need to offer a plan that operates within their parameters."

Tony growled—again.

"I have a vested interest in this succeeding," she reminded him.

"I have a vested interest, too," he countered.

Heat coursed through her at his assertion. His determination to find who'd placed the bomb, and his friends' support

—being here after a full day of training—told her she was no longer alone in this. They *refused* to let her be alone. It sparked a hope she hadn't felt in years.

"I hate to interrupt this lover's quarrel, but who're we puttin' in the body bag?" Dominguez piped in.

"Thanks for volunteering." Tony turned his attention to Dominguez.

"I wasn't—" he started.

"You're close enough in size, and in the bag, no one could tell." Lundgren's statement cut off Dominguez's protest.

"It should be me," she admitted.

"But you don't want—" Tony began.

"I have to get out of the condo some way," she pointed out. "That's where they'd expect me. Why risk the exposure by putting someone else in there? Better to go out *pretending* to be dead than the alternative."

"She's got a point." Lundgren's agreement shut down Tony's objections.

In a room filled with alpha males, Lundgren was clearly the top dog. Mack Hanlon and Tony fell next in the line of authority. The group dynamics went beyond rank. There was an undeniable bond between the men. A trust. Respect. A brotherhood. Though Tony and Dominguez butted heads at every turn, like real brothers, they put aside their differences to get the mission done.

"That frees up Dominguez. Mack?" Lundgren turned his way.

"We'll put him on the street with Rozanski. You up for that?" Mack asked.

"Heck, yeah," Rozanski answered.

"Gonna cordon off the area below her condo for 'repair work' to keep pedestrians clear. They'll have hard hats, but go easy on the ordnance," Mack cautioned Porter and Grant.

"You're sure you can limit the damage to just my unit?" Angela asked, unable to quell her worry over the risk.

"We might break a window or two. Knock a few pictures off the walls. But we'll use thermal imaging to make sure none of your neighbors are in the blast zone," Porter said in his smooth, professional voice instead of his we-get-to-blow-things-up voice.

"Liu is surveying the area to get a feel for traffic flow to determine the best time of day, but we'll wait as long as it takes to be clear," Lundgren added. "The rest of us will be on the lookout for any unusual activity afterward. It's a long shot, but if the hitman is local, he may come to observe. Key is to make it real and for the word to get out. Besides your friend, how many people in the D.C. office know about the bomb?"

"All the tech crew. The ordnance disposal crew. The forensics team." There were probably others, but listing half the D.C. field office made Lundgren grimace.

"Forensics able to narrow down the date of entry?"

"At least two days prior to my release from the hospital. It could have been over a week. Hard to tell since I'd been gone for nearly three months."

"Did anything turn up in the investigation of Vasquez's financials?" Lundgren's attempt at a reassuring smile fell flat.

"The family's got dozens of accounts. There are constant small transfers. Nothing that stood out, though." No half-million-dollar payouts. Mostly a few thousand dollars. Angela fought to hold onto the scrap of hope that they'd find who'd set the bomb and somehow put an end to the contract on her life. *If only …*

Their plan was solid, but would the Bureau buy into it? She hoped so. Because all the members of this elite Special Operations team had marshal credentials, which meant they could skirt the limitations placed on the military working on U.S. soil. Based on the mood in the room, the guys were going through with this plan with or without the Bureau.

A tingle started in her arms. It spread throughout her body. Once again, the idea of being a part of this community engulfed her. Despite the threat to her life, she'd never felt so protected. So cared for.

"This is our best shot. No second chances. We gotta sell it." Tony's gaze shifted from one teammate to the next. Each nodded. Championship game faces on.

THIRTY-FOUR

FBI Special Agent Bailer turned the corner to circle the block. It wouldn't be believable to get a parking space in D.C. on their first pass. Angela wouldn't mind circling a few more times, though that wouldn't calm the roiling in her stomach.

She picked out Ray Lundgren's blond hair when they cruised past the front of her building. She overrode the urge to lift a hand in greeting to Rozanski and Dominguez working on the segment of the sidewalk they'd closed for repairs.

When they turned back onto her street, Lundgren steered his sedan out of its spot. Bailer parallel parked, kicking the mission into gear. She waited while he got her suitcase from the trunk, then opened her door and offered his arm to assist her out.

She focused on walking to the entrance instead of doing surveillance. Half of Tony's team was out there—she needed to let *them* do their jobs.

This time she made it up the stairs without having to stop and catch her breath. She opened the door and stepped inside to find a different scene waiting for her today. Tony greeted her first. She'd indulged in visions of him here—but not like this.

While the Bureau agreed with most of the team's plan, they insisted one of their agents be her escort. Tony hadn't liked it, but she'd convinced him it made more sense for credibility and getting the word out. She hadn't admitted she wanted to limit him and his team's exposure on the public side of her "death." Selfishly, she didn't want to close the door to future contact with Tony—no matter how remote the possibility.

Tony led her and Bailer into the living area where Linc Porter and Devin Grant played cards, apparently done with their part since they'd snuck up in the gloom of night to start their work. Behind them, plastic sheeting covered the hallway leading to her bedroom. It took being in her home for the reality that she may never come back here after today to hit her. The familiar sense of loss sucked the air from her lungs.

"We're all set." Porter rose to his feet.

"My neighbors?" Had the would-be assassin cared that he might claim another innocent life? Tony stood beside her, so close his shoulder brushed hers, perhaps wondering along the same lines.

"Units above and below are empty as are the ones across the hall and next door. There is someone in the downstairs kitty-corner unit, but they won't be impacted. Well, maybe shook up a bit." Tony's fingers slipped over hers, anchoring her to the present, not what could have happened.

"To make it look real, we're going to need to add a few personal effects to the blast debris." Grant swept aside the plastic sheeting and led her toward the bedroom.

Nothing appeared out of order when she gave the room a quick perusal. Her gaze settled on the nightstand where a framed picture of her and Stephan sat. It had been taken at his college graduation. It seemed a lifetime ago. Without meeting Grant's eyes, she knew he and Porter had seen the picture, and Grant was asking her about keeping it safe during the blast.

Was there anything she needed? She had a duplicate of the photo in her scrapbook. *Her scrapbook.*

Her limbs dragged like she wore weights as she crossed to the bookshelf in the corner of her room. She pulled out her lone scrapbook.

Inside were baby photos, pictures from birthdays and holidays over the years. A few obligatory school pictures—her mother had always been happy when Angela had gone back to school. There'd been fewer photos the older she got. She'd added some from her time in Germany. More from her student exchange year in France. Then college. Pictures with Stephan. Maybe she could get a picture of Tony to add to the book later.

"Can you take this?" She handed the book to him since she'd be staying with him while she continued to recuperate. She sure wouldn't be able to stay here.

"Of course."

"We're ready once we get the all clear. Kitchen is the safe zone. Afterward, we'll have to stay out of sight of the windows and wait for the first responders. If anyone needs to use the latrine, now's the time." Porter got down to business.

"Give me a minute." Angela ducked into the bathroom. She closed the door behind her and leaned against it for a few moments. She ran her fingers over the cool white quartz countertop she'd selected. The gray flecks in the quartz coordinated with the brushed nickel fixtures. The pale aqua walls made the windowless room light, peaceful, and cheery.

She opened the cabinets, checking for anything she

might have left behind before going to New York. A light knock on the door announced Tony before he cracked it open.

"You okay?" He stepped inside.

"We need to stop meeting in bathrooms," she quipped, trying to buy another moment to control her emotions.

"I don't know. I've got some good memories of us in bathrooms." A smile played across his mouth. He took hold of her hips. Waiting, he stared into her eyes.

"It's harder than I thought. This is the first place that was mine." It'd been more of a home than any place she'd lived the past two decades.

"If you want, we can ship your furniture and stuff to my place."

Man, leaving him was going to be worse than losing her home. So much worse. She drew in what should have been a calming breath.

"It's not the furniture. That's just stuff. It's knowing where everything is in the local grocery. Knowing where to get the best pizza and sesame chicken in the area. Having a stylist who cuts your hair the way you like it. Seeing familiar faces." Ones that weren't a threat. *Good Lord, please don't let me cry.* "You know how it is when you're constantly moving."

"Yeah. The 'see the world' novelty wore off pretty quickly. A benefit of being in Special Operations is less moving. More stability for having a … a family."

Family. That word slammed into her like an iceberg.

Kathryn had assured her the Bureau would let her choose where she went next. Anywhere. She tried not to think about it yet. She was accustomed to the larger field offices, but smaller would work. Her preference would be for someplace warm. Miami, maybe. But did Vasquez have too many ties there? Charlotte was a decent-sized office. Good climate. Only a few hours from Fayetteville ...

She needed to do what was best for both of them. Not give Tony false hope. Charlotte was probably not the best idea. Too much temptation.

"Let's get this done," Angela said with all the bravado she could muster.

In the kitchen, Tony briefed Bailer on his expectations once they detonated the explosive. She had to give Bailer credit for not giving Tony attitude about telling him what to do. Then it was Porter's show.

He gave them a brief rundown before radioing the men outside to signal when all was clear.

Despite her nagging fears about what could go wrong, she held onto the tiny seed of hope that she could put this threat behind her for good. That *was* her best option. When the radio squawked after only a minute, she let go of her concerns.

As a precaution, the group took cover along the kitchen wall. Tony pulled her into his arms, shielding her with his body. She melted, looking into his eyes. His face lowered, and she turned hers up. Their mouths met, and tongues engaged.

One of the men gave a throaty chuckle, probably at their timing for making out. Tony kept her steady when the blast rocked the building. The brief muffled sound wasn't as loud as she'd expected. The shattering of glass served as a back-drop to the tender kiss.

Porter and Grant rushed to check their handiwork, and three beeps told her Bailer placed the 9-1-1 call.

Though she didn't see any dust when she opened her eyes, a burnt smell similar to cordite permeated the air.

Bailer identified himself as FBI and started in on an

Academy Award-worthy performance when speaking to the emergency operator. His voice faded as he moved out of the kitchen, then elevated with panic.

All was silent for a few seconds before he passed along the news of an intentional explosion and warned of the possibility of more devices. Even Tony's body heat couldn't ward off the ice that formed in her veins when Special Agent Bailer reported her death.

Porter and Grant slipped back, all smiles, and gave a thumbs-up. The group stayed out of sight of the windows. Bailer stuck to the plan, transitioning control of the incident from local authorities to the FBI. Minutes later, sirens pierced the air until the fire trucks roared to a stop outside. Bailer nodded to her and Tony, then exited the condo.

Angela envisioned the scene on the street below. More sirens announced the medic unit's arrival. She held her breath, hoping the plan worked, while Bailer kept them out until the Bureau sent in their team to secure the premises.

"Want us to deal you in? It could be a while." Porter shuffled the deck of cards.

"Would we be playing for money?" Tony asked.

"I don't play for money against Grant." Porter laughed. Tony nodded in agreement.

The tension eased, and she joined them at the table. *Might as well have something to take my mind off things while we wait.*

"Five-card draw," Porter announced. "Deuces are wild."

She waited until Porter dealt the cards before picking up her hand. She studied each of the men's faces and postures while they sorted their cards. They also studied each other and her.

By their fifth hand, she'd guessed Porter and Grant's tells. But Grant seemed to remember every card played, which explained why the guys didn't like to play him for money. She'd thrown Tony with a fake tell in the third hand, but he was on to her now, and she hadn't pinned down any tells for him, either.

They locked gazes as Grant shuffled. Whether Tony's intense scrutiny related to unearthing her tell or mentally undressing her, she couldn't ascertain. It sent heat radiating through her and blew her concentration for the hand.

Loud footsteps in the hall warned of someone's arrival. The door opened, and a figure in a bomb-disposal suit waddled in. After closing the door, the man pulled off the suit's headpiece and grinned at them.

"Hey, Hoffman. Good to see you."

"How are things outside?" Angela asked the FBI bomb-disposal tech, Morris.

"Explosion looks convincing."

"Of course," Porter stated.

"I had something to do with that." Morris spread his hands, palms up. "And defusing an unknown explosive is riskier than putting one together." The men didn't refute his statement, which appeased Morris enough to continue, "There's a good-sized crowd on the street. Bailer is holding off fire and medics. They're treating one of your team for—"

"Someone's hurt?" Her stomach dropped to the floor.

"Some minor cuts from the glass. They're bandaging him up to keep the medics busy. Think they were antsy to get up here and see if they could do anything for you."

Angela laid her cards down on the table and breathed only slightly easier.

"There's a news crew out there already. I'd better get busy and do a visible sweep so the media can get a shot for the news." He mugged as if posing for a picture, then put the helmet back on before heading down the hall.

She lost the next few poker hands. *How long would this take?* She tried to focus. Morris had to make clearing the scene and checking for additional explosives look real.

Tony cut his eyes to her when he dealt the next hand. She shifted in her seat due to his intense stare. If she stared at him too long, she might start thinking about what had to come. She could do this.

A shiver coursed through her when Morris called down to send up the forensics team—and a body bag. The table shook a bit because Tony's arms flinched, too.

It's okay, he mouthed.

She swallowed, not able to dislodge the lump in the back of her throat but nodded anyway.

Morris re-entered the kitchen carrying his helmet and hand shields. He wore a relaxed smile, though sweat matted his hair.

"That didn't take long," Porter commented.

"Took longer the first time. That was the real deal. Don't want the gawkers to get bored. You aren't going to be hanging out here after all this, I guess," Morris said.

"It'd undo all this for me to show up at the office next week." It'd take longer than that to make repairs to her condo.

The forensics team traipsed in and headed straight to the blast zone that had been her bedroom. Their voices carried to the kitchen while they went through the motions for any observer with a view inside.

Maybe if this went perfectly, she could come back some-day. For now, she operated under the worst-case scenario. Well, not the absolute worst-case—that would involve cutting ties to the Bureau and everyone and everything in her life to completely start over. A definite possibility that cast a distinct shadow of grief.

The card game continued, more as a distraction. It

didn't distract her enough to ignore when they brought up the gurney. Last hand: *Showtime*—with her in the starring role.

The furtive glances of two men in navy windbreakers emblazoned with FBI in yellow letters made her stand rather than wait for them to call for her. The open body bag covered the gurney's surface.

"It's not too late. We can get Dominguez or put Grant in there," Tony offered.

"No. Stick with the plan." She fingered the heavy black plastic. "Ready?" she asked the two agents.

"Yes, ma'am."

She perched on the gurney and lifted her legs onto the surface. "Remember, better *to know* I'm going out in a body bag than not be aware of it," she told Tony—and herself.

He kissed her again.

"I'll see you on the other side." She laid back.

He winced. "Yeah. You'll see me soon," he stated emphatically. Then he stepped back to let the agents zip the bag.

"It's important that you don't move, so we will strap you down. Normal procedures. Okay?" the forensics agent informed her.

The straps holding her to the gurney immobilized her. She closed her eyes as they zipped the bag closed. Darkness engulfed her, and she forced out a breath, willing her body to remain calm.

The gurney jolted over the threshold. Being carried out like a corpse hit her as symbolic. She'd changed her name after leaving the CIA. Angela was close enough to Angelique that she responded naturally. In a nostalgic moment, she'd chosen Stephan's last name for her new identity. Hmm, Angie Vincent popped into her mind as a potential name. Oh, like that wouldn't give Tony any ideas. Or make her think of him every day.

She gritted her teeth to keep quiet while they bumped down the stairs. Each step took her further from her old life. Further from Tony.

THIRTY-FIVE

SEEING Angela in the body bag nearly made Tony retch. He watched the two agents wheel her down the hall. This time she was conscious as they took her away—her heart beating strong—yet it still dredged up memories of when he thought Hakim had killed her.

She'd survived, only now another threat shadowed her. Not a spontaneous threat like Hakim. A deliberate, intentional menace motivated by revenge and greed. Not a good combination.

When the men and gurney disappeared, he prayed the assassin saw the publicity and bought this. It wouldn't surprise him if, on top of the news coverage and obituary, they had to hold a memorial service. The plan was for a cremation, so he wouldn't have to endure a public graveside service.

He wanted to get her back home—soon. The past few days, she hadn't been herself. He couldn't read her, and she'd glossed over it when he probed. He hoped once this ended, she'd relax, and they could take steps toward the future. What the bomb tech said about her leaving D.C. conjured mixed feelings. *Please have her want to stay with me.*

He rallied his strength and made his legs carry him back inside. Until they had a clear opportunity to get out of her condo, he, Grant, and Porter were forced to wait it out. Angela's photo album sat on the entryway table. Curiosity won out.

The early pictures were mostly of her with her mother. He could have mistaken her mother for Angela from a few years ago. Both had the same high cheekbones, delicate nose, narrow chin, and full lips. Similar brown-black hair fell in soft waves.

Only her mother's dark eyes radiated coldness versus the warmth Angela's held. Flipping through the pages reinforced that impression. A few pages in, he found a close-up of Angela with her father. She didn't have his eyes, either. In fact, she bore no resemblance to him. At all.

He kept turning pages, watching Angela grow. The backdrops changed, too. From her Louisiana home to the lush foliage of South America to the starkness of the Middle East. She became more alluring with age, though the sadness in her eyes grew. Occasionally there would be a picture of her with friends. The number of photos of her father dwindled to nothing.

With the move back to the States, her mother's beauty began to fade. Tony attributed it to hard living and drugs. It was a miracle Angela escaped that life.

He studied a picture of her standing next to a young man on a Harley. Brock? His muscles tensed as he recalled her story of Brock saving her from the biker's attack. Pictures from Paris marked her time in France and the return of the smile absent in the previous pages.

Circumstances forced Angela to mature early, but it took

getting away from her dysfunctional family for her to be happy. Based on the pictures of her during college, she thrived being on her own. Or maybe it had to do with being in love. There were pages filled with photos of her with her late fiancé. Then Tony got to the page with clippings of 9/11. An obituary, then no more pictures.

He needed to get some pictures of him and Angela together in hopes she'd add them to her book.

He flipped back a few pages, and it hit him. He already guessed she might have trust issues, but it likely went deeper than that. Every significant male in her life had vanished after a life-changing incident. First, her parents' divorce, and then she had to move halfway across the world from her father. Tony would bet a month's pay her "dad" wasn't her biological father, and both she and her dad figured that out at some point.

Did Angela blame herself for her mother's deception and the divorce? He'd also bet money her stepfather hadn't done jack shit in her life—at least not in a good way. Brock paid the price for sticking up for her. That may have pushed Angela toward law school and a career pursuing justice. Then her fiancé dying in the terrorists' attacks—after he came to see her—that had to suck.

So, on top of trust, add abandonment and survivor's guilt to the list of issues in her life. It was a lot even for someone as strong as Angela. Jarrod screwing her over didn't help, either.

"Vincenti, we dealing you in, or you sneaking down to do surveillance duty?" Porter called out.

"Coming." He closed the album. It might take a while for him to overcome all the issues in Angela's past, but this kind of challenge was worth risking his life—and his heart—for.

THIRTY-SIX

"I'll get the dishes," Tony said when Angela moved to clear the table.

"I'm not really dead. I can manage to load the dishwasher."

The hint of defensiveness in her tone made him stand down. They hadn't gotten any leads after faking the explosion in D.C. yesterday, and both were on edge.

"I can see that. Maybe I want you to save your strength for other lively activities." He held out his plate but didn't release his hold on it, and with his other hand, brought her body against his.

"Sorry." She turned her face up to meet his mouth.

"Damn," he grumbled when the phone rang, and she broke the kiss. He wanted to ignore it and continue the present course that would take their mind off the waiting. He had a few fantasies that worked in the kitchen.

"Go ahead and get it."

Her hand trailed over his chest, which certainly didn't motivate him to stop for a phone call. That's what voice mail was for. It was likely his folks making their weekly call, and he could call them back later. Or tomorrow.

When she took a step back, his hand moved from cupping her butt to her hip.

Great. Nothing like a call from Mom to kill a romantic mood. It's like she had video surveillance to know when to interrupt and save him from breaking a few commandments. His eyes scanned the kitchen for any hidden camera before he moved to answer the call.

It wasn't his parents' name and number displayed on the caller ID, but a 212-area code. Hope shot through him at the possibility they'd hear that Vasquez had wired the money. As he answered, it clicked that 212 was a New York City area code, not D.C.

"Vincenti. It's Jarrod," Carswell returned his greeting.

"What's up?" *Jarrod,* he mouthed to Angela. That Jarrod would call instead of someone in the D.C. office triggered a warning in his brain.

"I heard about Angela. I can't believe it after what she'd been through. We're all in shock up here. I know you two were close, so I wanted to see how you were doing."

"I can't believe it myself." He caught himself before saying too much. Of course, Jarrod wouldn't know about Vasquez and the contract—hopefully—since only the Bureau's D.C. office participated. Better to keep it that way since Jarrod had a big mouth.

"Did you hear anything about who they think is responsible?"

"Not yet. An agent picked her up at the airport. If I'd ... I planned to go up this weekend." Tony walked to the family room, away from Angela, to keep his concentration.

"Do you know details on a funeral?" Jarrod asked.

Shit. Would Jarrod seriously consider going after the way he'd treated her?

"They're going to—" He paused, drawing in a breath for effect. "They're going to do a cremation and hold a memorial service. The obit's supposed to run tomorrow with the time and place. The D.C. office is handling it."

"I'll check online then. Again, I'm sorry, man."

After they ended their conversation, Tony sat on the couch, letting the hostility brewing in him subside. Glasses clanked as Angela loaded the dishwasher.

"What did Jarrod have to say?" She joined him in the living room and sat beside him.

"Called to offer his condolences." Though had he said that? What did he really want? "He didn't try to start things up again when you were in New York, did he?" He had to ask.

"No. It would have been a moot point anyway. I have no attraction to Jarrod. None. Not after I found out what he was really like. When we were working in Afghanistan, I asked him if he was married on more than one occasion. Each time he misled me. Didn't outright lie, but when I brought up a wife, he said 'Wife? You don't see a wedding band, do you?' or 'What? Do you only have a thing for married men? I'd hate for that to spoil the possibilities.'" She shook her head, her mouth set in a dismayed twist. "I should have known from the way he ducked giving a direct answer."

"He lied, even if he didn't say 'I'm not married.' It's not your fault you believed him." Typical Jarrod. Tony wanted to beat the shit out of his former teammate. And he thought Dominguez played games when it came to women.

"After the ambush, they shipped him home to the States. I felt bad, so I went to the hospital when I got back. Coming face-to-face with his wife …" She shook her head. "I did my best to cover. I told her we worked together. I'm not sure she bought it."

"Again. Not your fault. All Jarrod thinks about is himself."

"Yeah. I certainly learned that—too late. He gave me a headscarf he bought at the market in Khost. Then he got mad when I didn't wear it. It was handmade and distinctive."

"If someone identified it as the one he bought, that would expose you." *Duh. What the hell had Jarrod been thinking? Oh, about his pride. And his dick.* Tony kept his mouth shut. Questioning her choice of Jarrod as a romantic partner wouldn't help when she clearly regretted the relationship.

"Exactly. I pointed that out, and he still acted as if I was making too big a deal. He said only the woman who made it would know. Anyway, I'm not Jarrod's favorite person, either. I didn't know he was leading the mission in New York when I went up. And he sure as hell didn't know it was me coming in to help until I showed up."

"Hmm?" He didn't follow how Jarrod wouldn't know.

"He knew me as Angelique Gilbert. My given name. I changed it when I left the CIA. It seemed safer considering the contract. Anyway, New York was strictly a working rela-tionship. Jarrod needed me because the first undercover agent, who *he* selected, nearly exposed the Bureau's interest in Hakim. Jarrod is smart and charming on the surface, but it's crystal clear that he only cares about one thing. One person: Jarrod. He's not near the man you are in any way. Being involved with him was a mistake, so I'd rather not give him any more of my time—especially when we were right about here."

She shifted on the couch to lean in and invade his space. "And I think your shirt was coming off." She gave a playful tug to the bottom of his T-shirt.

God, that sultry look in her eyes shut out any jealousy pricking him about Jarrod. Considering his past, Tony couldn't hold hers against her. Not when what they had was so damned perfect. And what was under her shirt was so damned perfect, too. Blood drained from his upper body and headed straight to his groin.

Time to forget Jarrod and give Angela his undivided attention and more incentive to stay.

THIRTY-SEVEN

THE HUM of the garage door opening set off the same giddiness of a high school girl with a keep-me-up-at-night crush. Angela's fingers froze on the laptop keys. She wanted to think her reaction to Tony's arrival resulted from having someone to talk to after being alone throughout the day. But it was more than that.

For years, she had no problem being alone. It was Tony. Spending time with him made her want more. Want the things she'd given up after joining the CIA. The longer she stayed, the harder it got to separate the present from her future.

Imagining Tony's brawny arms was enough to make her lose her train of thought. His eight-pack abs—yeah, his body sported not six, but eight—packed a wallop of desire whenever he appeared in a towel.

Or a pair of jeans.

Or in uniform.

Or naked.

His keys clanked against the kitchen countertop, and seconds later, Tony strolled into the family room. She closed the screen of her laptop, and her body temperature shot up.

He made the plain tan crewneck T-shirt sexy with the way it emphasized his arms and broad chest.

A new kind of tingling started when she noticed the bag in his hand. "What's that?"

"What? This?" His grin broadened. He pulled a gift-wrapped box out of the nondescript bag. "Just something you'll need." He held the box in his hand, not yet extending it to her. "I figured you might be tired of being cooped up in here most of the time. Thought when you're up for it, we'd get out and do something fun."

She squirmed on the couch but refrained from reaching for the gift. It wasn't her birthday or any special occasion. Based on the size of the box, it wasn't lingerie—not that she would have minded. A fancy dress and dinner didn't suit either of them. "What'd you have in mind?"

His eyebrows waggled playfully. She smiled back while her mind shifted away from the gift.

"You want to open it now or, uh, later?" He stepped closer, then laughed as she debated how to answer. He took a seat on the couch, then laid the box in her lap.

She ran her fingertips over the satin ribbon.

"Go ahead." He grinned at her.

She couldn't wait any longer. The box was heavier than she expected. Like a kid on Christmas morning, she shook it before pulling the ribbon to undo the bow. Her hands shook as she peeled back the layers of tissue paper. She gasped when she saw what lay inside.

"I thought we'd go riding soon," he said.

Her fingers glided over the jacket's soft, supple leather. She couldn't bring herself to lift it from the box. "You shouldn't have. It's too much."

"I haven't had someone to spoil in a long time. Unless you count my folks and nieces and nephews. Try it on."

The mention of his family, people he cared about and needed to protect, jabbed at her.

She took the riding jacket out and held it up. "But I won't be here much longer."

He started to speak, then stopped, taking an exaggerated breath. "You know ... it's not a good idea to go back to D.C. —even if you are 'dead.' It could get back to whoever ..."

"I know. That's why I'm working with Kathryn to transfer to another office."

Tony's mouth tightened. "I hoped you'd stay here."

"And do what? Sponge off you? I can't do that."

"There're plenty of businesses that need translators."

"Not to sound conceited, but I helped stop a bombing. I saved lives. Becoming a translator for the courts, a hospital, or defense contractor, that's a big step backward."

"Defense contractor might pay better than the Bureau," he grumbled.

"And would you take a job with a private contractor?"

"If it meant giving us a shot, I'd consider it."

Whoa. That was the last thing she expected. She sank back against the couch and laid the jacket on the box.

"What about the Bureau's Charlotte office?" he suggested.

It was her turn to sigh. Time to bring out the sledgehammer. Make it sink in—for both of them. "And what about a family? You want that, don't you?"

"Yes." Tony didn't hesitate.

"If I'm a few hours away, and we get together every couple of weeks—"

"That's not what I had in mind—"

"Exactly! Tony, I ... I *can't* have a family. Not with my past. Somebody put a freaking bomb under my bed!" Her voice broke, and tears staged a surprise ambush.

"I know. I was there. But we stopped it. We're going to get whoever did that."

"We don't know who it was. It might be tied to al-Shehri or the Vasquez family. They aren't the only ones who have a score to settle with me."

"Whoever it is, we'll stop them. I can protect you." His firm voice didn't waver.

"You can't take out everyone who might want to hurt me. And you can't be there all the time." She shook her head. "What if ... what if we had kids? Some of these people are ruthless. You'd be targets. I can't live with that."

"I can take care of myself. Maybe we don't have kids ..."

Kids? Dammit. Why did I bring up that possibility? Where did it even come from? *Because I love him.* Yes, she was flat-out, gobsmacked, down-the-rabbit-hole in love with him. "I can't ask you to give up everything you want."

"This would buy us time to figure things out. Make a plan."

"People don't get everything they want. And what if we tried? Then say one day you come home, and I'm gone. Maybe the place is torn up. There's blood. Or maybe there's nothing out of place. I'm just ... gone. And you don't know if someone took me, or I had to leave to keep you safe. Then what do you do?"

For once, Tony had nothing to say. He sat there, his mouth open, his head shaking.

"You have an exit plan," he finally said. "Okay, you tell me where and—"

"I can't. You know that."

His mouth turned into a grim line as she countered every objection. Anger flashed in his eyes.

"You're talking like this is a sure thing. You're willing to walk away on the chance that someone will come after you."

"They already have. I couldn't live with myself if someone died because they were close to me." Saying it broke her control; her throat constricted, so she could hardly breathe. Tears scorched the back of her eyelids.

His mouth was tight, and anger rolled off his body, but he didn't get up and stalk away. Not yet. She couldn't blame him if he did. He had given her an expensive, thoughtful gift. The grown-up, Tony-version of a promise ring. And what had she done? She stole his joy—not just about the gift, but about how their relationship was progressing.

It hadn't been her original intention, but she had to find out if her assumptions about him wanting a family were on target. It wasn't fair to mislead him—not when he was talking about *their* future.

She didn't say more when he pulled her into his arms and held her against his chest. When the jacket slipped to the floor, neither of them moved to retrieve it.

"This isn't over. You have to give us time for this to play out. Find out who and shut them down."

She didn't expect him to give up without a fight. That wasn't in his nature. For now, she'd give him time to process the whole picture. Once he did, he'd come to accept it. That gave her more time, too. Time to stock up as many memories of Tony as possible to carry with her when they had to part.

THIRTY-EIGHT

THIRTY-THREE. Thirty-four. Screw it. Tony lowered the weights and let go of the hand pulls. He strained to hear Angela's voice. She must have moved into the kitchen after getting the phone.

He grabbed his towel, then pushed up from the bench. Wiping his face, he stepped out of his home gym and paused, listening again. What was he afraid of? This was his home.

Strolling to the fridge, he studied Angela's face. Distractedly, she tapped a pen on a legal pad. A few lines of notes were scribbled near the top. Under those, swirls of ink formed a dark cloud.

"It sounds like they bought the explosion being successful." She glanced up but didn't hold eye contact with him. "I won't hold my breath on that. Thanks, Kathryn."

While he drained a glass of water, she continued tapping her pen on the pad.

"Kathryn Barnsley?" That explained Angela's rush to answer the phone while they were working out. Only she didn't appear happy with the outcome of the conversation.

"Yeah." Her hand stilled. "Four-hundred-and-fifty-thousand dollars was wired out of a Vasquez account yesterday."

The hair on his sweaty forearms stood at attention. "That's what we wanted. Now we know who." Finally, things were moving forward. But obviously, she didn't share his enthusiasm. Why?

"You want to cash in on that action?" She managed a grim smile.

"Not nearly enough. Especially for you." He winked, then took a seat at the kitchen table.

"The money was wired to an account in Singapore."

"Shit." *Singapore.* Not only was it offshore, but banking privacy laws meant the Bureau wouldn't be getting any info on the account holder. Someone had the brains to make it hard, if not impossible, to trace the money.

Angela's mouth pursed, and her head shook in agreement. "They did get a name from the wire transfer on the Colombian bank's end. So far, no hits on an Austin Cooper in the FBI database. Or Homeland Security. Or Interpol."

"Austin Cooper?" The name rattled around his brain. "Isn't he that actor who did the show pranking other celebrities?"

Angela shrugged, reminding him she rarely watched TV. "Without access to the identification used to open the account, the Bureau's hitting a brick wall. It's a waiting game to see where the money goes next. Which, if it's a professional hit, could be a while. It reinforces what I've been thinking."

Her tone as much as her words pulled him forward on his seat.

"Maybe it's just as well if we don't find out who." Her shoulders sagged.

"What?" She couldn't mean that.

"Currently, the Vasquez family thinks I am dead. They're out a chunk of change, but it's not as if they don't have millions more. If the assassin thinks he completed his job, he's moved on."

"You want to … let them off? They tried to kill you!"

"And they didn't succeed. Not this time. If we find who set the bomb and put him on trial, everyone learns I'm alive, and I've got a bull's-eye on my head again. This way, I can move on, too." Acceptance of her situation showed in her eyes.

She had a point, but the idea of someone getting away without repercussions incensed him. He slouched back into his chair and took a long, deep breath. Then another. It didn't ease the pounding of his pulse or his head. "I don't like it."

"Me, either. But we can't charge the Vasquezes or an assassin with murder if I'm still alive. Attempted murder, yes, but … It's a trade-off. They get away with it; I get to live without looking over my shoulder all the time. The Bureau can set me up with a new ID, and I can start over somewhere. Maybe they'll find evidence to convict the assassin of another crime or murder."

Or Tony could find this Austin Cooper and kill the son of a bitch with his bare hands. The guy hadn't killed Angela, but he was killing his shot of a future with her. Every time she brought up leaving, it felt like a knife butchering away part of his heart. How the fuck was he going to convince her to stay instead of shutting him down and out?

He pushed back from the table. "I need to get a shower before I go into work."

She stood, blocking his exit. "I think you need to expunge some of this hostility first."

He didn't respond though her suggestive smile implied she didn't mean going back to finish his workout. "I'll shoot things." He wasn't in the mood to be pacified. He debated forcing his way around her—until her hand rested on his stomach. The spark in her eyes held him captive.

"Shooting stuff was not what I had in mind."

"Sex doesn't solve everything."

"No." Angela's victorious smile grew. "But I've got some frustration to work off, too. Angry sex might make us feel better. It won't hurt. Well, maybe a tiny bit. In a good way."

Oh, Lordy. So much for not being in the mood. In the two seconds he closed his eyes and swallowed, her shirt pulled a Houdini. No point countering her argument when he couldn't help but get a hard-on anticipating how she might plan to work out her frustration now that she was solidly on the road to recovery.

THIRTY-NINE

TONY JERKED the note off the training room door. He crumpled the paper and shot it into the trashcan before hustling out of the command post. Down at the dirt clearing, the team stood outside the ring where Dominguez and Porter circled, armed with training knives.

"Nice of you to join us, Sergeant Vincenti," Lundgren remarked.

"Sorry, Chief." Excuses were for sissies.

"Why don't you help out Porter?"

He didn't question Lundgren's order, though the odds were definitely in his and Porter's favor. He'd only taken a few steps into the ring when Lundgren tossed a blue training knife to Grant, evening up the odds.

Tony turned from his approach to Dominguez to face Grant. The sex helped somewhat, but his need to release more frustration had his adrenaline revving at the starting line. *Let the dance begin.*

He let Grant move close enough to attempt a strike. A hop-step back had him clear of Grant's reach. His own counter strike missed as well. In his peripheral vision, he kept watch on Dominguez and Porter. Grant made a bold charge, forcing him back two steps.

Suddenly, Tony was flat on his back, looking at the sky, his legs draped over another body when Grant plunged the collapsible knife blade into his chest.

Shit.

Someone—it sounded like Shuler and Mack—chuckled while Rozanski crawled free.

Grant extended his hand, and Tony reluctantly grasped his wrist for the assist up.

"Your enemy won't announce he's sending more guys into the fight. Gotta maintain situational awareness," Lundgren said with the men echoing the oft-heard phrase.

Tony dropped his head to stare at his boots. He couldn't afford to be distracted like this on a mission.

"Shuler. Your turn. With Liu."

"Any updates from the FBI?" Rozanski asked Tony when they stepped to the perimeter of the ring.

"Ang got a call this morning that Vasquez wired out nearly half a million dollars yesterday."

"That makes for some expensive booty," Dominguez said.

Tony wanted to knock the smirk off Dominguez's face, but he reined it in. "Only the money went to an account in Singapore."

"Oh, man. Isn't Singapore like the new Cayman Islands of banking secrecy?" Rozanski said.

"That's what Carswell called it when we were working on that assignment with the intel leaks to North Korea," Mack chimed in.

"Yeah. It's looking like it could be a dead end." Instead of the team helping to put Austin Cooper out of business— permanently—they could be sitting on the sidelines doing nothing. And his future with Angela could evaporate when she did.

"Speaking of Carswell, what was the deal with him and Angela."

Tony glared at Dominguez. Was he trying to goad him?

"I noticed him watching her, too," Rozanski said in Dominguez's defense. "And he snapped a few pictures of her before the paramedics took her out of Hakim's. It was creepy."

Rozanski's statement gave Tony a this-is-gonna-be-bad-shit feeling.

"I thought the two of them had a thing going the way—"

No, you don't... Tony lunged for Dominguez before the asshole could diss on Angela.

Rozanski managed to catch Tony's arm, throwing him off course. Dominguez leaped back so that Tony's right hand only swiped at him.

In a flash, Porter pulled Dominguez away. Rozanski planted himself between the men.

"Chill! Look at me. It's not worth it." Rozanski used his wiry strength to hold Tony back long enough to make him think rather than act on pure emotion.

"Break it up," Lundgren ordered in the authoritative voice that made Tony cringe. "Keep it in the ring. Vincenti. Dominguez. You two earned everyone a five-mile run."

"Me? I didn't do nothing. All I was saying—"

"Seven miles," Lundgren cut off Dominguez.

Porter threw up a hand in front of Dominguez's mouth, effectively silencing him for the moment. "You should try *thinking* before you go 'saying' sometimes."

Tony stepped back, rolled his neck, and shook out his shoulders. He nodded to Rozanski, who lowered his arms.

"What are y'all waiting for? Me to make it ten miles?" Lundgren barked.

Tony jogged toward the trails through the woods without waiting for anyone. The routine seven-mile run didn't qualify as punishment for shoving Dominguez, but if he was subjected to more chatter or insinuations about Carswell with Angela—well, better to pound the ground than Dominguez's face.

Stampeding through the woods, he used the change in scenery to come at the problem of someone learning Angela's identity and location from a different angle. What changed that they'd found her after all these years?

Five miles in, he gave up. It was that or bang his head against a tree, except that wouldn't give him workable ideas. Just like he was freaking stymied on how to make Angela feel safe enough to stay. He had to give her *a reason* to stay. A purpose, until she admitted he—or more accurately, them together—was enough of a reason.

FORTY

TONY STEERED his Harley to the vacant spot near where Angela had parked his SUV under the shade of a Bradford pear tree. Heat shimmered off the parking lot's blacktop surface. He hung his helmet over the handlebar, then strode to the restaurant entrance.

She parked far from the front door, a reminder that each day she regained more strength. That she was another step closer to independence. Energy hummed through him. This had to work.

Inside, his gaze shot to his usual booth in the back-left corner. Angela sat in *his* preferred booth, in *his* spot, giving *her* a sweeping view of the room. Another reminder of how compatible they were—even if she stole his seat.

She watched him, her face projecting her curiosity about the request to meet him for lunch. He prayed the idea he'd finally gotten during his run led somewhere.

"Tony!"

He turned in the direction of the enthusiastic voice before thinking.

Oh, shit. The brunette waitress skirted a table, targeted

right on him. He hadn't recognized the voice, but he recognized the face. *What the hell was her name?*

"Hey. I haven't seen you since that night at Jumpy's." Her eyes moved from his chest to his face and sent heat rushing up his neck—not in a good way.

"I've been out of town." *Tish? Andrea? Jessica? Heather?* Why couldn't the servers wear nametags?

"I hoped you'd call me." Her voice dropped low.

Three more steps and he would have been in the booth. *With Angela.* Who could now overhear every word coming out of the brunette's mouth. *Shit.* He needed to shut her up. "Yeah, well, I'm, uh, involved with someone."

The woman's eyes narrowed. "You're not married, are you?"

"No."

"Then you should call me. We can have a good time again."

Seriously? He needed to man up and shut her down—without being an ass, or more of one—in front of Ang. "Uh, I'm looking for something more serious."

"Oh, I'm serious."

"Excuse me." He turned away and stepped over to the booth, not that this could get any worse. He slid onto the bench beside Angela—where he didn't have to face her. "I'm sorry about that." A sickening sensation churned in his gut.

"I can understand why she wouldn't want to give up without trying." Angela nudged him with her shoulder. "Look, we all have a past we can't change. No matter how much we may want to."

He had no clue what to say. True, she had a past with Jarrod he didn't want to think about. She might not seem bothered now, but how many more women from *his* past were going to be thrust in her face if she stayed here?

Would she trust that he'd stay faithful? He dared to meet her eyes.

She scooted closer. The kiss she pressed to his cheek helped ease his self-recrimination. Her face lingered. He kissed her back, wishing he could kiss away the reality of his past flaunted in her face.

"Ahem."

Shit! His one-night stand—*Holly!* That was her name. Wasn't it?—cleared her throat.

Water sloshed onto the table when she set two glasses down. "Are you ready to order, or do you two need another minute to look at the menu?"

Every molecule in his body fired off warning shots. So, yes, it could get worse. He could deal with spit in his food— he eyed the water glass—but if another woman who knew him that way walked up …

"I'll have the club salad. Oh, I asked *our* waitress, but if you could bring some sliced lemon, I'd appreciate it." Angela handed over the menu, impervious to the attempt to get under her skin.

Tony ordered, then turned his shoulders to face Ang, blocking out Holly and everyone else. If it weren't too late to salvage things, he'd better charge ahead.

"It's been years since you worked for Vasquez. What changed that had someone looking to cash in? Do you think you could have been identified in New York?"

"I've been trying to figure that out. I was constantly on the watch there. Nothing stood out. Even if someone recognized me as Raquel Decaino, there I was Sabine Deschamps. I can't see them making the connection to me and D.C. It had to be something before New York."

"But how—"

"Here you go." A bowl with a few lemon slices rattled onto the tabletop. Holly made eye contact with him.

Holy shit. Holly had unbuttoned one, if not two, buttons to expose her pushed-up cleavage and a peek of black lace. *Why did I think coming here would be a good idea?* He should have waited until tonight when they had privacy at home.

"Thank you." Angela flashed a clearly fake smile, her voice full of sweetness and sunshine. She dismissed Holly by reaching for the bowl.

"How would they know the timing of you being out of town?" Though Holly walked away, he kept his voice low.

"Maybe they didn't."

"The folks in the Bureau's D.C. office knew you were gone. How many of them knew about the contract?" he persisted, though she rolled her eyes.

"Three. Four if you count the former Assistant Director. But none of them would be involved in—"

"You can't rule them out."

"They're law enforcement. They wouldn't risk their reputations and careers."

"Half a million dollars is a lot of temptation." There were plenty of people he'd encountered who would kill for way less depending on the cause.

"Maybe to some people. With someone I know—it'd have to be personal. I don't buy into it. They've got no reason."

"Then who made the connection? How?" Tony had to do something to conquer this helpless feeling. Usually, Intel did the grunt work and found the target. Not this time. Only he wasn't coming close to doing the job, either.

EVEN THOUGH ANGELA had been through it dozens of times in her own mind, she patiently answered the questions Tony threw out while he wolfed down his sandwich.

She knew Kathryn, had dinner with her, her husband, and two sons on more than one occasion. While criminals and terrorists wouldn't want Kathryn setting her sights on them, she was an honest, upstanding individual who wouldn't consider setting up a hit.

With less than two years of service remaining to collect his pension, Harkins, the current assistant director, wouldn't risk turning on his own people. There might be a notation in her personal file, but access to it was restricted, ruling out other personnel.

She tried to recall anything that stood out as suspicious or out of the ordinary her last few months in D.C. She took a bite of salad to buy herself more time. Maybe it wasn't someone in D.C. But who? How?

In the background, the flirty waitress talked to the original server for their table. The women's heads were close together, and both snuck glances in Tony's direction. Good thing she wasn't the jealous type since the waitress had the subtlety of a wrecking ball.

A twinge of sympathy for Tony accompanied her admiration for how he handled the awkward situation. He polished off the last of his sandwich and turned to their waitress, who immediately noticed his focus on her. She strutted over.

"Can I get you anything else?" She aimed a sultry smile at Tony.

Underneath the table, Angela's feet flexed, but she kept her hands relaxed.

"I need the check, and do you need a to-go box, babe?"

"Please." Angela glanced up in time to see the flash of disdain on the server's face. *Sorry, honey, not handing him over to you even if I'm gone soon.* "In a hurry to leave?" she asked him once the woman sauntered off, hips swaying, despite Tony not watching.

"Can't be late twice in one day." He winked.

"Sorry." Shocks of electricity fired through her at the memory of this morning's ardent sex.

"No, you're not," he returned with a snorted chuckle. "And I'm not, either. Though after that, you—" He broke off as the server closed in on them.

"Here you go. Nice to see you again. Come back soon." The waitress set the check at Tony's elbow, then slid the Styrofoam container toward Angela.

Angela scooped the remaining salad into the box.

Tony didn't wait. He stood and pulled out his wallet. "You can keep the change—and your number." He handed over both the money and the green ticket with a phone number written on it. "I'm flattered, Holly, but like I said, I'm involved. And even if I wasn't, I'm a changed man."

"It's *Molly.*" Finally, she balked at Tony's refusal to play her game. Her mouth tightened, and her blue eyes narrowed. "Changed my ass," she grumbled, drawing the attention of guests at several nearby tables as she spun on her heel and walked away.

Angela edged out of the booth, then slid her hand into Tony's and nudged him to move.

"It hasn't been a month," Molly tossed over her shoulder.

Tony's head jerked, and his jaw jutted forward, but he kept his head held high, shoulders back as they wove through the tables to exit.

Once outside, he held the door for the couple shuffling up the sidewalk. The white-haired woman's age-spotted hand gripped her companion's arm, and she used a cane to assist the slight dragging of her left leg.

"Thank you." She beamed at Tony, though only the right side of her mouth turned up.

He watched the couple pass by. The expression on his face warmed Angela's heart.

His gaze shifted to scrutinize her after the couple went inside.

"What?" she asked.

"Nothing." He released the door, then guided her with a hand on her back.

Though he didn't say what was on his mind, his face reflected sadness. Longing. She'd bet he was envisioning his future.

How long had the couple been together? Fifty years? Sixty? Or maybe they'd only been together a few years. Maybe they'd found each other late in life.

Maybe one day, she wouldn't have to examine every face and situation for danger.

In ten or fifteen years, she could look Tony up. Only by then, he'd be married. Have a couple of kids. Be on a second career. Have a dog. She couldn't expect him to wait for her. Life wasn't fair.

She could always get a dog for protection and company. Better for safety than turning into a cat lady with a dozen standoffish felines.

The silent trek across the parking lot ended at his SUV. Neither opened the vehicle's door.

"I love you. We are going to figure this out." He pulled her into his arms, rocking slightly and stroking her back.

As if the heat and humidity weren't enough to make her melt into a puddle, his words made her insides quiver and her heart stop. Though she opened her mouth, her vocal cords suffered from sudden paralysis. Yeah, she loved him, too, but why did he have to say it? Not when she couldn't stay.

Dammit. She'd accept her own heartbreak. She didn't want to drive a stake through his heart, as well.

He turned up her face to meet his. The kiss was tender, gentle, and totally consuming.

"Meet me in the garage when I get home. Wearing your leather jacket."

"We going for another ride?"

"Kinda. If you're willing to give it a try."

A try ...? Oh! "Oh. And should I wear anything besides the jacket?"

"Your black lace thong would be good."

Tempted to back him up against the SUV right there in the parking lot, she took a half step out of his arms. He opened the door for her to get in.

"Text me when you're leaving for home."

Putting on his helmet, he shot her a libidinous grin. She checked the dashboard clock. Four hours until he got home. *What am I supposed to do for four hours?*

He roared off on the Harley before she could compose herself enough to insert the key in the ignition.

Why did he have to keep turning her world inside out, upside down, and spun around until she was dizzy?

Navigating down the boulevard, she played with new options for her future. She had enough money and convertible assets saved and stashed to live comfortably in Central America or the Caribbean under a new name. There she could buy a house or even a boat. Living with Tony on a sailboat, traveling to different exotic locations, definitely had appeal. They could offer day sails and snorkeling or scuba trips to tourists.

It was an alluring fantasy.

Only that life would cut Tony off from his family. They were too close for her to ask him to give that up. She couldn't ask him to give up his career, either. In a few years, he'd have in twenty years of service to retire from the Army with a full pension *if* he wanted. Though she didn't see him leaving then. Or being ready to spend his days lounging on a boat—even with her.

No. She needed to stick with the plan. Find a Bureau office where she'd feel safe enough. Create a new name. Since Angie Vincent would be too obvious, maybe Angie Davidson. Or Dalton. Tony's cover identity from their original assignment was less obvious than Vincent. Still, it would make her think about Tony every time she heard or said it. Not that she wanted to forget him—ever.

FORTY-ONE

AFTER LAST NIGHT'S ADVENTURES, Tony parked in the garage, lingering a moment in the event Angela appeared for a repeat performance.

Guess not. Okay, so his bike might not have been the most comfortable place to try and do it, but it had been creative foreplay. And hot.

Shit. Now he'd be walking inside with a hard-on. He didn't want Angela to think he wanted her sticking around only for the mind-blowing sex. Though her dangerous, adventurous side sure didn't hurt. He could spend a lifetime with her and never get bored. He shouldn't have texted her when he left post. She read him too well—probably knew what he was thinking, hoping.

As soon as he opened the door into the kitchen, he inhaled an unfamiliar but delicious aroma. The sweet scent of apples mixed with cinnamon and pastry. Angela paused from slicing up a head of red cabbage to stare at him. Yup. She'd seen the text based on the look she gave him.

"Smells great. You're not overdoing it, are you?"

That only amused her more. "I'm fine."

"What are we having?" He dropped his keys on the counter and moved closer. What looked like a strudel sat on a plate off to one side of the sink. On the stove, breaded cutlets sizzled in a frying pan.

"Tonight's dinner is a traditional German meal. You get Wiener schnitzel, parsley potatoes, cabbage, and apple strudel for dessert."

"This is great. What inspired a German feast?"

"I heard something today that reminded me of Germany. You've been taking such great care of me, I wanted to do something nice for you—that didn't involve sex."

"I'm not complaining about that. And I don't mind cooking. My grandmother and mom taught me to cook. It's in my blood." Or maybe it was marinara sauce in his veins.

"While you're a great chef, I'm pretty domestic, too. I didn't exactly get that passed down, but I've been cooking and taking care of myself since I was a teen." She turned back to the stove and stirred the cabbage in another skillet. "I enjoy cooking and learning new dishes. Tomorrow I can cook either a Middle Eastern or South American dish."

"Hmm. I think you should dress up, too. Got a belly-dancer costume?"

She chuckled. "Based on where I've been in the Middle East, I would be completely covered, including my face."

Her statement triggered memories of his last tour in Afghanistan. His forefinger traced his surgically repaired nose. "That doesn't work for me."

"So, a Venezuelan dish?"

"Sounds good. Especially if you keep up that sexy Spanish accent."

"Voy a hablar sólo en español si lo desea."

"Oh, baby."

"¿Ahora? ¿O después de la cena?"

Why did an accent have to be such a turn-on? Now or after dinner? Based on the dirty pots in the sink, she'd spent most of the afternoon fixing the German feast. Satisfy instant raging hard-on or appreciate her other gifts? "Got a German-wench costume?"

"Keine." She smacked the back of his head.

"No" was one of the few words of German he knew. "Sorry." He grinned at her, picturing her in a low-cut white top, short skirt with a white petticoat underneath, tall white stockings, hair in braids, and a stein of beer in her hand. Who would need other women when Ang could be them all? When was the last time he'd been this comfortable with a woman—in every way? Never.

The stare Ang fixed on him made him suspect she read his mind.

"You going to wear lederhosen?" This time she eyed him as if she pictured him in the leather shorts and silly suspenders.

"Yeah, uh, no."

"Too bad. You've got nice legs."

"I could be talked into a gladiator costume."

"Kinda stereotypical."

"But I could plunder and take you hostage."

"You're pushing it, Vincenti."

Several more insinuations came to mind. He held back to avoid being cuffed again. He loved the playful interaction—which they could both use right now—and for the rest of his life. "What can I do to help?"

"Grab plates, and I'll serve it up."

His mouth watered at the enticing smell of bay leaf and onion. Identifying everything by its German name, Angela loaded up generous portions. It made a colorful presentation with the cooked red cabbage, schnitzel, and roasted potatoes.

He finished off half his plate before he slowed down to ask what had been on his mind most of the afternoon. "Did you hear any updates from the Bureau?"

"Yes, only no new useful info. The bank in Singapore isn't willing to give any information on Austin Kufer that they got to open the account and—"

"Wait? Austin *Kufer*? I thought it was Cooper."

"I heard her wrong yesterday. It doesn't matter. They still aren't finding anything. I can keep looking at surveillance video captures, but…"

As she talked, he couldn't dismiss the name.

Kufer.

Austin Kufer.

It sounded familiar beforehand, but more so now.

He heard a female voice saying that name.

Taking another bite, he closed his eyes and tried to remember the place and person. Why had it stuck in his brain? Had he been a target on a mission?

No. A target he'd remember. Maybe an alias?

A mouthful of parsley potatoes became mashed potatoes by the time he swallowed them. He took a bite of schnitzel, chewing until no flavor remained.

Angela was silent, allowing him to trek back in the recesses of his mind.

He went to stab another piece of meat, and his fork clattered to the table. He hurriedly swallowed his food, so he could speak.

"Did Jarrod know about the contract on your life?"

"Yeah. I kinda slipped. He brought up us taking a trip to Rio together, and I mentioned returning to South America wasn't a good idea. That there were people there that wanted me dead. But I never mentioned names."

"Did he have access to your personnel file?"

"I don't know. Maybe with him leading the New York assignment. What are you saying?" Her brows dipped close together.

The initial rush of energy from connecting the name to the memory faded, leaving him drained like an empty pool. "I think Jarrod … I think he's Austin Kufer."

"No way."

"Why not?" He asked himself as much as her.

"Why would he? And I can't believe someone I slept with, your friend, would tell the cartel where to find me."

"First of all, he wasn't exactly my friend. We worked together—not by choice. As for telling the cartel, Jarrod has the skills to build and place that explosive himself." Each step his mind took down this path increased the sick feeling in his gut. "You said yourself, if it was someone who knew you, it had to be personal. Jarrod blames you for losing his gig with the contractor and—"

"I'm not to blame for him losing the job. He—"

"*He* sees it differently. Jarrod mentioned being axed because of you not wanting to go along with the mission you quit over. *And* he got hurt …"

"Again. Not my fault."

"But he's Jarrod. He has a history of taking risks and blaming others for anything he can."

"True, but…" She dropped her gaze to the far end of the table and bit her lip. "Not liking him aside, what makes you think it's him?"

He needed to push her beyond what she wanted to believe. Now if he could do it without revealing classified information.

"A couple of years back, Jarrod led a mission in Libya. You plan for everything, only this was one of those missions where everything that could go wrong did. Walt Shuler tangled with a Libyan operative and got cut up. We patched him up best we could." Tony skipped over how that turned out for the Libyan operative.

"We got to the airport, where things got worse. I created a diversion so Jarrod could get our package through security. Airport security hauled me off and threatened to throw me in prison—not what you want over there. But I managed to, uh, 'get released' from security and make a later flight." One to Brussels before the airport security guards got free and put out a security BOLO on him. "When I made it back here and debriefed, Jarrod said he ditched his backup passport and credit cards. I didn't question it at the time. Sounded plausible. I swear Sergeant Jewett said, 'We'll retire the Austin Kufer identity' and Jarrod said something like better to retire the ID than him."

By now, Angela's mouth hung open, her eyes fixed on him. The slight rise of her chest assured him she hadn't stopped breathing.

"Jarrod had already planned on taking a private security job rather than re-upping. His poor planning and the risks he exposed the team to showed he'd already mentally checked out. The colonel gave the next mission to Charlie Company. It was Carswell's last mission on the team."

"Ouch," Angela commiserated.

"Yeah. Private companies offer referral bonuses to get Spec Ops guys. After Jarrod left, he and his wife, Cheyenne, tried to recruit a couple of the team. The idea of working for Jarrod—with no rules of engagement—and him thinking he didn't have to answer to a chain of command …? He didn't get any takers." You couldn't spend a huge paycheck if you were in jail or weren't alive. "The way Jarrod always covered his ass, I can see him stashing away an ID for an emergency out. Especially if he thought it would be untraceable."

Angela pushed away the food she hadn't touched since he mentioned Jarrod's name. "I may not be his favorite person, but trying to kill me … I don't see it."

It poked him like a sharp stick that she defended Jarrod. He inhaled and started counting in his head. By the time he reached seven, he could see her point. Maybe his personal biases made him see things that weren't there. He wanted so badly to protect her. How hard should he push?

Angela stared at her plate, worrying her bottom lip. She'd been trying to convince him it was too dangerous for her to stay—and he didn't want to accept it. Now, he'd flipped the tables. If he could persuade her to trust him on this, and he was right, it might be the breakthrough he needed to convince her to give them a shot.

FORTY-TWO

ANGELA SLID out from under the sheet, trying not to wake Tony now that he'd finally stopped tossing and turning. She scooped up his T-shirt and pulled it on. In the family room, she sat on the sofa and hugged a throw pillow to her chest.

Faint light shone in from the front porch light. The refrigerator hummed in the kitchen, and her mind whirled.

She lost track of time as she sat in the dark, trying to get in Jarrod's head. Tony padded into the room in only a pair of gym shorts. She hadn't heard the bedroom door open.

He plunked down beside her. "Couldn't sleep?"

She shook her head.

"Hope I wasn't snoring."

"Nope."

"Then you were thinking about Jarrod."

"I doubt you're shocked."

He shrugged. "You willing to consider it's possible?"

"How sure are you about the name?"

"Pretty damned sure."

She didn't doubt his memory, even when it came to

obscure details like favorite coffee flavors. "A name that he may or may not have had an ID for isn't evidence."

He rested his forearms on his bare thighs, staring down at his joined hands. "There's something more. It's not evidence per se, it just ..."

"What?"

He exhaled, and his face muscles relaxed and sagged. She waited, scarcely able to breathe. The lumps in her stomach grew like aggressive cancer.

"When Jarrod came to see you in the hospital—"

"He did?" Had she been so zoned out on meds she didn't remember?

"You were asleep when he came. The way he acted ... at the time, I thought he still had feelings for you. Looking back, I can't help but wonder ..."

"If he came to kill me?" It seemed like a stretch. She wanted to believe it was a mile-long stretch.

"It was the middle of the night—like the dead of night—not long before the shift changeover. He made it sound like he'd come from the office, but he'd changed out of his suit and wore a ball cap. I didn't think about it then. I was kinda out of it myself. He acted all concerned about your recovery with the coma and all. It didn't feel authentic. Like he was digging for info."

She had trouble envisioning Jarrod coming to check on her—even if she'd once done the same for him. "It's not proof. I can't ask the Bureau to investigate one of their own without something more substantial."

"We can't have the Bureau involved."

"Why not?" She didn't like where this was headed.

"Because if it is Jarrod, and he gets tipped off that we suspect he's involved, he's got the passport and half a million dollars to disappear. Along with the skills that guarantee we never find him."

Fuck. "You're right. So, we look for him on the tape?" Knowing when and who to look for could narrow it down to a doable task. Maybe.

"He's too smart for that. He would've hidden his face. Used the back entrance to avoid cameras. He wouldn't leave a credit card trail."

Again, Tony was right. Damn Jarrod. Between his time in Special Forces and the FBI, Jarrod knew what they'd be looking for to track down an assassin. "And you're sure he could bypass my alarm and set the bomb?"

"I know I could," Tony said with no trace of doubt.

She saw the prospect of concrete evidence pulled back out to sea by a tsunami. "What are our options?"

"I'm not sure. We need to get some sleep and think on it." He rose and extended his hand.

She let him pull her to her feet. "Come on, then." She tugged him toward the bedroom. "It's going to take some very angry sex before I get any sleep." Even that might not work.

"So, you're going to use me for sex?"

"You got a problem with that?"

"Yeah, right."

She stopped in the middle of the hallway and pushed him against the wall. Going up on tiptoes, she molded her body to his and pressed her lips to his mouth.

His lips parted to welcome her tongue. His fingers tangled into her hair, forcing her head to comply with his directions.

Need pulsed through her, and she ran her hands along his smooth, hot flesh, then underneath the waistband of his shorts, pushing them down past his hips. He hiked up her leg, grinding against her. The kisses grew fiercer, more demanding. He lifted her from the ground and spun them both around so that he had *her* pinned against the wall.

"You're so beautiful." He paused, staring into her eyes— only her eyes. "I love you."

"I love you, too." She didn't hesitate to tell him this time. No matter how this turned out, she needed to give him that gift.

Despite the frenzied need of seconds ago, they remained still, their eyes locked on each other. Smiles on their faces as they focused on here, this second, and let the moment sink in.

Tony's eyebrows rose hopefully.

Oh, yeah. Back to where we were.

———

TONY'S BREATHING had fallen into the heavy, steady rhythm of sleep. She tucked into his shoulder, and her head rose with each breath. Normally, she didn't want anyone touching her when she slept. Tonight, she took comfort in the contact.

The first time, in the hallway, had been fast and furious. Hot. Satisfying. Definitely memorable. But it only stoked the fire. Her body still rode the wave of orgasmic bliss, the wave cresting but not breaking, after Tony carried her into the bedroom where he'd taken his time.

It worked. Cleared her head enough to gain a fresh perspective. Though she hated to ruin the serenity, she set her thoughts to the possibility Jarrod had tried to kill her. If so, it torpedoed her plans to stay with the Bureau. Eventually, he'd find out she was alive. Then what? Staying with Tony held the same risks—and extended them to him.

If it was Jarrod, her only choice might be to disappear.

Play dead.

Let him win to survive.

She made out Tony's profile in the darkness, praying Jarrod had nothing to do with the attempt on her life.

ANGELA SHUFFLED INTO THE KITCHEN, her eyes barely open.

Tony waited, watching as she poured coffee into the mug he'd left for her on the counter. He gave her a moment to take a few sips of the potent brew. "Good morning."

"That's debatable," she said, her voice raspy. She plopped onto the seat.

"I guess it's my fault you didn't get much sleep."

"Directly. And indirectly."

"I prefer the direct method."

With one eye open, she smiled over her coffee at him. "Me, too."

"Need to let that coffee kick in before we have a strategy session?"

"We need to go see Jarrod."

He resisted the urge to jump to his feet and head out.

"I'm hoping he's not involved, though," she continued. "And if that's indeed the case, I don't want to subject him to a witch hunt and taint his career with unjustified accusations."

Tony lost his battle to keep his mouth shut. "Why don't you want it to be Jarrod?"

"Because if we bust him, it gets out I'm alive, and I'm back to having a price on my head. I have to go underground."

Damn. Now he didn't want it to be Jarrod, either. That wouldn't solve their problem. It made it worse. Way worse. Only his gut wouldn't let it go. "But if he is …"

"Just because we walk in, Jarrod isn't going to confess.

"It might take a while, but I could persuade him to confess."

"You can't torture it out of him."

"He's trained to endure it, but he doesn't have a real high threshold for pain."

"He could be innocent," she said like the devil's own advocate.

I still wouldn't mind beating the shit out of him for the way he treated you. "I'm not going to kill him. Or cut anything off." *At least nothing vital.* She fixed him with a stern expression reminiscent of the strict nuns from his childhood. Had he been thinking aloud? "How do you propose to find out if he's involved then?"

"Jarrod has a tell. Not when he bluffs in poker—he knows you're watching for one—but when he lies, he has a tell. And I know what it is," she said with absolute confidence. Light glinted in her eyes.

Tony listened, though waterboarding Jarrod was still an alternative. Or pulling out his teeth. He'd start with an incisor since Jarrod was a vain prick and would hate that. "Say you decide he is involved, what then? Will it be enough to get the Bureau to hold him? I'm not letting the son of a bitch slip away."

"Might want to bring along flex-cuffs. Or would he be able to get out of those as easily as handcuffs?"

"I'll bring enough to subdue him. Though getting them on him might be a challenge," he admitted. "Jarrod would rather die than go to jail. When we were overseas, he joked that if he ever got captured, Mack was to take him out with a clean headshot rather than let him be tortured. He doesn't like confined spaces, either. Liked to ride with the windows down. Taps his fingers when he's in an elevator. The reason he didn't join the Navy and become a SEAL was the possibility of being on a ship in those eighteen-inch berths or, God forbid, he had to be on a submarine."

"I'll let you cuff him and put him in a dark closet until the Feds show up if he's guilty."

That sounded good. "How soon until you're ready to hit the road?"

"You want to leave this morning? What about planning?" she asked.

"We'll do it in the car. You can sleep afterward. I'll drive. If we can get there in daylight. Catching him at home gives us an advantage over showing up at Federal Plaza."

"I can be ready in half an hour." She didn't debate the wisdom of winging it.

That gave him time to do a little investigative work. Blood raced through his body, providing energy and building his urgency. For this, he'd take the chance the team wouldn't get called for a mission, and he'd be back Monday morning for work.

He strode to his bedroom. Cuffs. Kimber. Vest. Recorder —he could use his phone. Binoculars and better pack the night-vision goggles, too. He added two changes of clothes, MREs, cash, and a fake ID to his mental packing list as he pulled a bag from his closet.

He paused for a moment. *God, give us a hand here.* He still believed in the power of prayer, and right now, he needed some divine intervention.

FORTY-THREE

OUTSIDE JARROD'S house on Staten Island, Tony sat lethally still. The tree-lined street of neatly maintained clapboard houses was quiet. The leaves and tree branches swayed and danced due to the pending summer storm darkening the sky. The good thing was the weather might keep any nosy dog-walking neighbors from calling the police to report a suspicious vehicle parked on their street.

It'd only been about five minutes, but static energy filled the SUV. The distant flash of lightning and rumble of thunder increased the nervous tension and made Angela's limbs ache. They were here and needed to follow through—only would she like what they found out?

On the first part of the drive up, she and Tony had run through scenarios for confronting Jarrod. They'd were on the same page with showing up in the hope that seeing her alive rattled him. That'd be key for her discovering if he'd been involved. From there, the rest of the plan was freer flowing than she preferred, but she trusted Tony—trusted him with her life, even after all the years of trusting only herself.

"I say we go now." His hand moved to the door handle.

"Lights are on. TV's on in a back room. The minivan's gone. Jarrod wouldn't drive it." Tony tapped a finger on the Google map image of Jarrod's house.

"His wife could be out, but she may have left the kids here."

"That could work to our advantage."

Tony had a point—though, with Jarrod's impulsive nature, it might not impact his response. She took several deep breaths and debated the possibility of kids in the house. "We look inside. If we see kids, we knock."

"Agreed."

With the goal of a face-to-face with Jarrod, spending time sitting here wasn't going to garner any vital information. Time to get this over with.

A simple head nod had Tony out of the car. She kept an eye on the street while he dug through his gear. With her back to the SUV, she tucked her Glock into the waistband of her jeans and pulled her top down to conceal it in case the neighbors were watching. Tony seemed less concerned as he put on his Kevlar vest and pulled his shirt back on over it.

He stuffed a couple pairs of flex-cuffs in his jeans pocket. "If we don't need them for Jarrod, sure we can find another use for them later."

The suggestion took off the edge enough to draw the full breath she needed. It gave her something to look forward to once they got past dealing with Jarrod.

They crossed the street and approached the house from the far side of the narrow drive separating Jarrod's house from the one next door. Tony glanced in the window of the dark sedan parked between the houses before striding to the front porch.

They scooted past the sidelights, using the solid door as shelter. Tony turned his phone in a semi-circle in front of the glass, videoing the interior, then examining the clip. "It's clear."

She reached out, but he stopped her before she pressed the doorbell. Releasing her arm, he tried the knob. When it didn't turn, he dropped to one knee, then swapped his phone for a leather case containing lock-picking tools.

"This is so illegal," she stated.

"Not as illegal as murder."

True, but the end didn't always justify the means. Talk about being a hypocrite.

Tony rose to his feet. "Go ahead. You can say you found it unlocked."

Like Jarrod would believe that. She was still an accessory to breaking and entering. They turned on the record function on their phones before pocketing them. She turned the knob and gently pushed the door open, listening for children's voices or the telltale beep of an alarm system. Nope. Good to go.

Tony entered first. He glided silently through the foyer, past the stairway leading to the dark second floor. The front room had only a small desk with an office chair and floor lamp, giving off a Spartan vibe. She'd expected living room furniture or toys.

An announcer's muted voice came from whatever sporting event was on the TV. They moved down the hallway, past a closet, and the open door of a half bath. A framed family picture sat on the hallway table along with a set of keys, a bowl of change, wallet, and pieces of mail.

The full impact of invading Jarrod's home hit her. She wanted to grab Tony and get out. Do this another way. Her heart beat so hard her body shook. What were the chances she could change his mind?

She froze when Tony crossed the entranceway into the next room.

A deep, startled hoot sounded along with glass hitting the hardwood floor.

"What the fuck? Vincenti? Jesus Christ. I could have shot you. What the—"

She stepped forward. Jarrod's words stopped, and his mouth dropped open. His hands hung at his sides. No gun. Thank God. A beer bottle lay on the floor, a foamy puddle glistened in the light.

"Angelique. You're ..."

She cringed to hear Jarrod use her birth name. The name she'd gone by when they'd been together. "Alive?"

"Obviously. It's great, but what happened?"

"When I took her back to D.C., someone had disabled her security system." Tony's voice possessed a calm, controlling quality.

The left side of Jarrod's mouth twitched as Tony sketched out what happened.

"You remember the Vasquez family put a bounty on her life?" Tony continued.

"Really?"

Her arm jerked of its own accord. "It's why I said I didn't want to go to Rio," she responded.

"Oh. Yeah. You never mentioned who. You'd think they'd have dropped that after all this time. So, what happened?" He tried a classic-Jarrod redirect. His gaze darted around, not making contact with Tony or her.

"I called the Bureau in, and they found a bomb in my condo."

"Jesus. It's good you found it. So, you fake your death. Smart. I get you want to keep it secret, but you could have called to let me know instead of breaking in my house."

Jarrod took a step away from the couch, his face wearing a smile like a plastic Halloween mask concealing what lay beneath.

"That's not why we're here." Tony's voice dropped, his tone laced with malice.

A shiver ran up her spine. Right now, she could envision Tony killing to protect her.

"What? You need some Bureau resources to investigate? I can make a few calls."

"The Bureau's already traced the money from a Vasquez account to a bank in Singapore," Tony told him.

"Damn. You able to get any info then?" Jarrod bent over and picked up the beer bottle from the floor.

She couldn't see his eyes, but her gaze never left him as he set the bottle on the end table, not that it'd be much of a weapon.

"Account's in the name of an Austin Kufer. That ring any bells?"

Jarrod appeared to contemplate, his mouth pursed, and his head shook slowly back and forth. It took several seconds for him to visibly breathe. A chill spread through her despite the heat radiating off Tony's body.

"They run the name through Interpol?" Jarrod asked.

"They did, but no hits. Not that I'm surprised. I don't think that alias was ever used. Didn't you say you ditched it after the fiasco at the airport in Libya?"

"What are you talking about?" he gruffed out. "You think I'd forget a cover ID?" Jarrod took another step closer to the bookcases that lined the back wall.

"No. I don't think you'd forget. And I'm sure Staff Sergeant Jewett kept a record."

It was like watching two animals readying to battle. Jarrod had answered every question with his own—leaving no doubt in her mind that he'd been involved. How deep, she couldn't say.

She held onto the microscopic hope that he'd only fed them her name and location. That Jarrod hadn't grown so callous that he'd kill for money. Yet remembering his willingness to torture innocent civilians in Afghanistan, she knew it wouldn't be a huge leap to cross that threshold of justification.

Jarrod's eyes narrowed, and one side of his mouth turned up in a cold sneer that made her skin crawl.

"I told you, I dumped a passport in the airport trash can on that mission. Couldn't risk both of us getting nabbed by security with multiple IDs. Now, if someone found it and used it, I can't be held liable."

"That's gonna be your story? Or that someone set you up?" Tony mocked Jarrod.

Hate brewed in Jarrod's darkening eyes when his gaze shifted to her.

"This is all your fault. This vendetta to *fuck up my life* like you have every guy you let get in your pants. You should watch your back, Vincenti."

She lunged to shut the bastard up. Only he maneuvered to grab her around the waist, using her momentum against her. She crashed to the floor, then struck the paneled doors of the bookcase. Her head exploded in pain, and sparks of light clouded her vision.

She reached for her Glock. Her hand came up empty. When she turned her head to see what was happening, more pain resounded through her skull. Jarrod had moved out of reach, his arm extended. His hand held *her* weapon, pointed at Tony's head.

"Don't try it." Jarrod's voice was a savage growl. "Put your weapon on the floor and kick it to me. You were always too predictable, Angelique. You let emotions get the best of you. Thanks for that."

Tony held his Kimber by two fingers and leaned over to set it on the floor. His eyes darted to where she lay a few feet away on Jarrod's other side.

The same icy fingers gripped her throat as when Hakim had beaten her to her purse. Only this time, the gun was pointed at Tony by someone with everything to lose. This was her fault, and she had to do something.

"Stay down, Ang, or I will shoot him."

"Why? Why would you decide to kill me?" She tried to draw Jarrod's attention her way.

"Killing you wasn't originally my plan. But you were shot, flatlined twice, and the surgeon said it didn't look good. I figured I should cash in on your death. Claim *I* killed you. Only. You. Didn't. Die. You already cost me my job by running your mouth. Fucked things up letting my wife know about us—"

"That's on you. You lied—"

"I told you what you wanted to hear. But that wasn't enough for you. You had to blow my first solo case with the Bureau and let al-Shehri get away. You owe me. And since Vasquez paid me a retainer, either I do job, or he kills me. The explosive in your bed was supposed to finish the job. But, this time, you lose.

"You won't get away with this." Tony hadn't kicked the gun away, but he'd taken a step backward.

"Watch me. Wait, you won't get to." Jarrod sounded nearly delusional in his conviction.

"What about your family?" Angela took a stab at any remaining humanity to get his focus on her and give Tony an opening.

Jarrod scoffed. "A little late for that. Cheyenne took the

kids and moved out weeks ago. Just as well with all her bitching about me not being a good husband or father. Not a good enough provider."

Her hope of Tony kicking the gun her way died when Jarrod motioned to Tony.

"Now back up." Jarrod squatted to pick it up.

Tony was a blur of motion. His leg struck Jarrod, knocking him on his ass. Before he could aim, Tony was on him. The two rolled across the floor, tussling for control of her Glock. A hand shot out, reaching for Tony's Kimber. It skittered further away from her. She pushed up onto her knees and launched forward.

Two shots rang out before she reached the weapon.

Her hand grasped the gun. Her fingers instinctively wrapped around the textured grip and slid over the trigger. She flipped her body, raising her arms into firing position.

One body lay prone.

Tony's body.

Jarrod, weapon in hand, lurched to his feet.

Tony emitted a guttural groan—it was better than silence.

Blood dripped from Jarrod's nose down his chin. He lifted his arm, aiming at Tony's head.

"Don't do it!" she ordered.

As if playing out in slow motion, Jarrod turned his head her way. Not a trace of fear shone in his eyes. He smirked at her, then turned back to Tony.

She didn't hesitate to pull the trigger.

Jarrod's head snapped to the side. The pounding in her head and the strong recoil from Tony's Kimber caused her second shot to go wide. Or it missed because Jarrod's arm dropped. The gun tumbled from his hand, and his body crumpled to the floor.

Angela scrambled over and secured her Glock. Nudging

Jarrod with her foot produced no movement. Though his chest didn't move, she didn't trust him. She kept out of reach, training her gun on him as she moved around to his face. His mouth gaped open, and his eyes stared unseeing. Even Jarrod couldn't fake blown pupils.

Still holding her breath, she spun on her heel. "Are you hit? Where?"

Pain contorted Tony's face. "Vest. Be … okay. Gotta … catch my breath. Your head?"

"Rang my bell is all."

"You weren't … supposed to rush him," he scolded through gritted teeth. "Should've stayed behind me."

"He pissed me off."

"But I had on the vest."

Thank God he had it on. Her hands trembled as she lifted his shirt. Relief flooded through her. Two flattened slugs were embedded side by side in the vest. However, they'd been fired at such close range they could inflict blunt force trauma, especially so tightly grouped.

"Lie still. We need to call this in. I hate to do this to you, but I need your phone."

"What? Ooh." He grimaced when he raised his hips, and she reached underneath to pull his phone from his back pocket.

"Gonna need you to make the call, too. Better not to have my name or voice on the 9-1-1 call." Great, how was she going to avoid being exposed when the cops showed up?

The shattered screen on Tony's phone evidenced his struggle with Jarrod. But, hallelujah, it was still recording. Damn brilliant call on Tony's part. She pulled out her phone to get the Bureau's New York number.

Jarrod's lifeless body looked smaller sprawled on the

floor, less threatening as she searched for the number. "I didn't want him dead."

"Jarrod wasn't goin' to jail. He didn't give ya a choice. Took the coward's way out." Pain punctuated his words.

She dialed Tony's phone and held it to his ear. Listening to him make the call to the Bureau, she let his assurance settle in. Jarrod knew she'd shoot him to keep him from killing Tony, but would he have shot his former teammate? The two rounds in Tony's vest said he would. And she would have been next. She had to take him out first.

Tony requested they get in touch with Special Agent in Charge Grochowski, masterfully delivering urgency while providing the minimum information necessary.

"Now, we're calling 9-1-1, and you are requesting an ambulance for yourself."

"It's only a cracked rib. We should wait. Give the Bureau a head start on getting here," he said.

"The neighbors probably called the police. Better to get ahead of it. And you may have a collapsed lung, so you're getting checked out."

"I know what a cracked rib feels like—"

"Don't piss me off, Vincenti."

Tony gave a short laugh, *"Ow, ow, ow."* He winced. "Yes, ma'am. Saw what happened to the last guy who pissed you off."

"Shut up and kiss me." She bent over until their lips met.

The adrenaline surge faded. Though she had no desire to remain in the room with Jarrod's body, she didn't dare move Tony or risk compromising the scene. Instead, she slumped to the floor, resting at his side while he made the 9-1-1 call.

The sound of sirens stirred her too soon. Off to stonewall the cops, and hopefully not end up in handcuffs.

FORTY-FOUR

THE MEDICS HAD TOLD Angela which hospital they were taking him to, so where the hell was she? Tony couldn't call her since he'd turned his phone over as evidence.

He swung his legs over the side of the hospital bed. Waves of pain shot through his chest and radiated to his side. He gritted his teeth to get through the agony.

Okay, he'd give it another half hour, then he'd find a phone and call the Bureau. Then the police. Hell, despite the scary fist-sized—and spreading—bruise, he'd walk out bare-chested, though it could make getting a cab tricky. She had to be somewhere. He eased his legs back onto the mattress—but he wasn't closing his eyes. And if the nurses tried to give him pain meds again, he was getting out of here, paperwork or no paperwork.

When the door opened after what seemed like an eternity, he put on his game face, ready to throw down with whichever doctor or nurse tried to keep him here. Instead, Angela appeared.

"Thank God. I was afraid they'd taken you in." He switched from combat mode to stand-down.

"No, but they did have a lot of questions."

"Have you got my clothes?"

"They're in the car. Are they releasing you?" She winced at the bruise as she came to his side.

"Now that you're here, I can go."

She cocked her head, studying him, then pressed the call button.

Damn.

"Can I help you?" The nurse sounded exasperated.

"Is Sergeant Vincenti being released?" Angela fixed him with her no-bullshit stare.

"We're preparing his Discharge Against Medical Advice papers now."

Busted.

"That won't be necessary. He's spending the night."

"Come on. They can't do anything for cracked ribs." He struggled to sit up, only her hand pressed on his shoulder and pushed him back. It took an effort not to flinch.

"Well, I can't leave town yet. Grochowski needs to have the Bureau's investigators go through the evidence, and the police need your statement. Did they send someone over?"

"Yeah, a local detective." *A prick.* "I told him the FBI would be handling the investigation due to security issues. He insisted on running a GSR test to see if I fired a gun. You worried?" With Angela here, he started to relax.

"No. Grochowski said he could overlook the breaking and entering considering the circumstances. Released me on my own recognizance. He did ask me to stick around until tomorrow. And you need to take it easy." She pressed the call button again. "Can you bring Sergeant Vincenti some pain meds? Make it a big-ass needle."

"Ha, ha. I'll sleep better away from this place. We can get a hotel room. You don't like hospitals."

"Not when *I'm* the patient. But if you end up with a collapsed lung, they're better able to help you than I can. Deal with it. My turn to sit by your bedside."

He'd be pissed if it were anyone else insisting on keeping him here. He guessed he could take a dose of meds now that she was by his side. "You can climb in and—"

"With your cracked ribs? I don't think so."

"Can't blame a guy for trying."

Angela leaned over. Her lips brushed his on the first pass. Then her tongue wet his lips. His right hand copped a feel of her breast. She stopped him when he attempted to slip his hand under her shirt, but didn't stop kissing him until the nurse came in.

The glint in the nurse's eye warned him she aimed to deliver a little karma of her own over his being a difficult patient. However, Angela being safe made it worth the pain when the needle jabbed him in his ass. The blonde in scrubs departed with a masochistic smile.

"You know, with Jarrod dead, he can't hurt you or say anything to anyone."

"We also don't know how much information he gave to the Vasquez family. Names. Background. He had to convince them he had the right target. It's why I wanted him alive."

Shit. They were screwed with Jarrod alive and could be just as screwed with him dead. Could be. Maybe they'd find something in their investigation. The pain started to fade, and numbness took hold of his brain, lulling him to sleep.

"Don't let them cut me open or change my face."

"I won't. I like you the way you are."

Her face became blurry, and the room got darker. "Stay with me." His lips were thick, the words slurred.

"I promise. I'll be right here when you wake up."

"No, I …" *I mean forever.*

FORTY-FIVE

T ONY CLIPPED a shooting target to the line, then put on his ear protectors. It was good to be at work, even if this morning's five-mile run made him think over not sleeping in and lounging around with Angela for another day or two. Spending time together while he'd been sidelined the past week kept him from going stir-crazy, though they still danced around a final decision on their future.

He emptied the magazine, smoothly reloading his Kimber to fire again. The air hung thick with smoke, and the sound of gunfire surrounded him. He pulled in his target to examine his hits. Though shooting produced a slight throb of pain, his cracked ribs hadn't affected his aim.

Striding to the table holding the ammo, Tony stood next to Mack and reloaded his emptied magazines. Chief Lundgren's shrill whistle pierced the air. The gunfire died out while the operators got each other's attention. Lundgren motioned for the men to follow him.

While a sudden changeup in their daily training didn't necessarily mean anything, Lundgren's brisk pace toward the command post triggered an urgency that made the rest of the team hustle to keep up.

Inside the conference room, Colonel Mahinis waited. An image of two men, both in traditional Middle Eastern garb, projected on the board.

Mack stopped to analyze the picture. "Is that El Waddi?"

The colonel nodded.

"Who's that with him?" Dominguez took a seat at one of the long tables.

"We don't have a clear shot of his face," the colonel said, clicking to another image of Mohand El Waddi, an Arabian sheik known for funneling millions of dollars from his oil profits to extremist groups. The next picture showed the profile of the other man.

Tony's body went frigid. "That's al-Shehri."

"We don't have a good enough picture to run facial recognition; however, Intel believes *it is* Samir al-Shehri. They were spotted by a CIA operative just after ten hundred hours our time," the colonel said.

"Where?" Lundgren asked.

"Hotel in Riyadh, Saudi Arabia."

Not exactly a friendly country from which to extract a non-willing detainee, Tony mused.

"They went to a room together. After their meet-up, El Waddi stayed, but al-Shehri—if it's him—left the hotel. The operative was able to tail his party to another hotel."

Yes! Goosebumps erupted on Tony's arms.

"Probably not staying at the same hotel for security reasons. El Waddi has reservations for two more days. We don't have information on al-Shehri. It's likely he used an alias, but the Agency is trying to get a photo to run facial recognition to confirm his identity. In the event it's him, we want a team in place. We can't afford to lose him again." The colonel paused to let that sink in. "Charlie Company is on short call, but I'd like Bravo to come up with a plan and—"

"Hell, yes," Lundgren stated. "We want this."

The team echoed his sentiments.

Except for Tony.

"May have to shadow him to a new destination where we can do a grab-and-go." The colonel surveyed the group.

"Not a problem. We've got a vested interest in this." Lundgren crossed his arms in an authoritative manner that said Charlie Company would spend their time hanging around at Bragg.

"I figured as much." The colonel showed a rare smile. Throughout the room, heads bobbed in agreement. "That file's all we've got for now. Start working up your plan. Intel will feed you anything else we get. I'll brief Charlie Company when they get in from the field."

The colonel handed the files to Lundgren, who handed a folder to each man. The team scurried to take seats.

Except for Tony.

Chief Lundgren and the colonel stared at him.

He didn't speak. Not yet. He swallowed, moving the lump lodged in his throat down an inch. "Are you going to need me on this?" *Damn, did I really ask that?*

"Your ribs bothering you?" Lundgren asked.

"No. The ribs won't slow me down." His hand rubbed over the bruised area. "It's Ang."

"I thought she was doing well considering ..." Lundgren's genuine concern made this harder to put out there.

"She's doing good and hoping Doc Rivers gives her the okay to go back to work soon. But, with the whole pretending she's dead, she's not going back to D.C. We want to give things a shot, so if I could transfer to Lewis or MacDill, she could go to the Bureau's Seattle or Tampa office."

"You want to leave the team?" Surprise tainted Colonel Mahinis's question.

Mack's head jerked up. "What?"

The entire team's attention locked on Tony.

"I don't want to leave this team, but I will if that's what it takes for me and her to be together. Charlotte is too far to commute. It might not be the top tier, but at least I'd stay in a Special Ops unit." The job wasn't enough anymore. Not since Angela turned his world inside out. He'd go on loan to the SEALs in DEV Group if needed. Hell, he'd join the Air Force, Marines, or work as a freakin' mall "cop" to keep her in his life.

"Isn't it early to make that kind of commitment?" Lundgren asked.

"I want her to know I'm all in. If it doesn't work out, I could come back, if you'd have me."

"She works great with our team," Dominguez said.

"Even though she'd be an asset, we're not adding a woman to the team," Lundgren stated, clearly amused.

"She's using my language CDs. Her Pashto is already nearly as good as yours." Tony threw that out there since they desperately needed women translators to deal with Afghan locals.

"Besides the rules and regs, she'd be a distraction."

"I know." Damn, did he know. "Maybe it's time to move to the next phase of my life, and if this is what it takes …" He couldn't live with the what-ifs if he let her go.

"With where we'll be, we're going to need you on this. You're our best shot at getting close to al-Shehri. We need to grab him without it becoming an international incident. Can you wait to decide until you get back?" Lundgren pressed.

"Alternative is to go ahead and send Charlie team," Mahinis reminded them.

Pressure weighed on Tony. The timing sucked. He didn't want to let the team down. He wanted to get al-Shehri. But he needed time to convince Angela they could have the future they both wanted despite the threats from her past.

If he deployed now, he could come home to an empty house. An empty future.

Every member of the team was top-notch and highly trained. Only he was the one with the best ability to blend in where they were going.

Where *they* were going.

He'd already decided. Yes, he had to see this mission through. Then he could leave the team with peace about it.

TONY PASSED through the kitchen to the family room. He heard Angela repeat a phrase in Pashto.

Startled at seeing him, she pulled off her headset. She paused the program on her laptop and set it beside her on the couch.

"Accent sounds good," he said.

"Thanks. Words are similar to Arabic, but the different sentence structure takes some getting used to. What time is it?" Her brow wrinkled as she glanced around.

"Almost fifteen hundred. Something came up. I need to go out of town."

"Today?"

He nodded. "We got a lead on al-Shehri's location."

"Seriously?" Angela leaned forward, her eyes wide. "Is he in the States?"

"I can't say," he answered, though he shook his head.

"But you get to bring him in?" Excitement shone in her eyes.

"Hopefully. Sorry I won't be here to take you to see Doc tomorrow."

"I can manage fine on my own."

He forced a smile as her independent nature roared. Working on her Pashto kept her mind occupied, but he knew she needed to feel useful. "Will you promise me you'll be here when I get back?"

"How long will you be gone?"

Tony shrugged, not liking that she'd responded with a question instead of the promise he needed. "A few days, at least. Likely longer." Hopefully not longer, but al-Shehri was enough of a high-value target that if they did find him, they'd stay on his ass as long as it took to get him.

"I'm expecting Doc to release me, then I can have Kathryn check on openings."

"Has she mentioned anything in Seattle or Tampa?"

"She's waiting until I'm cleared to contact them. Don't want to have to explain I'm on leave after being shot. Fewer questions the better with establishing a new ID."

"Are you willing to wait for an opening there?"

"She knows those are my top choices."

Tony fought against the escalating frustration. "I want us to be able to discuss this, not to come back and find you gone."

"If something is open, I'll let you know where I am. It's not like I'm going to disappear."

He broke eye contact, wanting to believe that. The Bureau hadn't found anything else on the communication between Jarrod and the Vasquez family. Nothing beyond the texts on a disposable cell phone with pictures of her and the obituary identifying her as FBI. It'd been sufficient for Vasquez to pay Carswell half a million dollars. There hadn't been anything out there to identify Carswell and make the family suspicious that he was also dead. Tony hoped it was enough to reassure Angela.

"I love you." He spoke it with his voice. His eyes. His heart slowed as if it might stop. He meant it with all his being.

"I love you, too."

It reassured him that she didn't hesitate to say it back. But was it enough? Did she trust she'd be safe. Did she trust him?

"Come on." He tugged on her hand. "I've got an hour to pack before I have to leave. I can pack in fifteen minutes."

"Mmm. You have something in mind for the other forty-five minutes?"

"I have *someone* in mind." He pulled her with him to the bedroom. Time for a reminder of what she'd be missing out on if she left.

FORTY-SIX

THE TEAM REMAINED SEATED as the jet taxied to the private terminal adjacent to the King Khalid International Airport in Riyadh, but their energy crackled in the cabin.

Tony gave Mack and Chief Lundgren another once-over. He kicked himself for not bringing colored contact lenses, but if they kept sunglasses on, no one would see their blue eyes. The *ghutra* cloth covered their hair, and Tony had applied make-up to darken their fair skin. From a distance, the mascara on their eyebrows and fake facial hair looked natural.

The one problem he couldn't do anything about was the chief's height, which tended to draw a second glance. Attention they didn't need.

The rest of the team had been easier to camouflage by simply donning the traditional white *thwab* and headdress and some foundation. They just had to make the short trek through the terminal to the vehicles the Agency had waiting for them. That part should be easier than most of their missions. They still needed to get eyes on al-Shehri before they could formulate a plan to bring him down once and for all.

Tony had waited so long for this. Was risking so much. The Intel had to be good. He couldn't let al-Shehri slip away again.

The moment their pilot lowered the steps to the tarmac, heat blasted into the body of the aircraft. Welcome to Riyadh, where a hundred-and-ten degrees was the norm. Still, better than Kandahar, with its IEDs and mortar attacks to contend with. As long as local authorities didn't pick them up, they'd be good—but finding al-Shehri was likely to come with a slew of complications.

Each of them grabbed their suitcase and the bags with their gear and weapons from the jet's cargo hold. They passed through the Saudi Aramco terminal without a problem, finding the two white SUVs the Agency left for them in the lot.

Even with the dark-tinted windows, the interiors of the vehicles were like a furnace after a short stint parked in the sun. Mack started the engine of the one he slid into and cranked the air conditioner to full blast while they loaded their bags. When Tony climbed in the back seat with Grant, it still had to be a couple hundred degrees. It only added to the fire in his belly. Let the hunt begin.

From the airport they passed through a mix of architectural styles, and closer to the city, palm trees lined the streets. In the distance, several impressive modern buildings rose above the rest to stand out against the skyline.

"The building with the hole is the Kingdom Centre. El Waddi is staying there in the Four Seasons Hotel." Lundgren pointed out the windshield. "We'll do a pass-by, but head to where our CIA contact is staking out al-Shehri."

After a quick loop around the Kingdom Centre, Lundgren

plugged in the GPS coordinates to take them to their destination. The further they went, the more the atmosphere changed. Less Western influences. The few women, covered from hair to toe and most with veils, struck Tony as odd and oppressive but signaled to him that he had to get in the right mindset for this role. Accomplish this mission, and he could get home to the woman who mattered most.

The way Grant stared out the window, taking in the sights, amused Tony for some reason. Their recent tour in Afghanistan had been Grant's first time in the Middle East, and Kandahar offered a stark contrast to Riyadh.

"You're right about half the men dressing in these robes," Grant said.

"Modest dress is required even for men, and they're ready for daily prayers," Tony said. "Does make it easier for us to blend in, but a bitch to follow a target in a crowd." Out of habit, he leaned over to check the side-view mirror. It took him a minute to pick out Rozanski driving the other SUV. With the vast majority of vehicles being white, it would be just as easy to lose a vehicle they were tailing.

The GPS directed them to a crowded commercial area in the Batha district. Some businesses included English signage, and Tony made mental notes of what was around the building the CIA operative was camped out in. After cruising the block a second time, Mack pulled the SUV over. Tony, Lundgren, and Grant exited the vehicle, then headed past the hotel where al-Shehri was reported to have entered and was hopefully staying.

They kept a standard pace but did a visual security check. Tony didn't get a decent view into the lobby, though, to determine if they had any type of guard they'd have to avoid.

The trio crossed the street at the corner and made their way up to the second floor of a three-story office building.

Lundgren checked the surroundings before knocking on the door three times with a pause between each rap. He waited. Then three more rapid taps: God, Bless A-mer-i-ca.

Land that I love. Tony silently sang the next line.

A low voice from the other side of the door spoke in Arabic, asking for the day's crash code. Lundgren answered, and the door swung open. The space they slipped into was the size of a typical American family room. Tight quarters for eight.

The operative stuck out his hand. "Jon Smith. No *h*. You're looking kinda light."

"Didn't want to draw attention coming up together."

Smith nodded his approval. A deep dimple showed in his right cheek as he stroked his beard.

Chief Lundgren gave his name, then made the rest of the introductions. "So, this is it?" A large corner-unit desk was the only furniture. Probably too big to get out of the office when the occupant vacated.

"Best we could do spur of the moment. Didn't want to lose track of the guy if it was al-Shehri."

"Have you had eyes on him since he went into the hotel?" Lundgren stepped to the side of the sole window and looked down the street.

"No, the guy who I am convinced is al-Shehri hasn't left. But I have seen one of his bodyguards leave and return with food."

"What made you suspect it's him?" Tony thought it was him from the picture, but wanting it to be, didn't mean it was, and it would majorly suck if it wasn't al-Shehri.

"I couldn't get a decent shot without drawing attention to myself, but I got a good look. That face is in my nightmares. Saw the scar below his bottom lip."

Tony liked Smith's confidence. He changed places with

Lundgren. The angle wasn't great, but they could see the front of the hotel and a good bit of the street.

"Is there a back entrance to the hotel?" Lundgren asked.

"Delivery entrance. I couldn't cover that solo. Best not to be spotted loitering, even in garb." Smith indicated the robe and headgear he'd shed.

Lundgren gave a grim nod. "We'll get a camera up there once it's dark."

Grant handed two energy bars and a bottle of water to Smith, who drank a long swallow. Considering the guy had been on al-Shehri's tail for twenty-four hours, they could give him a minute before pumping him for information. He hadn't finished the first bar when Mack and Porter arrived.

"Dominguez and Rozanski are scoping the area and will bring up food and supplies." Mack set two oversized shopping bags on the floor near the wall. "Liu and Shuler are keeping an eye on our vehicles until we can get the rest of our gear up here."

"Does al-Shehri have a car, or did he take a taxi from the Four Seasons?" Lundgren asked Smith.

"Taxi."

"Did you overhear any of what he and El Waddi were talking about?"

"No." Smith shook his head. "El Waddi and a few others from the billionaire-sheik club are in town for this huge auto show. I was keeping my ear to the ground when I spotted our guy having tea at the Four Seasons. When he saw El-Waddi in the lobby, he beelined for him. The sheik seemed surprised —not in a good way. They only talked for a minute. He pretty much blew off al-Shehri and left with his entourage."

"Interesting. If they didn't have a meeting planned, what would motivate al-Shehri to come out of his hidey-hole to Riyadh?" Grant mused.

"Even from his profile, he did not look happy in the picture," Tony said. "Think about it, the planned Fourth of July bombing was a total bust. Didn't even make the news. He's lost Hakim, his crew, the radioactive material. He probably needs money, and it sounds like there are several sources of capital in town he may try to meet with."

Lundgren nodded. "Makes total sense. But how long will he stay?"

That was the million-dollar question. Their time window might be tight if he left when the sheik did.

"Was al-Shehri alone when you spotted him?" Lundgren asked.

"He was with two others at the hotel. I think they're his protection detail. I got pictures."

"We'll need those."

Smith shared the photos of the bodyguards, and Lundgren forwarded them to the team. At least they were wearing traditional Afghan attire, so they stood out from all the Saudi's in white robes or more Western attire.

"You guys might want to check the alley down the street as a possible location for a snatch-and-run," Smith advised.

"Washington wants us to tail al-Shehri to his home base to get computers and potential intel."

Lundgren's statement was met by uncomfortable silence. Tony ground his teeth together. What the hell did the suits in Washington know about tailing a terrorist? Al-Shehri had the intel they needed—about the damn bomb. If he got away— again—they had nothing. A bastard in the hand, was worth two in the bush.

"Course I want to win the lottery," Lundgren continued, "but I don't like the chances of that happening, so if we can get al-Shehri alive, we take it."

Now the chief was talking. Tony was not going back to

North Carolina and telling Angela they'd failed to get al-Shehri or information on the second bomb. No way.

"What if alive isn't an option?" Mack asked.

"Dead is better than him getting away, but we *need* details on the bomb. We've got to get ears on what he's talking about and who he's talking to."

"I'm on it, Chief." Porter pulled his laptop from his satchel and inserted a secure hotspot.

Smith gave him the name of the hotel, and Porter typed away.

"I'm in." Porter went from shaking his head to low growls. "I didn't expect him to be under his name, but the hotel doesn't have security cameras on the floors to give us eyes."

"Not surprising. A lot of shady dealings in this district. Lack of that kind of security is actually a draw," Smith said.

"Flipside is they won't have eyes on us if we go in," Mack said like an eternal optimist.

"We need to know where to go, though," Lundgren groused.

"We can use the drone. Peek in windows," Porter suggested.

"You don't want it spotted, and after dark, the curtains are likely to be drawn," Smith said. "Though if the drone can read heat signatures, and we spot one of his guards making a food run, we can track him."

"That's a possibility," Lungren agreed. "Though we still have to get access to hear, and if al-Shehri isn't going anywhere…"

"Bribe a maid?" Grant threw out.

"I wouldn't risk trying that. More likely, they'll tip him off." Smith shut that idea down, and he knew the area.

"For now, we'll observe. Gather intel and try tracking

anyone in his party to come up with a plan. But it will likely be on the fly," Lundgren warned.

Rozanski and Dominguez were filled in when they brought up more equipment. Since the team had no idea how long they'd be holed up, they might as well be as comfortable as possible under the circumstances. Before nightfall, they'd used thick tarps to partition the room into a sleeping area with four travel hammocks affixed to the wall studs, a living area with four camping chairs, and the observation nest.

Smith happily settled into a hammock, and Tony claimed another. Smith's even breaths started within minutes. Tony couldn't have been asleep long before jolting awake to Mack's voice.

"We've got the younger bodyguard exiting the building," Mack said into the radio. "He's heading east. Need you to confirm the ID, Smith."

Smith swung out of the hammock and hurried to take the binoculars from Mack. "That's him."

"I've got him," Kyle Liu reported.

It wasn't al-Shehri, but it upped the chances he was still here. And if he were planning another bombing attempt next month, he could be so desperate for money to pull it off that he'd make a mistake. Adrenaline flooded Tony's body at the possibilities.

"Tail him, but don't attempt contact," Lundgren ordered. "Let's see where—let's call him Ibrahim—goes. Rozanski, go to the roof and get the drone up. Shuler, give a signal when you see him return."

Their training taught them to wait patiently, but Tony couldn't stay put. He wanted to be on the street. Doing something.

"We got this," Lundgren said through clenched teeth as Tony prowled around their cramped space.

"I'll go to the roof and be his lookout." Tony jerked a thumb to Rozanski, who was pulling on his *thawb*.

"Good idea," Lundgren agreed, probably more to have Tony out of his hair for a few minutes.

Tony dressed in a flash, then peeked into the hallway to make sure all was clear. They took the stairs up to the flat roof. The sun dipped low on the horizon, casting long shadows, but the temperature hovered in the mid-nineties. The dry air parched his throat.

He did a surveillance scan before Rozanski opened the case and took out the high-tech drone. In seconds, the spinning blades emitted a low whir and went airborne. Rozanski piloted it like a pro, sending it so high Tony lost sight of it.

Even once Rozanski lowered the drone so the hotel filled the screen, the images from the heat-detecting camera were blurry blips. Maybe they could determine what floor the guy went to based on the size of the figures. Grant could probably calculate that, but they still had to get a listening device in the room.

Or did they?

Tony's brain whirled.

Angela replaced the sim card in Hakim's phone, so they could hear both sides of his conversations. Surely, the guards had cell phones. If they cloned one, they wouldn't have to get into the hotel room.

He ran through scenarios on how to make that happen. They needed a situation they could control, or at least manipulate.

Shuler reported the guard they'd dubbed Ibrahim was about to enter the hotel with sacks of food. After Rozanski landed and packed up the drone, Tony put the finishing touches on his plan. A plan that would utilize his skills, putting him right in the thick of the action.

Back in their space, Tony sat on the edge of his seat while they waited on Liu for the rundown. The fact that Ibrahim made a mundane food run and occasionally checked his six for a tail didn't give them anything useful to work with, so Tony took the opening.

"I have an idea. If we clone the guard's phone, could you use it to listen in?" he asked Porter.

"Yeah, as long as it's a smartphone and has a speaker app. They all come preloaded with speech recognition now."

Lundgren's head bobbed. "How close would someone have to be, and how long to clone it, though?"

"Real close and I don't know. Not as fast as they do in the movies. Maybe a couple of minutes."

"If you got trapped in an elevator with him, that might work," Grant threw out.

"I don't know about that," Smith said. "Might make him suspicious. If he's alone, he might not even get in the elevator with a stranger."

That shot down one of Tony's ideas, but he had another. It was a little more complicated. And a little more fun. He kept his delivery professional, watching the chief and Smith's expressions.

"It's a stretch," Smith said when Tony wrapped up. "But it could work. Show him a soccer video, but be sure to call it fútbol."

"Porter, we have any of the long-range trackers that look like Euros?" Lundgren asked.

"Sure do."

"We're going to need those because we're going to piggy-back on Vincenti's idea." Lundgren shook his finger for emphasis.

"How soon do you plan to try this?" Smith asked.

"Tomorrow. Can't wait when we don't know when he

might blow town. This is our shot at getting the intel we need to plan our next step. And if anyone can pull it off, Vincenti's the one."

"I'm gonna leave this in your capable hands from here. If you need anything else, text me," Smith said.

Tony leaned back in the chair with a smile. He wished he could tell Angela the plan but knew that was out of the question.

"Ow," Angela complained.

"That hurts?" Doc Rivers let up the pressure on her side.

"It does when you press that hard, considering I got shot there five weeks ago."

"Exactly. Healing takes time. Do you need a refill on pain meds?"

"No, I'm only taking one at bedtime, so I can sleep through the night."

"You're tough," Doc said, "but don't overdo it or let Tony push you too hard."

"He's not. He oversees my rehab strength training like a pro." Or a mother hen. She couldn't help smiling, thinking about the way he watched over her.

"Sit up. Let's check the range of movement in your shoulder." Doc pulled the ill-fitting medical gown back to cover her side.

She maneuvered to an upright position and let Doc manipulate her arm.

"Show me how high you can raise it. That's better than I expected," he said when she complied. "Tony must have you working on that."

"You could say that." Her cheeks heated at the memory of

Tony guiding her arms over her head to remove her shirt yesterday.

Doc cocked his head. Understanding dawned in his expression. "I thought he'd come in with you today."

"He had to go out of town."

"Code for deployed on a mission." Doc grinned at her. "Why don't you come down for dinner at our place tonight?"

"I can manage fine. You're releasing me for work soon, remember?"

"Yes, but that's what we do on the teams. Take care of family. We've been neighbors with Tony for years. He plays ball with my boys. Helped me coach their soccer team when their head coach moved. You're the first woman we've seen at his place. I already had orders from Shelly to invite you both for dinner," he admitted.

Family. When was the last time she'd been thought of as family? She didn't have a clue what to say, yet a pleasant and comfortable acceptance drew her to its bosom.

"If you aren't at our house by eighteen hundred hours, Shelly will send Lacey and me down to escort you."

"Sounds like resistance is futile. Can I bring anything?"

"Not this time. When we have you and Tony come, he can bring his famous cannoli."

Would there be a next time? God, she hated the idea of tearing him away from his team, his friends. The job he loved.

The weight in her chest returned. What was she going to do when Doc cleared her? This was going to be the hardest decision of her life.

FORTY-SEVEN

"DAMN, Vincenti, that hawk's beak is more noticeable than your old nose." It took Dominguez all of two seconds to start in on the prosthetic.

"Good. I *want* to be memorable. Does the scar look realistic up close?" Tony stepped over to Mack.

"I'd buy it's real," Mack said.

"Grant, you have a finger splint?" Tony wanted to ensure if either of al-Shehri's guards saw him again, there'd be no resemblance, so the more memorable, the better.

Grant dug in his medical pack and produced a padded silver splint. "Which finger?"

"Put it on the middle one." That got a snort from several of the team.

"Phone's loaded with a couple of soccer videos." Porter handed him the cell they'd picked up that morning. "I loaded some contacts and apps just in case he gets a look at it."

"Perfect." Tony checked the phone's home screen.

With Tony's finger wrapped and Rozanski and Grant ready to play their parts, all they had to do was wait—and hope that Ibrahim or Rashid did a food pickup today.

The morning dragged, and the afternoon passed by agonizingly slow. Tony tried reading the book he'd brought but got lost in thought about the pending mission to the point of rereading the same page and still not knowing what he'd read.

Maybe the hotel had a continental breakfast buffet as the team had eyes on both the front and back doors, and neither al-Shehri nor his two known bodyguards had left those ways. But what if the hotel had an underground passageway? That would be like al-Shehri. Or was there another guard they didn't know about?

If they didn't see anyone from his party today, he was going to press Smith to see if they could dig up building plans or suggest to the chief that they send someone in to check out the hotel.

Dominguez and Liu headed out to relieve Mack and Shuler after their stint on surveillance in the brutal afternoon heat. The two came in soaked in sweat.

"We got pictures of anyone coming and going from the hotel." Mack set down the food they'd brought up, then stripped off his headgear and robe. "There were two who appeared to make food runs. Could be a fourth in al-Shehri's party."

"Makes sense to provide twenty-four-hour coverage." Lungren sighed. "We'll see if Intel finds anything on the pictures of the two who we know about. If one of the others ventures out again today, we'll tail them to see if they pick up anything. We might need to get someone in the lobby to try and determine what floor they're on, then we can use the drone to see how many are in the room. Maybe we'll get lucky."

Tony had a helping of rice and chicken with cashews and raisins, then settled into a hammock. He hadn't yet dozed off when the afternoon Azan blared over speakers, calling people to prayer. He checked his watch. Nearly three-thirty local time. Eight-thirty in the morning back home. What was Angela doing? Eating breakfast? Working out? Showering?

He should have told Mack and the chief to have Kristie and Stephanie invite Angela to lunch or a movie to keep her from being alone. Getting her tied in with the wives to feel like a part of the unit would be a good idea.

As the people began their prayers, Tony lay in the hammock and thanked God for Angela's survival and for putting her in his life. Then he prayed something would convince her that staying wouldn't put him in more danger than he already faced.

"Rashid is exiting the building."

Lundgren spoke rapidly and loudly enough that it roused Tony out of his light sleep. He rolled out of the hammock and slid on his sandals, then took a second to adjust the coils securing his headscarf. Inserting his earpiece, he heard Liu acknowledge that he was tailing the guard.

"See you in a few." Tony nodded to Rozanski and Grant, dressed like European tourists, then slipped into the hallway.

He hit the street and kept his pace brisk, following the directions Liu provided. This was just the first step. They had a long way to go.

"He's going into a little market shop," Liu reported when Tony had gone about a block.

Things rarely went according to plan on a mission, but the news still prompted him to growl. Tony slowed his pace, debating whether to continue past where Rashid had stopped. Instead, he ducked into a shop and browsed the prayer rugs.

He scanned the store, but nothing caught his eye as a gift for Angela. Outside, he caught sight of Rozanski and Grant strolling on the opposite side of the street.

"He's exiting now. Looks like he's headed back to the hotel," Liu said.

Shit. Not what he wanted to hear.

"Wait, he stopped at a trash can." Liu paused. "He's opening a carton of cigarettes."

Fine, take a smoke break. He had all night.

"He's heading north again."

That was good. Tony continued down the main thoroughfare.

"Bingo! He just went into the restaurant with the blue sign. Picture of a basket of fruit on it and the name starts with what looks like an *S* in red."

Tony spotted the sign and watched the door for anyone else entering.

Precision timing essential, Tony counted the time it took entering the restaurant to walk to the counter. Two of the six booths in the brightly lit dining area were occupied. Rashid waited behind another customer, who waited for his order at the farthest of the three benches facing the cashier. At least he didn't take the middle and ruin the plan.

When Rashid stepped to the counter, he gave a name, not an order.

Tony pulled out his phone and texted: To go, giving Rozanski and Grant timing details for staging themselves. Tony gave the menu board a cursory glance and sent the "NOW" text after Rashid took two bags from the cashier.

As Tony gave his order, he heard the impact. When the cashier turned to investigate the noise and raised voices, Tony peeked, too. He missed how they'd pulled it off, but one of Rashid's bags lay squashed on the sidewalk with food spilling from the containers.

Rozanski got to his feet, and Grant was playing peacemaker as he held something out to Rashid.

Take it. Take it. Yes! Tony fought the smile when Rashid accepted the money and came back inside carrying one bag of food.

After placing his order, Tony took a seat on the middle bench, where he overheard Rashid complaining about the "stupid tourists" to the cashier. Tony activated the cloning program on his phone, then started watching the soccer video, grumbling that a penalty resulted in a free kick.

Rashid slumped onto the empty bench and started typing on his phone. He looked over when the Saudi goalie blocked the kick, and Tony cheered.

"What a block," Tony exclaimed in Arabic. He turned the phone toward Rashid. "Watch this."

"Who's playing?" Rashid's brow dipped.

"Al-Nassr. I missed this game in the spring. My cousin is a center back for Al-Nassr." Tony grinned proudly, then scooted to the edge of the bench. He queued the video back. "Watch this." He fumbled with the phone, extending the splinted finger before handing it to Rashid.

"It's started syncing," Porter reported over the comms link.

"Watch for number four." Tony pointed at the screen when Rashid started to hand back the phone.

He watched for another minute. This time when he handed the phone back, Tony took it but angled it, encouraging Rashid to keep watching.

The cashier called a name, and the man on the other bench got up and took his bag.

Take your time with my order.

Porter didn't give a progress update, but at least he hadn't given any warning about losing the connection. Tension took a joyride through Tony's body as he watched the soccer game like he cared. A great header and run kept Rashid engaged.

"Almost there," Porter crooned.

Might not be close enough. Tony's jaw locked as the cook put a Styrofoam container on the serving ledge.

The counter clerk came and looked at the ticket. Instead of calling a name, he waited, talking with the cook through the window. When a second order was up, the clerk bagged them together. Still no go-ahead from Porter.

The clerk called a name—not the one Tony had given. When Rashid got up, Tony did, too. The clerk's gaze shifted from one to the other. "Nabil?" he repeated.

"That's me," Rashid said.

Tony laughed and pointed to himself. "Nabil Mohammed. What are the chances, my friend?"

"Shawarma and falafel," the clerk read.

Nabil took the order and gave a farewell nod.

"Let me get the door. Don't want you to have another accident," Tony offered.

"Idiot tourists too busy taking pictures to watch where they were going," he said in the stilted manner of speaking a secondary language.

"Got it!" Porter said in time to keep Tony from turning into a stalker.

"May Allah have mercy on you," Tony said, then went back to wait for the food.

———

Tony ducked in the back entrance of the office building and made his way upstairs. The room was crowded with everyone there, besides Dominguez, who was keeping an eye out to make sure Tony hadn't been spotted returning.

Mack gave a slow clap. "Another Academy award-winning performance."

"I'd like to thank my supporting cast." Tony motioned to Grant and Rozanski. "He take the Euro trackers?" He handed the phone to Porter.

"Yeah, called us a few choice names in Pashto, then we gave him more than enough to buy more food so he wouldn't spend those," Rozanski said.

"Good job. And I'll take al-Shehri in prison over an Oscar." He unwrapped the tape and removed the finger splint and tossed it to Grant. Then he peeled off the prosthetic nose.

"We'll keep your name off the Hollywood Walk of Fame since your performance might draw some critics." Lundgren gave an approving nod.

Tony chuckled and opened the food container.

"I thought you ate before you went out." Grant eyed the sandwiches.

"When is Vincenti not eating?" Walt Shuler laughed.

"When he's sleeping," Mack said. "But, thankfully, after his rhinoplasty, I don't need earplugs."

Tony didn't mind the ribbing. Successful missions left him famished, though, so he picked up one of the lamb wraps without apology.

"Karma, we have contact." Porter grinned wickedly less than ten minutes later.

The room went silent. Porter pulled off his headphones and played the audio for the team to hear.

"That's the TV," Lundgren said.

"I'm recording everything. I'll start downloading any messages saved on the phone."

"As soon as you do, send them to command to be translated," Lundgren ordered.

"And have Intel see if they can dig up any known associates with the name Nabil. He didn't give his surname.

If they need help translating, Angela is available," Tony threw out.

Lundgren studied him for a drawn-out moment. "Pass it on," he said to Porter.

Lundgren's affirmation made Tony feel close to Angela as he climbed into a hammock alone, rather than into his bed with her.

FORTY-EIGHT

THE KNOCK at the door made Angela's heart beat faster, though it didn't send the same panic through her as the time Kristie and Darcy Hanlon had shown up. *It's probably Doc's kids popping by.*

Dinner with Tony's friends two nights ago had gone unbelievably well. By the end of the evening, she was picturing more get-togethers with them, and she'd offered to tutor the older two in Spanish.

She approached the door from an angle, but instead of kids, she caught a glimpse of a camouflaged sleeve. Living close to post, she'd become accustomed to seeing men and women in camouflage; however, an assassin could pick up fatigues at any surplus store to get her to let her guard down. She opened the drawer in the entry-hall table and gripped Tony's Beretta in her hand.

Before opening the door, she took a quick perusal of the soldier at the front door. His salt-and-pepper hair was shaved on the sides and slightly longer on top. His craggy face had the olive hue she associated with the Mediterranean. Would

Vasquez send an Italian or Greek hitman? No, the man's posture assured her he was the real deal.

She tucked the gun into her waistband before opening the door.

"Agent Hoffman, I'm Colonel John Mahinis. Sergeant Vincenti's commanding officer."

Her curiosity morphed to a different state. She could think of only one reason he'd be here. One that made her knees buckle. She grabbed hold of the doorframe to keep from sinking to the floor. "Tony? He … Is he hurt? Or …?" She couldn't draw air into her lungs.

"He's fine." The colonel's hand under her elbow steadied her. "I'm here to see you on a professional matter. I'm sorry. I didn't think you'd—"

"You could have started with that." Her knees became less like jelly as she drew in a few ragged breaths.

"Let's sit you down."

The intensity of her reaction to the possibility of losing Tony hit her like the proverbial two-by-four. She thought she could leave Tony if that were best for him. Man, was she wrong.

———

PORTER FOUND LITTLE STORED on the guard's phone, which showed they were careful about deleting texts and messages. Though they now had the number of someone else in al-Shehri's party from the text Nabil sent while the restaurant replaced the ruined food order.

Tony had fallen asleep hopeful they'd get a needed break. He woke to the news that Intel had not found anyone named Nabil on the watch list, but they had managed to restore a few deleted texts and hacked into the phone records for a log of calls.

Using the cell's microphone, they were listening to everything the men said, which confirmed there was an additional bodyguard with al-Shehri. Though the addition didn't concern the team, they hoped it'd be easy enough to identify him if he made a food run today.

Tony could use a good run himself, but couldn't risk it or even running the stairs, so he settled for sit-ups, push-ups, and wall sits. He'd started a trend with the rest of the team, who rotated in the cramped space to exercise and relieve their boredom.

The chief and Rozanski flanked Tony, and the three were engaged in an unofficial wall-sit showdown when Shuler, who had listening duty, waved for quiet.

"Got an incoming call."

Lundgren pushed off the wall first. Tony looked to Rozanski, whose gaze extended the challenge.

"Which phone are they calling?" Lundgren asked.

"Not Ras—I mean Nabil's," Shuler said. "One of the others."

"Let's stick with calling him Rashid since we wouldn't know he's Nabil." Lundgren took the headphones from Shuler. He motioned for a pen and began writing notes.

Curiosity and quivering quad muscles made Tony acquiesce and stand.

"Thank God." Rozanski leaned forward and limped away.

Lundgren's frown deepened as he tuned out everyone else and listened for several minutes before pulling off the headphones.

"To summarize, El-Waddi is checking out of the Four Seasons and has *not* agreed to see al-Shehri, who's staying— for now. They're contacting some cousin who has a connection that may *help*." Lundgren ended with air quotes. "It's vague but backs up the idea he's trying to raise money. So, we're holding here as long as they do."

"WHAT'D I MISS?" Tony walked back into their lair after a trip to the bathroom to find Lundgren listening through headphones again.

"Got a response from that cousin about a meetup," Mack said.

Already? It hadn't even been two hours. Hopefully, it was a fast and hard pass on helping. Then al-Shehri would decide to pack it up, and the Bad Karma team would track him home, do a little cleanup for the good of mankind, and he could go home to Angela.

"I don't know who the hell Azam is, but he wants to hear al-Shehri's pitch," Lundgren filled them in.

"Meeting here or al-Shehri's?" Tony refocused.

"Neither. Azam is having his jet pick up al-Shehri tomorrow afternoon. Which doesn't give us much time if we're going to get him here. Have Intel look into this Azam. He's got a private jet, so sounds like he can afford to fund terrorist activity."

"ALL RIGHT," Lundgren said loudly enough to get everyone's attention without being overheard by the pair who'd shown up for work in the office next door. "Intel has a line on Azam. As the number-one son, Azam Khalid inherited his dad's oil company, and his billions, three years ago. He lives in the port city of Jeddah and owns a Lear jet, so that fits. He's got no known ties to extremist groups, but his wife was cousin to one of the 9/11 hijackers. Their third child, a son, is named after him."

"Honoring a mass killer? Isn't that sweet?" Shuler scoffed.

"We have to make sure Azam doesn't transfer money to al-Shehri so he can launch a second attempt at whatever US target he has in mind. So, how do we get close to him before he jets off?"

As the team tossed around ideas, Tony tried to think outside the box. What had Angela said about getting close to Vasquez? His sister had hired her as a nanny. Wait. No. She hadn't applied for the job. Vasquez's sister had hired her *away* from a friend. Likely the Agency intervened to ensure those families needed a new nanny. That same play with taking out one of al-Shehri's guards wouldn't work for them, though. He walked it back in his mind.

"I know how we can do this," Tony cut through the chatter. "We get al-Shehri to come to us."

"Sure. Shall we call or send a formal invitation?" Dominguez's mocking tone grated on Tony's nerves.

"He's already got his invitation—from Azam Khalid." He paused. "Think about it, they use cutouts rather than talking directly. They'll get a text or call with the time to be at the airport. *We* have a jet."

"I'm liking it. Go on," Lundgren encouraged.

"We do the telemarketer trick of spoofing a phone number, one they recognize, and we text to bump up the time to meet Khalid's jet."

"It's not even kidnapping if he gets on of his own free will," Mack reasoned.

"Let's work out details. As long as we get a time, we've got a plan," Lundgren said.

"CHANGE the time for the flight to two seventeen," Rozanski said. "It's more believable. Like a real flight time rather than saying two-thirty."

"Good catch," Lundgren agreed.

Porter sent the text with the new time for al-Shehri to meet "Khalid's" jet, then waited for a response. If the terrorists used a different phone instead of replied to the spoofed number, their plan was dead in the water.

Lundgren listened to the conversation being broadcast via the cloned phone and broke into a smile. "Pack it up. Game on."

"They bought it! Hot damn." Rozanski gave Tony a fist bump.

"I'll monitor things here until they're all away," Smith said. "Well done. Good luck." He stuck out his hand to shake the chief's hand.

"We owe you big."

"You know how it goes. A lot of leg work and waiting, and sometimes you strike gold."

"When you make it back to the States, get in touch. We'll take you out for a day or two of fun," Lundgren promised.

"I'll do that. And I want a picture of Samir al-Shehri in cuffs."

"It'll be my pleasure," Tony said.

"We need to get everything loaded on the plane before they show." Lundgren gave a let's-go whirl of his hand.

BEFORE ENTERING THE PRIVATE AIRPORT, the team ditched their robes and headwear. Inside the otherwise-empty lobby, the two Army pilots looked every bit their part. Their white button-downs had navy epaulets with gold bars, and blue ties matched their dress pants. Gold aviator-style sunglasses dangled from the pockets on their chests.

Tony reviewed the plan with them while the rest of the team loaded their gear into the plane.

"Weapons and cuffs are stashed on board," Dominguez updated him when the team trooped back in.

Shuler pulled on his suit jacket and began strutting around to get into character. Tony and Dominguez put on shoulder holsters, tucking in their handguns before donning coats.

"According to the time Smith said they left, we've got about ten minutes." Lundgren sent Rozanski and Grant out, so they didn't blow this if Rashid recognized them from outside the restaurant. "Hopefully, Rashid won't be the one who boards with al-Shehri since he should have the trackers, but don't tip your hand. We can try following without them."

If all went as planned, they'd get al-Shehri tonight, and maybe find his base of operations, if his guards went there. It was worth a shot.

Porter and Mack trailed Lundgren out of the terminal to set up observation when reality set in. Al-Shehri was on his way here. After years, Tony would be face-to-face with that murderous son of a bitch. He'd play it cool, get him on the plane, then smile when he wrestled him into cuffs.

Al-Shehri would spend the rest of his life locked up. No easy way out. No martyrhood. Was that a word? It didn't matter because it wasn't happening.

"Eyes on our guys. They're getting out of a taxi now. Party of four," Mack reported in.

Tony signaled the pilots, and they stepped out to the tarmac.

Seated in the lobby, Shuler spoke to Liu with a German

accent. Ibrahim and Samir al-Shehri entered the terminal after a cautionary survey of the small waiting area. Rashid and the third guard trailed with the suitcases. They paused at the empty counter.

Come on in, said the spider to the fly. Tony's heart pounded in his chest at al-Shehri's nearness.

One of the pilots approached Shuler and Liu.

"Your luggage is stowed. Even though this is a private flight, no firearms are permitted on board the aircraft. If your men are armed, we need to secure the weapons in the cargo hold." The pilot gestured to the metal lockbox he carried.

"You can't be serious?" Shuler answered in English but laid the accent on thick.

"Yes, sir. Sayyid Khalid's mandate and we do have another party for the flight."

Shuler hesitated, looking around, then gave an exaggerated nod to Tony; Liu waved to Dominguez.

With a gruff, Tony made a show of unbuttoning his suit jacket and removing his handgun. Dominguez followed suit. Each placed their weapons in the box.

"Thank you. We'll be boarding shortly." The pilot turned his attention to al-Shehri's group. "Are you Khalid's other party?"

"Yes." Al-Shehri moved two steps closer.

"Which two of you are the ones coming?" the pilot asked, reaching for the suitcases.

"We are all going." The slightest hesitation came through in al-Shehri's reply.

"According to the manifest, we have four in Herr Wälde's party and two in yours."

Al-Shehri spoke lowly and angrily to his group before turning back to the pilot. "There has been a mistake, my men come with me."

Though Tony reveled in al-Shehri getting rattled, he kept his expression neutral and prayed they wouldn't bag the trip.

"If you would like to contact Sayyid Khalid regarding a change, we only have twenty minutes to update our flight manifest with the tower."

"Perhaps, we can compromise, and they will leave one man also." Al-Shehri pointed to Shuler and Liu.

Shuler shot to his feet. "Our meeting has been scheduled for weeks. Azam is expecting my engineer and I and our translator and aide."

Rashid's skepticism played out in his expression as he locked eyes with Tony. His narrowed gaze dropped to Tony's left hand and returned to his face long enough to raise a degree of concern that he recognized him from the restaurant.

Tony countered with a dismissive once-over.

"I am authorized to transport two of your party, or none. Would you like me to load your bags or not?" The pilot played a verbal game of chicken to see who would veer first.

Straining to hear the brief conversation, Tony picked out a few Pashto words and phrases. *No choice* and *go home* being ones he liked—though would they go to their home or al-Shehri's?

When Rashid handed two suitcases to the pilot, then stepped back to take hold of the one remaining, Tony did a silent victory whoop.

"And if either of you have any weapons, I'll need those now," the pilot addressed Ibrahim and al-Shehri. "There is a metal detector." He motioned to the entrance to the tarmac when they hesitated.

Both men produced compact handguns from under the loose-fitting shirts that hung to just above their knees. They complied, placing them in the metal box.

The pilot locked it. "Thank you, gentlemen. You are free to board." He stood next to the doorway, waiting.

Shuler took the opening, with Liu on his heels. They passed through the metal detector with no issues, but Dominguez set off the metal detector and stepped back. He handed the pilot a set of keys and passed through.

Tony stepped back and motioned for al-Shehri to go ahead as he removed his belt.

Ibrahim reached into his pocket and discreetly handed what looked like a knife to Rashid under the guise of a traditional Muslim goodbye hug that Tony didn't buy for a second. *Nice try.*

"May Allah bestow his blessings on you," Rashid said, embracing al-Shehri.

"Glory to Allah," the other bodyguard said in parting.

"After you." Tony gave a wave of the hand because there was no way in hell he was moving until al-Shehri headed to the plane. He'd knock him out, toss him over his shoulder, and carry him if he had to. He released the breath stored in his lungs when al-Shehri moved forward to pass through the metal detector.

"What business does your boss have with Sayyid Khalid?" Rashid asked.

"He designs custom racing cars," Tony threw out over his shoulder in an Italian accent, dropping his timbre to further differentiate from the role he'd played in the restaurant.

He handed his belt to the pilot, strolled through the metal detector, then took back the belt and walked out the doors, not caring about the blazing heat as al-Shehri climbed the stairs of the jet owned and operated by the United States Army. *Hoo-ah, motherfu—*

Al-Shehri froze on the top step.

No! Not now, not now!

Tony pretended not to notice and marched up the steps. He held his position on the step below Ibrahim. If they'd changed their minds, they'd have to jump or go through him.

The pilot set the lockbox in the cargo hold. When he lifted the first of al-Shehri's suitcases and loaded it, al-Shehri ducked through the opening into the aircraft.

Mission almost complete. Tony settled into a seat with his team in the front of the plane and breathed a sigh when the pilot pulled the door closed a minute later with the lockbox under his arm.

Ibrahim and al-Shehri settled into the rear of the plane.

"Welcome aboard. This is your captain, Timothy Crites. Please fasten your seatbelts as we'll be taxiing in just a minute. Today, we'll be cruising at 38,000 feet, and our flight time to Jeddah will be approximately one hour and thirty-five minutes. We may run into some turbulence, so keep your belt on while seated. Thank you for flying Con-Air."

Tony snorted at the captain's movie reference. He was right about the turbulence—they'd hit it about the time al-Shehri and Ibrahim realized they were not landing in Jeddah.

An hour into the flight, Ibrahim went into the bathroom.

"I get the honors," Tony said.

Dominguez opened the storage compartment next to his seat and pulled out the Tasers and flex-cuffs.

Tony tucked them in his suit jacket and unbuckled. He stepped to the galley and retrieved several water bottles. Strolling back, he handed one each to Shuler and Liu and slipped the Taser into his free hand. He carried waters back to al-Shehri.

When al-Shehri reached to accept the waters, Tony fired. He smiled as the leads made contact with al-Shehri's torso, making him shake violently as the electricity coursed through him and rendered him incapable of moving.

It was almost too easy slipping the flex cuffs over his wrists. Tony stuffed a rag in his mouth, so he couldn't cry out. That would also save them from listening to any crap coming out of his mouth.

Dominguez edged past them and waited by the bathroom door as Tony tightened cuffs around al-Shehri's ankles. Dominguez hit Ibrahim from behind before he could see al-Shehri. He collapsed at Tony's feet.

Once they had the guard bound, Tony took a picture to send to Lundgren to forward to Smith. It'd be a better gift than some trinket for Angela, too.

Tony tapped Liu for the first watch before he alerted the pilots that the two were restrained. Next stop, Guantanamo Bay to drop off their guests at an exclusive club. Then home.

Stretching out on the jet's couch, Tony closed his eyes and pictured Angela. Time for some sleep and good dreams.

FORTY-NINE

TONY TURNED off the engine and coasted the Harley up the driveway. Moonlight bathed his house, but no lights were on to welcome him home. No porch lights, either. Not that he'd called Angela to tell her they'd landed—she'd be asleep at this hour—and he still feared she wouldn't answer because she was gone.

He punched in the code to open the garage door, then rolled his bike in and parked it next to his SUV. He laid a hand on the car's hood. The coolness didn't offer any reassurance.

Entering the kitchen, he looked for signs of life. The counters were bare and clean. The sink empty. He stood there, unable to venture further. His temples began to throb. His lungs strained instead of working naturally.

For this moment, he had hope. Hope from all the prayers he'd said the past few days.

Turning to place his keys on the counter, he saw it.

Angela's purse.

Warmth and life seeped back into his body, brought up a

smile from deep in his belly to land on his face. Laughter rumbled in his throat, and his eyes got moist.

Filled with renewed energy—and purpose—he carried his suitcase to his bedroom.

The door was ajar, and inside, asleep in his bed, wearing one of his T-shirts, was the most beautiful sight ever. She didn't stir while he stripped down, nor when he slid under the sheet and snuggled up to her.

"Thank you for being here," he whispered into her hair. "I love you."

She murmured something unintelligible, her breathing maintaining a steady cadence. For the first time since he'd seen her bleeding in Hakim's apartment, Tony's mind downgraded to DEFCON 5—normal readiness. He closed his eyes and inhaled her spicy essence before he succumbed to much overdue sleep.

TONY SENSED Angela's presence before she moved into view in his workout room. Or maybe her scent wafted to him. He turned to face her.

Wow! He hadn't seen her wear that pale-pink lingerie before. Lace edged it in just the right places. A slit rode up the side to her hip. The hand weights slipped from his grip to the floor with a thud. Probably the effect she wanted.

"When did you get in?" She took a step closer, though stood out of reach.

"Around three." *Come here.*

"You should have woken me."

"I tried."

"Sorry. I'm still taking a painkiller at night. You should have tried harder."

Harder? That was already happening. "I needed some sleep, too."

She moved closer. The sweet floral scent grew stronger. Not only had she changed out of his T-shirt, her brushed hair fell like sheets of silk over her shoulders. For him. *Yes.*

"I wasn't expecting you back so soon." She stood, straddling the bench in front of him.

"Sometimes it takes a while, but eventually the sun comes out and burns off the fog."

"You got him!" A wickedly victorious smile lit up her face.

"Alive. The mission was a success." So far, they had two prisoners, two laptops, and four cell phones, plus the cloned phone. With Lundgren and half the team tailing the other two, they might win the intel lottery. That might keep the team busy.

"I love you, Tony Vincenti." She kissed him with the same raw passion and acceptance he had for her.

His hand glided up the outside of her thigh. Damn. No panties. Even better.

"Mmm," she murmured, pulling back to look in his eyes. "I am glad you're home safe. Your colonel gave me a scare when he showed up."

"My colonel?" His hands froze mid-journey to her cup her ass.

She nodded and draped her arms over his shoulders. Her statement didn't make sense, but between lowering her body to perch on his thighs and her barely covered breasts brushing against his chest, he couldn't focus on anything except being inside her.

"I was afraid something happened to you." She shivered in his arms, intertwining her fingers in his hair.

"Nothing happened. I'm perfectly fine." He'd happily show her just how fine.

"I see." She scooted closer and nestled against his erection.

"So, why did the colonel come here?" He nuzzled the base of her throat, then ran his tongue along the hollow.

"He didn't have my number to ask about having me do some translation work for your team."

"Really? I mentioned it but didn't know if he'd do it."

"One of your translators, Captain Patil in Operations, is out. She's pregnant—"

"Yeah. Hard to miss."

"That's because she's having twins."

"Whoa. Didn't know that."

"Neither did she until they did an ultrasound. She has to go out on medical leave soon, and Colonel Mahinis thought I might be able to fill in during her absence."

"And …" A geyser of hope erupted.

"I had to pass a language-skills test."

He had no doubts. "You passed."

"I missed a word on the Pashto. The sentence didn't make sense."

"One word? You passed!" The urgency for answers trumped all his other needs. He didn't want to breathe until he knew.

"Yes, I passed. But when the colonel told General Barden about my proficiency in Spanish, Arabic, and so on, he offered me a commission and permanent spot in Special Operations Command."

If she hadn't been on his lap, Tony would have leaped from the bench to do a victory dance. "Tell me you accepted."

"No."

"What?" His entire essence deflated with that single word. He wanted to beg her to change her mind. He wanted to cry. Yet she sat there with an endearing, loving—yeah, loving—smile. Why? He wanted to understand. He *needed* to understand.

"A commission would lock me into a contract. A time-of-service commitment. I couldn't leave if I needed to."

Damn. Weren't they past that by now?

"More importantly," she continued, "a commission comes with rules and regulations. I'd have a real problem with that one about fraternization between the ranks."

"We could get around that." Mack had, though Kristie was in a different unit—not under Special Ops Command. His mind whirled, trying to come up with a workable option.

"True." Her smile got bigger. "As a civilian contractor, those rules and regs don't apply to me. I don't get the great health benefits, but I don't plan on getting shot again."

"You took it?"

"Of course, I did. When I thought …" Her eyes misted, then closed. She drew in a deep breath. Another. Her mouth opened to release that breath. Her eyes opened to stare into his. "When I thought you'd been hurt. Or worse …" Her head shook slightly. "I love you. And I can't imagine my life without you anymore."

"I love you, too." The world seemed brighter—from her glow, not from the sun streaming through the blinds.

"I can get my own place if my staying here would cramp your style."

He laughed and pulled her hips closer. "Your moving out would hamper my love life a lot more. You're staying."

He kissed her shoulder and pushed the pink satin out of the way. With al-Shehri in custody, Tony had a new mission.

To make sure Angela felt loved and safe enough to stay—not just for now—but forever.

THANK YOU for reading *A Shot Worth Taking*. I hope you loved getting to know more about Tony and meeting Angela as well as seeing Mack and Kristie and Ray and Stephanie from *Deadly Aim* and *Desperate Choices* again. You'll get to see more of them in the rest of the series along with the other heroes of the Bad Karma Special Ops team—whose love lives are as dangerous as their missions.

I appreciate your help in spreading the word about my books. Tell a friend. Share on social media. Post a review on Amazon, Goodreads, BookBub, or your favorite book site. Reviews are like hugs to authors, and I love hugs.

Higher numbers of reviews will help other readers find me and know if this book is for them. It doesn't even have to be a five-star review—though those are certainly welcome and what I strive for.

I don't want to disappoint my readers, so I spend time researching and hire editors. We're human though and miss things. So, if you find mistakes and want to tell me in a nice way (not like the perfectionist acquaintance that takes glee in pointing out errors,) email me so I can fix it and I will be grateful!

And I'd love for you to join my newsletter list which is the best way to hear about new releases, sales, giveaways, and receive FREE and EXCLUSIVE content—including Undercover Angel, the backstory of how Tony Vincenti and Angela Hoffman first met. If you didn't read it before diving into *A Shot Worth Taking* but want more Tony Vincenti, sign up to join my newsletter on my website https://www.tracybrody.com/

Next up is *In the Wrong Sights*—another Golden Heart Winner. They are stand-alone novels with a common cast of characters, though reading them in order eliminates spoilers. I hope you'll fall in love with the leads in these books as well.

The weight of the casket and lifeless body of Master Sergeant Hal Boswell matched the heaviness in AJ's soul. If he hadn't been the one to discover Hal, to press two shaky fingers to the cold flesh of his throat, he might not have accepted the death of his mentor.

A heart attack. AJ's jaw locked recalling what the coroner had speculated. No way. It had to be something else. Hal was as fit as when he'd served on Special Forces teams. He'd endured multiple tours of duty. Survived too many dangerous missions to count. For him to die of a heart attack was like surviving a gunfight, then dying from the flu shot.

AJ wanted this to be a bad dream. Instead, he joined five other elite warriors—men Hal had molded into the best of the best—and moved toward the open grave. Even at eleven hundred hours, the heat and humidity of a cloudless North Carolina morning made sweat trickle from the rim of his dress uniform hat, down his neck, and under the crisp collar of his shirt. His white-gloved hand gripped the casket's handle as he and the other pallbearers took short, precise steps. Steps closer to the void in AJ's life left by Hal's passing.

Had he done enough to show his appreciation while Hal was alive? There'd be no more weekend trips to Hal's fishing cabin. No more wrangling over who caught the biggest trout. God, he hoped Hal had no doubt of his respect and the father-and-son type of bond that went beyond Hal's mentoring.

The forty or so mourners seated were other lives Hal had touched: members of the Army's Special Forces community; former teammates; members of the Selection cadre; men he mentored. All of them turned out in uniform to pay their respects.

However, there were no grieving widows at this funeral. Chief Lundgren contacted at least two of Hal's ex-wives, but the few women among the group were wives attending with their husbands. No true family to hand the flag to.

A flash of movement to his left drew AJ's gaze to the lone woman in running shorts and a T-shirt. Her long, lithe limbs churned, and her dark-red ponytail swung as she ran along the asphalt drive bordered by tall pines. Right toward them.

Protesters at military funerals usually had signs and typically didn't come solo. Was she curious? Her questionable choice of locations aside, with its acres of white tombstones standing like rows of dominoes, why intrude on the one ceremony taking place?

Jeez, lady. Have some respect. His teeth clenched. This wasn't a show. Hal served his country and deserved better than gawkers.

The runner disappeared behind a small mausoleum. AJ focused on his duties as the honor detail set the flag-covered casket onto the lowering stand beside the grave.

"Order arms!"

The honor guards moved to stand in formation for the service.

In the shade of the mausoleum, Cassidy labored to draw a breath. She slipped the ropes of the gym bag down her arms and pulled it off her back. The stitch in her side kept her bent over while she dumped the bag's contents on the ground. She shook out the dress before grabbing the bottle of water. After she downed half of it, she pulled herself upright and drew in another gulp of the humid air.

She'd made it. Despite her mother's lack of urgency in relaying the news. Despite having to drive all night. Despite the blown tire two miles from the cemetery. She had made it.

A scan of the cemetery turned up no one but the mourners gathered for the service. She yanked off her sweaty shirt, used the remaining water to rinse off as much of the perspiration as she could, and hastily dried herself with the workout towel. She'd stink, but there was nothing she could do about it.

She was drenched in sweat from trying to loosen the lug nuts. Swearing like Hal hadn't worked any magic for her and waiting for AAA would have taken too long. She hadn't driven the whole damn night to miss Hal's funeral. She had the rest of the day to worry about the car and getting back home.

Okay, not exactly *home,* but the only home she had until Flores went to trial.

She took another scan of her surroundings, then stripped off her shorts and tugged the black knit dress over her head and sticky limbs. After she shoved her dirty clothes in the bag, she traded her running shoes for black pumps, undid her ponytail, and secured her hair with a clip.

Ready.

Almost.

She inhaled, closed her eyes, and slowly exhaled. Her racing heart calmed but still beat—despite the hammering of grief it'd taken.

She stepped out from behind the shelter of the mausoleum. Not as many as people had turned out as she'd hoped for her to go unnoticed in the crowd. Most of Hal's old teammates had retired, probably moved on. Just as well. It lessened the chance she'd be recognized. Though if someone did recognize her, Hal hadn't told anyone her story. Being recognized here wouldn't put her in jeopardy.

As she crossed the grassy expanse, her insides quivered. She took the vacant seat at the end of the last row of chairs. *It'll be okay.*

Except her gaze settled on the flag-draped coffin holding Hal Boswell's spiritless body.

Cassidy's heart revved again from how close she'd come to missing this. Her mother had passed along the news almost as an afterthought at the tail end of their bi-weekly call. *Oh, I got a call that Hal died.*

Dead?

He seemed invincible. The shock of his death had slammed her like a tsunami. *Did I make enough time for him?* College. Moving to Chicago for work. Two years ago, he'd insisted she come visit. When he balked at her mention of bringing her boyfriend, Parks, she'd postponed the trip. Then an EMT wheeled Reynaldo Flores into her Emergency Department and screwed up her life six ways to Sunday and Monday and Tuesday.

She'd lost two years of her life she'd never get back, and now she'd lost Hal.

While her mother hadn't bothered to note the details of the service, Cassidy found the online obituary with a simple internet search. It'd taken her less than ten minutes to pack a bag and hit the road because she *had* to be here.

This wasn't how I wanted to say goodbye. But I'm here. Would it give her closure?

Tears welled once again. Her hands shook, not from the caffeine flowing through her veins, but from the loss of the one man, the only man, who'd invested his time in her. He'd made her feel she mattered.

Even after her mother and Hal divorced, he'd been there, continuing to help with her college tuition, which enabled her to get her nursing degree. He called on her birthday. Had been there when she had important decisions to make. She trusted his clarity of breaking things into a "this is right; this is wrong" analysis—even when the outcome had cost her.

A snuffle escaped. Several heads turned in her direction since no one else was crying. She sniffed hard but surrendered to scrounging in the gym bag at her feet for the pack of tissues. With a fresh tissue in hand, she closed her eyes against the bright sun and listened to the eulogy that captured the essence of Hal. Though not a perfect man, a decorated soldier. One who gave of himself far beyond the service required. She drew comfort from the accurate description of the man who sought no glory for his actions.

With her heart rate and breathing almost normal, she relaxed a bit on the folding chair. Though it had been years since she'd lived in Hal's home here in Fayetteville, North Carolina, she searched for familiar faces around her. She recognized a blonde seated in the front row, but the woman likely wouldn't remember her. Then she picked out the woman's bear of a husband standing at parade rest with the honor-guard detail. He met her eyes and gave her a slight nod. She returned a wavering smile, trying to recall their names.

Another pallbearer, a younger man with a strong jaw and well-defined cheekbones, stared at her. His narrowed eyes and the stern set of his mouth made her shift her gaze back to the chaplain and sit straighter to keep from squirming in her seat.

Even with her hair pulled up, AJ recognized the runner. She'd changed into a black dress—where?—and sat in the back row, a seat apart from everyone else. What the …? Another thing about this day that made no sense to him. The chaplain's voice carried through the still air. AJ's gaze shifted to the tissue wadded up in the young woman's hand. He tamped down the irritation in his gut, determined not to let her arrival distract him further.

When the chaplain concluded, Chief Lundgren assumed his position at the head of the grave. AJ and the other pall-bearers came to attention. The funeral director asked the mourners to stand for the rendering of honors.

AJ had attended over a dozen military funerals since enlisting—too many thanks to Iraq and Afghanistan; however, the protocol still moved him.

"*Pre*-sent arms!"

Seven rifle bolts slid into place with one metallic click.

"Ready! Aim! Fire!"

The expected crack of rifle fire still made his body jerk. The sliding of the bolt to chamber the next round preceded the second call to aim, fire, then the simultaneous volley of shots. By the third round, the instinctive jerk became a mere twitch.

The bugler began playing *Taps*. Sunlight glinted off the gleaming brass instrument. How could anyone here not feel the honor that accompanied the solemn ceremony? No matter what anyone said, AJ was damned proud of his service. What he did. Sure, sometimes it meant doing ugly things to prevent others from perpetrating cruelties and injustices, but, as Hal pointed out, where would the world be without men like them to ensure balance and justice? He and his team were part of that equalizing force. Raining down bad karma on those who deserved it. He stood straighter—if that was possible—his eyes fixed on the coffin.

The last strains of *Taps* faded. AJ and the detail took their positions alongside the casket. Lundgren nodded. They took hold of the corners of the flag, gently lifted it from the coffin, and pulled it taut. They folded it in half lengthwise, then again before turning it on the triangle. The fold man tucked in the end and inspected it to ensure no red showed. As the casket team leader, AJ ran his hands over the edges to "bless off" on the corners and squeezed the flag tight to his chest before bringing it down to hand back to the fold man— another Special Forces member Hal had mentored.

The men passed the flag down the line of pallbearers to Chief Lundgren, the presentation man. After the three-second salute, Lundgren turned the flag, preparing it for presentation.

AJ tried to swallow the hard lump in his throat. It stuck like a wad of chewing gum. Normally, the flag would be handed to family. A spouse. A child. Parents. A sibling. Hal had none of those. He had family forged by blood, sweat, and gunfire.

I want that flag. It means more to me than anyone else.

Lundgren had been silent on the subject of disposition of

the flag. He turned on his heel and walked toward the seated mourners. AJ ground his teeth. Lundgren strode past those seated in the front row, then turned and proceeded down the aisle. AJ squinted into the sunshine. At the last row, Lundgren dropped to one knee—beside the redhead.

What. The. Hell?

WANT TO KNOW WHAT HAPPENS NEXT?

Find *In the Wrong Sights* here.

And I'd love for you to join my newsletter list which is the best way to hear about new releases, sales, giveaways, and receive FREE and EXCLUSIVE content! Including the mission where Tony Vincenti first met FBI Special Agent Angela Hoffman.

JOIN MY NEWSLETTER HERE.

Coming Fall 2020

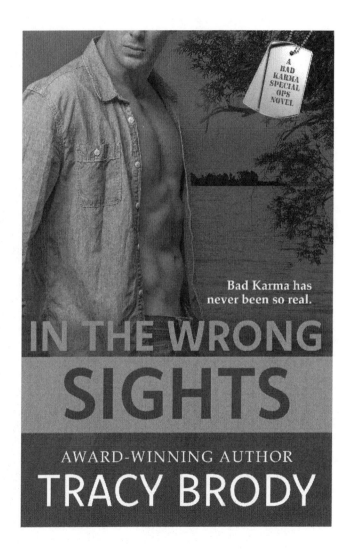

A BAD KARMA SPECIAL OPS NOVEL

Bad Karma has
never been so real.

IN THE WRONG
SIGHTS

AWARD-WINNING AUTHOR
TRACY BRODY

ACKNOWLEDGMENTS

Thanks once again to MSG Dale Simpson (US Army Ret.) for responding to my calls, texts, and messages asking for your military and Special Ops information. Any errors or artistic liberties are my own. If any Special Ops guys want to help me get things right, invite me to spend the day training with you, and I'll bring my freakin' awesome brownies for everyone.

Thank you to my critique partners and beta readers, Paula, Kathryn Barnsley, Carol Thorton, Karen Long, Becky Eien, and Judy Eien.

To my friend LTC Kathryn Barnsley (USAF Retired) for those initial copy edits when I entered this manuscript in the Golden Heart® contest, where it became a finalist and won!

The validation of being a finalist, and even winning RWA® chapter contests, kept me motivated to continue learning and writing. But it was this story becoming a Golden Heart finalist in 2015, that was a life and career changer. The friendships that came from being a part of the Dragonfly group was, and still is, a huge blessing. I love you ladies and wish you all happily-ever-afters. I went on to become a member of the Mermaid, Rebelle, Persister, and Omega Golden Heart groups. Each unique group and writer added to my circle of friends, and I always love to see writers who encourage and help and lift up other women and show how love can change things.

Thank you to my developmental editor, Holly Ingraham, for pointing out what I needed to add to make my story better and my characters richer. I hope you enjoy the addition that you suggested the story needed. I had fun writing it!

Christy Hovland, you did another fabulous job on the cover and gave Tony the perfect tattoo and scar. Sorry that we didn't get to show his abs and chest.

To JJ Kirkmon, I am so thankful I invited you to write with our group. My productivity is up since I wake up earlier to work alongside you (well, pre-Covid-19). You make my manuscripts flawless (or nearly so, since I tinker), and I love that we are so in-sync in how we think and get along.

Most of all, THANK YOU to my family. My awesome husband has always supported my increasing number of writing retreats, often telling me to attend conferences, especially when I was a Golden Heart finalist. My daughter, Kristen, is my biggest cheerleader. My son is my tech expert, and now I have a daughter-in-*love*. We're all so glad you found each other, Brandon and Lauren. Also, my sister, Kathy, who watched and cheered when this book won the Golden Heart and always tells her friends about her sister, the author.

Thank you, Lord, for opening my heart and mind to accept You and for the gift of this overactive imagination.

Also by Tracy Brody

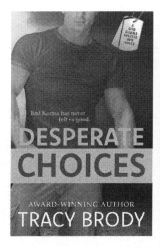 

For updates on the Bad Karma Special Ops team,
sign up for my newsletter. You'll receive free
exclusive content including the mission where
Tony Vincenti meets Angela Hoffman.

https://www.tracybrody.com/newsletter-signup

ABOUT THE AUTHOR

Tracy Brody has written a series of single-title romances featuring the Bad Karma Special Ops team whose love lives are as dangerous as their missions. A SHOT WORTH TAKING and IN THE WRONG SIGHTS won the Golden Heart® for romantic suspense in 2015 and 2016. DEADLY AIM was a four-time finalist in the Golden Heart.

She has a background in banking, retired to become a domestic engineer, and aims to supplement her husband's retirement using her overactive imagination. Tracy began writing spec movie and TV scripts, however, when two friends gave her the same feedback on a script, saying that they'd love to see it as a book, she didn't need to be hit over the head with a literal 2" x 4" to get the message. She joined RWA® and developed her craft and is still working on using commas correctly

Tracy and her husband live in North Carolina. She's the proud mother of a daughter and son and now a mother-in-law. She invokes her sense of humor while volunteering at the USO. You may spot her dancing in the grocery story aisles or talking to herself as she plots books and scenes while walking in her neighborhood, the park, or at the beach on retreats with friends.

You can connect with me on:

https://www.tracybrody.com/
https://twitter.com/TracyBrodyBooks
https://www.facebook.com/tracybrodyauthor
https://www.instagram.com/tracybrodybooks/
https://www.bookbub.com/authors/tracy-brody

Sign up for my newsletter at https://www.tracybrody.com/ newsletter-signup if you'd like to hear more about the Bad Karma Special Ops team and upcoming projects. Free exclusive content including the back story of when Tony and Angela first worked together.

- facebook.com/tracybrodyauthor
- twitter.com/TracyBrodyBooks
- instagram.com/tracybrodybooks
- bookbub.com/authors/tracy-brody
- goodreads.com/tracybrodybooks